Where Are The Snows

Also by Maggie Gee

Dying In Other Words
The Burning Book
Light Years
Grace

Where Are The Snows

MAGGIE GEE

HEINEMANN : LONDON

William Heinemann Ltd
Michelin House, 81 Fulham Road, London SW3 6RB
LONDON   MELBOURNE   AUCKLAND

First published 1991
Copyright © Maggie Gee 1991
The Author has asserted her moral rights

A CIP catalogue record for this book
is available from the British Library
ISBN 0 434 28747 4

The author wishes to thank
the Hawthornden Foundation
for their hospitality during the writing of
Where Are The Snows.

Printed and bound in Great Britain
by Clays Ltd, St. Ives Plc

This book is for Nick

... mais où sont les neiges d'antan?
FRANÇOIS VILLON

Caelum non animum mutant qui trans mare currunt ...
Quod petis hic est.

They change their sky, not their soul, who
run across the sea ... What you seek is here.
HORACE

Prologue

I

Mary Brown

Was it sex, or love, that mysterious thing they seemed to have more of than anyone else?

And why should it bother me so much?

The charge in the air, or in me, when I saw him pass close to her, as if accidentally, but really to rub against her back and run his hands across her shoulder-blades.

Stroking my daughter's silk shirt last week before I sent it to the jumble sale, it began to purr and crackle faintly as if the universe were coming alive. And I thought of Christopher and Alexandra. Alexandra and Christopher . . .

2

Alexandra: London, 1986

I don't look at other people very much, unless they're beautiful or interesting. But yesterday, as I waited for the money, I looked at the other people queueing in the bank. They were neither beautiful nor interesting, a dozen or so of the shadowy strangers who pass down the margins of life every day.

They were worried, preoccupied, impatient, grey with London air and ordinary ill health, with too many bags or too many papers. The queue was stalled, as usual. They were standing still, of course. But they seemed to trudge uphill as I looked. They were going uphill into the darkness.

The men looked back at me, hard, which is only to be expected; men have always looked at me, all my life – I suppose they always will.

And I thought, every one of you would like to be me. Every single one of you would ditch your life if you could do what I'm about to do.

I'm flying away with my darling.

From the chores and the queues and the dirty light.

We're going on holiday and never coming back, and life will be a fairy-tale.

The last few days have been made of lists, lists on every scrap of paper. I tried to get Chris to draw up lists, but he said my lists would do for six. I started to get tired and cross. We started to dislike each other, Chris and I, Chris and I who adore each other.

It's the tension, of course. We're a little afraid, of other

4

people's sorrow and too much happiness. We're afraid we are trying to be too lucky.

I haven't slept well these last few nights. I've nothing on my conscience but I haven't slept well. Chris has decided to block everything out; he's slept too well, and snored.

Last night – the very last night at home – was the longest night I have ever spent. The Newsons' dog howled like a wolf, three gardens away, and a small child sobbed . . .

On this final morning I woke feeling frightful and lay for a moment with my eyes half-closed, trying to grapple with a horrible dream. I had to recall it or I'd never escape it. When dragged to the surface it was about a little girl with a pretty smile and an empty suitcase.

She wants me to buy her a Japanese doll. She holds up the doll she wants me to buy, which is puggish, with slanted eyes, not pretty. I say so, and she explains it's a dog. I tell her the dog has to be put down. She cries, and folds herself into the suitcase. She promises they will follow us.

It's perfectly meaningless. The morning is beautiful, I smell my bacon cooking downstairs, the dream is no longer frightening.

Things start to seem more promising.

The suitcases, packed but not yet locked, stand in a line along the wall. Joy of the place-names that will fill those labels. The lists have all gone into the waste-paper basket, each with its long smug line of ticks. I've had my injections, collected the money, ordered the cab for the airport. I make one final triumphant list. Apple, paperbacks, flask full of brandy, in case we get stuck at Budapest airport and the barman has no Rémy Martin . . .

And I start to feel it, a foretaste of fun, a shiver of ecstatic anticipation, the first of a thousand unknown bars, just the two of us alone together . . .

This morning I'm avoiding the children – postponing the children, shall we say – until I have enough caffeine inside me.

5

Yesterday evening they both became suddenly (strategically?) sad, though they weren't a bit troubled when we'd told them we were going.

– They are just being sad to upset me. Isaac's nineteen years old, after all, and studying art at St Martin's. You'd think he'd be glad we are going away, you'd think he'd be glad of a bit more freedom . . .

Isaac doesn't talk a lot, or not to us, but he has a way of hanging about that I find intensely irritating, partly because he's a clumsy boy; there are always little thuds and crashes and sulky muttered apologies, and the carpet is covered in coffee stains, and I haven't the energy to replace it. He sighs a lot as well. You can't see his face with those gigantic blue glasses. I've tried encouraging him to buy lenses but he thinks the glasses are fashionable, which they probably are, but he looks a fright. He sits there reading his art books, which he could perfectly well do upstairs . . . or he watches James Dean on the downstairs video, he has an obsession with James Dean which is probably an art student's thing about style; we gave him a VCR of his own for his eighteenth birthday, but he didn't take the hint, he likes ours better. Well now he can do whatever he likes, now he can have the run of the house, so why must he give us a hard time for leaving?

I suppose the children are secretly green with envy, just like everyone else . . . It's nothing to worry about. They'll be celebrating the minute we're gone, inviting people for an all-night party . . .

– A moment's qualm, which I dismiss. Mary Brown will keep an eye on things – dear Mary, she's a good friend to us. Though I hope she's not going to fuss too much and bother us with every little detail. She said she would write, I hope not too often . . . The daily will come in three times a week, the best china is stored in the attic . . .

They're sensible children, in any case.

I'm quoting my own bland statements to friends. No one could call Susy sensible. Limited yes, sensible no. She's nearly seventeen but she seems much younger. Thank God for the unconditional place she's been given at the Poly of Central London by a tutor who said *sotto voce* that she looked like a Rubens woman.

It was Isaac who assured her this was complimentary and meant she was certain to be offered a place. 'They're gormless things with enormous bottoms. Rubens women are quite disgusting. But most people seem to think they're beautiful.'

Yes, the children are certainly fond of each other, we know they'll look after the house and each other, they'll thrive on independence, it will be good for us and good for them ... All quotes from my public statements. Not that I don't believe it. Oh yes, and we'll be back in September, in any case, in time for the beginning of Susy's first term – Chris has more or less promised the children as much, and I haven't the heart to contradict him.

Nothing too much can go wrong by then.

Ah, here's Chris with juice and coffee and a plate of over-cooked eggs and bacon. That wonderful cock-eyed smile. I still find him devastatingly handsome, tall and thickset with thick dark hair and a great bear's chest I can rest upon. He kisses me slowly, tenderly, as always, forgiving me for all the lists, the timetables, the worry, the temper. He must feel just like me; ready to be free and happy. No breakfast to cook for a very long time. We'll lie in state and be waited on and make love twenty times a week.

11am. Time ticking away. Cases in the hall, hand luggage packed. The telephone never stops ringing; people wanting to say goodbye. Isaac's gone out to take a video back. He loses track of time in video shops. I emphasised that we were leaving in an hour and his father would be most upset if he's not back in time to say goodbye ... He stared at the ground and said nothing. Possibly irritated, possibly sad, it's so hard to know with teenagers, I normally don't bother to analyse but leaving home makes me take them seriously, thank Christ you only have to do it once.

I've promised Chris to make time for a long talk with Susy. I don't begrudge her it, though talks with Susanna always seem twice as long as they really are. Talking to sixteen-year-olds is never plain sailing. But today I grudge her nothing; impending freedom always makes me generous.

I hear her slopping around upstairs in Christopher's slippers, which are much too big, though her feet are big enough. Slap, slap, an unharmonious sound, a nagging reminder that she's there.

(While we're away she'll never bother to get up. She'll answer the door in her dressing-gown. Must talk to her about that. Isaac will have to answer the door – for the vision of Susy, flushed from sleep, a pink and nubile teenage girl, clutching her dressing-gown half-heartedly round her as she answers the door to the goggling milkman, is not a calming one.)

11.45. Put down the phone. I'm travelling in the cream shantung which, despite appearances, does not crumple. And the cream silk blouse, and Chris's pearls, the ones he gave me on our wedding day. Instead of going up to deal with Susy, I find myself polishing my beige kid shoes, which don't need polishing. I put them on, and tap upstairs.

Even with those heels on I'm smaller than her. Sometimes she makes me feel flimsy.

'Susy?' I stand outside her door. No answer, just a shuffling, like an animal at bay.

'Susy, I want to talk.'

'Oh.' The tone is heavily neutral. A few seconds pass before I hear her push back her chair and pad to the door. She opens it. She is a very large girl. Her yellow hair springs out like straw.

'Do you want to come in? Or do you want me to come out?' She implies she herself is eager for neither. And yet, she's shy, as well. And perhaps there is a hint of wistfulness in the downcast eyes, briefly lifting, falling. And she's got some clothes on, *before twelve o'clock*, on a day when she doesn't have to go to school, as if she is making a last-ditch attempt to convince us of her maturity. Black mini-skirt and straining t-shirt – never mind, *she's dressed*.

'I'd thought perhaps we'd have a chat . . .'

The children never like it when we say things like that. I perch on the bed. She inspects my clothes. Those long green eyes can look very sharp.

'You look terribly smart.' Said like that, it's an insult.

'Susy, are you going to be *all right*? – with your work and everything? You know, *all right*?'

'Why shouldn't I be all right? You and Dad think I'm a cretin.' She yawns elaborately, and fluffs her bright hair.

'Of course we don't. But your father worries . . .'

'Maybe he could come and talk to me himself.' Pain shows through; she bites her plump lips. She's right of course, he can't face her.

'Of course he will, before we go. But he had to make one last trip to the office . . .'

'He always has a good excuse.'

I rush on. 'Look will you be all right for money? Up to a hundred and twenty pounds a week. Just draw it from the bank. The bills are all paid by standing order. Your father would hate you to be short of money.'

(You see, we haven't been irresponsible; we've nothing to feel guilty about, yet it's as if Susy can smell our guilt. Not *my* guilt, his guilt; I'm not their mother. Stepmothers aren't supposed to feel guilt.)

'Thanks.'

Silence. How to begin?

'Are you getting on all right with Tim?'

Tim is Susy's current boyfriend. There have been others worse than him. He's smaller than her, but so are most people. He has a job. He doesn't smell. He doesn't appear to be a heroin addict.

'Yeah. Thanks for asking.'

She's not going to help me, that much is clear.

'Susy. When we talked before . . .'

She doesn't say a word. She stares at me, green eyes perfectly blank, then her full lips open, as if to speak, and I am just willing her to do so, quick, when I see it is turning into a yawn, another monstrous slow-motion yawn, glittering adenoids, a sexual tongue, rows of tiny regular teeth.

'You remember . . . when we talked about babies.'

9

'Yeah. Well we talked about it, didn't we.' She gets up from her slumped position on the bed with an uncharacteristically decisive movement and pretends to look out of the window, at the browned rhododendrons and the monkey-puzzle tree and the flaming hibiscus, my pride and joy, which I planted to make the garden less boring, flaunting its flowers like red silk birds by the gate through which I shall fly away ... *our* view, *our* garden, which we'll soon be leaving, no longer boring now it's touched with nostalgia, the scattering of sparrows on the telephone wires, the distant silver of the Jennings' poplars.

– Her front is voluptuous but her back is plain fat, the back of a fat sulky adolescent girl, the back of the sort of girl who'd get herself pregnant. I suddenly feel brisker, stronger, crosser.

'What did you decide about contraception? If you are going to sleep with Tim.'

She talks to the window, not me. 'It's none of your business, is it? It's horrible, your going on about the pill. My mother wouldn't have gone on about the pill – '

Her mother is dead, and can't help her, and I'm in a tearing hurry to be gone. ' – I just want to know if you went to the doctor.'

'I asked her about the pill.'

'And?'

'She doesn't advise it.'

'Why the hell not? You're very young. And it's practically foolproof – '

' – Meaning I'm a fool.'

'*Susy*. I was on the pill myself till I was thirty-five or so. It didn't do me any harm.'

'It's not very feminist to go on the pill.'

She's the least feminist girl alive, but she likes to use it to needle me since she knows I am a feminist. I begin to lose my temper.

'Forget the fucking pill. What else did she suggest?'

She stares at me levelly to show she hates swearing.

'She was keen to know if I really loved Tim.'

'I suppose you sneered at her for that.' Too late, I try to pull myself back. We mustn't have a row just before we leave.

'Well you're wrong. I like Dr Larch.' (Clear implication: I don't like you.)

She half-turns to deliver this deadly thrust, and as her mouth turns down and her round face flushes she suddenly looks so very young, a giant model of a six-year-old, that I soften; this scene is ridiculous; she's innocent; she isn't grownup.

'I like her too. I'm glad you went to see her. Whatever you decided is fine.' I go over to where she is sitting on the edge of the table and put my arms round her broad shoulders and my cheek against her prolific hair. It doesn't feel comfortable, but we hug. She doesn't move away.

I want to tell her, let's drop the subject. At least I've established that she's been to the doctor, at least I have a crumb to offer Chris on the plane . . .

The plane. Chris will have to come back soon. He might have slipped in while I've been upstairs . . . and my heart starts to lift with happiness, for there we shall be, in the sky, side by side, with nothing to do but talk to each other, and laugh at the toytown food on trays, and be a little pissed, and a little romantic, and all this nonsense will be left behind.

Now I've dropped the subject, Susy feels thwarted.

'If you want to know – ' she says, ' – but don't pass on any details to Dad – '

'Guide's honour,' I say. I was sacked from the Guides for having two boys in my tent.

'I haven't ever done it,' she says. It's obvious what she is talking about. 'I sort of – want to know – if I love Tim. Like Dr Larch says. I really want to know. And if I decide I love him. If he hasn't given me up by August. I think we might start after my birthday.' A long pause. I will her to speak. 'Only . . . I know this is wrong, I mean I know it's not right. But I sort of feel that if I love him . . . I might want to . . . well, don't get annoyed . . . but I might want to . . .' (she is blushing furiously) '. . . I might want to have his baby . . .' Her eyes dart up, agonised, see my horrified expression, fall in shame. 'I know it's wrong,' she repeats, dully. 'I will make sure I don't have a baby.' I nod, frantically. She presses on. 'I think that – you know – rubbers are best. If he agrees, if he can use them. He hasn't ever done it, you see . . .'

I feel pity and irritation and worry; if she's telling the truth, she's younger than I'd dreamed. She hasn't ever done it despite our fears. And, she's going to do it when she's seventeen, *if* he hasn't given her up, that is, as if all boys would give her up . . .

But that isn't funny. It's what she feels. It must be our fault, her bad self-image (and again I have a flash of the inside of a plane, the kind stewardess who will erase all worries, filling my glass with oblivious gin; blank blue windows, smiling strangers).

'Anyone can use them if they try,' I say, attempting to sound crisp and encouraging, but not too crisp, or *immoderately* encouraging.

'That's not the thing that worries me most . . .'

– The physical contact, so rare between us, seems to have released a different girl, a confiding, dependent, needy girl we might have been grateful to know last week . . . Now, however, is a bad time to meet her. In under ten minutes the cab will arrive.

'. . . Do you mind if I ask you something?'

'Please.' (But why didn't you do it before?)

'How do you know . . . don't laugh. How do you know if you love someone?'

Suddenly feet bound up the stairs. Her door swings open, and Chris rushes in. He looks amazed to see us cuddling each other. 'The cab's outside. Are you ready? And where the hell is Isaac . . .'

'You're interrupting. Go away.'

'What do you mean . . .?' He gazes at me. I project the fictitious desire to be left alone with Susy that the occasion demands. And to my surprise it isn't wholly fictitious; I almost feel like a mother, for once, yet at the same time I've split neatly in two, for another self, overcoat flung round her shoulders, steps out of the door and runs down the path, leaps straight through the taxi and into the sky.

Chris turns on his heel, exasperated.

The mood is broken. She edges away. I look her in the eyes, and try. 'It's very hard to say. I love your father. As soon as I saw him I wanted him . . .'

' – You mean, when he was still married to Mother.'

'Sorry. I'm trying to be truthful. Love is . . . oh, it's *everything*. Not just wanting someone, needing them. Needing to have them to yourself. Wanting to protect them, sometimes . . .'

(Wanting to protect Chris from you and Isaac. Needing to take him away from your mother. Wanting to take him away on a plane.)

'. . . Feeling they love you completely. Knowing how much you matter to them.'

Susy is staring at the floor, where the sun makes a brilliant pool on the carpet. 'I feel I'll never have all that. You're the sort of person who gets all that . . . You're the sort of person who'd get Dad. It's all right. I'm not blaming you.'

And she smiles at me, a defeated smile, looking more grownup than she ever has. I turn and kiss her on the cheek.

'Look, if you love this boy, you'll know. You wouldn't have to ask me.'

– Susy comes down to say goodbye, pounding docilely behind me, Susy who's never been known to run, and rarely bothers to say goodbye.

(But where is Isaac? Hopelessly selfish. All teenagers are hopelessly selfish.)

Chris hugs her, engulfingly, passionately. His eyes over her shoulder are full of tears. At the very last moment, as we open the front door, Isaac comes panting up the street, an ungainly boy, very slightly knock-kneed, gleaming blue specs and flying hair. He is blowing like a fish, and trying to smile, and shouting something through the noise of the traffic . . .

It all turned into a scene from a film. Years later, that is how I remember it. For a brief moment we were all there together, all four of us by the hibiscus bush, blinking and cavorting in the sun, falling over cases, trying to hold each other, trying to say things that might last.

'Take care.' 'Good luck.' 'Take care of your sister.' 'Take care of each other.' 'Don't drive the car.'

The sun was so un-English (as we thought then) that Chris put on his holiday dark glasses, and the children laughed at him; 'Poser!' 'Rock star!'

– He looked like an actor but he wasn't acting. For a moment there we were a normal family, standing on the edge of another world, where we would simply have fitted together and gone on together into the future, the children growing bigger and brighter, us getting smaller and fading away; it was not too late, we could have changed our minds . . .

And then we turned, my eyes searched for Chris's, a hibiscus bloom was reflected in his lens, then Susy and Isaac, smaller, distorted; the red silk bloomed on the back of his lens, a giant hibiscus, a tiny family; our fingers met, our fingers twined, we were leaving together for paradise.

In the quiet of the taxi we sat holding hands. The driver was in a tearing hurry and swore at a pudgy little dog who walked self-importantly over a zebra crossing.

It reminded me of the horrible dream with the dog-like doll and the empty suitcase.

But it seemed to come from another country, and besides, the little girl was dead.

'What are you thinking about?' Chris asked, as we screeched to a halt at Heathrow airport and he brushed the hair away from my cheek, ran his finger down my cheekbone.

'You, my darling. Me and you. I can't believe we've got away.'

'Twenty pounds sixty!' shouted the driver. Chris still took the time to kiss me, tenderly.

The gins we drank at the airport were large; we didn't eat lunch; we were too excited. And a little tense, as well, having watched the queues of travellers filing like pack animals to the

14

check-in desks. They were neither beautiful nor interesting; they were harassed beings from an alien planet, the dreary planet we were hoping to leave, people frowning at watches, counting their luggage, checking the papers in their briefcases. When a telephone rang in an empty booth, some of the zombies started staring about them, looking in the direction of the shrilling then casting round helplessly for someone to answer it, as if the ringing were a cry for help, as if it were somebody calling us back; as if it were somehow wrong to be leaving.

'For whom the bell tolls,' said Christopher.

'What do you mean?'

'It's just a quotation. It came into my head, the way things do.' His smile was insouciant, reassuring.

Christopher: darling Christopher. I decided to ignore everyone but him. He was certainly beautiful and interesting. Perhaps a touch heavy, but I like heavy men, big men who know how to look after themselves. And me of course. I like to be looked after. His bones are fine; they can carry their flesh; a good square jaw, and an aquiline nose with well-cut bridge and nostrils. Sensual lips. Amused, slightly crooked. Frequently bored, but never with me. His eyes are hooded, a clear sea-grey with touches of yellow around the pupil. Sun on the sea: traveller's eyes. He was my St Christopher . . .

I was a little tipsy; I stared at him, the detailed clarity of his face printed on a haze of faceless strangers. Only he and I were real, I knew. Christopher and me, a world of two.

As the plane climbed and the earth receded he pressed his clinking glass against mine. 'Christopher and Alexandra for ever,' he said, and his other arm encircled my body, his hand under my jacket gently stroked my left breast, rubbing the silk against my nipple.

'Alexandra and Christopher,' I breathed.

And we were away. We had got away. Stepping across into another life, flying away into our dream. This was where it started, the fairy tale. This was where the happy ever after begins.

*

In the old life we would never have considered making love in an aeroplane. It was something people only did in novels: childless, carefree, fictional people. But this was the new time, fairy tale time.

We could go anywhere, do anything. And so the thought flew into our heads through the blind and brilliant blue of the window.

Alcohol and chance helped it to grow. Our seats were in the very front row of the plane, by the window, and the flight to Hungary was only half full, dotted about with businessmen and people in cheap, outmoded clothes who were probably Hungarian, poor things. The steward and stewardess were less than officious. The ice-cubes in our glasses stayed stranded.

'Maybe they're up to something back there.' They had both disappeared into their little galley way back in the rear of the plane.

'I wish *we* were up to something.' We were kissing idly; no one could see us, though in the row of seats just behind and across, two stolid businessmen discussed aluminium. I pushed up the arm between our two seats. The kisses opened, became less idle.

Open kisses are curious things. Two little animals, wet and warm, tumble out of their caves and fall on each other, sliding and rubbing, naked, juicy, and everything between them is melting, easy, so they send out a message to the bigger animals: this is delicious. You do it too.

The longer we kissed, the louder the message.

Christopher took and squeezed my hand and brushed it across the front of his body. I felt what he wanted me to feel.

'Too bad,' I said. 'You'll have to wait . . . *Christopher*, we've been married twelve years!' For Christopher's hand was between my knees, nosing dog-like up under my skirt. I was weak with laughter, weak with gin, weakening as lust ran through my body, rushing faster than alcohol.

Things were confusing; things were confused; drink, desire, a dazzle of sun flaring through the low windows of the plane. On other seats there were only shadows, whereas we were urgent, we were real. In this new life we had only just met, we were only just meeting, 40,000 feet up, flying together near the dangerous sun, soaring way over the storybook clouds.

Christopher draped his beige spy trenchcoat over the gap between the backs of our seats, then his other hand was inside my thighs. His face was familiar, flushed and intent. I forgot where we were, I forgot who I was, I pressed myself down upon his hand, I licked his cheek, I half-closed my eyes.

Almost too late we heard the stewardess's snappish offers of drinks approaching again, and the hurried tinkle of money and glasses. Swearing, Christopher removed his hand, I turned towards the window, his body cupped mine, he tugged the coat down to cover us up and with one accord we feigned sighing sleep, though my cheeks were hot, and our sighing excessive. The stewardess asked sternly for our orders, but when we said nothing her voice receded.

I half-opened my eyes into dazzling sun. Christopher's breath was loud in my ear. We were making spoons. We were making love. The enormous blue looked in at us. We were flying together, drunk with light. His finger slipped inside again. Not his finger. Oh not his finger.

I was due to menstruate next day, but he didn't know, only I knew that; he was an idiot who wanted to make babies, he was an idiot who loved me. I pushed down over him. I took him in. Miles below was a silver fleece of clouds, miles below that a tiny planet existed only for our pleasure. 'More,' I sighed. 'Yes. Oh yes.' We moved very slowly, then slowly faster.

Hot skin of the seat on my own hot skin, the blazing sun, we were burning, swelling, I squeezed my lids as I started to come, there was only a bright red greedy blindness, then the sun burst through me as I was transfigured, gasping, impaled in thin blue air, staring amazed at a tiny plane which passed below us, diamond-edged, as I shook with Christopher's dying moments.

We died together. We dozed. We dressed, furtive and sleepy, then dozed again.

Till the chimes awoke us; time to fasten our seat-belts. We

17

cocked a cautious ear behind us; the two grey men were talking tin.

'What if we just made a baby?' Chris asked. His tone was playful, but it wasn't a joke.

I didn't disillusion him. Let him dream.

We circled Hungary, in fairy-tale time.

3

Mary Brown: London, 1995

My name is Mary Brown. I know it's dull, but I'm fond of it. Actually Brown is my husband's name, but before I married him I was a Smith, so you see I hadn't a thing to lose.

– I prefer Brown to Smith. It seems more solid, and I like solid things. Having been brought up in a feckless family, I'm not very drawn to drama . . . at any rate, I used not to be drawn to drama. I'm not so sure of myself as I was.

A lot of things have changed in the seven or eight years since Christopher and Alexandra went away. I've suddenly started to think about ageing; my husband Matthew is younger than me, but I never used to think about my age. I still can't believe that I've stopped having periods and can't have any more children . . . my own children are enormous strangers who've learned to say 'sorry' and 'thank you' at last.

I was always what people call 'a good mother'. Matthew used to say I was a good wife. When I was young I was told I was a very good student, with composition my forte. I sometimes wonder where my goodness has gone . . .

But I don't think about myself much. When I compare my life to other people's it's lacking in stature, or substance, or I am, playing a bit part in my own life. So I don't have a story of my own to tell. I can only tell you about my friends . . .

Alexandra and Christopher. Because they're not here their names have somehow acquired a melancholy ring. Yet when they first came to live in Islington, and the four of us made friends – almost too quickly – just the sound of their names on the phone cheered us up. 'Mary? It's Alex. You've got to come round.'

They were very soon our best friends. Always dropping in,

always cheerful and reckless. Especially at first, before Penelope killed herself. They seemed to grow younger as their kids grew up. We had two as well, so that was a link.

Chris and Alex's two – not really Alex's, of course, Chris's children by his first wife Penelope – would have been around six and eight when they first came to live across the road from us. They were just married, and besotted with each other. For over ten years we were as thick as thieves.

Although my husband never admitted it, he was a little in love with Alex. It wasn't her fault, she seemed awfully young, and a lot of men must have fallen for her . . . I couldn't dislike her for her beautiful face, though I sometimes felt she was a dreadful mother. After a while they were simply there. We saw them so often she became like a sister.

Now they write to us from extraordinary places. The first year or so we heard every other week; we were keeping an eye on their children for them. Then naturally the cards slackened off. No complaints, it was kind of them to think of us at all. But we must have been becoming less real to them, getting smaller, the wrong end of the telescope.

Usually Alex would scribble a poste restante where I could reach them, and I wrote at once. Yet I never felt sure my letter had arrived. The next card from them never seemed to respond. I suppose our news wasn't earth-shattering, whereas they were travelling all over the world.

So we weren't really talking to each other any more. It didn't matter, they were still our best friends. We longed to see them, though. Twice Alexandra sent photographs.

We were happy to have the first one. Alexandra in Malta with a pigeon by her foot, crouching in the sun. That enviable red-gold hair. Christopher smiling, crinkling up his heavy-lidded eyes at the brightness. All Matthew said was 'I'm glad she hasn't cut it.' I didn't like that. I'd cut my hair that year. I thought I was too old to have long straight hair, but I fear it looked even more ordinary, chin-length.

It was the second photo that upset us. A snap, not quite in focus, of the two of them sitting on a low yellow rock that

20

looked a bit like a sleeping lion. Behind them, one of those long white bays that seem to go on for ever. The light was so bright that their faces were bleached. It made them young, almost featureless, and Alex's hair was like blown sand; the sun had taken away its red. She had cupped his hand between her two paler ones, their feet were touching, they were looking at each other . . .

I enjoy sex more than my husband does, but it's not in my nature to be jealous. Matthew and I would feel silly holding hands.

Chris had scribbled something on the back which seemed rushed, or careless, and perhaps that's what accounted for the disappointment. As if he didn't mind what he wrote.

'*Turkey is great. Photography by a maniac Alex found hiding in the dunes. Alex says I'm a bullshitter. So you see nothing has changed. Love C.*'

Matthew stood and looked at it. I remember it was raining great heavy drops. It was sixish, a summer evening, but we had to have the light on.

'What does he mean, "*nothing has changed*"? What rubbish! They've just buggered off. We haven't seen them for years – '

'Matthew – '

' – I haven't even told her about my kidneys.'

'That's not their fault. I couldn't put it in a letter.'

'I didn't say it was their fault. But I miss them. Alex used to brighten things up. Oh hell. It's just the weather.'

That year the sun didn't shine at all in England. A volcano had exploded somewhere in the world. Perhaps we minded that Chris and Alex weren't there to suffer with the rest of us.

Or perhaps it was the hands and feet that upset us, the way they couldn't stop touching each other. Everyone wants to be loved like that.

As time goes by, I think Matthew minds less. He still dreams about Alexandra, though. Perhaps even more than he tells me he does. We are very good friends; we tell each other things. I'd rather he told me. I understand . . .

Indeed, I wish I could dream about Chris, but I tend to dream about supermarkets, with occasional attacks by wild animals, and yes, I do know what that means. Chris is a 'dish', or used to be a 'dish' – my daughter tells me my language is dated. His jaw was always blueish dark, although he claimed to shave twice a day, and he had lots of black hair, whereas Matt is bald . . . I admit I regret that Matt is bald . . . but by now Chris is probably balding as well. And despite that photo with its blank young face, Alex must have wrinkled like the rest of us. That very fine skin, I'm sure it would wrinkle.

I must sit down and write to them now at once. It must be six months since we last heard. They'd flown to Tasmania for Christmas, and I wrote straight back, but there was no reply. She had said they were going to spend summer in Toledo. They often seem to spend summer there.

Summer in Toledo. It's another world.

And I suddenly wish I could join them, never mind the garden and the grandchildren, fly off and join them just like that. Pack one small bag and go, the plane headed straight into sun like a swallow.

But of course I couldn't leave Matthew behind.

We could go together . . . we could.

But we never had the thing that links them. That weirdly intense romantic thing. Or perhaps it's just sex, something tangible, electrical, that rustle in the air when they moved close, something I know they will never lose, and *hell oh hell I'm jealous.*

Part One

4

Christopher: Venice, 2005

I miss my darling. I miss my love.

I lived for love. Love left me.

The sheets where she once lay beside me, the lip of sheet where her thin arms lay, always one arm outside the covers, thin gold fingers plucking, pulling, turning the sheet to a fold of skin – her part of the sheet is flat as snow. Desolate, untrodden snow.

I never wander across the bed towards her ghost; I stay this side, staring across at the stupid whiteness when I wake up and look for her.

I can't help it. Too old to learn. She slept beside me for a quarter of a century. Now she sleeps with – *madness*. Madness to think of her now.

Alexandra left me. Or I frightened her away. A messy, humiliating scene with a gun. She should have understood. I was desperate. What else could I do? We no longer talked, but she was my life.

All the same, what I did was stupid, wrong. I knew it was over when I glimpsed her face, the split second that I pulled the trigger and changed our lives for ever; amazed, disgusted, embarrassed, afraid, but not, as in my dreams, admiring, not a vestige of sexual thrill, no hint of the look I'd known so well and longed above all to see again, the narrowed bands of hazel light she turned on me when life was young.

Better to pretend Alexandra is dead. Better drink my brandy, then another brandy, then droning with golden noise to bed, deaf to the cries I sometimes hear, *Chris, come and find me, Chris, I'm lost, Chris, you promised we'd never part, Christopher, what happened to us?*

Because if I hear those terrible cries. Coming from the other side of the world, from Brazil, perhaps, from Bolivia, from the land-mass where I would never take her because I knew she would only suffer, heat and flies and cruelty and children begging for the last of your steak, swarming over each other like frantic bats, dirty shirt-tails held out as a pouch for leftovers – if she calls to me from the land of fire, if I hear her cries on the edge of my dreams, I shall start to believe she will come back.

I know my darling will come back.

– I know that I know nothing.

I sit in Venice, in Guido's bar, dark and hot but with windows on the sea and enough loud flies to disquiet the tourists.

Tourists. Scum. They will cover the earth until there is nothing left that shines. We were never tourists, Alex and I . . .

But there aren't so many as there were last year. Not half so many as five years ago when we last came to Venice together, in 1999, the year before she left me. There had been great works in the early 1990s, drainings and diggings and shorings-up and spectacular quarrels in the world press. Then things quietened down and it was business as usual. Around the millennium, the world flocked to Venice.

I remember she panicked in St Mark's Square. You could hardly see the red colonnades for the sweaty press of jostling bodies, snapping away as if the world were ending. She was sickly white beneath her tan, her pupils shrank, her mouth was a hole, her nails were pincers on my arm. 'Help me, help me.' She needed me. Later, of course, she forgot all that; she only wanted to get away.

Now the tours are bypassing Venice again, with the water-level rising and grave men telling us our half-drowned ballroom will slide into the sea. My beautiful, poisonous, turquoise sea. It stretches away from this rotted window, dazzling under the lemon-bright sunlight . . . will that cloudless sky really see us vanish?

26

The tourists are frightened. The old are not. I love this city of cats and secrets. Its endless flux of inhuman tears renders my own more bearable. I am old. I hope my travels are over (but if she called, if I were sure she needed me, I'd go to the utmost ends of the earth. I'd choke my way through the burning forests, *I'm coming, Alex, I'm coming . . .*)

Embarrassing. I am on my feet, I said her name. They are looking at me. A cough, that's all. Since the waiter's staring, I'll have another brandy.

We were never tourists. We were travellers. Travellers are people who never go home. Epic travellers, world explorers, although we stayed in the best hotels. We stayed away for half a lifetime. We went on holiday and never came back. Our life was a great adventure, you see, a story to tell our grandchildren, if we had happened to have grandchildren, if I'd managed better with my son and daughter, if we had been – luckier. (I hear Alex hissing that I'm a liar.)

Alex didn't care about grandchildren then. When we could have had children, she didn't want them. She always said how lucky we were. She said we had everything – looks, love, money. Soon there will be nothing left but the money . . . but don't underestimate the power of money.

The brandy I drink is the very best. I'm a smart old man, one might say immaculate, a seventy-year-old who could pass for sixty, with a smooth tanned face and a daysuit of exquisite old-fashioned cream linen, soft to the touch and five times as expensive because it has not been texed or dirt-safed, real breathing linen like they used to make, torture to iron after every wearing . . . Lucia tells me this, with a smile, for the money ensures that I never have to iron.

The money means I can be sad in comfort. I have space to be sad, and time to talk, though these days there is no one to talk to . . . strangers, servants, I can always find, but they grin and listen without understanding, *si signor, no signor,* and I'm too proud to make them see.

It's here, inside me. Maps, pictures. A map of the world, our life together. Seas and mountains and grains of sand. A thousand beds, a thousand bars. I don't want the images to die inside me, I don't want our story to be lost.

(Is it just a story? Can it really be over?)

Alex was always the talker, not me. Women often complain that men talk too much, but that's not how it was with us. I never minded how much she talked. You see, she talked for both of us. She put my feelings into words.

Very late in life I realised I'd let her do too much talking for me. However much someone loves you – and it's not a delusion that Alex loved me, she loved me a lot, she can never deny it, *no, you bitch, don't you dare to deny it* – they don't see things from your point of view. Why should they? They have their own to look after.

But we felt so close, the boundaries got blurred, we started to think and speak for each other.

– You can get lazy.

– You can get lost.

– You can get so close you are taken for granted. You can trust too much, and be betrayed, though I don't think she ever betrayed me before . . . before the final total betrayal.

A decade ago. In Toledo, in Spain. Those Spanish summers in the 1990s. Alex kept wanting to go back. There was a tall shy man I worried about. He and Alex were friends, I think just friends. Stuart and his wife had a flat out there. Then the fear receded. We were safe again. Years ago he dropped away.

People fall from my life like snow, these days. So many white-haired tiny bodies sinking beneath their obituaries – I refuse to use the term *obitfile* – or dying as quiet as snow in letters. Friends who were slightly older than me, friends who were thirty, certain, jaunty, in their prime when I was twenty. There's hardly a letter without a death.

– Why did I think she would never leave me?

– Why was I sure we should never die?

*

Now at the age of seventy I want to say things for myself. Maybe she'll read it, if I manage to write it, instead of mumbling to myself. After I'm dead. She's so much younger . . . She never liked to dwell in the past, but surely she'd want to read our story?

Yes, she'll read it, and contradict, or add some details of her own. Beware of that; she was always a liar.

I ought to know, I admired her gift, when she started to add to the travel pieces I sent to the papers in England. The details were marvellous, but untrue. She would take these rotting bleached-wood windows; distil the smells of seaweed, sweat and beer; capture one fly, erratically loud; transport the whole to Rimini.

'So wonderfully vivid,' the editor would scribble. 'You never fall into clichés of place.' I didn't, he was right – this was Alex's carefree fictional geography.

If she tries to change our story – *my story, mine, it is I who stayed faithful* – I hope they'll have burned and scattered my body so thoroughly that I shan't have to know. I don't want to haunt the margins of her fiction, bitterly disputing times and places, bodiless, impotent, a hissing ghost, reminding her of how much she loved me, reminding her she grew up with me and I grew happily old with her, that we grew together, and into each other, how much we laughed, how I made her laugh, how many times I entered her, she took me in, we cried out with pleasure . . .

Seventy years old, in a stifling bar, alone among strangers, stiff with longing. Stiff as a boy under my cream linen daysuit. The brandy fills my throat with fire. I toss it down, and stand, awkward. My cock feels young but my knees are old . . .

If she ever comes back, I'm ready for her.

5

Alexandra: Esperanza, Bolivia, 2005

I saw Christopher yesterday – *my husband Christopher*.

That phrase was an experiment, but it didn't sound right, he's no longer mine, though we've never bothered to get divorced, he isn't anything to me. I'm always telling my lover that.

But that's a lie, too, I suppose he still means something. A patch of scar tissue in my brain. Even the sparrow on the white verandah means something, pecking the *empanadas* I throw him . . . I lie to Benjy because he's young.

(I suppose it's an ant-bird, not a sparrow. They all eat garbage, they're all the same.)

Christopher's not my husband, except in name and on paper, and it all happened so long ago, it was all so *twentieth-century*, for Christ's sake, so juvenile, so old hat.

In any case, yesterday he looked ridiculous. The telsat screen made him look fat and small. He had a thick black fringe and a pudgy face and his hair was almost shoulder-length. He was wearing what they used to call a 'kipper' tie, so wide you could hardly see any shirt between the lapels of his velvet jacket, and when he stood up and gestured at the map his hands were stagey and unnatural-looking.

They were showing an extract from an ancient documentary Chris made in the 1960s, before I knew him – God, I'd never have let him dress like that! 1967, they said. It was his first film, which I'd never seen. He must have been in his early thirties, but he seemed adolescent, and so did the title, 'Path to the Untrodden Snows'.

– What snows there were then, I was amazed to see them,

extraordinary expanses of snow, incredibly bright on the black and white screen. I can't believe we ever took it all for granted. But it's no good getting sentimental now.

Chris always said he'd take me to those snows one day. It was the last great adventure we had in mind, but we'd started to grow apart, you see, we kept putting it off, and the snow was shrinking . . .

Then our future disappeared. In a blaze of gunfire, a mess of heat. The stupid fool, he did everything wrong, it was all his fault, the klutz, the moron!

– My temper's bad today. I have a hangover, the heat's appalling, the hotel's never heard of bottled water and the tap water tastes of blood or iron as well as those foul little sterilising tablets. It makes me long to be back in Europe or anywhere that isn't here . . .

Seeing the film brought a lot of things back. Chris must have told me a million times about that '60s trip to Tibet, the extreme clarity of the air, so you could see every hair on the head of a horned sheep in the valley below, the sharpness of the edge where the ice met the sky . . . what did he call it? – 'immaculate'. (Imagine it glittering, the blue-cold ice. You can long for ice with such intensity here.) The mountains had a wonderful name, 'Abode of the Gods', that was it, and I'd imagined him as god-like, too, young, slim and impossibly handsome, climbing up into the mountain sunlight, climbing away from the old dull life of accountancy and wife and kids . . .

I never imagined him grey and uneasy, in fatuous clothes and a shaggy-dog haircut. He was tall, for god's sake! Not short and fat! I hated him for looking so awful . . . it was his first film, of course, he got better later, but I was furious that Benjy laughed at him. (By the way, I loathe the name Benjy, though everyone's always called him that. It would be perfectly charming for a little boy, but for a six-foot grownup man it stinks. It makes him seem even younger than he is, and God knows he's young enough already.)

Benjamin was lying on the bed eating peanuts and throwing

the shells on the carpet; he'd drunk too much beer, which makes him aggressive. We'd fucked but he hadn't satisfied me.

We switched on telsat. There was yet another programme about the dispute over the ice-caps, *boring*. Then all of a sudden Christopher was there. Chris, who I lived with for twenty-six years.

'My God,' I hissed. 'That's fucking Christopher.' (I'm sorry, my language has gone downhill since I've been living with Benjamin. One of the boring things about the young is that they swear non-stop.)

Benjy shot upright, spilling his beer. 'I don't believe those *clothes*,' he said. 'I don't believe that *hair*! You really went round the world with that man?'

'Everyone looked frightful in the 1960s . . . in any case, don't be so fucking superficial.'

He didn't reply, he didn't need to, we both know it's me who's obsessed with looks. There was Christopher in long shot waving his arms, Christopher with flared trouser-legs flapping. Benjy began to titter and snigger.

He's insecure, of course, now it's clear he has failed to make me pregnant. I loved him because he could make me pregnant, I loved him because he would give me a child. I went on hoping, I hoped against hope . . . even now the blood keeps coming each month . . . less than before, but I still bleed . . . all the same, I know, and he knows, he's failed me. A great strong boy of thirty. I try not to let my frustration show.

He's insecure, and it makes him spiteful. And we've been cooped up together too long in this third-rate hotel in this fifth-rate town, while we wait for news about the most important and beautiful event in my life to date . . . shh, it's bad luck to think about it. I try not to count on it too much.

Benjy is thirty, I'm fifty-five. Perhaps I'm lucky to have a young lover (but I don't look my age – I don't think I do, I still get ogled when I walk alone). I ought to be patient, because he is young, but I can't be patient, I was never very patient. I won't have him sneering at my past.

I suddenly felt something – crumbling, I suppose. As if, like

Venice, my past could slip in a second under the sea, and I'd go with it.

Rubbish, I've just got a hangover, it's not like me to mope and moan. The old life shouldn't matter now. I've a new young lover and plenty to hope for. I've always believed in happiness; when it goes sour, you just move on.

But this new happiness, a little voice whispers, the latest happiness has soured as well. Don't pretend, Alexandra. It's true. And maybe you can't move on for ever. Even if you do, you might need your past. Or else you'll end up aged sixty with nothing.

Even you could be lonely, Alexandra.

Perhaps I need to go over my story. So I'll have a story to tell the child, when the child I long for comes to me.

My life-story is beautiful, beautiful, an amazing, lucky, adventurous life . . . My Dad used to tell us stories. Winter tea-times, after our bath, he would tell us about his childhood in Stepney as we dried our hair by the fireside in that poky little house he thought was a palace . . . when he was a boy they had been so poor that even his shoes were castoffs. And he told us sagas of my mother's family, epic stories with monsters and demons and cream-skinned Irish heroines who he said looked 'exactly like your mother', though her own face curdled as she tried not to hear and later she'd warn us against his 'nonsense'. We sat by the fire while he told us these wonders, staring into the friendly flames . . . I wish he had known that I would be rich. It was why I loved Sundays, those fireside stories.

Now fire is the thing that everyone fears. Fire is gutting this monstrous land.

Your story's not suitable for a child, the burnt breeze whispers, the small sour wind.

6

Christopher: Venice, 2005

This is my apartment. She has never seen it, it has never seen her, it is mine, all mine. I never — hardly ever — think of her here. The flat belongs to another age, like me. Tall and cool and elegant.

— Lagoon-like mirrors with a blackened bloom that I've asked Lucia to leave untouched. The ornate plaster ceilings are too high to see clearly, ideal pale gardens, unpopulated. The windows soar effortlessly up from the green canal to the pigeon-pocked roof-tops. They are windows taller than the tallest woman and swagged by my orders with umber velvet, tied with strong cords of twisted silk which would hang or strangle the man who took her . . .

Get out of it, Alex, it's my turn now. I'm going to tell the world, you see, I'm going to tell the ones I love, whatever that means, whoever is left. The children — the child — perhaps. My friends. Who are my friends? There is the sorrow; we lost our friends.

I'm going to pretend that everyone cares, that nothing on earth can matter as much as remembering what my life has been.

I do believe it, in a way. I do believe that each life matters. What do they say? Not a sparrow falls . . . Christopher Court must count more than a sparrow. I shall sing as I fall, in any case, I shall finish my song to my own satisfaction before the sea swells up and sucks us down.

I have to find out who I am, you see, before I sink back towards non-being.

*

34

Christopher Court is an invented name, which isn't a good start when I want you to believe every word I say. It's an anglicisation of Czaycowski, a Polish–Jewish name. My father believed in caution, though he refused to believe persecution existed. Desperate to be ordinary, he pooh-poohed anti-semitism.

And indeed my beginnings were ordinary. I was the only son of a prosperous Jewish accountant and a pretty, clever, English-woman, daughter of a county family and therefore uneducated (and perhaps that's why I loved my half-educated wife, for my mother was always sweet to me, my mother loved me till the day she died . . . I should have killed Alexandra before she could leave me).

An only child; my beginnings were lonely – I longed for someone to make me complete.

My mother and father met in London when she was being finished. He told her the time in a dusty garden square in the 1920s. My mother told me there were starlings and daisies. She forgot her handbag because he confused her with his shiny black hair and curious accent; my father saw the bag and ran after her, catching her up by the dark wood chalet where they sold pink-iced penny buns and tea. They talked about the birds in the garden, and buses, which in fact my mother had never used, but she stared at the icing and talked about buses and thrilled to my father's Polish twang.

(My father denied all memory of this. My mother recounted it lovingly.)

They fell in love poor and fell out of it rich. By the time he died they were estranged, though they still lived together in a farmhouse in Surrey whose only claim to be a farm now rested on an aged plough, restored and polished, a foil for the roses, its neat brass label giving date and provenance. My mother always meant to remove that label, but the effort was too much for her. The house was too big, and they were too different once my childish presence no longer linked them, but they stayed together because they had promised.

They stayed together in retirement, she stayed with him after he had his stroke and at the end when the nightmares came, when my father realised they were not alone. In the middle of the night he heard bellowing ghosts of slaughtered cattle in the empty outhouses, and then he began to grieve at last for all the deaths he had tried not to notice. He blamed my mother for not being Jewish, for making their home near the plough and the roses.

– They stayed together because they had promised. It was ordinary, then, to stay together. They stayed together, he died with her.

Yes, Alexandra. They stayed together.

– But this came later, when I had left home. My boyhood and youth were as solidly ordinary as my father could have wished. I was what they call a good all-rounder. Arts and sciences, top of both. Which meant I was in for a tug-of-war, since my father assumed I should follow him and become a partner in the family firm, whereas mother – my dear, sweet, casual mother with her sudden swoops of inspired kindness and her brief exhibitions of intense concentration – remembered each poetry prize I had won, each school play I had postured in. 'You're so handsome, darling, don't be an accountant. Don't bury yourself in that awful fug.'

– No one ever said that my mother was tactful. But she understood about happiness. That's why she loved Alex, from the start, when she should have disapproved, when she should have been loyal to my first wife Penelope, the mother of her grandchildren, after all, the wife I was married to when I met Alex . . .

(I'll get to Penelope later. No time now.)

I compromised. I read Greats at Oxford, the education of a gentleman, training me for nothing, committing me to nothing. I thought I was elegant and urbane (in retrospect, arrogant, rude and narrow). Girls fell in love with me, *real* girls, beautiful undergraduates, not the larger underclass of secretaries and husband-hunters . . . life would be flavourless without a little arrogance.

I was suddenly as handsome as my mother had said. And an actor, just as she had hoped. A student actor, Romeo, Antony, Tristan in an adaptation of the lovers' legend that I helped to write, or overwrite . . .

Ah, you will say. So that was the start. A hopeless romantic, even then. In fact, my thoughts were not at all romantic. Once I lost my virginity I couldn't believe I had wasted twenty years not having this bliss. I wanted to have it every day, I wanted to have it three times a day. But the girls were shy, even when they were loving, and codes were strict, and walls were high, and beds, when you got there, horribly narrow.

(Don't think I am callow, or crude. Since then I have called myself a feminist. But I was young, and ignorant, and plagued by erections when taking exams. I've been plagued by erections all my life; they were only a blessing when Alex was there . . .)

Despite all this, I got a good degree, and was President of OUDS, the Dramatic Society. A job with a theatre company was fixed. I was packing my trunk to come back to London, where I meant to find rooms near theatre-land. Then everything changed, without warning. My father had his stroke.

I had always thought my father a bore, and the conviction had grown with the Oxford years of prancing about with golden children. My friends were the sons of lords and poets, land-owners, dashing entrepreneurs. If the parents appeared in term-time, they greeted their children with loud assured voices.

My father was dull and quiet by comparison. He'd only come to visit me once, and that was in my very first term. I looked down upon him from my second-floor window, his dark coat hunched around him as he walked across the quad; I was too mean to greet him, wishing him dead as he peered up anxiously at other people's windows to see if they were looking at him. I didn't call his name even when he unfolded an inch of white paper to check which staircase and it blew away and he scuttled after it, sideways, humbly, tripping and slithering, a tiny beetle on the great gold quadrangle.

I remembered that moment three years later when the phone call came about my father's stroke. At first it seemed he would never walk again. His mind was untouched, but his speech was gone. He wrote me a letter, a strange new father, in a spiderish, chaotic hand, explaining my terrifying new duty.

I still don't know why I did what he asked. I had never been

37

a boy to do what was asked. I am awkward, stubborn, still. But I thought he would die at once, and I thought I was somehow guilty. I dashed off a letter to the theatre company, melodramatic and apologetic, and another, longer, soberly phrased, proposing myself as he had suggested.

The good life vanished like a dream. I was articled to a rival firm of accountants, so I could enter the family firm in due course as a conquering lord, not a fallible minion.

My-son-the-accountant-who-went-to-Oxford.

'You were mad to agree,' my mother said.

I can hear her still as clear as the limpid lap-slap-lap of the waves down there. Louder than usual this evening. The tides are higher every day, pushing up under the bridges, through the crevices, under the grey-pink walls . . . 'Mad to agree . . . mad to do it.' It's mad to stay in Venice, now. Probably mad to stay alive, but we all cling on. I love life still.

What I did all those years ago wasn't mad. It was an act of love, perhaps the only one I ever performed for my father. Fifty years later I don't regret it.

'You and your father. Mad as hatters.' There's her voice, liquid, fluting and all her life with a hint of the debutante who said 'How kind' to my panting father, as he skidded to a halt with her handbag in his hand, that day in the square in the 1920s, sending up a shower of gravel and pigeons.

Outside my window the gulls are competing with pigeons for fish-heads and heels of that coarse brown bread. My cook Lucia is throwing her leftovers into the canal just out of sight. I see a hand, a fountain of pieces, then the birds sweep across, their heavy bodies briefly gilded by the evening sunlight, then harsh sea-calls and the clapping of wings join the lapping water. Hard strong wings.

Gulls and pigeons are dirty birds, opportunists who should not be encouraged. But this is Venice. It belongs to them. To gulls and pigeons, cats and rats.

To drowning palaces and mad old men.

*

Here is my supper. Slivers of delicate pink-brown liver and pale pink fungus, a tomato salad in a pale green bowl. The wine, thank God, is red as blood, fit for a hero, not the timorous invalid the rest suggests. Lucia thinks I need mothering, or rather, since she is half my age, Lucia thinks I need a nurse-maid. A glass of wine, quick, then another. Fill me with coarseness, blood and iron. Forget my parents, my dutiful past. Forget I am a child of England. Let's skip a little, all those boring years when I earned my living, got married, bred, left my wife and found true love . . .

Let me tell you about my life as a hero. It's just possible that you think you know me, for I had a certain renown . . .

Too pompous. Try again.

I enjoyed a certain temporary fame after the drama of five years ago. People thought they knew all about me. About us. About me and Alex.

Let me tell you they know nothing at all.

People lapped up the newspaper stories – the wife, the lover, the smoking gun, the white-haired avenger ranting and weeping . . . Not seeing that the things that happened bore only the thinnest relation to what might have been. To all the potential of that one moment. (I might not have shot. I need not have shot. If I'd simply flourished the gun and threatened . . . or I might have aimed better, and smashed him to pieces.)

The mystery is always what didn't happen, but nobody found us mysterious. They thought we were gamblers, high rollers, the rich, extravagant players in bloody dramas.

There you are, you see, I was a hero for them. A cuckold, perhaps, but dashing, violent. I like the image, but it wasn't the truth. On the day of the shooting I wrecked three lives, and didn't even manage to kill the intruder . . . There was nothing heroic about that day. My heroic act had been fifteen years earlier.

I can't remember any more if it was Alex's idea or mine to go away and never come back . . . nearly two decades ago. How young we must have been.

— Young enough to be forgiven, perhaps, by all the people we must have hurt?

No, because fifty-two is hardly young. It starts to seem young, you see, as I nose up from three score and ten . . . At the time I recall it felt old. So old I was almost panicky. I felt it was then or never if we were ever to do what we longed to do. A last-minute break for freedom, that's what I thought we'd done.

Before we took the terrific step, in the last few years we were living in England, there were moments when I'd look at Alexandra, perhaps sitting on the staircase, reading a book, at the loose treble clef of her seated body, and I'd think to myself, she's still young. And I still felt young — I was in love, you see, whenever I had time to notice, which is a way of staying young. And I wanted us to *live*, not exist, while we were still young enough to enjoy it, while Alex still looked like a swan waking up as her head looked briefly up at the skylight, and my hand still ached to touch her long white neck. I thought, we don't *have* to grow old.

I'm not claiming we were so special. Surely everyone must have moments like that, moments of longing, premonitions of regret, when you see life closing in on you, or death, I suppose, to be exact.

(While we're on the subject of dying, I don't want anyone to fly me 'home'. Bribe Lucia's husband to spirit me away. I want to be scattered over my sparkling, lethal Venetian sea. Or across one of the lesser-known squares at sunset, when all the children run about. They can brush me off their shoes at bedtime. I'd like to be dust on the children's shoes . . . other people's children are sweeter than one's own, easier to love, less critical.)

My kids said we were selfish to go. Down the years, they must have said it again and again. But maybe selfishness isn't all bad. Selfless people are empty people. When people say some-one's selfish, they usually mean they're jealous of them, or wish they had the nerve to act the same way.

— It's selfish to be true to yourself. Selfish to suffer less than everyone else. It's selfish to be too happy.

So Alex and I were selfish, yes. Having made our bed, we

40

refused to lie on it. We didn't accept that we should stay home and grow old. We didn't accept it was the children's turn now (because it never would be their turn, would it, if they had children too?) Women have done it for centuries, lived for the future of their children. And where has it got women?

Precisely nowhere. Those tired sad faces.

But Alex and I went round the world.

No, it's all right, I'm not upset. I'll pause for a moment to light the candles. The sky in the window, clear blue, reminds me. I am upset, you can see I'm crying, and I see myself, striking in the ruined mirror, a silver-haired actor with shining eyes, still playing Tristan now in my dotage.

I know I'm absurd, but it's right to cry. I'm remembering the greatest deed of my life. I'm remembering the triumph we both felt when we realised we had done it, when we sat in a tiny bar in Budapest and looked ahead into uncalendared weeks, weeks without deadlines or dreary duties.

Time was suddenly on our side. Time became ours, and infinite. A bell was ringing in the clear blue night. We looked through the door at a completely new skyline, tender declivities, yearning spires.

That was when we knew we would never die.

Because life, which had been narrow and episodic, endlessly divided into crowded rooms, had opened up, in one effortless movement, into all the world and the air beyond.

Alex, my love. Do you remember?

She must remember.

Alexandra.

7

Alexandra: Esperanza, Bolivia, 2005

I've been travelling for twenty years but I still miss the English newspapers. Even the word has a marvellous nostalgic flavour, it sounds like the comfortable rustle of pages and the hiss of a coffee percolator somewhere, lovely sounds from the twentieth century when there were a dozen daily newspapers in London, not two ... New York still has four, but only one worth reading. I've stayed loyal to my past in that respect, though lazier people and the new non-lits prefer to pick up the Dayscans on their computers.

I hunger for a newspaper now, this evening, which is too hot for walking and in any case unsafe for me to walk the streets on my own, with Benjamin sulking God knows where. I'm too tired (again) to write the letter to Mary Brown that I've owed for going on two years. Writing is dangerous, it makes you think, whereas reading fills up emptiness.

I could lie here with my pisco sour and my newspaper, stretched out on the shaky little sofa which is the most comfortable piece of furniture in our room and indeed in the whole Hostal Libertad, the whole wrecked, bald Bolivian hotel so laughably proud of its telsat system though the lavatories are a disgusting joke and the shower is never more than half-warm – I could put my feet up and spread my red hair over the sun-bleached cushion and look both preoccupied and spectacular to Benjy when he comes back drunk (he's still in love with me. Poor foolish Benjy). I'd devour the paper cover to cover, politics, scandals, health, psyche, not forgetting the fashion, if you can call the new cottons fashion ... what bliss it would be, sipping and reading, though a pisco sour is not the same without ice.

Lovely, lovely print. Of course I love it, it made me rich, print was what I worked at, never awfully hard, until we turned our lives into theatre. Even now I might go back to it one day. Sometimes I jot down a note or two. Names of flowers, or birds. I do research. I walk a lot. I take an interest. I thought I might write a travel romance, but life's too distracting, and I lose heart. One day, though. One day I might do it ... If things don't pan out. If I can't have my baby.

So long ago now it all seems like a dream ... To think I once made money, instead of just spending it. The most frivolous woman in the world, that's what Stuart called me a few years ago ... Seven years ago. How they stretch out. 'Alexandra, you were born to be a lily of the field ...' Men always underestimate women. I made us rich, I could do it again, I could do anything I choose, I'm not a back number ...

OK, everyone has forgotten me, but one day I shall astonish them. Five years after Chris and I went away the publishers were still begging me to write another book, chasing us from poste restante to poste restante. But I didn't bother to answer, and the film of *Gold Cards* was never made ...

No one but me remembers now that in 1985, my annus mirabilis, my picture was featured in every magazine in Britain. I still keep the photo they used in my handbag. I get a little thrill of something – shock, pride, grief, amusement? – telling myself that was really me. A sunny photo Christopher took on the lawn after Sunday lunch one day – how fucking English my life once was! I look so innocent and girlish! – I was in my thirties, but I could be eighteen, with a sea of red hair around my face, the living incarnation of *Red Gold* ... I think people were amazed to see all writers weren't ugly.

Looking back on it now the whole thing was absurd. I started the first book almost as a lark. Poppy, my mate at Klingfeld and Wish – (dear Poppy, I wonder what she's selling now? Not books, at any rate, the world has moved on) – who'd put a lot of freelance editing my way over the years, inspired the whole thing by saying one day, as we drank acid wine in a sandwich bar, 'It's mad to be an editor. Wrecking your eyesight over other

43

people's messes when you could be in their shoes earning lots of lovely lolly. And be famous to boot.'

'Are the authors I edit rich or famous?' The books she gave me to edit were mainly obscure books about European subjects, Venetian glassware, Italian design. We had known each other at college, you see, where I read modern languages until I dropped out. She did business studies, and thought I was a highbrow. We rather lost touch during my Harrods period, but after Chris wangled me the little job being decorative in a Bond Street gallery I got in touch again, and she was duly impressed. I found editing easy, but very poorly paid.

'The money's in bestselling novels, darling. Ever since Sally Flanagan made millions out of *Bodies*. Now everyone says they're going to write a bestseller . . . I'd do it myself, but I'm not a bit creative.' There was a tacit assumption that I wasn't either. To this day I remember the spasm of anger and joy that ran through my body. *I am creative, I've always been creative.* Besides, I'd read thousands of novels – I felt I was something of an expert in novels. I read them still. What else is there to do?

'I could write one,' I said. 'About my mother's family in Ireland. I could write you a lovely saga . . . with creamy-skinned heroines and demon lovers. Rags to riches, except they missed out on the riches.'

Poppy looked at me consideringly. 'You've got the looks,' she said. 'For publicity, I mean. But it won't do if they don't get rich.'

'OK they will. Then maybe *I'll* get rich.'

I'm sure she didn't take me seriously, and I had no idea if I could do it or not, but her disbelief, and Chris's teasing – and I'm sure the kids must have joined in as well, they missed no opportunity of tormenting me – drove me on over the pages. I wrote *Red Gold* in just under six months. It was hard labour – my God it was hard. I take it back that I've never worked hard. My head ached, my back ached, my eyes were a torment . . .

Poppy said she liked it, and so did her superior, but they both suggested I rewrite it completely, and then they rewrote it all over again. When we had arrived at a final draft they flattered

44

me grossly and took me out to lunch, not in a sandwich bar this time but in a sugar-pale interior with too many waiters. They didn't pay me a huge advance, which would have been more flattering still. And then a giant stroke of luck intervened.

(I had so much luck, perhaps I used it all up. I suppose I must be happier now. But I'm not so sure that I'm lucky any more. I've spilled my drink. A refill, quick.)

Chris had been in television news for donkey's years and most of his colleagues were amiable drunks. One of his oldest mates was Terry Fraser, a producer who drank rather more than the norm but who'd always shown me his charming side. His latest project was *Hot Frox*, a 'young' series on ready-to-wear fashion; I'd given him a contact, a friend of mine at Harrods – Angela and I once sold coats together in the lean years after I dropped out of college.

(The lean years, the desperate years when I sometimes sold rather more than coats. I was never quite a prostitute: too pretty, too arrogant, too ill-organised. But it was easy to meet rich men in Harrods, rich men who were eager to give me presents, and later, of course, it was hard to forget.)

When the presenter of *Hot Frox* got some horrible disease – shingles? syphilis? can't remember – not long before shooting was due to begin, Terry came round to our house drunk as a lord. 'Fucking stupid bitch, why does she have to get it *now*? Three months ago we could have replaced her, no problem, six months hence she could drop fucking dead!'

I too have my less charming side. Benjamin has found that out to his cost. I've grown more savage than I used to be, but I think I was savage enough with Terry. I told him what was wrong with his attitude, and graduated to what was wrong with his programme. He began to look at me very oddly, with a weird intensity I put down to drink.

Then he said, without answering any of my points, to Chris, who was listening anxiously, 'Listen, could she do a camera test? Has she worked before? She could be the answer.'

After he went we laughed at him. We didn't see ahead; we laughed at him. But I was interested too. I like new things, I get tired of routine, I like a change (Chris should have been warned; *I like a change*).

Next morning Terry was late and bad-tempered, ready to pretend he had been joking. But the camera loved me. It was all very easy. Terry's rudeness turned to an ecstasy of gratitude.

Success, success, I was a sweet success, the show and I were a terrific success. The media loved my face and hair and one journalist raved about my husky voice, so all the others copied him. RAW SEX ON FROX, screamed *The Sun*. I framed that cutting and stuck it in the loo. Suddenly I was a cult. I bought a Panama hat and enormous glasses so I could go to the shops in peace, but a *Sun* photographer spotted me, and after the front-page photograph young girls went out and bought Panama hats. The media acclaimed the 'Alex look'. By the time my book was published I was seriously famous, and Chris's children weren't speaking to me.

Red Gold sold ten thousand in hardback and a quarter of a million in paperback, helped by the hinted libel in reviews that the lesbian affairs were my own – affairs I'd dreamed up at Poppy's suggestion. The viewing figures for the programme doubled.

I loved it all; I lapped it up. It was glorious to make money on my own. We had always been comfortable on Chris's salary, but now we were extremely comfortable, with the paperback advance stashed away in the bank.

But that was it, so far as I was concerned. It was an episode, over, not the start of something. When Terry asked me to do another batch of *Frox* I refused without a pang. All I had in mind was a holiday.

My agent soon disabused me. Three months after *Red Gold* was published, he rang me to tell me my publisher had offered a fabulous sum for a two-book contract. £100,000? £200,000? Whatever it was, I fell silent, amazed.

'Alexandra? Are you OK?'

'But I haven't even *thought* about another book. What are they offering all that money *for*?'

'Your name,' said my agent. 'You're bankable.'

'Why? I'm not doing any more television.'

'You're not serious – '

' – I am.'

'Well they don't know that. Take the money and run.'

I signed for one book, actually. No one was going to buy my future. *Gold Cards* was a blockbuster about prostitution, its ritzier, soft-focus end, as you would guess from the working title, *Kept Women*. The film rights were sold before the book was finished. But things didn't go according to plan this time. I meant to write the book I had promised, but someone else seemed to take over my brain. A past self, a buried self. I began to write about lies and misery and pain and humiliation.

For a while after dropping out of college, in my early twenties, in the jungles of Knightsbridge, I had dropped out of the normal world. I was very young, I was very pretty. Fresh and round-faced in the photographs, my smile out-shining Harrods' plate-glass though I functioned on pills and alcohol. My nights were night-clubs, discos, casinos and private suites at the big hotels where I faked orgasms for rich Arabs. The only bits I liked were the money and the dancing, but they didn't make up for the aching mornings when my body and brain felt dirty grey, as if cigarettes had been stamped out all over me.

I put it all in. There were pages of ash.

There was a fictional version of the terrible birthday – was I twenty-two? – I think I was – when my brother travelled from Ireland to see me. They'd all gone back over when my Father died, but I chose to stay in London: I was barely Catholic, I'd never felt Irish, even my name was chosen by Dad, not Mum. Seamus was a strange, heavy, sulky, loving boy, five years older than me. I was his favourite, not Brigid, who was the spitting image of Mum.

He came to see me as a birthday surprise. The flat I shared with another girl was too full of the evidence of how I lived. His watery grey eyes darted about him. He made me nervous; I started to drink, not beer or whisky which he'd have understood but vodka martinis in a steady chain. The phone rang too often. The doorbell rang twice, both times men I have now forgotten.

Seamus got into a steady rage. There was a dreadful row, muddied with drink. He called me a whore, I called him a moron.

His face was beetroot when he got angry. I suppose one day he will die of a stroke . . . perhaps poor Seamus is dead already, for since then I have only seen him once. He and Brigid, appalled and vengeful, came to the hospital later that year when I gave birth to a daughter and caught some stinking postnatal infection. The doctors insisted on next-of-kin, and my mother's legs were too bad to travel. My daughter lay silenced by the glass of the nursery. I'd decided long before to have her adopted, but the hospital hadn't explained to them. Perhaps they'd come hoping to reclaim us both, and shower love on their new little niece . . .

She wasn't their niece. She wasn't mine, either, she was dark and minute with a face like any of the Arab men who might have been her father.

I was very weak, but I stood up to Seamus. I've always known how to stand up to men. I told him I didn't need my past, I didn't need my family, or the Church, or guilt, or a future as the mother of a fatherless daughter. He called me a devil, and they cast me off. I was hardly out of the hospital when the letter arrived from my mother in Ireland, in her raging, ignorant round hand.

Perhaps they thought I would beg for forgiveness. But I'd never felt like one of them. I was quicker, thinner, more intelligent; they were stew and potatoes and sweet strong tea whereas I had been mad for prawns and champagne since I had them at a wedding when I was fourteen. I didn't look like them or talk like them or dress like them. Only my flaming red hair came from my mother. I loved my father, the sweet shabby man who had fallen in love with Mum's Irishness; from him came the stories and my eyes and mouth and my hunger for things he never had. After he died they didn't seem like my family.

I didn't miss them for nearly a decade, and then I noticed an emptiness. No guilt of course; why should I feel guilt? I did nothing wrong, but they cast me off. All the same, their absence

48

left a tiny chill which even Christopher couldn't stop growing ... for a while he was my father, my mother, my brother ... Now he's gone, like nearly everyone else.

I wonder if my mother ever read my novels. I wonder if Brigid ever saw me on *Hot Frox*. I wonder if Seamus squirmed with horror as he read the sex scenes in *Red Gold*. I wonder if he recognised me in *Gold Cards*; I wonder if he remembered the row.

At least I made use of my dreary family. At least they helped to make me rich. I wrote the truth, not the sparky inventions I'd promised Poppy when they drew up the contract.

The public were surprised and offended, the public didn't like truth in their books, and *Gold Cards* sold less well than *Red Gold* ... what did it matter? I'd banked the advance. I had the money. What did any of it matter ...

I quit my family, I quit writing novels. Why should it seem to matter more now?

Why do I drink when I think of my family? I made my fortune, I made myself free ...

Take the money and run.

That phrase used to echo in my brain when Chris and I were nerving ourselves to get out of England. We were both what Mary Brown would call *quitters* I suppose if she hadn't been too fond of us to make judgements. Too fond of Christopher at any rate, I was never quite sure what she felt about me. Mary and Matthew; they were our best friends. Now Matthew is ill, and I haven't written ... It's been two years. He might be dead.

I don't like illness, I don't like to be near it, I've been allergic to illness since the horrible millennium when half my days passed in a stinking sickroom ... it was one of the reasons why I wanted Benjy, his firm young body gleaming with health. I've never gone in for illness myself, though in this wretched place it's a miracle we're not dead of the heat or the disgusting food ... can I ever have thought fried plantain exotic?

I'd always wanted to go to South America, but Christopher

always made excuses. I imagined the jungle as flamboyant and brilliant; I hadn't quite imagined the killing heat or the red mud after the rain falls, sucking at your shoes, sucking at your ankles, turning to choking dust when it dries. No one who hasn't actually been here could imagine the number of biting things or the utter poverty of the villages. Not that there are many villages; even Bolivians disdain these lowlands. That's why we've come here, because they're poor. Because poor people will do things for money, though so far nothing's gone right for us.

The *servicio higienico* . . . nothing was ever more misnamed. We've been here for months but I still can't believe that the lavatories can't cope with toilet paper. If you're lucky there's a wastebin to drop it in. In our first hotel I complained to the manager that our wastebin was nearly always full. 'Tiralo al suelo pues señora,' he said. *Drop it on the floor!* And that's what they do! They're animals, and besides, they thwart me. We brought them our dreams, Benjamin and I. Our dreams and our money, but they make us wait. I've never liked waiting. It makes me angry.

Luckily the local booze is good. I like my drink, I need it here. I don't get drunk, I despise drunkenness, but I drink a little more than I used to, when life was easier, when I was . . . younger.

I don't want to say *when I was young*, because I'm not old yet, I don't look old . . . why doesn't Benjamin come back? Why is there never any ice for my drinks? If I think about ice I can almost come, imagining it sliding down my forearm, imagining it sliding between my hot breasts and over my nipples which ache with heat . . .

If Benjamin was here we might make love. This rat-hole's unbearable on my own, if nothing is settled within the week we shall have to get out, I'll have to get out, I'm a quitter, you see, a fly-by-night.

Why does everyone think it's weak to escape? I've always thought it took tremendous daring. Christopher and I escaped. The pisco is making me sentimental, but it's not just the drink, we were of one mind, we were travellers, we loved to move, we were in love with the world as well as each other, I haven't forgotten, I merely pretend . . .

And we did escape, it was glorious.

8

Christopher: Venice, 2005

Burning thirst in the middle of the night oh God I need water horribly alone . . .

Three in the morning; the most hopeless time. No more sleep for me tonight. Yet I fell asleep so happily, big with alcohol and sentiment. Now I am worthless, shrivelled, small. Now no woman would look at me.

If I could have two minutes with Alex. If I could see her face to face – (I hope it is lined, and sunken. I hope South America has yellowed it. I hope that no one else would want her, no, I am mad, she is beautiful, of course she is, she could not change) – I should make her answer me.

Alexandra, you must answer me.

Was it in New York, in the burning heat, with the klaxons blaring and the petrol fumes drifting sourly in through the open window, with the deafened silence after the blast and her thin voice screaming from another planet – was it then that every-thing went wrong? Or was it long before? Have I forgotten, did I not understand, was I blind? – You used to say all men were blind.

Did something happen, long ago in Toledo, that I should have seen and understood? Did you want me to be jealous, did I fail to be jealous, was there something real to be jealous of?

(Maybe I was jealous, and have forgotten. A decade ago, or a dozen years, make it thirteen, that's more unlucky. It starts to leak back, a taint of jealousy, that unforgettable, metallic taste. An old foul taint of fear and need.)

Last question. Answer and I'll let you go. I won't wrap those cords around your neck, those strong silk cords, twisted cords,

52

and tighten, tighten so you'll never leave. Answer, my love, and you shall go.

Was our end in our beginning? Was it my stupidity in taking you away that led at last to this loneliness? Did I plot to keep you to myself and delude myself that it was what you wanted?

— There is the nightmare; that she wasn't ever happy.

How can I sleep till she answers me?

9

Alexandra: Esperanza, Bolivia, 2005

The beginning was so simple, such wonderful fun. Looking back on it now it's hard to believe that life ever felt so light-hearted. That incredible sense we both suddenly had that the future was now, that we didn't have to wait . . . that's how I remember the beginning. A dizzying shift from feeling bogged down and frustrated by duties and domesticity – not that I was ever domesticated, but I felt bogged down by all I didn't do – into another life where everything was light. Freedom, freedom. We were going to be free.

Houses and families are deadly I think. They're what everyone wants, but they eat you up, they waste your time, they weigh you down. It's why the very young are so delicious; they're not dragging all that dull baggage around.

We both suddenly knew that we had to get away, which didn't mean three or four weeks in the sun but a real journey, a real escape. We'd both lived in England since we were born, after all (what a penance, to spend so much time in England! What a waste of planet, what a waste of life!)

All our adult lives there had been too much clutter and we'd gone on expecting it would clear away, one day, any day, it couldn't last, the muddles were purely temporary. Soon there would be more time and space. But since we'd been married things had actually got worse; the phone rang non-stop, the callers kept calling, the irrelevant letters kept dropping through the door, outdated friendships we couldn't evade, outdated promises we had to abide by, bills, ads, requests for donations, the endless bleat of good causes at breakfast, *plant more trees,*

54

save the whale, give to the starving, the sick, the crazy, fill another form in to save the world ... Great fat envelopes bulging with virtue. No one sends letters like that to hotels.

The children were another problem. Chris's children, that is, since they never felt like my children (I won't know for sure till I have one of my own, but I'm sure my child will be adorable). Susy and Isaac were five and eight, and rather sweet, when Chris and I married, but later they grew larger and greedier, for time and love and money, for advice on acne, help with their calculus, admiring responses to their thoughts on life.

– Not that I gave them all this without a fight, except the money, which was easy to give. I was adept at being both cool and jolly, and I made a tactic of being too young. As they grew older, I grew younger; by the time they were ten I was much too immature to do their washing or ironing.

But Christopher did his best, and tormented himself that it wasn't good enough, trying to make up for leaving their mother. Weekends were a whirlwind of educational outings, which the children outgrew long before their father; he didn't notice they were growing up, they didn't bother to tell him what they wanted. They didn't seem to want to go out at all. They preferred to stay at home and be bored, and blame us because home was boring. I watched Chris grow more tired and drained as the children grew surlier.

Home *was* boring, they had a point. Home-owning is a monumental bore. The house made dully insistent requests to be looked after. Things I haven't had to think about for twenty years, but I still get a headache when I try to remember, or else I have drunk too much pisco, which is Benjamin's fault for being late, I shall lose my looks, it will all be his fault, I shall have to get out ...

There was an endless whisper of things decaying. Paint, plaster, drainpipes, gutters ... things one should never have to waste one's time on. I remember the despair when I looked into a cupboard and saw my beautiful black feathered hat had a faint frosting of mould, and I knew I had to worry about the damp when all I wanted to do was buy a new hat ...

55

Each week there was more rubbish, old shoes, old coats, old jewellery, outdated timetables we never used but never threw away ... Chris spoke the truth for both of us one day, as he craned out of the window trying to see if a crack had spread and the house was subsiding; suddenly he exploded, 'Alex! My neck is bloody killing me! I can't spend the rest of my life in this dump!'

– It was hardly a dump, by the way. It was a five-storey house in Islington, London, crammed with rather good furniture and pictures and plants. (I still miss three tiny Burra drawings I bought in the early '80s when they were still cheap.) And then there were all the electrical goods which Chris bought compulsively and then got bored with, the latest VCR, the latest CD player, the latest – what was it? – *camcorder* (how dated all those terms sound now!) ... they were such fun new, and such hell when they broke, and gathered dust mournfully, waiting to be mended. Every corner of the house had its ghosts, my 'Speak Russian' cassettes, my trampoline, Isaac's skating boots, Susy's oil-paints, things I had half put away, half-used, and paper and dust and old-fashioned dirt.

The piles of paper multiplied after *Red Gold*. Each draft was the hardest work of my life, and I couldn't yet bear to throw them away, any more than I threw away my fan letters or the invitations to open supermarkets which lay in the study in dusty sacks.

The cleaning women, naturally, never stayed, and I had no talent for housework. Chris got home much too tired, and of course his mother never taught him how to do it, any more than I taught Chris's son.

'I wish we could live in a hotel,' I said. 'We could almost afford it. We could afford it. It would leave more time for the important things.'

'I wish we didn't live in London. I wish we didn't live in England.'

'Of course, there's your job. We have to stay here.'

It wasn't strictly true. After *Red Gold* and *Gold Cards* we had enough money to keep us comfortably till we died. But neither of us quite believed in that money. It had come too easy, and we were too used to Christopher being the breadwinner.

Then fate pushed us hard in the right direction. Chris's mother died, which was a pity in a way since she was vague and amiable and very fond of me, and didn't expect me to be a housewife. She was suddenly dead of a heart attack, and the house was left to Chris. It turned out she hadn't been totally vague. The farm had twenty unused acres, and just before she died she'd got planning permission to build an 'exclusive' modern estate . . . The land sold for over two million. Now no one could deny that we were rich.

Chris was bored with his job, in any case. The more promotions he got the less creative he felt. He no longer went out on stories, no longer wrote scripts, no longer made programmes. Instead he advised about other people's programmes; he sat in endless meetings talking about nothing, took decisions about 'balance' and 'political judgement' and hated himself for knowing the rules. He had watched his contemporaries get older and sadder and told himself it wasn't happening to him, until one day he couldn't pretend any more.

I remember the day we decided. He had come home early, which wasn't like him. The kids weren't even back from school, and I was dozing on the sofa in the drawing-room when I heard his feet on the stairs. I asked him if he was all right, but he didn't say anything, he wouldn't sit down. Then without warning he was saying what mattered.

'You once said you married me because I was honest . . .'

' – Two liars in one family would be too much.'

' – *Listen* to me Alex, this is important. I haven't been honest for years and years. Everything is trimming, playing by the book. I can't go on like this till I die. I'm fifty-two, I've only got thirty years left . . .'

I hated to hear him talk like that. I went and put my arms round him, but he wouldn't be deflected, he wouldn't even look at me. Normally he liked to look at me. Light from the side made him lined but handsome as he stared at the sea-green velvet of a chair over which his son's pajamas straggled mournfully, thin and twisted as a long-drowned corpse. Everyday chaos, everyday mess . . .

'I wish we were in Venice,' I said.

'We have to get out,' Chris said. 'I mean it.'

I was a little frightened, for surely he was happy . . . surely he had been happy with me? Happier than I was, surely? I hadn't noticed that he had grown desperate.

We talked about the pros and cons. There were our friends. It's not easy to make new friends. Mary and Matthew were our best friends. True, she was dull (Chris didn't agree), but terribly kind, a wonderful listener, and 'far from stupid', Chris said. And Matthew was witty, and adored me. Probably still does, if he hasn't died.

But friends aren't enough to keep you at home. They improve your life, they don't live it for you. That day Chris was perfectly certain what he wanted. 'I loathe living here. The kids don't need us. They can't stand us. Let's go on holiday and never come back.'

It was partly bravado, of course. Chris didn't mean it, about never coming back. It isn't so easy to lose the past. When he thought of the children, he vacillated, and asked the company to take him back. I wasn't having it, I said I would leave him . . . I was already making our travel plans, I was already enjoying a foretaste of freedom. I admit I pressed him, for his own good. I knew better than he did what he wanted.

Terry Fraser rang up drunk one day and tried to tell me that Chris was going through the male menopause, and when I said it was none of his business he said I had always been a ballbreaker, and I told him to fuck off and dry out.

Chris resigned again, this time for good. I was happy again; we were happy again. But I think the question of how long we were going for was fudged, between us and the children. Not in my mind, though. I knew this was it. I had decided to say goodbye to little England.

When Chris promised the kids we would be back in September I didn't say anything. Nor did they. They didn't seem to mind, at first.

We went away that summer. I can't recall exactly how many years ago. A mist came up between us and home, a mist came up between us and the children . . .

I thought about them over the years. Even before they pursued us, I thought about them. I'm not as hard-hearted as people say. I thought about Isaac's awful degree and whether what happened was all our fault.

And I thought about the other folks back home. I think about them sometimes still. Mary and Matthew, our friends. I try to visualise Matt twenty years older. He made me laugh, which is wonderful. I think I missed him at first, I'm beginning to forget. And now perhaps he is dying – dead.

I remember good old Mary. I suppose by now her hair is quite grey. I wonder what they thought about us, and if they forgave us for what we did, since a lot of the problems fell on them. She has gone on writing over the years, affectionate letters in that mouse-grey hand.

I wonder if I'll ever see her again . . .

The pisco makes me melancholy.

I want to be touched, I want to be fucked.

– Toledo was every human shade, an encyclopaedia of flesh-colours. The city was on a hill. From the opposite hill where our parador stood you could look across the whole sweep of it. At siesta time there was no one about, just rose and fawn, peach and pink, tawny gold and dun and brown, a vanished painter's dream of flesh. The doors and windows were little dark eyelets, but we knew no one to ask us in.

– So we were free, of course. Chris said 'That's what freedom is.' Knowing nobody, not being known.

I wasn't sure, I think I wanted something else, I've always wanted everything . . .

We first went to Toledo in '92, an early summer of glorious heat. I saw Stuart sitting in a cafe with his son. He was beautiful. I wanted him. After that I made sure we went back every year.

(My head starts to ache. It wasn't my fault. My heart was always true as steel. The swords of Toledo are remarkable, thread-thin steel which can bend full circle.)

Outside in the dark the cicadas go crazy, breeding like locusts in the savage heat. Rats and insects are happy now, coming into their own in the twenty-first century . . . Toledo seems so long ago.

A warm breeze blew between the parador and the opposite hill where the city stood. I think of that breeze with longing here where the heat is three times as intense and for days and weeks not a breath of wind and I've nothing in the world to do but wait, in the sticky bloody heat, cooped up with a boy I no longer love . . .

And I think about love. Romantic love.

People tell you romantic love is 'unreal'. 'It's just the icing on the cake,' they say. They assume they're confirming what you already know, that all right-minded folk agree.

They must have different blood. They must have different bones.

There are women who live their lives for their children who would be appalled by what Chris and I did, leaving the kids for each other . . . Because 'you can always get another husband. They don't need you like your children do.' And if I turned and said to them 'They weren't my children, they were *his* children, I have no children of my own,' they wouldn't know whether to feel pity or outrage, and once I would have said 'Go fuck yourselves, bitches, what do you know, you withered old cows,' but now, curse them, I'm beginning to agree with them about the pity of childlessness. All the same, I think most women are virgins, and jealous of the ones who are truly loved . . .

You see how hard it is to talk about love without all the other shit breaking in; wifehood, motherhood, responsibility, notions that turn me rigid with boredom.

I'm trying to talk about passion. Adult love, sexual love, between a woman and a man (Isaac would bridle at that, poor boy).

I think about love because I know about it, even if it has deserted me. In other areas my knowledge is patchy. There are

60

facts about the world which escape me, yes, but I know about people. I know about life.

There have always been those who call me ignorant. Men, I mean. They clutch at it, to protect them from my intelligence, which was measured when I was eleven years old and had a mental age of twenty-one, an IQ of something near genius level. I'm not a genius, I know, and the teachers at secondary school all said I was lazy and cheeky and wasted my promise . . . but I'm quick; I'm sharp. Not many men like it. Quicker and sharper than most of my men. And so they fall back for reassurance on my ignorance of this and that – the stock market, computer science, positions of the continents upon the globe, politics, moral philosophy, the kind of thing I should have acquired at school when I was too busy doing gym and dancing and waiting for the bell at ten to four when I'd be picked up just outside the school gate by young men with motorbikes or (preferably) sports cars, giggling wildly when they asked me to marry them, considering the matter when they asked me to fuck. Not that they ever called it that. Learning a lot about love. That they loved me, but I needn't love them.

– Nearly forty years ago. You see, it is possible; forty years of fucking.

Aged eighteen I sat incredulous when my mother tried to tell me the facts of life, a lot of which focused on 'not working men up'. There was nothing I enjoyed like working men up, nothing so exciting as their desire.

It's hard to get used to the lessening of that, as the hormones taper off, in my fifties, though Benjy still says I'm beautiful . . . but that merely annoys me, it's sentimental, he didn't know me in the days when people stopped talking when I walked into a room. In Paris when I was twenty-five a taxi-driver passed me in the Latin Quarter, screeched to a halt, jumped out, staring, ran to a flower-stall, snatched up some roses, thrust a note at the gaping stallholder, ran back to me and went down at one knee as he gave me the flowers; kissed both hands; and ran back to his cab without another word, where an amazed passenger sat waiting for him. If I ate alone, men sent over champagne; I never had to wait at a zebra crossing; customs men never searched my luggage, which generally contained a surprise or two, and policemen were lenient with me for speeding . . . A lot of it was crass and boring, but all the same, when it goes, you miss it.

Sexual love; romantic love. Chris kept it going for a quarter of a century. We went round the world to keep it alive, we fucked in Athens, Rome, Berlin, Mombasa, Lusaka, Tripoli, in Santa Fé, in Amsterdam, in a tiny hut on Mount Kilimanjaro . . . we did unspeakable things to each other in a cable-car swinging up a Swiss mountain, we gorged on each other in the cabin of a boat that swayed along the River Nile. We knew every inch of each other's bodies; Christopher always rejoiced in that.

'No other man could ever make love to you as often as I have now. Even if you left me tomorrow. Of course I'd kill you if you did . . . no one could ever know you so well. No one could make you come as much . . .'

Desire seemed irrevocable to Chris, a way of programming himself. He saw our love as fated. 'No one else but you could have made me happy.'

What does he say now, I wonder?

Mrs Simpson and the Prince of Wales. They get most people's vote for sticking it out, making the original gesture worth it. For marrying and staying married, remaining, the while, good-looking and young. She was even romantic in extreme old age, romantic in her senility, for she was still thin, still tragic . . .

The world well lost for love.

No one could say we were unworldly . . . we travelled first class to first-class hotels. But Chris gave up a world, I suppose. His family, his job, his will to win. Not that there was ever a race worth winning down those hateful fluorescent corridors. His friends. Our friends, but he cared about them more. Mary and Matthew; he thought he would miss them, which seemed strange to me at the time we left when there was so much to look forward to, though they were perfectly agreeable. More

62

than that. But you can make new friends . . . I wonder why we didn't manage it?

Chris gave up the old life for love of me.

I'm telling you he loved me. I tell you that as a preliminary. And I was grateful, and loved him back, and didn't stop loving him for twenty-five years, and I can't think of anything more real than that. I loved him, you hear, for a quarter of a century. What I say next can't alter that.

– We loved each other in different ways. Not at first. It was after we left home that I became so much more of his life, replacing the children and the office and all those glamorous lunchtime women . . . Things changed, for then I felt sure of him. He said I was everything to him.

And part of me was humble and grateful. I did realise how lucky I was to have a man who loved me so. But my love wasn't like his. I won't concede that he loved me more, but certainly more totally. His love was based on one idea. *This is the woman that I love. Love, in this world, for me, means her.*

It was how he justified the choices he'd made. Leaving his wife and upsetting the children. It wasn't just a fantasy, though, he lived the emotion day by day. He couldn't bear me to be hot, or cold. He would never have brought me to this stinking place . . . He never shopped without buying me gifts, roses, a beautifully textured sweater, a pair of pale yellow ballet-shoes with the absurdly low vamp I loved. He ordered raspberries and cream for breakfast. He said he loved me nine times a day. And he did make me happy, he did, I've never forgotten that we were happy . . .

But how do you protect it, last year's present, sucked into the howling tunnel of the past? How can I explain myself?

For me, romantic love means desire, and desire means longing for something over there, something utterly delicious, almost out of reach, enjoyed but not possessed.

And when I think about romantic love, it isn't Chris I'm thinking of.

(And yet I loved him, I did, I did.)

*

There was another man (there were other men, but only two who mattered, in the end, and the other one was Benjamin).

There was another man. His name was Stuart. Stuart is such a hopeless name, a prunes and prisms Scottish name with no acceptable abbreviations, a name that makes you purse up your mouth. He was married, of course. After thirty, all the men worth having are already married. No wonder people feel smugger in their twenties, when there are more free agents and more room for virtue.

Stuart's father was Scottish. He'd never lived in Scotland and yet he had chosen a Scottish wife, partly, I'm sure, out of loyalty to some dim conception of Scottish blood. Stuart denied that; he said that he loved her, but men aren't perceptive about their motives. His two children were caricature Scots, a tough little girl with scarlet hair and oatflake freckles and sky-blue eyes, a ferocious boy with the small neat nose and heavy black eyebrows Stuart had, the features already cut from granite although when I first saw him he was three years old.

I met them in Toledo, just Stuart and his son. I wonder how much I'd have saved myself if my very first view had included Kirsty, still big from the two young children, her hair a brighter red than mine, cut in a tight cap round her head as if hair might spread diseases . . . Perhaps it would all have been different if Stuart and his son had been protected by her motherly figure, forever bent to child level, always stooping to soothe a pain or pick up a ball or replace a sunhat, a low-based, gentle triangle who usually stuck to her man like a shadow.

When I think about her, which is rare enough, I try not to see her eyes. Naked eyes which screwed up at the sun. The whites were pure as albumen. Kirsty didn't drink, unlike her husband, and I never saw a hint of red in those eyes, not until later when the weeping began . . . The irises were a severe grey-blue, or they seemed severe when they turned on me, but I suspect they were only shy. All the same, they were nun's eyes, and unprotected, and please God keep those eyes away.

Don't think I feel guilty. Why should I feel guilty? Preserving

64

a marriage is the business of the married; whatever happened was Stuart's fault, *I* had no obligations to Kirsty.

She wasn't with them, that first morning. It was my first morning in Toledo, too, on the first of so many visits. It was early for me, before 9am; I'd left Chris in the swimming pool and taken a cab across to the city.

I remember waking up that day. A tide of sunshine flooded the room, and I got up rubbing my eyes and went over to the balcony. We'd arrived in darkness the day before. A mile away on the opposite hill the long slope of the city unfolded upwards, a miraculous sequence of pinks and golds, not a modern building to jolt the eye. 'Come and see this!' I'd called to Chris. 'Come and see *this*,' he answered. What he had to show me was a lovely erection, so I wasn't frustrated on that morning walk, indeed I was glowing with everything good, a good sleep, a good fuck, a good big breakfast, a great new city to explore . . .

There was a little cafe at a turn of the road so steep it was like an elbow, the tables crawling out into the road because the angle of the pavement wasn't wide enough. There was quite a lot of traffic; people going to work, it seemed outrageous that they had to work with the day full of cedars and bells and starlings, the air still cool but promising heat, the sun making sculptures of every surface . . .

I sat down at a table. The streets were cobbled. I wasn't wearing sensible shoes. I fancied a giant *café con leche* while I rested my feet and watched the people, I could do what I wanted, I was young and free.

And I turned to pity a harassed young man who sat in the sun three tables away with a little boy who was making a fuss. Their belongings were piled round the table, a collapsing island of plastic bags. The little boy had a strawberry icecream. Because he didn't speak very clearly, it was a minute or two before I realised they were English – no, Scottish.

'Don't want it,' he was saying. 'Don't like it. Want a vanilla one.'

'Don't eat it then,' said his father, patient. 'I told you it was too early for icecream.'

65

'WANTA VANILLA ONE.'

'Have a biscuit.' The father began to search through his bags, at first hopefully, then in a despairing fury.

'Wantit NOW! Mungry, mungry . . .'

So it went on, for quite some time. I gloried in my childlessness – yes, I tell you, I gloried then – my baglessness, my singleness, though of course Chris waited for me in the shadows . . . Whereas this poor man was perhaps divorced . . . perhaps a widower.

All I managed to see was his lean muscled back, plus a perfect view of the sexual characteristic I've always found obscurely appealing, the back of his neck, a masculine neck, thicker than a woman's and yet vulnerable when the neck hair is cut short enough to show it. This young man's hair was short and dark and ended in a minute duck's tail, curving to the left, not upwards, then pale skin and gleaming white shirt. They must have come away very recently; so home was still there, for people to leave . . . we had been away from home five years, and though I had recently given up sunbathing my skin had acquired a dense pale gold colour from living in the sun day after day. I wished the young man would turn round and admire me. My hair was pulled back in a tight red bun which I thought made me look like a ballerina.

'Thass Mummy!' said the little boy, suddenly very loud again, pointing at me, then with perfect illogic 'Not Mummy, no. Want Mummy. Want a wee wee. Wanta go home.'

When the young man turned, he wasn't so young, perhaps my age or even older. I registered his extreme good looks. He hadn't an ounce of spare flesh on his face; he had a fine-cut nose with a narrow tip, a strong Scots jaw, and heavy eyebrows which hung like pines over large blue eyes. It was a very masculine face, but his mouth was wide, soft, full, and ready to break into a smile, as it did when he registered that this was Mummy. If I'd known what she looked like I'd have seen why it was funny, since she was never out of an anorak, or in summer a rustling cagoule, for she always felt at risk of rain. I wore a brief straight dress of yellow silk and the delectable primrose shoes Chris had given me.

I smiled with all the force of my approval of his handsomeness, all the joy of sun and sex and the morning and my first glimpses of the flesh-coloured city. He smiled back, a marvellous smile (Chris's one bad feature was his teeth, too small and very faintly discoloured, so I always admired a set of white teeth; these gleamed at me briefly in the sharp sunlight).

'I'm English,' I said, to make things plain.

'Sorry,' he said. 'This kid adopts people. His Mummy has red hair.'

My heart sank briefly to know there was a Mummy. He smiled again, and my spirits rose. 'Do you think your little boy would like one of my biscuits? I mean, if he won't eat that icecream.'

'Well — that would be wonderful. He wouldn't touch his breakfast, and I promised Kirsty I'd make him eat something . . .' Kirsty must be Mummy then. Not a very attractive name. I wished very hard they might be something distinguished, something I wouldn't be forced to find boring. He could be an actor, a painter, a musician . . . We could ask him to eat at the parador. And his wife and son, all three of them, or perhaps she'd prefer to babysit. We enjoyed distractions. His looks were distracting.

I handed over the vanilla fingers the waiter had brought with my coffee. Unsmilingly, the child took them. 'Thank you,' his father said. The biscuits disappeared with remarkable speed; he was Stuart, I was Alexandra, this was Robert, I had a husband called Chris, we 'lived abroad', he was fascinated, he was fuckable, I mustn't think like this.

I asked him what he did, dreading the answer. But it turned out he taught Film Studies and was writing a book about the cinema of Carlos Saura and Hector Pañol. They had friends with a flat in Toledo; they had lent them their house in Finsbury Park for the summer. So they knew Toledo quite well already. I accepted these items with grateful joy. They were valid credentials to pass on to Chris, who might not have been too delighted if I'd asked a civil servant to dinner.

Perhaps I was giving off that curious miasma that clings to the satisfied flesh after sex. He was watching me very acutely, despite the demands of the child beside him who wanted icecream, Mummy, love. Indeed he had suddenly turned on me an absolute quality of attention, as if I were someone he had always loved and been away from half a lifetime. He looked at my hair, my eyes, my hands as if he were logging minute changes on which his life and mine might depend.

His eyes were very blue. They looked at me, surely, much too hard. Perhaps he was merely cocky, or rude. I stood up briskly.

'Oh,' he said, a little moan of unfeigned disappointment that told me he was not smooth, nor rude, nor a womaniser, nor anything bad. 'Do you have to go? I mean . . . what I mean is, we're going too. Come on Robert. We'll walk with you.'

Walking with them was such a different thing to the sauntering stroll I'd had alone. Robert was tired, and wouldn't walk, but felt demeaned by being held, so was up and down like a jack-in-the-box. He glared at me. I smiled at him. He put his tongue out. Stuart didn't notice, and I pretended not to notice either.

Stuart bent down to pick up Robert's toy plane, and I looked at the tender pale back of his neck, then saw he had paused to stare at my naked legs in the pale Italian shoes. It was only an instant, but our eyes met, he knew I saw, I saw he knew, he had found the plane, he was back on his feet, we walked side by side up a bright cobbled slope that led into a narrow neck of shade, I no longer knew what the child was saying, our arms touched briefly as we went into the dark. It was very cold. I drew in my breath.

The street was only seven feet wide, medieval houses which rose four storeys to an even narrower ribbon of sky. 'Look above your head,' he said. Suddenly my eyes grew used to the dark and I saw it was full of garlands.

'It's Corpus Christi,' he said. 'They carry the Virgin Mary down here.'

But I felt the garlands were there for me, their colours burning into the dark. The Virgin had little to do with it. Stuart and I had met, and the flesh-coloured city broke into flower.

Is it shocking that I felt such sharp desire on a morning when I'd just fucked my husband? But desire doesn't live in the sexual parts. Desire lives in the mind. Desire lives in the soul . . . yes, I have a soul like anybody else. I was ready to fall in love that morning, with the new city, with being alive, with being myself and desirable, with being, if not young, not old.

– I wanted to be surprised. Chris could adore me, but not surprise me. The force of Stuart's hunger as we stood on a corner and said goodbye, at last, after trailing Robert through half the streets of Toledo, caught at my breath with its novelty. Yet nothing was said or even hinted and afterwards I feared I had imagined it, the merest projection of my lust.

But we had a date. The most innocent date. 'My husband would really like to meet you . . . sometimes he longs for an English voice. You're Scottish, of course, but that's just as good . . .'

'Better,' said Stuart, 'but I'll forgive you.' Both of our voices were insincere, overhasty with suppressed excitement.

'You must bring your wife. We'll go out to dinner. Our treat. Let's eat at the parador.'

'That costs the earth,' said Stuart, kindly. 'We'll go somewhere local. Anywhere. The food isn't what matters, after all.'

Instantly both of us were heavy with embarrassment, as if he had just declared himself, though the words were innocent enough. I forced my attention back to the venue.

'It's OK, really . . .' (But how can I say, 'As it happens, Chris is a millionaire . . .'?)

We made a date for Saturday. I don't think Stuart's mind was working at all, for he looked astonished when I called him back to ask him if he had a sitter for Robert. If not, perhaps a maid at the parador . . .

'What am I thinking of?' he said. 'For a second I forgot about the children. It's not just Robert, it's his sister Fiona . . .'

There was a sister, Fiona. This was not getting easier.

'That won't be a problem. We'll pay the girl more.'

– I felt that 'girl' slightly grated on Stuart.

'Well actually, you see . . . Kirsty doesn't like to leave the children with strangers.'

'But what do you do when you go out?'

'Well actually we hardly ever do.' This confession caused him great discomfort.

In the face of that I grew bossy and rich. 'Well tell her she has to go out. Everyone does, or they go crazy. The parador cooking is marvellous. Tell her she owes herself a treat. The children will be under the same roof so she's hardly leaving them, is she? . . . We'll expect all four of you on Saturday. Eight o'clock. Everything will be arranged.'

He looked up suddenly, looked me in the eye, our glances held with grappling hooks – we stood three feet apart, hands by our sides, imagining we were naked, touching.

'I'll be there,' he said. 'We'll be there. Robert, kiss the lady goodbye.'

Robert didn't want to. His Dad held him up. At the last moment he shrugged his mouth away, and his sulky jaw and cheek were presented. Stuart watched as I kissed him, tenderly, twice. I think he knew who I had really kissed.

Love and lovers, lovers and love. Believe it or not, I was glad they were gone; I was free to go my own pace again through the magical streets, smiling at people. I had my secret to hold and polish. And when the afternoon got too hot I was happy to go back to the grand hotel and creep into the high-ceilinged room where Chris was napping behind drawn curtains, kick off my shoes, kick off my dress, curl into the comfort of his half-clothed body.

'I met a man,' I said. 'English. Well, Scottish. Interesting. Writing a book about Spanish cinema. With a boy of three . . .' Chris was very keen on three-year-olds. Susy and Isaac, so he affirmed, were angelic at three, and perhaps they were.

'He has a wife?' He turned lazily and started to stroke the

inside of my thigh. I thought about Stuart's hand. I moved my thigh appreciatively.

'Yes, my love. Red-haired like me.'

'I adore red-heads. Ask them to dinner.'

'Yes, my sweet. I will.'

Lovers and love. Nothing is simple. I tell you, I loved Chris no less. Water was running outside the window, filling something up or draining away, things were moving and changing inside me, we lay together in an unknown city, loving each other in different languages, for all I said had become a lie. Except that after we made love again I said 'I love you', and 'Thank you', and nothing had ever been more true; I loved him more, and more gratefully, because I had been so far away, because I had played with our past and future, and yet he was still here for me.

I wanted to talk about love that day. Love and lovers, lovers and love. I wished I could tell Chris everything, and make him see how marvellous it was that I wanted this man so much and come back to find nothing changed between us . . . But although I like talking, I'm not a fool. I knew that I could never tell him.

Instead I talked into his thick black hair as the world outside began to stir, recovering from the siesta. But sex had made us sleepy again; after all, we didn't have jobs to do.

'Thank you for being here,' I said. 'It's wonderful you're always here.'

(Yet that, in a way, was the trouble; constant presence erodes desire. You can't long for something that's always available.)

– I took so much for granted then.

'You know I'll always be there for you.'

I wonder if he's still waiting. He'll be out of prison, I suppose. I wonder if he has other women. In any case, he must be seventy now. Perhaps he's impotent – *no, can't bear it.*

I can't imagine him with other women. I never had to, you see; Christopher never made me jealous . . .

Can that be true? It can't be true. For milliseconds, maybe, in the distant past. Something drifts back, the smallest flotsam. Occasionally, before we left home, though it was ludicrous, I felt the slightest bit jealous of Mary Brown. *Mary Brown*, of all people. One of the plainest women you ever met. Because she was *good*, there's no other word for it, and Christopher liked her – *motherliness*. She was always very good with the children. That made me jealous, God knows why. Maybe he loved her, in a way. But not sexually, of course. You couldn't feel romantic about Mary Brown. I don't think she knew how children are made. So there was no sense in my being jealous.

What does it matter, in any case, now none of us care about each other any more – *(how is that possible?)* – except Mary, still doggedly writing letters. It must be a sign of an empty life.

That phrase has an unpleasant ring. It echoes in this empty night.

– If only I could go back again.

– If only I were young enough to make amends.

If only we were all still here, and young, in garlanded Toledo.

Ah, there's Benjamin, stumbling on the stairs. Humming as he comes, the great buffoon . . . but my heart quickens, all the same. A hotel room can feel very lonely.

I shall keep my temper, but I wish he'd stop humming . . . I don't know the tunes that Benjy hums. Younger people know different tunes.

I wonder if I shall ever go home.

IO

Christopher: Venice, 2005

Today I thought of Mary Brown. After a gap of decades, I thought of her. But first things first, the great news first. Today I have been bad again. Good, good, bad again!

Her name was Caterina. But that's probably her trading name. I spotted her by chance as I walked down the Piazetta dei Leoncini in the five o'clock sunlight. She stood by the fountain, pulling her thin yellow skirt against the curve of her buttocks, heavy buttocks above slender legs, pausing for a long glance over her shoulder . . . this certainly wasn't an innocent Venetian girl early for the *passegiata*.

Her brows and eyes were black as soot. She trotted beside me like a little pony, black fringe bobbing, rouged mouth smiling.

Inside I offered her a glass of wine. I amused myself by offering this rough child a glass of exquisitely round Barolo. I am no fool, I had one too. She drank hers down in two or three gulps and grimaced slightly. Soon I should have her! I rolled the rich red around my mouth.

'I like sweet wine,' she pouted.

'I have something here I hope you will like.'

We played together for over an hour in the dark bedroom twelve feet above the spotless kitchen where Lucia was working, singing to herself, cursing the cat. Had she known, she'd have worried about my heart; too pure to worry about AIDS, and I am too greedy, and long past caring.

Lucia, I didn't strain my heart. I was a grand seigneur all afternoon, lordly and idle, sitting there groaning with pleasure as her small mouth took me.

I paid her extra for being quite naked. Thump, thump in the

73

kitchen below, Lucia's great bare golden arms beating the sirloin wafer-thin. There would be olives, white butter, bread . . .

Somehow the image of my stately and virtuous cook got confused with my naughty girl. At the moment of exploding for the second time – the second, hear that! At seventy! Notice I use the verb 'exploding'! So much sperm, it must be full of babies, Alex was wrong to despair of me – at the end of my second orgasm I was suddenly intensely sad. Below me, cutlery clinked like bells. In the distance, a real bell rang for the faithful.

Knives and forks and good fresh bread.

Who said that women should be good like bread?

Women should sit with you at table; love you, feed you, stay with you. I must have been thinking about my mother. Neither of my wives has ever done that.

– 'Cover yourself,' I said. I paid the girl double and she slipped away, suddenly ugly, obsequious.

Alex was never good like bread. She was good like shellfish or langues de chat or perfectly cold champagne in summer. I thought of Mary Brown. I suddenly thought of Mary Brown. Mary Brown was good like bread. A good wife, a good mother . . .

As I washed myself and applied cologne and smoothed my actor's silver hair I started to think quite differently. A good woman can also be bad . . . I found it unimaginably exciting, conjuring up sweet Mary Brown, her frank pale eyes and thick pale skin and ample, accommodating body . . . I confess I defiled her memory.

(Three, I tell you! Don't be depressed! It was my highest score in three times as many years, and tomorrow I quite expect a reaction. I shall be fragile, an invalid, and my good Lucia will bring me broth and offer to say a prayer for me. I shall nod, benign. I need to be shriven.)

Mary Brown. Not the one in my spasm. Mary Brown, the real live woman . . . at least, I hope she's still alive. Ruth's letter just said Matthew was ill.

Perhaps I should write to them. I recall that Mary was keen

on letters, firing them off at my selfish wife, who probably never bothered to read them.

Oddly enough I did. So Mary didn't waste her time. She wrote a good letter, an excellent letter. Good sort, good woman, good friend.

If it's not too late, I'll write.

Perhaps my money would help them. Did they have any money? I can't remember. It takes a lot of money to help you die. It takes a lot of money to speed the passing — *ease* the passing, I must mean.

Matthew might already be dead, of course. I could offer her my sympathy. Later we would play at widow and widower . . .

No, don't think me cynical. I'm just high-spirited, because of my score. The truth is, sometimes I get lonely. I've drinking partners, I've sexual partners, but sometimes I long to have — a friend.

Besides, I could talk to her about Alex.

Excellent. That's the dinner-bell.

For a man like me, a whole clove of garlic, a side of sirloin, a meadow of peas, a ransacked glasshouse of fat tomatoes . . .

Open the second bottle, Lucia. A tired athlete needs his wine.
Good. I have been bad again.

Part Two

11

Alexandra: Esperanza, Bolivia, 2005

Look on the bright side, at least we're going, at least we're getting out of this shithole!

Down below it's pandemonium, the manager screaming at the maids, the cook raging at all of them because yesterday her mangy cat gave birth and she doesn't want quarrels to upset the kittens – all seven of them billeted in the kitchen. Blind, disgusting, I know what they're like, somebody ought to wring their necks, kill all babies before they're born, strangle their mothers before they have them!

Everyone's angry because we're going. They hoped the rich gringos would be here for months, paying through the nose for dubious meat and rice in virulent pepper sauce – probably cat, that's why the cook's so protective – and telephone bills and taxi rides from the manager in his rattle-trap Daihatsu jeep. But no, it has all gone wrong, we're going.

We thought everything was fixed at last. We had met the family recommended to us by the crippled miner in Concepción, their cousin, he said, as he asked us for money, this part of the world is riddled with cousins. The mother was pregnant and spoke only Quechua, or else she pretended, the cunning cow, but the father spoke Spanish fluently and he seemed to like us OK. No wonder he liked us, we'd paid him thousands of dollars in bribes to prove we were 'serious' – thousands of dollars for fucking nothing, for the bitch of a mother has changed her mind!

He had four daughters and said they couldn't decide which one to let us adopt. Each time we visited we took more dollars. The children had uniform Indian faces, broad flat noses, unreadable eyes. Any one of them would have suited me. Of course they were alike, they were young, they were babies, what could it matter which one they chose!

Babies, babies. I came here to find one. Let's be brutal, I came here to buy one, but it all went wrong. Now we have to get out.

This little town sprawls in a hole in the forest. It presses all round you, especially at night, repulsively fertile, crawling with life, the rubber trees oozing yellow milk ... The rain-forest knew we were wasting our time. Two more stupid pale-faced tourists leeched of their money and sent away. You could hear the monkeys laughing at us, screeching with laughter in the sweltering dark.

Don't worry, I'm not defeated. *I have never been defeated.* All this is only delaying the moment when my glorious plan becomes a fact, I'm not too old, I'm not ... I am vigorous, I am only fifty-four – well, fifty-five, because I've just had a birthday, but only last month I was fifty-four – I run and dance like a very young woman, I tell you it's true, ask Benjy.

Benjamin is packing in the room next door. We have two rooms; in this grubby little hotel there are no suites, so we took two rooms and made them unstick the communicating door. It was obvious we had to have a sitting-room, but they looked at us as if we came from Mars.

The maid kept giggling as she struggled with the lock. She was a fat little thing, bursting with hormones, her upper lip hairy and beaded with sweat and those awful stinking jungly armpits.

'Ask her to go away,' I told Benjy. 'She makes me feel ill. You're strong, you could do the door, no problem.'

Benjy was smiling at her straining rump. 'Leave her alone, she's rather sweet.'

The door suddenly yielded with a clanking shudder, the maid tumbled sideways, Benjamin caught her. His Spanish is ten times better than mine because he once lived with a Puerto Rican. She was grinning and speaking volubly. I went into the bathroom and ran the tap but only a trickle of brown water came out and the pipes ground hideously.

He came in and touched my shoulder. 'Have you got any change? We should give her some money ... She shouldn't really do heavy work, she's pregnant. And she's got three children under five to support.'

– See how they try to torment me. This sweaty little pig, bursting with babies. I remain quite calm, I shall not be maddened.

Benjamin is packing noisily, crashing drawers, clattering doors. Last night he drank too much *alcol*, the disgusting drink of the very poor, so strong that they use lighted matches to burn off some of the alcohol before they drink it, but Benjamin wanted to hurt himself, Benjamin wanted oblivion . . .

We were sitting outside with the night all round us. The air was close, soft as damp fur, and sweat ran down between my breasts. His face was beaded as if with tears, glittering in the lamplight. That cretinous maid had told him the *campesinos* drank *alcol* to drown their sorrows. I took one mouthful and spat it out but he pretended to like it, he was macho and stupid and drank all the more when I tried to stop him.

I confess I was impatient. Surely the grief and loss were mine?

'I feel – as though we've lost our future,' he said. 'We would have looked after her together. I wanted her too, you know. You're not the only one who wants a child.' (Odd that that hadn't occurred to me. I really thought he was just trying to please me.) 'I loved my brother's kids back in New York. If I had a chance, I could be a good father . . .'

This perspective seemed an absurd intrusion. I'd have thought he'd have the decency to comfort me, but the young are very selfish . . . I wanted to get away from him.

'I'm afraid I'm going to lose you, too.' He was drinking steadily but not yet drunk. 'I don't want to lose you, whatever happens.'

'I want a child.' I evaded the issue.

'Do you want me?'

I couldn't answer. His honesty makes him seem so young. But he *is* so young, my beautiful Benjy, that's why I came away with him . . . I said perhaps we needed space. We'd been cooped up together too long, the humid air was stifling me . . . I tried to be kind. I said how fond of him I was. I said perhaps he was just too young.

And so he got drunk and began to abuse me, thus sounding younger than ever, alas.

'You only wanted me for a stud because that murderous bastard couldn't put one in you. Ever since you resigned yourself to not getting pregnant – '

' – You haven't understood. I'm not resigned. All I want from life is a child – '

' – Ever since you gave up on me making you pregnant you haven't looked me in the eye.'

(True. I used to look into his eyes and see babies, a luminous future with fine twin babies, for older women are more likely to have twins, oh yes, don't worry, I know the facts, there was a time when I read so many books, so obsessively, about having babies . . . Once upon a time I knew all the statistics, I read and dreamed for three or four years, I was positive Benjy would pull it off . . . For a year he made love to me every night, sometimes more, night after night.)

I still had eggs, but they never ripened.

So Benjamin was wrong for me. Or maybe my eggs were already dead . . .

– I know my eggs weren't dead from the start. I did conceive all those decades ago, I refused an abortion, I had my daughter, but there was no father to support me, I had no life to offer her, I had her adopted for her own good . . . I was a child myself, what else could I do? I decided never to think about her. I decided never to think about children. I told Christopher I would never have children.

Then the mistake, the accident, what good does it do remembering . . . And we tried again and failed again. Blood on a flower in a Turkish wood.

Maybe my eggs all died from neglect. Maybe that's why it

only came too late, this piercing, tormenting wish for a child. Maybe it's true, what he said last night, the thing I've been trying not to recall . . .

It was horrible, unforgettable. Something that shouldn't be said to anyone. It sounds in my head again and again with the circular hum of a long-trapped wasp, maddened, dangerous . . . I could smell the poison as he leaned across to say it, too much booze and stinging green pepper, bitter alcohol and green regret.

'Now you've given up on your fucking womb I'm no fucking use to you, am I? You're a cold fucking bitch, you're hard as nails, you're so fucking – *sterile* – '

He meant something else, he didn't mean that, but it will never be unsaid till I have a child.

We were alone on the verandah in the harsh light and dark from the brilliant insect-repellent lantern. I was stone-cold sober, drinking bottled water, I had stayed quite calm as he stormed at me, I knew the aggression was just hurt pride –

– I stared at the ugly cast-iron legs of the table under which his long legs would not fit, I concentrated on the vulgar iron, I examined the bruised black patches on our clothes where the sweat-soaked cotton clung to the skin, I thought of our cream-smeared arms and legs which gave the night its curious smell, something half-sweet, half-medical – I tried to hold on to these small hard facts in the enormous night that bore in on the lamplight –

– Then the jungle howled inside my head, it sobbed, it cried, I sat and wept, clutching the table, seeing nothing, deaf and blind, a thing of water, and all I wanted was to be dissolved, for the first time in a long life to be anyone but Alexandra, anything but a sterile woman.

(I still feel a little strange today, blurred at the edges, not myself. That curious, terrible wish not to be. Maybe I feel – but it seems so silly by sensible daylight with the brisk cross sounds of packing next door, and the squawking row going on in the kitchen – I feel as though I had waved to death, in that single moment of despair, and now it is still looking at me.

Rubbish, fuck off, get away! In future the rich will never die, the technology virtually exists already . . .)

After I wept he passed out in his chair, woke up in the early hours and crawled into bed, cold – I'd forgotten that flesh could feel cold – shivering, gloomy, begging my forgiveness, wanting to know that I still loved him.

I've heard it all before, alas. I've lived a long life, I'm not sentimental, and not at my best at two in the morning. I told him to go to sleep.

'But I love you. I want to marry you.'

'Two hours ago I was a *fucking old bitch*.'

'I was drunk, I was mad, you'll have to forgive me.'

'I'll have to go to sleep. We're leaving tomorow.'

And so we're leaving, still unreconciled. When he passes the doorway I can see his face, young and proud, divinely sulky, downcast eyes with that thick fringe of lash. He's tall and slim but his cheeks are still round, smooth and faintly plump with youth, there was a sweetness about him I once loved, but he's turned against me as all men do.

And then he calls from beyond the partition. 'Shall I go down and ask them to send us up a snack? They might have some turtle eggs, if we're lucky, a bit of *charque*, some beer . . .'

And here he is. He's forgiven me for not forgiving him. Or else at all costs he wants to make friends. His mouth's soft and timid, no longer sulky. His eyes drive mine down to the stained wooden floor, nameless stains and casual damage . . .

When I want something I want it all the time, just as long as I want it, which may not be for long, and I still have the passion for *charque* that I conceived when we first came to South America, although it's on offer day in day out from the roughest vendors in the poorest *mercado*. They thrust the *charque* under my nose, hard black strips of sun-dried meat, salty and strong as bulls' pizzles. I like to chew on those great dark thongs, but the hotel offers it already sliced up into delicate little appetisers.

'Bring everything but the beer.'

'I've done the packing. We can leave after lunch.'

– And I feel it tug at the corner of my heart, a small rush of

hope at the thought of departure, an echo of all past hopefulness, all those leaps into the unlived future.

Outside the window, the hotel cock, whose internal clock is a
torment to him, shrieks for the dawn at midday. It's appallingly
hot; our blinds are drawn, erratically brown wooden-slatted
things that look as though they date from the 1950s . . . The
sun makes white prison-bars on the floor.

'I'm glad we're going.'

We kiss.

'So'm I.'

He does bring beer, after all. Below us, the fury dies away;
they've accepted it, we are already gone, distress swoons into
the stunning heat. The hotel sleeps. For them we are over.

Pathetic gringos who came to them with a feeble dream of
buying a baby. They've seen it all, including us. We pass like the
tiniest cloud at noon.

In case you've forgotten, I'm an optimist. Quite uncharacteristic,
all this gloom. Christopher always praised me for it, *unsinkable,
unquenchable*.

— Before we left, we were laughing together, Benjy and I, in
that rickety room. The beer released us from opera. Besides, we
were moving, weren't we? Stepping out together, fellow-
travellers . . .

Thank you, I thought, *the pain has gone*. The warm beer
made me invulnerable, just a tiny bit clumsy but entirely happy
as we climbed into the manager's white-hot jeep and rattled off
over the baking mud, paying extra for driving through the
siesta.

I thought I might have caught one final glimpse of my family
of daughters staring blankly after me, their narrow-eyed *mestizo*
faces seeing only the jeep, not the mad pale lady, but there was
no one, everyone slept.

I didn't care, I was flying, I was drunk, it was all a dream,
with another one tomorrow. We laughed so loud that the hotel
manager, who must have heard our row the night before, turned

round and stared over his white-flecked shoulder and scraped the side of a sleeping bus.

This ebullience got us to the railway station, and then the train itself took over, for I've loved foreign trains with a passionate love since the British railways withered away. Elsewhere in the world in the last decade the railways have boomed as governments turned against the motorcar . . . This particular line, which runs from Riberalta across the border into Brazil and down to Pôrto Velho, was dreamed up over a century ago as a way of making up some silly feud between Brazil and Bolivia – South Americans are always quarrelling, and *totally* unreliable, as Benjamin and I have found to our cost – the Brazilians, you see, never bothered to finish it, and the track would simply have rusted away if it hadn't been completed a few years ago on nothing more than a gangster's whim, a Bolivian cocaine baron buying good will, or so the maid told Benjamin, she was sly, she was always talking to him . . . How can you deal with people like that? Dreamers, idlers, gossips, crooks . . .

I'm glad we're going. A toast to cocaine. The original line cost six thousand lives, one for every hundred sleepers. I discourage Benjamin from tiring me with facts but I admit that this has an epic dimension, as if our carriage were surging through the rubber forest on thousands of straining human shoulders, with me above them, urging them on . . .

Benjamin doesn't like that image. Benjy has no imagination.

South American trains are wonderful. There are steam-trains (*steam-trains!*) still in service, or so they say, though I've never seen one; I'd adore to find one of those iron giants and rattle through the remains of the rain-forest. I've heard there are some at Pôrto Velho, if we manage to get as far as Brazil.

Even the diesel trains are marvellous fun. The vendors serve warm gassy drinks and *pukacapas*, *picante* cheese pies which somehow taste wonderful because you're moving. People travel with sheep and garrulous chickens and shout to each other in the shuddering bursts of light and dark as we shoot through the trees, past a wall of fire into untouched stillness where a troop

86

of macaques pauses, startled, the babies clinging to their mothers like bats, then the smoke sweeps everything back into darkness.

Not everything. I am left with the babies. Little soft paws which grope and cling.

And so the pleasure of the beer turned sour. If I'd had a gun, I'd have shot down the monkeys, aiming unerringly back through the flames. *God will help me; I must be avenged.*

But we stopped in the sun — someone dead on the tracks, a protester, they said, against the burnings — and the killing heat on the side of my head made me sleep, heavily, and dream black dreams, and when I woke up the rage was gone.

I swear I no longer felt angry, but the train had jerked at the wrong moment so I woke as I rose through a spiral of time, unsure which level I was on.

Someone was talking and kissing me.

'Wake up, Alex. It's nearly our station.'

' — *Christopher,*' I said.

I thought I was with Christopher, we were travelling, we were nearly there . . .

It wasn't the initial confusion that hurt him. Benjy says he could have accepted that. It was what happened as I woke up properly, narrowing my eyes against the blaze, and he saw his reflection in my pupil, saw me register who was there, and the pupil contracted with disappointment.

Little black stones. Of course he was lonely.

So I am lonely, and he is lonely. Not parting yet, just moving apart.

And we've only been together five years . . . how little life there is in us.

Christopher. Do you remember? When we lived together, there was so much life. For twenty years we honeymooned.

We loved each other till the day we parted. Some small mad part of me loves him still . . .

If I weren't a realist I'd love him still, but time and the world have left us behind.

Hotel Magdalena, Guayaramerín. Another town, another hotel, so near the banks of the Mamore river that we hear the frogs singing all night long. I hear them, at any rate, because I can't sleep. Benjy is sleeping youthfully.

All the hotels start to blur together, and all the names of South American towns. This one at least means nothing to me. When this dream began, long ago in New York, when I pored over the maps that Benjy brought me, I saw so many towns called Esperanza, so many called Concepción, others promising us Exaltación . . . at the time I was jubilant, I thought it was a sign, but now I see it was just their joke.

I think of memory like toothache, or the pain in a long-ago broken bone where the join is not quite effortless; a small piece lost, a connection gone. Days of departure ache the most, because they were the days when Chris and I felt closest . . .

Leaving somewhere and moving on, leaving behind the brief new friendships, proving yet again that only he and I mattered, a unit of two against the world. Drawing an arc into emptiness as the plane sheered away from the things we knew and straight up into a cloudless sky. Disappearing into a blank silver screen. Then we made pictures, beautiful pictures . . .

Alex and Chris in Poreč, in Istra, where so many things were a shade of gold, the glittering mosaics in the basilica, the orange roofs, the apricot juice we drank ice-cold in a tiny cafe as soon as we got off the train, the sweet tawny Prošek wine we had later as the light turned gold for the end of the day; Alex and Chris in Buenos Aires, in evening dress and gangster shades; Alex and Chris in Bermuda, where everything seemed painted white, the roofs of the houses, the powdery sands, the languorous tail of a tropic bird he said reminded him of me; Alex and Chris posing in Cairo, drinking gin slings in the setting sun, the light blazing pink through the rims of the glasses . . .

Everything was so bright, so light. An adventure film, an

artifice. We enjoyed each other and enjoyed ourselves and didn't think about much else . . .

(Nothing could be that simple, surely? Of course it can, of course it was.)

Now the world seems suddenly all too real. Dirt and squalor and flies and disease. The desperate need that drives me on. My changing body, my lessening blood. Things going wrong, things that have gone.

Why must things change? I ask myself, lying in the dark beside my lover, the smooth-skinned lamb I no longer love, and he moans gently and turns towards me, dumbly trying to clutch my hand, and I ease away, trying not to wake him, because if he wakes he'll want to talk and there's nothing left to talk about.

I no longer want him here, and that's that.

– In the morning I'll have to see us in the mirror, another mirror, another hotel, I'll be fifty-five, he'll be thirty and eager, nothing we've said can be erased, the sun will photograph the skin of my arm, a map of microscopic rifts and valleys, and we'll quarrel mildly and go down to breakfast, an older woman and her sulky young lover . . .

But tonight, in the dark, I can lie and dream.

I can fly back through time.

That first departure. The true beginning.

Try to remember, Alexandra.

I2

Christopher: Venice, 2005

I loved to make her come with my mouth. I loved to make her come in any of the dozen ways I made her come, but with my mouth, with my mouth, oh god . . . my lips are dry at the thought of it.

I loved her smell. She was never shy, whether she had washed or not, because she knew I loved her smell, because I loved her completely, her piss, her shit, when we shared a bathroom, the rank smell of her sex when I knelt above her in the hot countries we travelled through. Her sweat was delicious, a red-head's sweat, peppery, musky, animal. She gave herself to me, when we were together, completely, totally. You must understand, it was why I loved her, the way she melted when we made love, she no longer talked, she no longer bullied, she opened herself and became a life where I could be entirely happy, she opened herself and took me in.

— I loved to make her come with my mouth. That seaweed smell and her skin on my face, I can feel it still, her silky skin, the salt-wet smoothness so carefully folded between the rough curls of her long lips which I teased her she'd played with too much as a girl, and the landscape would change as my tongue glanced over it, the little peak would grow and yearn and harden under my gentle tongue, but she always wanted me inside as well, I loved the way she'd cry 'Please, *inside*', my tongue always had to push deep inside her, deep inside and then back again to the swollen ridge which probed for me like an answering tongue . . . and then less gentle, firmer, surer, now I could feel she was moving with me as the trembling began in her inner thighs and her buttocks tightened under my fingers and then her hands would be clutching my hair, pulling my

90

head against her need, and all of her would tense like a bow as she started to sigh and hold her breath and her body suddenly went haywire as small electric shocks shot everywhere, convulsing, shuddering across her, and the deep cries came, those wonderful cries which were wrenched from her as her thighs locked round me and I held her, I had her, we held each other, loud rough cries, she had lost herself.

Till the cries became purrs and sighs again. Deep soft childish sighs of release. And sometimes she would fall dead asleep, so deep that she'd wake and remember nothing . . . so I'd have to make her come again. I thought it would always happen again.

I loved it so.

Oh we loved each other.

Travel meant sex, for us. We went away so we could make love.

It was problematic at home with the children; we weren't naturally quiet lovers, and though the house was big the kids got everywhere. Feet would come padding up the stairs just when we had slipped away together and her cool fingertips slid under my balls.

'Dad? Do you know where the dictionary is?'

'Alex! Have you moved my red shoes?'

It was as if they knew. And although it's stupid, for we were married, after all, we'd freeze, and I at least felt guilty – Alex was never a great one for guilt. I wonder if she ever feels guilty now, when she thinks of the ruin of so many lives?

'It's *your* dictionary, *you* find it.'

'I put your bloody shoes *away!*'

I didn't want to upset the children, I never wanted to upset the children. We'd wait till bedtime, watching each other. But in the middle of the night, when we were finally alone, the house seemed nerve-wrackingly quiet, as if it and the kids were listening; the bed creaked; the clock ticked. I could manage to come with the quietest of sighs but Alex was never very piano and I used to clamp my mouth over hers, those beautiful, dark, exaggerated lips with the full lower curve which seemed so right for the thrilling low octaves her voice did best. She came contralto too – on the rare occasions when I didn't muffle her, or when our chaperones could be bribed to go out.

She wouldn't put up with this all the time, of course. Her condition for taking on me and the kids was that we'd go away together on our own every summer. The kids made a fuss but accepted it. Susy complained that everyone she knew had a real holiday with their mothers and fathers.

We tried a 'real holiday' at Easter and Christmas. The children became suddenly intensely competitive, it rained or snowed, they got tummy bugs, they disliked the hotel and each other and us; Susy obsessively posed us for photos, especially when we were rushing for planes, family photos that proved we were a family and made even Alexandra look ugly; Isaac unerringly left his glasses, his wallet or his dental brace in foreign hotels . . .

Family life remains as vivid as school, with its endless power to generate dreams. I'm an old man now but I still dream of school assembly, rushing down the corridor, always late. And I dream I'm back with Susy and Isaac, but they're still adolescent, sometimes even younger, I'm tying shoes or packing lunches . . . Those routines lived out day after day. They were my family; they're still in my head. I don't understand how I finally left them. Only bad men leave their children, and I'm not a bad man, I loved my kids . . . she must have bewitched me. She is a witch. Red hair, white face, black heart.

She hated those family holidays. In the end she decided to stay at home.

'But the children will miss you – '

' – Liar.'

' – and you love travelling, in any case.'

'It's not travelling, is it, if the children go.'

Travel meant sex, love, freedom. Every summer we sent the kids to relatives or friends and skipped off on our own. We did almost a decade of summer holidays before we decided it wasn't enough.

They were nice, those holidays. Small-scale, innocent. Guilt (my guilt) kept us close to home so we could fly back easily if

Isaac broke a leg (Isaac was always breaking things) or if Susy's cold turned to pneumonia, as she always threatened it would. We sent frequent postcards and brought back large presents, we had no reason to feel guilty then.

I'm talking about twenty-odd years ago. From the mid-1970s to the early 1980s. The Portuguese coast had only just been discovered, and nobody thought about skin cancer then. It became the place we went to be happy. And that's what we were, perfectly happy.

We went and lay on the blazing white beaches.

We went and ate fish in the little beach bars.

There was so much light. I remember no shadow, except the eventual need to go home. We loved those beaches, the long low dunes, the waves with the width and force of the great Atlantic stretching away behind them, dazzling. Alex always got drunk on light, her metabolism was hungry for it, and Portugal made her feel twice as alive, despite the knockout heat of noon.

This was before they started building in earnest, remember, before the great towers and 'aparthotels'. To us it was a kind of paradise.

Alex loved flowers. My darling loved flowers. In many ways she was easy to please. In the Algarve we found an extraordinary peninsula where every inch of turf was carpeted with flowers. She ran down the goat-tracks like a child, crouching to look at the little patches of brightness – some we recognised or thought we did, tiny indigo wild irises, I remember, flowers like a small deep purple sweet pea which smelled drowningly sweet and grew everywhere, white silky things she thought were dog-roses till I pointed out the leaves were wrong. And the trees were straight from Eden; pines, figs, almonds, oranges, mimosa trees so thickly balled with yellow that there was hardly any room for the shiny dark leaves . . .

No one was there but us and the goats. The air was scented with resin and herbs. We were Adam and Eve in God's garden. The flowers had sprung up after heavy rains which had washed deep gullies in the green turf; we found a sheltered place for lunch, completely hidden from the path.

93

'I love to see oranges and lemons growing,' I said.

She pulled up her t-shirt, pulled up her bra, gave me her dark-nippled breasts to eat, and I sucked them out so they were shaped like lemons . . .

I could hear the sea in the distance, a thin goat-bell, an alarmed bird. Her hair was thick and soft in my hands. Life was intolerably delicious. We were in shade, in the red soft earth, but we felt a great heat hanging above us, a dome of blue heat drawing everything in. I came very slowly, wonderfully slowly, luxuriating in her soft damp body, holding her breasts, kissing her forehead, which always felt cool, like marble . . . and when the last wave of it finally faded I said 'Thank you' and rolled over on my back and stared straight up into the amazing blue.

We were completely alive, and completely together.

Another of her passions was sunbathing. This was before we were all afraid of the sun, before we knew about skin cancer. Sunbathing seemed like such innocent pleasure, and Alex enjoyed it even more than me, perhaps because she spent so much time being active; she loved to doze and dream in the sun.

I was her attendant, her devoted masseur. I loved to rub suncream into her skin, it was a game we loved to play together. Innumerable times on those brilliant beaches . . .

I remember one time in Lagos. I was creaming her arms, which had just started to go pink. 'Lovely,' she whispered, and '. . . more . . . thank you . . .', sleepy whispers, she was going to sleep. I laid her on her tummy on the burning sand and spread out her limbs in an elegant X; then I stroked cream into every inch of warm skin, loving every dent, every hollow, every dimple, each sinuous muscle, each delicate bone, oh God, I held it all in my hands; she slept in the sun, entirely mine.

I shaded her with a beach umbrella and ran down to swim in the long lines of surf, maybe half a mile, three-quarters of a mile away. On the whole beach, which extended to right and left almost out of sight, there were only ourselves and two muscular boys leading horses, probably Portuguese. They had kept their shirts on, and looked at me sideways with hard black eyes as I ran past.

The water was gloriously cold, and I struck away from land on my back, the better to rejoice in the cloudless sky. I was a good swimmer. I felt strong and young – I wasn't forty then, after all – and on the sand she was waiting for me . . .

Then without warning a cramp seized my calf. I kicked out in agony and it eased, but the water was suddenly too cold for comfort. I was further away from land than I'd thought and I was all at once terribly afraid for Alex, those sturdy boys with their unfriendly eyes, why hadn't I seen what those boys might do . . . I struck out for the beach with big splashy strokes and I saw through the spray that they were both in the saddle and the horses had stopped beside her body, tiny black figures on the headachey white.

I ran up the beach, my legs oddly weak, uphill the distance was twice as long, the soft sand sucked at my feet and tripped me, I was shouting but the wind took the words from my lips, I stumbled onwards feeling weak and old . . .

They were robbing us. They had dismounted now, they had got my jacket, they were bending over her, of course I would have to die defending her . . . their muscular backs and greasy heads bent over her white unconscious body, short oversized calves like acrobats, what did they mean to do to her? Fifteen feet away I shouted again, and the worst thing was that they saw me coming but didn't stop, or run away . . . The horses loomed against the sun. I was the intruder, absurdly out of breath, irrelevant.

They had straightened up, at least. They spoke to me rapidly in Portuguese; they didn't seem so much guilty as reproachful. I spoke Spanish well, but no Portuguese, and the tide of speech just made me feel more impotent.

Alex woke up, turned over, sat up and stared at us, rubbing her eyes; they took in her beauty as she tried to understand. She had learned Portuguese at college. Within seconds she was smiling at them, with sleepy, dazzled, narrow eyes, she was flirting with them, these sturdy young men, she was nodding her head and they were all smiling. Her body looked terrifyingly naked, her breasts half-bare and dusted with sand, her thighs wide open, *cover yourself . . .*

They got on their horses and rode away, with a courteous nod to me.

'What the hell was going on?' I asked.

'They were so sweet. They were covering me with your jacket. They say you can burn even in the shade in this kind of heat. Locals never sunbathe . . . handsome boys, weren't they? Good riders.'

I don't know why I felt like a stupid child: I couldn't look after her, I was no good, she had stretched out her arms and smiled at them –

I was jealous, that was all, for the briefest moment.

We went back to the hotel and fucked for hours with the radio on to drown the noise and I made her come till my fear was gone, and then at last I came into her, deep inside her, on top for once, her white calves hooked up over my shoulders, her clever fingers tugging my hair, 'So thick,' she said, and I wasn't old, I was marvellously young and vigorous, and I'd been holding back for such a long time that the final orgasm was blinding and deafening and after it was ended everything was quiet, as if a part of my brain was gone.

A red moon had come up outside the window, unnaturally large, low over the sea.

We had a cigarette on our balcony. I wanted to sleep; she wanted to smoke. She wanted to walk, but I was too tired.

'I've got a headache,' I said. It was an understatement; it was shattering, behind my eyes, in the bones of my temples. 'You won't ever leave me, will you, darling?'

'Too much sun,' she said.

We half-saw figures far away on the beach; when the wind turned towards us I thought I heard hooves, then we saw them clearly for a second by the rocks, two horsemen dancing in the moonlight like centaurs.

'Beautiful,' Alex whispered.

96

She was talking about our love-making. I know that is what she was talking about.

— You see how completely happy we were.
— You see how insane my jealousy was.

Everything was perfect then. I treasure my memories of life before the fall . . . Portugal, our Eden.

They were only holidays, though. In those days we always went home to the kids; real life was grey, and somewhere else. Until we made our great escape, until we dedicated life to each other.

13

Alexandra: Guayaramerín, Bolivia, 2005

The odd thing is, when I really think back, leaving home wasn't in the least romantic. In fact it was bloody awful. *Escaping* was marvellous, leaving home was hell.

Because of the children, of course. Leaving your children isn't romantic. I'll have to start with the children, if anyone is ever to understand what we did, and the punishment which has come upon us, because sometimes I do think we're being punished – especially in the early hours, in the darkest, emptiest hours of the night.

It's three in the morning. The frogs have gone quiet. I miss them, they were company. I feel like the only thing left alive.

I even miss the children . . .

Susy and Isaac. For me the names were a pair. I thought they would always go together . . . quick, the children. Susy and Isaac. They were seventeen and nineteen when we left.

Isaac was the elder, and good at art. We rather hoped he would be a painter. I myself have always loved looking at pictures, though Christopher preferred the moving kind. From that point of view I was quite a good parent, praising the weirder things he did, occasionally taking him to galleries when it would have been more fun to have gone with a friend . . .

Some teenage boys are tremendously attractive, but Isaac wasn't one of them, I'm afraid.

He was clumsy, and tended to spots. He had thick black hair and quite nice eyes, but he always wore horrible heavy-rimmed glasses. His face was on the puddingy side, where his father's was rugged and interesting. He had his father's nose, but more crudely drawn.

He asked me if he was good-looking one day when we were standing at the gate of his school waiting for a boy who was coming to tea. I suppose he was comparing himself to all the other adolescent faces streaming past. I never lied to the children if I could help it. I said I thought he would get better with age.

'You'll be like your Dad, you'll see. The women will be wild for you in your late twenties.'

I got it wrong, of course, no teenager likes to be referred to the future, it merely reminds them of all they're too young for. His face got pinker and he looked at the ground. I tried to comfort him.

'If you like, we'll go clothes-shopping this weekend.'

'I'm busy this weekend.'

'Take it or leave it We'll go to Harrods.'

Resentfully, 'OK. If you'll buy me a black leather jacket.'

I was always happy when they asked for things, always happy to buy them things. I've always enjoyed giving presents. But it wasn't enough for Isaac.

He was a serious boy who did things slowly and wanted to know what they really meant. So he tended to get left out of conversations while more facile voices spoke. Mine, for instance, OK, I know. At the rare dinner-parties they deigned to attend, Susy and Isaac used to glare at me when I kept the conversation going, and left the room early, before coffee, with helpless downcast looks of distaste. Yet they talked and shrieked enough together when they were on their own up in one of their bedrooms . . .

I wish they still talked like that. I wish they could always have supported each other. It would have let their father and me off the hook if they'd gone on being allies, wouldn't it?

They had phases of liking me. We did best when we kept things light. I didn't let them draw me into any of the deep dark feelings adolescents love to drown in. Chris had to deal with those. I was just a kind of bracing, cheery older sister, attempting to drive them to the edge of the nest in good enough shape to fly away – though in point of fact, *we* flew away.

To be truthful, they frustrated me. Of course they weren't my children, but perhaps I had a feeling that if they had been they would have been more beautiful, more indisputably intelligent and gifted. They weren't exactly dull, but they weren't outstanding.

It didn't reflect awfully well on Chris, unless we blame it all on Penelope. But Penelope and Chris were both strikingly good-looking, and she took a First in Law . . .

Chris wanted Isaac to go to Oxford like he had, but Isaac said Oxford was out for art. So Chris said he'd heard there was rather a good History of Art degree at Cambridge.

Isaac said Chris was obsessed with Oxbridge. 'You wouldn't have told Van Gogh to go to Cambridge.'

'No, but I wouldn't call you Van Gogh.'

'You think you're so bloody clever and crushing,' Isaac said, very red, on the edge of tears. 'I'm quite a good painter, actually. You know fuck all about art.'

'Don't swear at your parents,' Chris said mildly.

'*Alex* swears,' Isaac said.

'That's because I'm ill-mannered, and older than you.' (I don't like quarrels; I like to make peace.) 'But I think you're right about Oxbridge.'

At junctures like that, Isaac would smile at me, grateful to have an ally.

He wasn't so tall as his father. He wasn't so handsome as his father. He wasn't good at games, like his father. He didn't attract the girls. I thought all this was hard on Chris, but it must have been worse for Isaac.

'I think he takes after Uncle Cedric,' Chris said one evening in summer, one long-ago summer evening – oh God where have those gentle evenings gone – as we watched Isaac come up the path to the door. It had rained, the sun had come struggling through, and Isaac pushed between the shining wet laurels which drooped across his way. His walk was always faintly dejected, and his school bag dragged him down to one side. With those heavy glasses and his heavy hair, a lot of his face was hidden, but there was still rather too much of it, sober cheeks and soft chin.

Chris was right, though I'd never noticed it before. I'd only met Cedric once; an eccentric bachelor who lived in Tangier. But his feet turned slightly in, like Isaac's, his shoulders were narrow, he bumbled.

' – Only in build, I mean,' Chris added, for Cedric liked limp brown boys. 'I hope he finds a girlfriend soon. Might, you know, sharpen him up a bit.'

I couldn't deny that would be an improvement. 'But don't ever say things like that to his face. It's a very sensitive age.'

A sullen voice behind us said, 'That's typical. Always patronising us. I'm going to tell Isaac what you said.'

And that, I'm afraid, was Susy, who had come into the front room silently and stood there eavesdropping. She must have been very cross to have bothered to talk. Susy was mostly too lazy to talk. It was her characterising trait, being lazy, not the most characterful characterising trait.

I find it hard to describe her, partly because of all that's happened since, but I always did find it hard to describe her . . .

There's no way of saying this which doesn't sound odious. Think the unthinkable. The truth about Susy is that she was very pretty in a slightly common way.

I'm trying to be truthful, not likeable. Susy herself was immensely likeable. Not to me or her father as a teenager, that would have been too much to ask, but to other children, when she was small, and their mothers, and teachers, and next-door neighbours, and dentists, and people choosing teams or partners or princesses for the school play. And she didn't look common as a child. No child looks common, however pretty – few things smaller than the norm look common.

When I first met Susy she was four years old with fair curly hair and dark red cheeks. It was summer, she had been out in the sun, her small pointed nose was prettily freckled and her mouth was what people have been calling 'a rosebud' ever since metaphors about lips began.

She smiled at me with all her might. The rosebud opened in a dazzling smile. Of course I wasn't her stepmother then, I belonged to the ninety per cent of the world whom Susy effortlessly charmed. I confess she looked like a bonus that day; I'd have Chris, with this lovely little girl thrown in . . . alas, her bonus-value didn't last long once she realized I would be replacing her mother. She was violently sick at our wedding, a stream of pink vomit, mostly jelly, all over the carpet and my good snake shoes.

She retained into adulthood one unusual feature, her long green slanted eyes, a direct import from her mother's face where they looked fierce and intelligent. But Penelope had a triangular face, cat-like, not at all like her daughter's. As Susy moved through her teenage years and grew larger and riper by the hour, her face stayed childishly round. She had melon-like breasts which made people boggle and profuse yellow hair which didn't darken till she was fifteen or sixteen, by which time she'd learned how to dye it. She was a statuesque blonde; men stared at her. Possibly it annoyed me a little.

My slenderness annoyed her too. Her green eyes, rather diminished in size by the heavy pink cheeks underneath them, would stare at my thigh in tight black trousers pressed flat on the table where I perched, pressed out to twice its normal width but still only the size of one of her arms. Her eyes would narrow, then she'd look away, and yawn dismissively.

At least in her teens she was not too lazy to take a bit of interest in her appearance. She favoured mini-skirts and fitted tops, which never did quite fit her. Perhaps I should have praised her more, for her interest in her looks didn't last. Later on, to judge from photographs and the rare and sorrowful times we met, she just grew bigger and bigger while continuing to dress in the fashions of the 1980s. On Susy's flesh this somehow looked tarty and cheap, not dated and spinsterish.

Naturally I was anxious when the breasts began to impinge on me. She was so immediate, so lush – she made me feel bloodless and insubstantial. And her transformation from a pretty little girl was so startlingly quick, leaving the rest of us thinner, paler.

It was Chris I was worried about. Here we were suddenly living in a house with an immensely nubile woman. She didn't stop sitting on his lap. She didn't stop giving him six kisses at bedtime; look at it another way, he didn't stop her. And her total lack of modesty!

I met her one morning skipping down the landing in nothing but a pair of pants, with a towel flung inaccurately round her shoulders so that two astonishing new-grown breasts stuck out towards me as she stopped to talk. *The nipples were three times the size of mine!* Susy didn't seem to know they were there.

'Is there any shampoo I can borrow?'

'No. I mean yes. You'll get cold like that.'

'You'll have to tell her,' I said later to Chris. 'She can't go round the house with no clothes on. It'll upset her brother.'

'You tell her. You're a woman.'

'She's *your* daughter . . . she'll think I'm jealous . . . I am a bit jealous, actually.'

Chris stared at me amazed. 'Jealous of my poor clumsy daughter? You must be mad. Of Susy? She was such a pretty kid, but she's turning into an elephant.'

'An elephant with tits.'

He winced. 'I don't like you talking about her like that . . .'

'*You* said she was an elephant!'

'I don't like the word "tits", not about my daughter. Oh come on, Alex, she's still my little girl, I feel protective about her . . .'

'Quite right. She's going to have to be protected. To start with, she's going to have to wear some clothes.'

His perceptions were oddly blinkered, I suppose because he censored any thought of sex.

One time we had Chris's boss Darryl to dinner. He was superficially loathsome, with no hint of depths beneath, and delivered his trite opinions in a loud unfunny monotone.

He delivered them to Susy, or Susy's forehead, since she stared at her plate, or tried to wiggle his opinions under her chin and towards the amazing shelf of flesh she was attempting to hide under her salmon salad. When he wasn't addressing her directly, he stared at her with that dreadfully embarrassing fixated glare which seems to consist of compressed sperm that will have to get out before they kill their owner.

But Christopher had noticed nothing amiss. 'Darryl was just being kind to her.'

'You're blind,' I said. 'He was crazed with lust.'

'I think you're weird, Alex. But I did notice that her clothes didn't fit. We don't want her to let the side down.'

'Don't worry,' I told him, 'she was a triumph. He couldn't have been more impressed.'

As she grew older she must have known her power. The boyfriends came in an endless stream. I'm sorry, that sentence was unfortunately phrased, and unfair to her; I am sure unfair — and yet all these years later I'm sure of nothing. Were they innocent, all those eager visits from boys bearing gifts of flowers and chocolates?

I think they were. I believe they were. I know now that I insulted her when I kept talking to her about contraception, and pointing out how important qualifications were in the modern world. She wasn't stupid, we told ourselves, not always convincingly. She had a sense of humour, and good taste in movies, and seemed to like boys and small children . . . she was brilliant with the toddlers our friends brought round, but there wasn't much else which seemed to hold her interest. She floated along in the middling stream of her middling private school.

'Maybe she'll do something with children,' Chris said.

'Yes. Have them,' I answered.

'Well — why not? There's nothing wrong with having children. Once she's grown up, I mean. Most women want children.'

I didn't pursue that one. I didn't like to be reminded that Christopher once wanted to have children with me.

— We had enough problems with the two he'd got. I did try with Susy, honestly. My feminism made me want to help her. I tried to tell her about feminism, too. She wouldn't believe that it wasn't an outdated extremist movement which hated men. That was what all her schoolfriends thought, if what they did could be dignified as thinking. They thought it meant not shaving their legs. She pointed out that I shaved mine. A terrible boredom sometimes overcame me when the children tried to discuss things with me.

In the end I gave up on feminism, but I occasionally tried to make her think. I didn't want her to sleep-walk into the world, eyes half-shut, half-naked, like the helpless girl in all the fairy-tales ... Cinderella, Gretel in the woods, Little Red Riding Hood ... I was a stepmother, OK, but I was never wicked.

Sleeping Beauty. How she loved sleep. Perhaps that was her passion. On school-days I had to drag her out of bed ten minutes before she was due to leave the house. She looked so happy, sprawled on the pillow. Hauled back to life she seemed bruised and lost, catatonic for the first few hours of waking.

We've come back to where we started. She was, or seemed, inverately lazy. She was labelled 'lazy' by her father, her teachers, me every morning, even her boyfriends, who from time to time could be heard attempting to take her for a walk or an outing ... But if she were forced to go outside, she preferred to lie in the middle of our lawn on a blue chaise longue, a dusty blue which made her look even more golden, entirely ripe to be swallowed whole as she swam in the shade of the monkey-puzzle tree, like a great soft peach sliding down into the darkness.

'Stop,' I wanted to shout at her. 'Wake up! This is the only life you've got!'

But maybe we were all just stupid. Maybe I somehow missed the point. Whenever I try to think about Susy I feel her slipping softly away.

I talked about her to my friend Drusilla, a psychotherapist, and terribly bright. She bridled at the word 'lazy'.

'There's no such thing as lazy, really.' She sifted me through the fine mesh of her gaze. 'People are "lazy" for a reason. They're unhappy, or unconfident, or unable to decide what they want to do. People go to sleep when they want to escape.'

She made me feel it was all our fault.

And it probably was. If not then, perhaps later. After all, there were hardly any problems to speak of in the period I am talking about, compared with the nightmares that followed, the awfulness after we went away.

But Drusilla would have said it's an illusion that life can be chopped into different parts. Our ends are in our beginnings, she said.

— More terrible when you know those ends.

I was not sentimental about the children, yet I could never bear to think of them dying. So maybe I loved them more than I thought. Or maybe everyone feels the same wrench, imagining the death of a younger generation.

Nothing they do should be irrevocable. They should be given more time, at least. Time to do things better than us. Time to realise some of their dreams.

That was what I used to think, when I knew that one or other of them was going out driving with another teenager, when the clapped-out sports car screamed to a halt outside our door, and off they went. *Please God no, not tonight. Give them time to leave home and be happy.*

Unbearable to recall it now, five years after the millennium.

Isaac dreamed of being a painter. He always . . . *never mind.*

Did Susy have dreams? I can't imagine. I think she slept too much to have dreams. That peculiar mist rises up and blinds and deafens me when I try to remember.

Yes, I suppose there was something, though hardly what one could call an ambition. Very long ago. A lifetime ago.

There was one thing she used to say, the only plan I can ever recall, though she wasn't much more than five when she said it, a round-faced child of five or six. They don't know what they're saying then. It couldn't have been serious.

I didn't let her have dolls. I'm not a hard-line feminist, but I think there's something disgusting about them. Little dead babies in female clothing, stillborns waiting to be looked after. I didn't want dolls in the house with us. We had just moved into the place in Islington and there seemed quite enough dependents without them.

So I threw all Susy's dolls away. They were scruffy things, in any case. I gave her farm animals, and lots of books, and encouraged her to be strong and active.

We played on the climbing-frame every day. I played; she sat on the grass and stared.

She said it as a prayer at bedtime, praying loudly when she knew I could hear her, and sometimes I couldn't get out of earshot. Sometimes I had to suffer it.

Please God let me go and live with my Mummy again and we'll have another baby, a sister. I want to go back and live with my Mummy.

Benjy is snoring fitfully, and mumbling a little, not happy. I don't seem to make people very happy. And I don't always notice when they're not happy . . .

Today we were walking down the main street, looking for someone who sold *chancho* sandwiches, although it was suffocatingly hot I was starving for the tenderness of hot fried pork, and when I'm hungry I have to eat – and a mud-splashed truck drove past us with bananas and a dark-skinned *chola* woman on top. It was going fast, and I almost felt that the driver was trying to frighten us, but in fact it was the woman who lurched to one side, her heavy skirts and bright apron flapping, and her bowler hat suddenly went skidding sideways and bounced across the dust towards us. Benjamin saw, ran like a sprinter, scooped up the hat, dusted it down on his trouser leg and as the woman wailed and the lorry slowed he tossed it back, briefly black against the sun, she caught it, smiled, waved the hat at him. He stood there until they disappeared, in the middle of the road, panting a little, and the sweat ran down his enormous smile as he watched the woman getting smaller and smaller.

When I saw his smile I realised it was rare. When I saw him run, suddenly charged with energy, I realised how hangdog his walk had been.

Too bad. The young are so easily depressed, I'm sure I was never depressed at his age.

All the same, I'm not happy he's not happy. Tomorrow I might try to cheer him up. After all, he's my travelling companion. Sometimes I think he's my only friend. And we're still in this together. Because I haven't given up, I shan't give up till we've tried every town in this shitty continent. I wouldn't stand a chance of a child with no husband. To be strictly practical, I still need Benjamin.

Maybe in other ways too. He did look – sweet, as he threw that hat. Gallant, as he used to be to me before I got impatient with his gallantry. And his smile, so warm, with such white teeth . . .

Bodies get cold in the early hours, as if the night's draining away their life. We're covered with the lightest *manta* which seemed unsufferably hot when we went to bed but does nothing to protect me now. My hands are cold, my heart is cold, my teeth begin to ache with cold . . .

Reluctantly and then gratefully I crawl over to Benjy and cuddle up next to him, burrowing under the blanket so I can fit my knees under the curve of his knees and press my belly against his warm buttocks. My face touches his back; from habit, from affection, I kiss it, very lightly so he doesn't wake up. I sneak my cold feet between his calves and my fingers inch under his elbows, stealing the warmth from his sides.

Benjamin, I love you after all, I love you for being here with me. I'm glad I'm not alone in this vast blackness. How did I ever come so far, did I ever mean to come so far, did I ever intend to end up here? Why can't I sleep, and dream of the past . . .

What did I do to deserve all this?

14

Christopher: Venice, 2005

We only went back to paradise once. We went back to Portugal in the late 1990s, when many things had changed, between Alex and me, as well as in Iberia.

As usual when May was drawing to a close she'd wanted to go to Toledo. But we were wintering in Tahiti; it seemed absurd to go back to Europe. I resisted, I was bored with Toledo, the magic had gone out of the city for me. We always saw the same people. Besides, I didn't want to go so near home.

'I need to see Europe once in a while, I'm *European*,' Alex sighed, as if I were a Maori, or a Solomon Islander.

'Since when have you had a good word for Europe?'

'I've always loved Paris . . .'

'OK, we'll go to Paris. *Not* Toledo. I'm up to here with Toledo . . .' Paris was where we had honeymooned; she was so young, she shone with youth, I couldn't quite believe she was mine. I half-felt I was still running after her, that I would pursue her till the end of our lives, panting behind her burnished hair past the silvery statues and lopsided fountains . . . the spring winds blew my words away. But she was mine at last, I took her home. It was all too easy to go home from Paris. We flew home together from innumerable weekends, to the children we had left with the nanny or the Browns – '. . . Forget it, Paris is too near home.'

Yet I wanted to get back to the good things we'd shared in the early days of travelling. I wanted Alex to love me again.

Naturally I thought of Portugal. Alex resisted, yet I could feel she was less keen on Toledo than in previous years, and eventually she agreed, if we could stay in places we'd never seen, and pop across to Spain for a week or so – I assumed that she meant both of us.

We decided on Lisbon and Sagres. My spirits rose once it was decided. We'd only ever spent one weekend in Lisbon, and that was nearly twenty years before; I remembered it intimate and slow, a good city for lovers. And we'd never been right down in the west to Sagres and Cape St Vincent, the south-west tip of Europe, the nearest point to America, the place where Henry the Navigator once trained his sea-captains to travel the world, Vasco da Gama, Christopher Columbus ... the starting-point for so many great voyages. I was full of hope. It meant a new beginning. It would carry us on into the twenty-first century, the dangerous voyage towards old age, she would be at my side, we'd be happy together ...

We flew in to Lisbon first.

'It's the perfect European city, just what you wanted,' I told her, as we circled above the gentle lights. I held her hand, my love, my wife.

Some things were left. I pointed them out. There were still narrow streets with open windows in which canaries swung in cages, above a brilliant display of petunias, there were still unripe lemons and arum lilies growing round the ruined battlements. The yellow trams had been phased out, but the taxi-drivers were more manic than ever, their pale green roofs flying uphill at twilight like terrified moths escaping hell.

But we had forgotten the earthquake. Worse than the earthquake of the 1980s. It was stupid, the papers had been full of it, but a year had passed and we had forgotten, the foreground always crowds out the past ... Alexandra blamed me for forgetting.

There was a lot of demolition work in the Alfama. The oldest buildings had suffered most. Some of the rebuilding was ugly new brick. Scaffolding clambered everywhere. The streets were full of sand and bricks. The air, which had once smelled of cooking and lemons, now caught at our throats and made us cough – new brick-dust, or disturbed dry rot? The sound of small birds was replaced by hammering.

On our last day we sat in the shade at a round metal table on the cobbles. We had found an alley far away from any builders. The table rocked, and was slightly too small, but the sky was lovely, the orange-pink roofs held their mustardy lichens up to the sun, the washing hanging from every balcony plumed in the wind, as white as sand . . . I felt nostalgic for our earlier selves, ten years younger, stretched on the beach, I was full of love for Portugal, for my wisdom, for the gin in my hand, first drink of the day well before eleven, so maybe something had already gone wrong.

A hammering; I heard it clearly, some way off, insistent, tinny.

'Do you remember, when we came to Lisbon before, we saw that little crowd round a dying pigeon?'

– It had been having some kind of fit in the street, convulsing horribly, wings askew. There were children watching and a black-clad old woman who looked so upset I thought she must be worried about the children catching some horrible disease, but she nodded sadly as they tried to touch it. Then a man picked it up, a whirling pecking bundle, and tried to balance it on a low wall. It sat there for a second, suddenly comatose. The man saw us looking and waved his arms at us hopefully, to indicate flight; you could feel the crowd willing the pigeon to fly, but actually it just convulsed again and fell backwards into a tin bowl of geraniums, where it lay still, slumped on its side. The sigh of disappointment was audible, as if the whole scene had been part of an opera.

'Do you remember how amazed we were at their kindness? That they genuinely cared about a filthy street-bird that Londoners think of as flying rats? – I was thinking, they must miss the birds. Do you notice, there isn't any birdsong to speak of. The building work must have frightened them away.'

She frowned at me; I was talking too much. She had a hangover, she wasn't drinking. 'I remember. They were horribly sentimental. Or perhaps they do it for tourists.'

That hurt. The Portuguese were either sentimental or false, and our younger selves were just tourists.

'You're in a bad mood.'

'You're ridiculous. Let's move, that hammering is driving me mad.'

While we talked it had got suddenly louder. Too much black coffee and then too much gin, my heart was thumping, I was afraid, but I knew the day would get better.

Alex loved shopping. She'd always loved shopping. We'd go to a market and stroll and stare and I'd buy her some perfectly chosen object which would show I knew her best in the world.

(Of all the anxiously narrow rituals that hotel life imposed on us, shopping was one of the oddest, though it never seemed so at the time. Alexandra had what's called 'an eye for beauty'; in other words, she collected things. Local handicrafts, weaving, carvings, silver trinkets, rocks, shells, rare skins and feathers, pottery, hats . . . but our suitcases couldn't carry it all. We left a stream of things behind us, gifts for the maids, who would have preferred money. Every new purchase displaced an old one. She had to have what she wanted, you see. Once we were rich, she had whatever she wanted, and when she got bored, she threw it away.)

We walked to the Feira da Ladre. I didn't really know what to expect except that it was a famous market where 'you could buy anything' . . .

What we found was very far from that. It was on a hill, and open to the air, blazing hot, with a few old trees. There were no actual stalls; the stall-holders just spread blankets on the ground, and their wares on the blankets, so we stared at sloping miles of blankets covered with every kind of object that had ever been made, or dreamed, or broken (most of them were broken), or lost (all of them looked lost). The amazing thing was that they were all on sale – not in Africa, or South America, but here in Portugal, in Europe. There were plaster dogs with one ear missing, plastic shoes, cracked records, an old mangle, old camera-cases, half-used scent sprays, odd buttons, old comics . . . miles and mile of solidified time, for all of them had fallen out of the past, beached as the tide moved on without them (I was loving it; it excited me; I felt I was looking at some kind of collage, I felt I was being taught something, though I hadn't understood it yet). The most hopeless blanket was entirely covered with empty tin cans – some Coke cans still, perhaps the report had been less publicised here or perhaps the cans pre-dated it, but mostly the distinctive green and gold cans of the *Fria* with which Coca-Cola Inc were flooding the world now no one sane would buy coke any more. In the sun the tins glittered like punk jewellery, beautiful as a blowfly's wings. It reminded me of scenes half-glimpsed as we had been driven through third-world countries. But this was Portugal, for heaven's sake. I had never realised how poor they were.

The curve of the hill was sometimes so steep that you expected everything to slide and go clattering and tinkling down to the bottom; why did it move me? Of course; it made me think of the curve of the earth . . .

I was so absorbed I forgot about Alex. It was ages since I'd managed to do that; I no longer felt safe enough to forget her, but briefly, there, I did escape. I was following my nose, fascinated, criss-crossing between the narrow aisles, nodding to the thin stall-holders, who smiled at me with a flash of filling, patient faces burnt black by the sun, crouching beside their empire of rubbish. 'English,' I said, apologetically, when they started a sales patter in fast Portuguese. 'Take dollar,' they said, and I moved on. 'Take traveller cheque . . .' I waved, placating.

The most disturbing things were the most personal; false teeth, outmoded hearing aids, glasses – broken glasses, lensless glasses, an optical nightmare of useless glasses – and not far away, with the bereft false teeth, what looked like an array of children's dental braces, what use was another child's dental brace?

All of a sudden I thought of Isaac. As if all the lost things in his absent-minded life had been reassembled here, but he was forgotten. His glasses, his wallet, the dental brace that had made his smile so sad, in his teens . . .

I stood in the blazing sun and felt cold. It was like looking at a pile of bones, and suddenly the whole landscape shivered and swam in the sun like a field of bones, blinding white, the dreadful remains of some final earthquake . . .

The sun went in. The moment passed. Nothing had happened, the salesman smiled, he had a daisy in the brim of his hat, the glasses were only glasses again. I realised Alex wasn't there.

I stared around me in stupid panic, the Feira da Ladre was covered in shadows, flitting silently from blanket to blanket, shadowy people with solemn eyes, poor Portuguese I had failed to notice, the salesmen were skeletons, leering at me, broken bicycles, a fork, a clock, had my whole life been as random as this . . .?

Then I spotted her coming down the hill above me, the sun came out, her hair lit up, but I was noticing her haughty walk, every bone and ligament discontented; she wore dark glasses but her mouth was set.

'Can we leave this ridiculous place?'

It was not like her to ask permission. 'Of course. I thought perhaps you'd already gone . . .'

That snapped a cord; she was suddenly raving. 'How the hell can I leave? You've got the fucking money! And the fucking keys! And the fucking map!'

'But – you didn't want to bring a jacket, or a handbag. I'm carrying them because you asked me to – '

'Precisely, so you have to think about me! You can't go footling off on your own! You can't just act as if I don't exist! I was lost, and then I was watching you, you were like a little dog going after a scent, you never looked for me, not once!'

And then I realised it wasn't just anger, the big tears rolled down from under her glasses, her narrow black glasses, so hard, so smart, and her painted lips collapsed, shivering, a small dark animal dying in the desert. She was wringing her hands and weeping, steadily. I was deeply moved; I was horrified. I had never seen her like this before. I put my arms round her shoulders and guided her away, stepping hastily over the crouching vendors who didn't look up, we were irrelevant to them, we had spent no money, we were going away.

I stopped a taxi; she huddled against me, no longer accusing but crying quietly. Her warm tears on my cheek and my neck, the wonderful wetness of my shirt, we were close again, we were close at last, for the first time since we'd landed in Europe.

'It's all right, it's all right.' I felt it was, as long as she leaned on me like that.

'I hated that place. It was like death.'

'I'm sorry, it was my idea . . .'

'Didn't you hate it?'

'Well . . . I was fascinated, actually.'

'But everything was dirty and broken and useless . . .'

'That was what I liked, in a funny way.'

'I don't understand you, Christopher.'

Later, in bed, where she clung to me, where we made love, where we made friends, I tried to explain to myself and her.

'It was like an enormous museum. About human life, or human artefacts. But all set up by alien beings, who didn't understand how to classify things . . . I liked the randomness.'

'It wasn't all random. There were those tins – '

'OK, and the comic stall, and all those glasses – '

'The dolls. That was what finished me off. They were so pathetic – disgusting, I mean. No one could ever want dolls like that.'

I'd seen the dolls, a field-hospital of dolls, lacking a leg, an arm, an eye, half their hair, a blouse, a skirt, yet each laid out lovingly by the vendor on its own small patch of blanket, so his goods might be seen to best advantage.

'. . . The way they were laid out. Like little dead bodies. Nobody would want them. They would lie there for ever.'

Extraordinary. Her eyes were full of tears again.

'Alex . . . what is the matter? You sneered at the Portuguese for being sentimental about pigeons, now you're getting weepy about a few dolls!'

'Nonsense, I hated them, I can't explain, it was the end of the world, that place. Nothing but the past. Everything – ugly. Neglected, broken, useless.'

She was still crying as she talked. I was missing something, not understanding.

'Never mind, we'll be in Sagres tomorrow.'

'I'm . . . overtired. I'm going to sleep.'

On the train to the south next day we sat close together; she wanted me to look after her, it was as if she were convalescing from something, no longer impatient or independent. I loved to look after her, I always had. I felt perfectly hot and perfectly happy.

– She was human, after all. I had started to think she was inhumanly strong, indifferent, unchanging, doing her exercises morning after morning no matter how hot or humid it was, walking and dancing when mere mortals like myself were stretched on the bed with a long cool drink, never ill except for her headaches, and those were more often a sign of rage . . .

Outside the window the terrain got brighter, harsher, sharper, more desert-like. Grey spiny *agave* was the only vegetation. The occasional human figure was bowed and ant-like, tightly contracted against the light. The houses crouched, flat-roofed and shuttered, white and blind in the punishing sun. I thought of South America, where I'd travelled as a very young man, but never with Alex, that was not for her . . .

Light poured in from the barren plain. She dozed against me and I stared at her. Funny how rarely you really look at the people you are closest to. I looked to admire, when we were promenading, I looked to enjoy, when she was naked, but I never looked to discover things. Now I wanted to learn about the rest of our life.

Yes, she was human, mortal. Her fine freckled skin had begun to wrinkle, there were little stretched fans beneath each eye, the eyelids were very faintly brown, and the bridge of her nose, so straight, so pure, was surely more visible than it once was, as if the bones were minutely closer to the surface.

I looked, I tell you, with absolute tenderness. I loved her more than I ever had as the glare revealed she would age like me.

116

Asleep, she trusted me completely; to look at her, to look after her. I kissed her gently, her hair and her cheek, still smooth as a flower beneath my lips, and she woke, and smiled, and slept again. *We should be together till the day we died.* A great exaltation rose in me, a certainty I had never quite had ever since she'd refused to bear my child some twenty years before, when we first fell in love . . .

It had been a refusal to give herself when she said she wasn't interested in children – *my* children, I thought, she doesn't want my children, how long is she going to want me? And the other thing, later, worse, much worse, as if she had killed a part of me, as if she'd decided to kill our future, unbearable still to think about that.

Yet Alex had stayed with me; she was forty-seven when we made that second trip to Portugal. On that slow hot train I felt at last that nothing now could take her away from me . . .

And everything I felt was folly.

The rest of that trip is a blur, with strange sharp fragments that don't fit together. It was a different country we'd come to. The people were inturned, dour, suspicious; the bleakness of the country was in them. This land was wide and high and harsh, rock and cactus and flat baked earth. The edge of Europe was entirely ungentle, a savage break between earth and sea over which the winds poured and the waters raged, flung back by the cliffs in torrents of spray. At Cape St Vincent grey walls of rock dropped perpendicular into the Atlantic. The lighthouse looked brave and small from a distance. You felt these people clung on to the earth by a mixture of courage and grim endurance.

– So how did they ever summon the flair to set off on those epic voyages? How did they dare to send their wooden boats acros the enormous curve of the earth? Was it possible that Alex and I would find new heart for our travels here?

I saw most of this alone. Alexandra was strange and lethargic, she who was never lethargic, and spent much of the time in our hotel room reading Portuguese scandal mags and watching television. We were staying in the *pousada* at Sagres, which was full of rich Americans. It was outside the town, an unreal place of anonymous luxury, slightly dated; its style and size could not have been less attuned to its surroundings. There were too many staff, who wouldn't meet our eyes. Everyone was dwarfed by the high ceilings; the lounge was a hundred feet long, and they'd chosen furniture to scale, so the guests looked tiny on the vast leather sofas. Our room had two massive dark wood beds, so large that they looked like two doubles. I made a joke about wife-swapping, and Alex said, 'I hate them . . . they look like funeral barques.'

We both slept in the same one, of course. One night I dreamed that Susy and Isaac were in the other one together, some frightful mistake, they were making love, it was too late for me to save my daughter . . . then they stopped and sneered at us, the same but different. 'It's all your fault,' Isaac said.

One dream-like memory I know to be true because it changed our life together. We were sprawled on the bed waiting for dinner, too lazy to dress and go to the bar, sipping the vast gins the maid had brought us. The evening cold that struck up off the sea was beginning to creep through the open window. We had switched on TV absent-mindedly and found a Portuguese soap in progress, which Alex insisted on watching, so I lay there companionably, reading my Baedeker. Recently she'd got addicted to soaps; they were international, she could find them anywhere. It was something I didn't care to share.

And then she was sniffing; I heard her sniffing. I reached without looking for the box of tissues which like everything else was giant-sized; I thought she was getting a cold.

'It's beautiful,' Alex said, or whispered, and the words seemed to come from someone else, for she was gazing entranced at the screen, the tears were welling in her hazel eyes, she wasn't talking to me but herself; '*Oh*,' she sighed, a little broken whisper.

She saw me looking and looked back, defiant. 'I'm *enjoying* it,' she said. The screen showed a hospital room, or a ridiculous set of a hospital room, all handsome doctors and exotic flowers.

And a woman miming ecstasy. And the cause of the ecstasy, and my wife's grief, a small, supposedly newborn baby.

And so I began to understand.

'Why shouldn't *I* have a baby,' said Alex, or someone else using Alex's voice, a little girl using my darling's voice. 'I could have a baby too.'

'You're joking.' It was utterly clear that she wasn't. Alex never played the little girl. Part of herself had broken loose. Part of herself was learning to speak. It told me something I didn't want to know.

'I'm not joking . . . I don't know what I'm saying.'

'But *do you* want one?'

She nodded, weeping, clutching her arms across her breasts.

'Is this something new?'

'I don't know . . . it's mad . . . no, I keep crying when I see pictures of babies. It's so stupid. I didn't want to tell you. I mean, I'm too old . . . aren't I? Am I too old to have a child?' Her voice gathered strength as she spoke, becoming less shame-faced, more Alex-like. 'Tell me I'm not too old.'

'Since when have I been able to tell you things?'

She suddenly flung her arms around me, laughing and crying at the same time, tugging at my hair, kissing me. 'Oh Christopher, let's try. It would be a wonderful baby.'

I didn't say 'You weren't very keen on Isaac and Susy.' I didn't say 'It wouldn't be your first.' I didn't remind her of the daughter she'd had adopted when she was twenty-two – before she met me, I wouldn't have allowed it. Nor of the child of ours that she killed. *It was our child and she fucking killed it* . . . Part of me will never forgive her for that. She was four months pregnant, he had eyes, ears, fingers . . . yet I went along with it, afraid to lose her.

Now I went along with another mad scheme.

A new chapter of our life began, a new and more difficult journey, not at all the one I had anticipated. We could travel anywhere in the world, we could use our money to do anything we wanted, but this took us into the interior, this drove us back against our own limitations. We were face to face with the ageing that travel had protected us from.

Her plan was mad, with a certain mad courage, and I agreed to follow it. I'd have followed her to the ends of the earth, and done anything to make her happy . . .

Anything I could, that is. She was forty-seven, I was sixty-two, we were much too old to start a baby . . .

But she was so eager, she had no doubts. Once the dam was broached, words poured from her at meal after meal and drink after drink, frenetic plans for our child, our children, names for our child, homes for our child . . . It was novel to feel sorry for her. I didn't entirely dislike the change, the new, more vulnerable Alex.

In any case I didn't dare crush her dream. Other men might have dreamed it with her.

And the sex was fun. The sex was marvellous. My darling was suddenly as eager as me, more eager than me, after years of coolness . . .

So this was the new beginning. Nothing is quite what you expect it to be, not Portugal, not the woman you love. We sat and giggled on the giant leather sofas, we fucked unprotected in the heavy bed; for the last week in Sagres, after Alex told her secret, we hardly seemed to go outdoors. My snapshots are all of Alex's face, Alex smiling, Alex in tears, Alex's face, which I now saw was mortal.

The American guests moved around us like extras, having unreal conversations in unreal voices.

'Say. Did Henry the Navigator *actually live here*?'

Because we had a notional relationship with the barman, the Americans thought we had superior knowledge.

'Pardon me. My wife would like to know, what does *Ovindo Mondo* mean?'

At least, that was what I thought I'd heard. The phrase meant nothing at all to me, though it vaguely evoked a brand of wine, or perhaps a Latin pop singer.

'Sounds like a name to me,' I said. 'My wife's good at the lingo. When she comes, I'll ask.'

When she came, I asked, and she frowned, puzzled, went over to the Americans. They showed her something in a tourist pamphlet.

'O *fim do mondo*,' she exclaimed. 'Is that what they call this part of the coast? "The end of the world."'

'Gee thanks, that's great!'

She came back to me. 'O *fim do mondo*. What a beautiful name.'

'I suppose it was the end of all the earth they knew . . .'

'So they sailed off the edge of the world; how brave.'

'So did we. No beginning without an ending.'

And how sweetly, how passionately she kissed me, how tightly she held me in her arms, how many times she told me she loved me when she set off alone for Lisbon next day, on her way for the week in Malaga she insisted she needed to spend alone.

15

Alexandra: São Benedicto, Brazil, 2005

Thank God we're in Brazil at last. Every time we move on I feel better for a bit. I began to have doubts at the border when I learned we needed yellow fever shots and the official started grinning a demented grin and assuring me he wished he could shoot me himself; then Benjy showed up and the creep backed off and we found they used an airgun to give us the shots, which was better after all than a dodgy needle. The motorboat puttered across the Mamore and we had arrived in another world; it felt positively . . . *metropolitan*, though now we're back in the wilds again.

But the wilds of Brazil are less *absolute*. One shouldn't be glad they've lopped down so much jungle, and the freshly cut areas are rather an eyesore, like a piece of burned skin through a magnifying glass, with singed stumps of hair sticking out of the redness . . . all the same it makes me feel safer, somehow, to know that human beings are on top.

In Bolivia I had nightmares for weeks after the little river trip we took, Benjamin and I and a Spanish-speaking guide, and there were piranhas and alligators and a colony of bats like great black ivy-leaves spread across a rotting stump.

'Don't they carry rabies?' Benjamin asked.

'Why did you bring me here?' I hissed.

True, there were butterflies and orchids as well and pink river dolphins that seemed positively friendly. But it was all so chaotic. The guide seemed surprised to see the alligators and utterly amazed when the boat broke down and he couldn't mend it for an hour and a half.

I should have seen then we were bound to fail, for nothing really worked in Bolivia, the jungle strangled everything. Even my hopefulness and energy. Now Brazil has put new heart in us.

The food. I've always liked my food. Food and sex are not unconnected. Afer Bolivia, the food is delicious. Wonderful fish in Pôrto Velho, fresh shrimp fried in olive oil and garlic, grilled dourado, vatapa – smelling of coconut, Africa, the sea. Food is a celebration again. And the meat is good for Benjamin. A big rare churrasco steak at night, plenty of cachaça to keep him cheerful and then two or three diabolically strong coffees, little *cafezinhos*, black as love, sweet and hot as Benjamin's mouth – he was inside me most of the night. He's still a good lover; I've no complaints there. I have plenty of complaints, but not about our sex-life.

São Benedicto is just right for us; a scruffy little town left beached by the gold rush. It was rich for a bit and now it's poor with scrawny dogs picking scraps on the street. No gold left, and the people will leave, for the tin mine can't employ them all. But they haven't gone yet. They've been waiting for us. There are children everywhere; I see them everywhere, small and bright-eyed, playing in the dust.

Benjamin's gone out to try the priest again – so he says, and perhaps it's true. Priests know who they've recently advised against abortion. If you pay them well and convince them you're Catholic – or convince them you're Catholic by paying them well – they will put out feelers, promising nothing. The whole process is terribly slow; we've been through it numbingly often by now. Money is no guarantee of success. Only inexhaustible willpower can do it, and Benjy has been deficient in that. Perhaps the steak will pep him up.

The trouble with Benjy – one of the troubles – is laziness. Sleepiness. He should be ashamed, doing nothing all day, with all the talent Isaac said he had. When I first met him he was always full of adrenalin, just finishing one picture and starting on six others, with paint-spattered clothes and restless eyes, looking about him to eat the world. He pretends to go out and

123

make sketches now, but he never shows me anything. There was one drawing of me, but that was appalling, entirely inept, made me look like a monster – for a second I was worried, but he just lacks practice. He sits around, listless, and drinks too much. It's not right at his age, barely thirty, at the beginning of his life.

Christopher grew idle too, I remember. All my men seem to tire in the end . . . but at least he was older, he'd worked all his life. And he still sent back regular pieces to the travel pages of the English papers. I helped him to make them more colourful, crisper, but he did keep working, after a fashion.

Part of him itched to make films again, though the longer he left it, the further his contacts lapsed, and any practical hopes of doing it. But he was an avid cinema-goer. In any town with a cinema he'd disappear in the afternoons; almost any kind of film gave him pleasure, because it was good, or because it was crap, because it was eccentric, or typical. He always came back in a good temper.

And it gave me some time on my own. Once I met Stuart that was very important, so I could be in a good temper too. In the end Chris grew less keen on going out and became addicted to video. Video films, video games. He could pretend to direct those electronic cartoons. In our last years together it was all Chris did: play computer games on borrowed screens or watch video films in dark rented rooms, and by then we no longer talked about them. By then we no longer talked at all . . .

But Stuart and Christopher loved to talk film. At first Chris took Stuart for an ideal audience, one of those Englishmen he loved to meet in hotel bars during those long days . . . we were happy, yes, but the days could seem long. There was nothing we had to do, you see, and I couldn't listen to him all the time, rehashing the old office grievances, reliving the old, faded triumphs, for part of him was in television still, part of Christopher had never left work, or wished he had not, and grieved for it (which was pointless – I mean, I never *forced* him to leave). He could impress other men with what he had done, especially if they knew a little about it, and everyone knows something about television. I was sometimes on the edge of such conversations, sucking in my gin and half-reading a novel, and I saw over the years how they began to falter as Chris became more out of touch with things. The names he dropped had a dusty air. Poor Christopher. He'd become a back number.

Stuart soon realised this, of course, so Chris couldn't lord it over him for long, the film-maker patronising the academic. To do him justice, Chris didn't much care. Here was a man who really knew about film, and film was Chris's first love after me. He could talk to Stuart in his own language. But Stuart's motives were less transparent.

Stuart liked to see films on his own, because it made the experience more concentrated — that's what he told Chris, at any rate. So he would recommend films to my husband within striking distance of Toledo, and Chris would drive off across the hot red plain. He would come back full of what he had seen, exhilarated by the long drive home past the fields of sunflowers and the olive-dotted hills. The last time it happened the programme times were wrong; we'd played that little trick once too often; he came back early and nearly caught us, he thought he'd passed Stuart driving down the road from the parador, but I affected ignorance.

'Not impossible,' I said. My voice sounded unnatural, my throat was dry. Perhaps Stuart had been having a drink with a friend, since the parador had the best bars in town; but of course those jeeps were very common in Spain. I was directing too much energy to the question. I thought, *he must hear I'm lying.* But he lit a cigar, and changed the subject.

'Bloody waste of an afternoon,' he said. 'I shan't trust Stuart's programme times again. Coming back was rather horrific. I ran into a hanging wall of orange butterflies, you couldn't miss them, they went on for ever, swarming all over the main road and all across the windscreen. Beautiful but disgusting. I killed a lot of them. Why didn't they have the sense to get out of the way?'

We always trod a very narrow line. The excitement was treading that very narrow line. It was exciting, too, to have a man with commitments, a man who worked and had a wife and children, a man who wasn't wholly available to me. We were both actors, both liars. I enjoyed the foursome (occasionally sixsome, when I couldn't dissuade them from bringing the children) outings almost as much as I enjoyed the moments we spent alone. Knowing both he and Chris wanted me. Sailing near the wind in the things we said, the way we looked, the tiny touches, apparently casual, but burning, burning. Whose foot was pushing mine under the table? The electricity ran from my toe to my groin as I eased my legs across one another, carefully avoiding my lover's eyes, knowing he was looking at me hard.

For me it was partly a game. Stuart was different, more serious, with a gloomy Calvinistic streak. The lying and acting caused him pain. I only felt twinges of fear, not pain.

'Christopher would kill us if he found out,' I said to Stuart one afternoon, half an hour after Christopher had left, ten minutes after Stuart and I shrugged our clothes off. Chris thought I was in the El Greco museum, Kirsty thought Stuart was working on his book. But he was working on me, with tender precision, his black head rooted between my legs.

'Can't hear,' he said, coming up for air.

'Christopher would kill us . . .'

'Don't *enjoy* it so much. Making them jealous. I feel guilty as hell.'

'I never feel guilty – don't stop, I want you – I just feel afraid. He's always been a jealous man. But why should we feel guilty, anyway? How can something so pleasurable be wrong?'

It began to feel wrong in the end. Partly because he was so agonised about it. We went on meeting for half a dozen years, and only missed one summer. He was hooked on me, but resented me. I suspect Kirsty was a bore in bed, and he'd never been unfaithful before. My orgasms were a drug for him, making him feel like a wonderful lover.

There were moments I shan't forget. One balmy May evening in the year after we met we were celebrating, in a false little foursome, meeting up again after twelve months apart. We were in the parador's restaurant, which is staid to look at and rather brightly-lit but offers extremely sensual food; I'd ordered sucking-pig, and it arrived, enormous, luscious pink flesh and a golden crust, enough to feed a city. The smell was wonderful.

'Is that all for you?' asked Kirsty, amazed. She had ordered sole; she was semi-vegetarian. 'How do you stay so scrawny, Alex?'

An awkward silence fell.

'She isn't scrawny,' said Stuart.

Kirsty blushed and covered her mouth. 'I'm sorry, I meant skinny.'

'Exercise,' I said, demurely, but because she had been rude to me I allowed myself a tiny smile at Stuart, a little look, a little longer than it should have been. Actually we hadn't had a chance to make love; Chris and I had only arrived the night before. When I rang to invite them to eat with us, Kirsty's voice had been anxious, a little unwilling, despite the friendly postcards we had exchanged.

She watched me tear into it with my teeth. 'Sucking-pig, you said. Do you think it means they're still being suckled? Do you think the poor bairns aren't even weaned?' Now her face looked rounder and paler than usual. I wanted to give it a little nip.

On cue, the baby-listener howled from the wall – we hadn't been able to get a babysitter, so the children were sleeping in our bedroom with a listening device plugged in.

'I'll go,' said Kirsty, the perpetual martyr.

'Don't be silly, love, I've finished, I'll go.' Stuart was a very good father.

'You won't be able to open the door, it's tricky,' I breathed, and saw his face twitch slightly. 'I can finish this pig in a second.' And I did. I ate ravenously, looking at Kirsty, taking big bites, with great enjoyment, sucking the juice from the succulent flesh. Then I followed Stuart from the room.

'Bring me my cigars,' Christopher called after us.

'Yes, my darling.'

We kissed in the lift. His tongue was long and thin and deft;

he pressed me so hard against the lift controls that we shot to the basement, then up to the sky. By the time we got to our bedroom door there was silence inside. We slipped in quietly. They were both tucked into our double bed, Fiona flat out with her little freckled arms spread wide on the pillow in an attitude of trust, Robert with his head on his sister's chest.

'Aren't they beautiful,' Stuart said, stricken.

I was irritated by his sudden stillness, his air of a worshipper returning to God. I let my hand slip down to his trousers, I felt his cock, I made it nudge against me, it was my cock, he was my lover, I demanded service, he was ready for me. Something crossed my mind; I began to laugh; I went and pulled out the baby listener that would have broadcast us through the hotel; then we were both laughing and kissing each other.

'Come into the bathroom, quickly.' He pushed inside me – I pulled him inside me – with my dress round my waist and his trousers round his ankles, the rim of the basin pressing into my hips, and I cried out softly at the first long thrust and began to fuck like a rider in the saddle, crazed with hunger for my orgasm.

'You taste of meat,' he panted, as he finally unclamped his lips from mine, as the moans he had muffled died in my chest.

'You're my meat,' I said, making my dress demure again, running my fingers through my hair.

'Am I good enough? Am I the best?'

'You're good enough. You're great. I mustn't forget to get Christopher's cigars . . .'

(Actually, after the initial novelty, I knew he wasn't as good as Christopher. Christopher had always been intensely sensual, and practice had made perfect, over the years. So why did I need Stuart? I like new things. I like a change . . .)

When things got difficult, I didn't need him.

'You're fantastic, Alex. Like no one else. Nothing like this has ever happened to me . . . you're like a drug. I'm hooked, you know that . . . but it's just selfishness. I blame myself. I hate myself.'

'As long as you don't blame *me*.'

128

But I knew he did blame me. You could sometimes feel it in the way he fucked, when he'd drunk a little at lunchtime and his dark blue eyes had an angry look. He battered my body into the bed as if he wanted to obliterate me even as he roared in orgasm.

That could be exciting too. Once or twice, but not as a habit. I thought the anger was becoming a habit. I don't like being blamed, or obliterated.

(And maybe I was just a little peeved that he'd never offered to leave his wife, his large-hipped wife and bad-tempered children – at least, they were always bad-tempered with me. He doted blindly on those kids, sniggering Fiona, beetle-browed Robert . . . not that I would have left Christopher, but I feel Stuart might have *offered* to leave. It deprived me of the pleasure of telling him not to.)

After five years I was tired of it. I was forty-seven, I was forty-eight . . . One year Chris didn't want to go to Toledo. He'd never shown that he suspected me, but he was very definite; Toledo was over. I found that I agreed with him. And I needed a baby, not a lover.

I arranged to meet Stuart in a little farmhouse I rented in the hills above Malaga. Kirsty thought he was on a lecture tour, Chris thought I needed to be alone after the crisis we'd lived through in Portugal. Stuart thought I needed to make love to him, but I only needed to end the chapter. I was eager to fly on to Christopher in Switzerland, our last port of call in Europe. The desire for a child had made me love him again. Stuart had become irrelevant.

The hills were dusty, lethally dry. The photo of the farmhouse had not included the gigantic pylon ten feet away, so the humming and singing and moaning of the wires almost drowned the frantic chirrups of the crickets.

He arrived tired and thirsty, ecstatic to see me. His face was faintly powdered with dust, which made his eyes very dark, theatrical-looking. I could see how much he wanted me. He hugged me, pulling my hips against him.

'I thought about this every minute of the journey . . .'

There wasn't any point in dragging things out. 'Stuart, wait – I'm sorry. The fun's gone out of it, my darling.'

And so the unpleasantness began. We argued for hours; the pylon echoed us, singing mournfully across the baked hillside.

'I'm glad to hear I was a bit of fun . . . I've been in love with you for seven years – '

' – Six, actually – '

'I've cheated my wife and let down my children. I did it willingly, but not just for fun. You can't just drop me, just like that, as if it didn't mean anything . . .'

I found he was right, it didn't mean anything. I always go cold when people bully me. I said I wouldn't meet him again. He grabbed hold of me by the upper arms and shook me against the wall like a rat. We were miles from anywhere, my head hit the cupboard, my neck whiplashed sickeningly. My heart started thumping. Fear and rage. *Don't dare to touch me, don't dare to hurt me*. I screamed like a banshee and kicked him hard, the satisfying contact of shoe and bone – how often we'd played footsy under the table – and then as I saw his face go pale and he grabbed my hair and yanked me towards him I did what I never thought I could do, for after all they had loved me tenderly – I grabbed his cock and balls and squeezed. I squeezed till the bones of my knuckles ached. His roar of pain was like the echo of an orgasm, it followed me as I ran outside, abandoning my book and my shoes, then Stuart came after me, half-doubled up. I jumped into the Land Rover and slammed the door and stared straight in front as he rapped on the window, trying not to hear the abuse he shouted – the engine caught and I revved like a demon up the slope that led to the long track down. I felt powerful driving barefoot up the hill, saving myself, at one with the machine, but the downhill track was a different matter, a switchback nightmare, narrow and steep, the slippery white surface only inches wider than the wheels of the borrowed Land Rover; I screeched down the hillside like a rally-driver, but giggling and frightened, smelling my own sweat, scattering dust and goats and butterflies, making a blue-clad farmer stare and spray the road instead of his olives.

I was relieved, of course. I'd had a narrow escape, he was obviously crazy. For a moment I'd thought that my luck was running out, I'd thought my sins were catching up with me. I even made a vow not to be unfaithful again.

I flew into Geneva cool and immaculate, two days earlier than I had first planned, and wept with joy to see Chris at the airport. I said to him, as he took me in his arms, 'You're the only thing in the world that matters. I haven't told you often enough that I love you – '

'You have told me. I know you love me.'

'And now we're going to be a real family.'

How sure I was, how stupidly sure, that he would be able to give me a baby.

Then the thing we had never expected happened; Isaac flew out to see us in Switzerland. Not the family I wanted, the family I had.

We were staying in Montana Vermala, a skiing resort in the Swiss Valais with spectacular views across to the Alps. Cool, cool, so cool and fresh, they still had snow, even in summer, I remember the way it flushed at sunset . . . It was nearly sunset when the telephone rang.

I was in the bath with a gin and tonic and the door open so I could watch the sunset through the spectacular arched windows in the bedroom. I remember my body felt warm and loose from the water and the day's first drink slipping into my bloodstream, I was back with Chris, we were safe from Stuart, Chris was reading the paper, everything was calm.

'Isaac *who*?' I heard Chris saying. 'Are you sure? . . . No, tell him to wait . . .' The pauses were long. I could hear him breathing. 'I'll be down in a minute. Ten minutes. He can wait in the bar. No, not now!'

When Chris put the phone down, he turned towards me,

staring through the doorway but not seeing me, and his mouth had a frightening old man's droop. 'I'm sorry, Alex,' he said. 'Isaac has come out to see us.'

'My God.'

'He must have got the address from the bank . . . we'll have to see him.'

'Of course.'

'He has no bloody right – '

'Most people would say he had.' I was shocked, but adrenalin was filtering through, I had to keep cool, I had to be strong. It had caught up with us, what we had done. 'Don't worry, darling. You look terrible. We can carry it off. We'll take him out to dinner.'

'You don't understand how I feel,' said Chris. He never usually said things like that. I got out of the bath with a movement that I thought would be decisive and graceful, like a swan taking off, but I only succeeded in drowning the floor. It wasn't like me; I hate clumsiness. I snatched up a towel, which seemed too small, it was the hand-towel: what was the matter with me? The skin on my legs was pink, half-cooked. My hair was a nest of dark rats' tails in the mirror. But I had to think about him, not me.

'I do understand. You've had a terrible shock.' Perhaps I sounded over-solicitous, for it only succeeded in irritating him.

'Well how about you, don't you feel anything? He's your child too – I mean, he lived with us.'

'Darling I *sympathise*. I'm on your side.'

He stared at me as if I were someone else. 'I feel so fucking appallingly guilty. I feel such a shit. I'm afraid of him. I'm afraid of what I'm going to see. I mean, what will he be like? What if he's horribly changed?'

'I should think it's us who will have changed . . . he's only, what, thirty, he's going to look fine. He never looked great in any case. Maybe he will have improved a bit . . . Don't feel guilty, darling. I always thought you were a very good father. If it was anyone's fault, it was mine, not yours.'

He didn't contradict me. His gaze was heavy. 'Very good

fathers don't go away. And I've hardly written. I don't like letters. In some families it's the woman who writes.'

This was completely outrageous. He was desperate, of course, he didn't know what he was saying.

'Don't be ridiculous. In any case, I have written, every now and then. Birthdays, Christmases, and so on.' I looked very naked in the mirror, my serpent's hair concealing nothing. 'When I've been in particularly wonderful galleries I always sent him a postcard. How often did your son reply?' (I knew it was false before I finished my sentence. He had written, at first, before he gave up. Every letter asked the same thing; when were we coming home? My cheery postcards never answered him. In the last few years he'd started writing again, but the gap was too long, I couldn't bear to read them.)

'So it's his fault, is it, that we buggered off?'

'What's the point of all this? We have to go down . . . or do you want me to leave you alone with him?'

'*No!*' It was a great explosion of anger.

'For heaven's sake don't get angry with me. It's not my fault your fucking son has shown up. From my point of view it's a fucking bore. Isaac was always a fucking bore.' There, it was said at last, the first time I had ever said it.

'Thanks very much. I happen to love him.'

'Hypocrite.'

But I could see it was true. Only someone he loved could cause such pain.

'I'm sorry, my darling. He isn't a bore, you're not a hypocrite. I'm just upset. I don't know what to wear.'

'That is the least of our worries.'

'I don't want to look too . . . frivolous.'

To my relief, Chris managed a smile, and a little bit of colour came back into his face. I went round behind his chair and kissed him, pressing my bare breasts against his back. But I meant what I said, in a way. My last memory of Isaac was as a first-year undergraduate, with those owlish blue glasses which should have looked modish but merely made him look a swot, reading books about Gaudier-Brzeska at breakfast. That boy had the power to make me feel frivolous.

Christopher and I went down together in the mirrored lift, staring at ourselves under the lurid light. I had put on a totally plain black dress which quite incidentally showed off my figure. I thought we looked nervous, but not really older. I was still very slim (might I have grown too thin?), Chris's hair was as thick as it ever was, and the wings of white merely looked distinguished. His skin was yellow, but that was fear. We were the same handsome couple we had always been (but there were horizontal lines scored across my forehead, and one of my earrings had fallen off and perched like a hard little tear on my collar).

Chris retrieved it, and kissed me. 'It's us that matters. We mustn't quarrel. I love you, Alexandra.'

We paused for a second in the palm-flanked doorway which led into the bar. There was only one figure to be seen; a broad square back on a barstool, the head bent over his drink on the bar, greasy brown hair lapping over his collar. He hadn't seen us. My heart kicked hard. A queer shallow ripple passed over Chris's features. I had a fleeting memory of a plump little boy with a solemn face and stern blue eyes refusing to say hallo to me, before the divorce, twenty-five years or so ago. And I had felt pity, for he was so small, and trying so hard for adult dignity. Now here was a great heavy grown-up man with a defeated weight of grown-up flesh. Inchoate questions rushed through my mind; how could it already be too late? After a painful moment, we went to greet him.

Small chin, long nose, red incurious eyes, thank God, it wasn't him.

'Hallo, Dad,' said a familiar voice behind us, and an unfamiliar man stepped forward from the shadow of the palm by the door. He had a round pink face, puffily round, though the rest of him was surely smaller, as if his skeleton had shrunk inside a thickening envelope of flesh . . . this couldn't be Isaac, but it was. The dome of his head was shiny, with a fringe of brown curls falling round his ears. And the glasses were gone; he must be wearing contact lenses; his eyes looked sharp, and unnaturally large, so perhaps those glasses had diminished them.

Chris half-hung there, clutching the doorpost. I thought for a moment he was going to faint. That helped me get a grip on myself.

'Isaac, how marvellous. Just for a moment – '

'I know, you didn't recognise me. It's the perm, it makes me look different.'

This information didn't help Chris find his tongue. But he managed to swing round like a boxer lunging and clutch at Isaac with great heavy arms. The two of them did a kind of lurching dance. The leaves of the palm hissed sharply as it toppled.

'We'd better sit down,' I said. 'You two are wrecking the hotel.'

I know how I sounded; cool and hard. Yet my heart hit the walls of my chest as wildly as their two bodies dipped and swerved.

At last they let go of each other. The middle-aged man that Isaac had become had suspiciously wet eyes. He seemed to see me then for the first time, and his lips pursed up into a kind of twitching navel before they suddenly unfolded again and he said, in a tone that was not complimentary, 'Alex, hi. You haven't changed a bit.'

I was sure he never used to say *hi*. It was a bit low-key after all these years.

The bar was cosmopolitan, coolly sidelit, a stage for people to perform gentle rituals and pass on, leaving no imprint. And we, who until that evening's phone call would have entered that theatre as of right, for these were the cameo parts we knew – we suddenly didn't fit in. I felt that there wasn't enough room for us there, though there must have been thirty bamboo armchairs to choose from. No longer a streamlined unit of two, we had grown enormous and clumsy, dragging an ugly, helpless weight of pain.

Isaac followed his father to a seat in a window. I brought up the rear, inspecting his back as we threaded our way between

135

the fragile tables. His small feet tripped against their bamboo legs. His thighs were big, his bottom bigger. The furniture swayed in the wind as he passed. There were hanging lanterns of simulated parchment which cast small pools of golden light. I thought about flayed human skin. Isaac's dome, as it swam underneath a lantern, became disconcertingly brilliant. Was it normal to lose so much hair in your twenties? Why was he bald when his father was so hairy?

The window was wide, with a deep padded seat. Isaac planted himself in the middle, then spread his hands out in what began as an inviting gesture to Chris and me, as if he had meant us to sit in a line, Mummy and Daddy with their boy in between, but in the middle of the gesture he lost confidence and his plump little hands fell irresolute upon the printed velvet.

We didn't meet his eyes as we sat down facing him on two bamboo chairs. I stared past his head at the last of the peaks, the snow on the summits still catching the sun, diamond-bright against the coming darkness. The snows would save us. I stared at them. Christopher would take me to the snows.

'Why are you here?' I asked him, as Chris went to order a bottle of champagne. It sounded offensive; I tried to soften it. 'I mean, why are you in Europe?' I'd forgotten that he lived in Europe.

He looked at me properly then. His eyes were definitely not very friendly.

'I'm usually in Europe,' he said. 'Except when I'm in New York. London is in Europe, you know.'

'Are you in New York a lot?' I asked him. 'How exciting. You must be doing well . . .'

'Didn't my last letter arrive?'

So that was the way things were going to be. 'That depends what was in it,' I stalled. 'The post is terrible, of course. But your father is always pleased to hear.' The truth was, I passed them on to Chris unread. He carried them round in his pocket; after a week or so, they disappeared. I never asked; he never told me. I really don't know if he opened them.

A terrible silence fell. Isaac sulked, heavily, staring at the carpet, presenting that lid of sad polished skin. Somewhere in the background, a tiny thud and an elaborate sigh as the champagne cork eased.

'Have you seen your sister?' I asked. 'I sent her orchids for her birthday. Well, not just orchids. Mainly orchids.'

'Didn't you get my message in Madrid?'

'I was never going to Madrid, I went to Malaga . . . alone. Is something wrong . . .?'

'It's because of Susy I've come to see you!'

'You used to be so fond of each other as children.' (I was trying to remember whether this was true. They had certainly fought over toys and books, but they were also a trades union of two, complaining about the employers. 'We used to get cooked breakfast at home,' Isaac had told me, accusingly, the week they arrived, when I was very young, but still not stupid, and Susy had nodded in bleak corroboration. I knew I had to sort them out right from the start. 'There are eggs in the fridge if you know how to cook.' And a dark look passed between the two of them; *this is what the chapel is going to have to deal with*. They were less than ten at the time. Children stick together when their parents break up . . . – And what if their father abandons them? They had probably grown closer with us away.)

'We aren't children any more,' he said. 'We haven't always been such good friends. There was a period when Susy objected to my lifestyle. She wouldn't let me into her house, she and her cabal. You know about them? She wouldn't see me, so I couldn't help her.'

Just at that moment Chris came back, preceding the barman with an icebucket.

The ritual of pouring and waiting for the froth to settle seemed to take much longer than usual. We sat in silence, waiting to begin, watching the dextrous movements of the barman. At last he was gone. We clutched our glasses.

'How is your sister?' Chris asked Isaac. His voice sounded hearty, unnaturally loud.

'Alex just asked me that. You're not going to like the answer.'

'No sign of her getting married?' Chris asked. He wasn't listening to what Isaac was saying. I tried to semaphore a warning look. It was a question about some distant relative, vaguely improper about one's daughters. Not that I could judge the proprieties; not that I knew how to behave to daughters.

'Why don't you ask about *me* getting married?' said Isaac, and the years seemed to slip away, we were back with sibling rivalry, his voice an amalgam of pride and resentment and something else I did not understand, a kind of excitement; *come on, attack me.*

'Are you about to get married?' Chris asked blankly, with an apologetic smile. I tried to erase the thought which flashed: *but surely he's too old to get married.*

'You don't know anything at all about me.'

This was awful. He was an angry small boy, disguised as a middle-aged man. Neither Chris nor I could speak. I gulped my champagne; wind in the gullet.

Chris put his hand on his son's arm. 'Look, I'm sorry. I can guess how you feel – '

' – I doubt it – '

' – what's done is done – '

' – thanks very much – '

' – but tell me why you've come to see me. Us. We can have a good evening together.' Chris's hand was kneading Isaac's arm, which stayed inert on the cushion of the seat. I looked beyond them and out of the window; the longing I felt was almost muscular, as if my gaze could have carried me with it far out across the unwounded snow.

'I must have thought it would be nice to see my father. You know how funny kids are about that. Every ten years or so, we like to touch base.'

'Of course it's – good to see you.'

'You would have died without trying to see me. Us. Of course Susy's got Jesus to keep her warm. She's a born-again Christian, you know,' he said, with malicious emphasis. The glass of champagne was easing his tongue. He knew we were both

138

allergic to religion. 'Replaced her family with the Heavenly Family.'

Chris was reeling from the blow. I think he had expected a veneer of politeness which might slowly wear through as the evening progressed. But this was immediate; knives at two paces. He filled up his own glass, splattering a little, not offering any to Isaac or me. 'She wasn't even confirmed.' He was bewildered. 'Isaac, you're having us on.'

'That's why she had to be born again. The house was a hotbed of evangelism. You would have been too godless to get in. They said grace before meals. They sang.'

'Do you mean your sister is living with people?'

'Precisely. Was, at any rate.' There was suddenly a sense of near-complicity. Isaac filled up his own glass, and mine. Then he seemed to regret being on our side. 'She must have been lonely, don't you think. She was only seventeen when you went away. That's not the best age to be abandoned.'

'She was just off to college,' I put in, knowing how weak it sounded. 'We didn't abandon her. I wrote. Your father made sure she had plenty of money . . .'

'Which she spends on nutters, and abortions!'

' – We kept in close touch after her abortion.' I heard my voice, shrill, hollow.

'Which abortion?' he asked, triumphant. 'You are just a teensy bit out of touch.'

Chris was looking very old. He hadn't said a word for some time. His second glass was already empty. 'You're saying your sister had another abortion.' His tone was dull. He reached for the bottle. The napkin flopped on to the floor, a defeated square of white.

'Susy had two abortions. At least, those are the ones I know about. Then she decided to sort herself out. Being born again seemed like a good solution. And they have a lot to say about abortion, these guys. She got very keen on the sacredness of life. She thought everyone should rear their Mongol. But she seems to have changed her mind, because . . . Maybe I should give you this a step at a time.'

(Who was he, this quick-tongued, spiteful man? What was so changed about his style? His tone was monotonous, downbeat, falling intonations that indicated life was a joke, he had it sewn up, this was how things were, you had to stay one step ahead of the bastards, you had to make the bastards pay. We were the bastards. We sat and paid. He had all the power of his terrible knowledge.)

'Shall I get another bottle?' Chris asked.

'I think we should go and eat,' I said. I was feeling faint, my thoughts spun wildly. Besides, the night might break his spell.

'Are there any decent restaurants here?'

(He never used to be a gourmet.)

'Yes,' said Chris, trying to rally. 'But we're a bit early . . .'

Isaac jumped in. 'We could have another bottle . . .'

'No,' I said. I had beaten him before, I had saved Chris before, I would save him again. 'I'll have to eat or I'm going to fall over.'

We walked through the streets. Clear sky, bright stars. It felt intensely cold, though it was early summer.

'It's hard to believe it gets colder than this,' I said to the air ahead of me, for I was leading the way; my limbs still functioned normally. I glimpsed the men following in single file in the glass of the expensive shop windows, mechanical dummies on blind manoeuvres.

'You could have worn your mink,' Isaac said. 'I assume you're travelling *avec les fourrures*.'

That was new too, the Franglais tag inserted with arch emphasis. I told him he was fifteen years out of date. 'No one is wearing real fur any more.' I noticed as he drew briefly abreast that he himself wore a long leather overcoat, bulging slightly at the middle buttons, a black leather coat turned up at the collar. How strange he looked, with his tonsured head and his little feet in pale tan moccasins.

The table we sat at was too small. It was Sunday night and we hadn't booked. All the other tables seemed to have decent Swiss families of several harmonious generations. The children were blonde and quiet and good. The grandparents lorded it over the parents. Although I had spent my whole life attempting to escape the stereotype involved, for a second I saw it in a different light. How admirable they seemed compared to us, two guilty people with a childless son.

The restaurant was efficient and brightly-lit, which depressed Isaac's level of malice somewhat. We all avoided the topic of Susy, though I could think of nothing else. For the first two courses and a bottle of wine Isaac managed to converse almost normally, asking us about the places we'd been, not exactly admiring the details we gave him but certainly listening, and filing them away. He seemed to have learned a lot about art. He made waspish comments about international galleries.

The dessert came, thickly piped with Chantilly, gentle, luscious, indulgent cream. The wine had moved fear further away. I thought it might be time to risk being nice, slipping in a little bit of flattery; it had always worked well when he was a teenager.

'Good idea to give up the glasses,' I said, appraising him as if he weren't ugly. 'You always had very nice eyes.' In truth they looked larger than when I used to meet him charging blindly to the bathroom on schoolday mornings.

'Are they soft or hard?' Chris asked. He himself had worn contact lenses since the divorce. I suggested it, and he conceded.

'You know what they say,' Isaac smiled, and at first I thought the flirtation had worked. 'Girls don't make passes at guys who wear glasses.'

— At least, that's what I thought he said, which was why I was astonished by Chris's reaction, for he paused with his spoon halfway to his mouth, and the cream began to slip down his chin till he scooped it back up with an angry movement. Something important seemed to have happened, for Isaac's face blazed with colour, and Chris was staring blankly at his plate as if he was concussed. I tried to smooth things over.

'Of course they do,' I said. 'I ought to know. I made a pass at your father . . .'

Somehow I had made things worse with this. Isaac gobbled

at me like a drowning turkey. He took a great swig of wine. Chris was picking at his cuticle.

'Well, you and Dad aren't gay,' he blurted.

'Of course we're not. What has that got to do with it? What have glasses got to do with being gay?' I started to realise as I finished the sentence, but my brain had given orders, the words kept coming.

'He's making some joke,' said Christopher. 'I think Alex misheard you. *Gays don't make passes at guys who wear glasses* is what Isaac said, my dear.' He sounded as if he was talking in his sleep.

Suddenly everything fitted, the voice, the clothes, the manner, the perm. I was flabbergasted, but I started to smile, I started to grin, I started to laugh.

'Oh Isaac. You must have thought us terribly dim.'

'He's having us on,' Chris insisted, dully. 'He's playing some awfully unfunny joke. How can you be gay? You were never gay. You don't suddenly *turn* gay, just like that.'

'Don't be stupid, darling,' I said. 'Don't take any notice of your father, Isaac. He's a bit surprised, that's all.'

'Shut the fuck up,' said Isaac, with venom. 'Don't interfere. It's Dad I came to talk to, not you.'

'Don't be rude to her,' Chris said. 'She's always been polite to you children.'

'Polite is just about it,' said Isaac. I suddenly realised that he was quite drunk, at the stage where frankness seems a glorious option. 'Polite is all she ever managed to be.'

(I smiled, but I was afraid. I had taken in a breath, but it wouldn't leak away again, it stayed in my chest, a hard, small fist.)

'She never loved us. *You never loved us.*' He turned his sharp blue eyes on me. Despite my fear, I observed it was makeup which made his eyes look bigger, less ordinary.

'I didn't want to try and usurp your mother. But I was very fond of you . . .' False to my ear, and to his. I was panicking. I hate being attacked. I wanted to appease him; I wanted to kill him. I wanted him to die and leave us alone.

142

'How sensitive and considerate,' Isaac sneered, lip curling to show faintly dappled teeth. I had never been strict about chocolate, even his teeth I had not looked after. 'My mother's been dead for twenty years. So you needn't restrain yourself any more.' Another deep swig of white wine. A little ran down his chin like lymph, as if essential fluids were leaking away, deep wounds opening to let it all out. 'Everyone knows you killed her, in any case, you and Dad between you.'

'Isaac! That's enough! You don't know what you're saying!' Chris was angry now as he scarcely ever was, big hands clenching, face drained of blood. I knew quite certainly he wanted to hit Isaac. I hoped for one mad second he would. Then I imagined Isaac's plump weak body collapsing. The ultimate horror; he killed his son.

I had to help. I had to make peace.

'We have to stop this. *Please*. Both of you. It's horrible. Forgive me, Isaac. I understand. I think I do. You and Susy must feel . . . I took your father away. And your mother's death . . . I suppose . . . it's inevitable you feel that. But I didn't break up a happy marriage. There are things your father wouldn't tell you. She was a manic depressive. Clinically. And she had affairs with his friends. Because she blamed him for her unhappiness. Then when she knew she was losing him, she suddenly wanted him back. And that was too late. He was in love with me. And everything else followed.'

'Please,' said Chris, no longer angry. 'It's all so long ago.' He reached out across the cluttered tablecloth and took my hand. The salt fell over, a small landslide of snow, but we were holding hands, life crept back between us, a quiet promise that we would survive. But what about Isaac . . . what had we done to him?

He sat deflated, scraping at his dish, the very last slivers of creme Chantilly. Even his hands were plump. Yet the awareness recurred that he had grown smaller, somewhere, hiding underneath the flesh. And Isaac was homosexual. The boy I had lived with was not as I imagined. Chris's son was gay.

'Why have you really come?' I asked. 'Let's have some coffee and some Armagnac.' I released Chris's fingers, and patted Isaac's hand. To my surprise he didn't brush me away.

'You have understood, haven't you?' he asked, and his tone was no longer aggressive, not even defensive, it was plain tired. 'Alex, you know I wasn't joking. I'm gay. I couldn't put that in a letter.'

'So that's why you came,' said Chris. He sounded as flat as his son.

'Not really.'

Over brandy and coffee the whole truth came out. We talked about Susy as though she were dead. Her story was dreary and predictable enough. The most recent abortion was two days ago, and this time the father was one of the Christians. I had somehow always known that she would get into trouble, but I'd envisaged babies rather than abortions. Isaac emerged well from it all, if his account was to be believed. He'd left various messages we never got, he had bribed the Christians to leave for good, and now he had come out to find us.

We had all grown quieter, almost formal. Chris asked remarkably few questions. Whatever had flared between us had gone. I caught Isaac looking at his watch. The blonde Swiss children had all gone home.

I sat almost serene, sipping my coffee, considering the problem in its abstract form. One thing was clear, to me but not Isaac; we wouldn't go home, I was sure of that. It was too late in the day for me to face Susy. Facing up to Isaac had aged me ten years . . .

But soon he would be gone. We could lie together and comfort each other in the velvety dark of our hotel room. We could try for a baby again. Our *own* child, our new beginning . . .

Then Chris astonished me. 'I'll go back tomorrow,' he said slowly to Isaac. Then he turned to me, his eyes met mine, perhaps asking me to understand, and he instantly jerked his head away, a movement of hopeless irritation, as if I had never understood a thing, and I suddenly felt he must be right, for this was unheard of, astonishing; the world rolled over and tipped

144

me off. This was the great betrayal — we had promised each other . . . we had vowed to each other . . . and I had just given up Stuart for ever . . . At that moment I wasn't sure what we had promised. I sat there, listening to distant voices, and didn't say a word. I could feel a pointless, untethered smile floating across my face, and dying.

Something very odd had happened to me. I have never been able to control myself; I see no point in controlling myself. Yet when we were finally alone I hardly said a word to Chris. We were drunk and exhausted, but it wasn't that. I felt stunned, wounded, beyond saying anything. We took off our clothes like zombies.

That night as Chris lay in bed and snored I stood by the window in our hotel bedroom, naked in centrally heated darkness, touching the glass, which was icy cold, looking across at the vanished peaks and the random pinpricks of hard white stars. Night was out there, and emptiness. And the snows, where no one talked, or suffered, where everything slept in frozen silence, and we wouldn't have to keep moving on. Maybe the edges were melting; the hotels were worried; the newspapers fretted; but the snowy heartlands were still there. They waited there, enormous, beyond the glossy little town, the expensive shops, the chic hotels, the ski-lodges and glow-worm trains which edged across the precipice.

There should have been a moon, three-quarters full. It was cloudless, and the moon had been big last night. I peered round the edge of the window-frame. I found myself praying it would be there; it would mean good luck, it would be a sign. If it wasn't there now it must rise soon. I stayed there hoping and growing colder.

I smoked one of Chris's cigarettes, though I hadn't had a smoke for many years. I did it to see the red glow in the dark, I did it because I craved nicotine. I did it because Chris had fallen dead asleep and I desperately needed something alive. I did it to make the moon appear. I felt I could draw down the moon with my breath, dragging in deeper, more desperately, reduced to stupid magic.

But the moon had already come and gone. I couldn't accept it; I stood and grieved. You need a man to have a baby. I couldn't have a baby on my own. How could he leave when I needed him?

By the time Chris woke, slurred 'Come to bed,' and fell heavily asleep again, I was shivering in violent spasms.

But I don't believe in suffering. I went and lay down.

And now I see that none of it mattered. We were never meant to have a child. My child was waiting somewhere here, in the teeming cities or the tiny villages, somewhere on the vast subcontinent, wriggling, waving, crawling towards me.

For everything has changed in the space of a morning. Benjamin is back, bringing good news.

I hardly dare hope after all the disappointment, but Benjamin thinks – Benjamin believes –

The signs are good. *The signs are good!* Movement at last after this terrible paralysis. Benjamin's so cheerful, a different man, sober, tender, making jokes again.

This time perhaps – this time I *know* –
We're due to meet her tomorrow.

16

Christopher: Venice, 2005

Too many *acqua altas* this week. Can't be bothered to decline it right. Duckboards in use day after day. The steps are a nightmare of slithering weed. Fogs like blankets; you can't see your ankles.

Acqua alta. It quacks and gurgles. *Acquae altae*? Decline, decline . . . Everything declining, settling lower. Surely this year will see us subside at last into our wrecked foundations.

I don't want to die. I'm not ready yet. You don't have to tire of life in your seventies. But damp and darkness infect my bones. I shall have to fly to the sun again.

Maybe I should go home.

An odd little voice, not really mine, for I have no home to go to . . . but you see, it never used to feel like that. Every hotel in the world was our home. Wherever Alex was was home for me –

Quick, the whisky. Pour it down. I shall not think of her again.

The house in Islington still stands. Susy lives there. We aren't in touch. Last time she wrote was a year ago to ask for money to spend on the garden. And she was thinking of taking a tenant; the rent would 'help', she said. Any other news was confined to a postscript. 'Have job, am managing. Hope you are too.' A postcard seemed on the terse side, considering how much money she wanted. Of course I said fine, and do take a tenant – no God squad though; perhaps a nice friend? Frankly I envisaged disaster – she would let it to criminals or hopeless cases, people who would never pay rent . . . But the house was far too large for her. It must have rattled round her ears. It must have been full of emptiness.

I know all about that, of course. My two lofty floors hang above the black waters, and on days like this is seems the emptiness sucks in the sour green smell of the canals and exaggerates the echoes of each small sound, so a cat tips a pebble with one cold paw and I hear things falling from great heights and drowning. Inside the house. Inside me.

When we were all at home in the house in Islington everything was so different. We felt we could hardly move without tripping over an adolescent limb. Kids start small, but they're soon too big. And Alexandra needed space. She had tremendous physical energy, whereas I've always been a bit lazy. She loved to dance, and run. Running upstairs, dancing down the hall, when there was room to dance down the hall . . . She hated clutter, it got in her way, and other people sometimes seemed like clutter, to her . . . she sat in strange, elaborate positions which gave her physical pleasure, stretched like a cat, flexing and turning, moving from one chair to another on incredibly light feet. You could never hear her in the house unless she was wearing high heels, which was only on high days and holidays, wasn't it, my cat-like darling, so lithe, so swift, so silent that you might still be here, prowling the marble above my head . . .

Of course she had to travel. She couldn't stay still.

I'm through with travelling now. Most of us are through with travelling now. Most of us accept that there's nowhere left to go. I've holed up here in this city of water because it's tired and old like me, with no painful dreams of paradise. There's beauty here, but it's in the past, it settles deeper but it can't disappear; having once existed it will always have existed. Whereas hope for the future can shrink to nothing.

These thoughts possess me on days of fog when life contracts to a nugget of ice, when the *acqua alta* outside the walls swirls with human cries and bones, a tide of lost people sweeping past the window, all the people we failed to notice . . .

The letter. Where is it? I must have it. The letter. Somewhere in this bureau. Begun and abandoned months ago after my epic day with the tart, Caterina, that stocky little girl with the split-peach arse and the leathery nipples I tweaked and pinched till they were hard as walnuts . . .

148

Aha, I'm not dead yet. A little rise on a day of gloom. But the letter. Where is it? More real than sex. I started it that day after supper. When I picked up my pen she was clear in my mind, Mary Brown, a half-smiling Madonna, but her flesh pink and solid, not at all translucent, her eyes a straight path of china blue to a safe destination near at hand . . . a faint shine in the dark, I can see them again, eyes which perhaps spell *warm* and *home*.

– She always liked me, Mary.

The letter! I have it! Wonderful . . .

Strange, it seems to peter out at line two, I'd remembered something of an epic . . . But now I recall that I lost heart. It suddenly seemed rather pathetic to be writing to someone who might have forgotten my existence. A woman in her sixties, moreover. That day I was proud, with my three great feats; did a hero like me need a woman in her sixties?

> *Dear Mary and Matthew,*
> *Friends! After all this time, and many sad changes . . .*

Today I am sadder, and less great. Today I'll finish and post the letter.

The 'and Matthew', of course, is just a courtesy. It's the oval-eyed Madonna that I'm writing to, with her large pale hands and nut-brown hair which now is probably silvery-grey. Even that thought isn't unpleasant. She'll draw it back in a queenly bun, and I'll have to persuade her to let it down . . .

No no. I run ahead of myself.

> *. . . After all this time, and many sad changes, I am*
> *writing to you from Venice, without Alexandra, alas . . .*

The terrible baldness of the words on the page. I feel my eyes prick with tears of self-pity to think how Mary will pity me. But would she already know about all the disasters which have come upon us? They didn't come to the funeral. I didn't do the invitations, of course. I suppose they couldn't have afforded to have flown to New York, in any case, just to watch a body burn. I wonder what Susy has told them . . .

> *. . . to say greetings, old friends, I hope all is well. I hope the floods will soon abate in London . . .*

(don't be pompous, it will annoy Matthew, if Matt's still alive enough to be annoyed)

> *. . . The Italian newspapers loved your floods, it makes them feel less despair about Venice. How are . . .*

Now I am really stuck. Their children. Alexandra would remember their names. Their children have turned out better than ours. But then, they had a better mother, and the same mother from beginning to end.

> *How are the children? By now perhaps there are grandchildren. I do hope so . . .*

I am sick with envy, thinking about it. Six stout grandchildren for Matthew to dandle, parade, play football with, confess to, if that starchy bastard has anything to confess. Six fine grandchildren to give him hope. And Alex and I haven't even got one.

> *. . . though of course they must make you worry even more painfully about the future. None of us ever envisaged these times, did we, in the far-off days when we were all young.*
> *Do you remember the fun we had with the children, on Jessica's birthday . . .?*

(That was it – Jessica! A freckled mouse, knock-kneed and brilliant, who went on to be a stockbroker and made a million before she was thirty. I shudder to think what she's doing now.)

150

. . . Way back in the mid-'80s, I suppose, when we went down the Thames, still a river, in those days, not a flood-plain, on a river-boat, and we took a monumental picnic (which must have been Mary's doing!) and four bottles of champagne, and the boys were not in the best of moods but they all started dancing to the piped music, Isaac and Jessica and Susy and –

(damn – I'll never remember it, put it in later)

. . . swooping round the other stodgy families in a glorious parody of Victor Sylvester, and Alexandra started dancing on her own . . .

– A more precise memory stays my hand. Actually the two boys weren't dancing, they were sipping champagne, which was quite against the rules since they were only fifteen or sixteen, but Alex had given them her blessing – 'Oh Mary, for God's sake, it's a *birthday* party!' – and they slumped in their seats, sneering and giggling as the two girls did their spirited tango, which parodied sex and yet yearned for it. Some way down the road to intoxication the strain of sitting still and watching other people dance proved too much for Alex, and she got to her feet, slipped off her shoes and some spotted skin jacket which I hope was fake but fear was not. She began to dance like a siren, with her blowing hair and skin-tight dress and the wind off the water caressing her body, holding an empty champagne bottle, the sun very bright on its green side and her red hair whipping against her bare shoulders . . . every man on deck was looking at her, everyone wanted to be that bottle. The boys stopped laughing and the girls stopped dancing and I knew all the children were ashamed but I still adored her; she was mine, all mine, and I knew that Matthew wanted her too. Susy's round flushed face, now sucking down smoked salmon with a steady, vacuuming motion, was a study of sour distaste, no longer transformed by her innocent tango. I remember something else; Mary moved over and rested her bulk on the back of the seat, just behind

Susy, and started to stroke her curls very lightly, and Susy stopped eating, and leaned against her, her eyes closed so as not to see her stepmother.

I remember the end of that outing too. Jessica was in floods of tears because no one had been nice enough to her, one of the boys was sick, Mary and Matthew had a mild dispute, Alex was on tremendous form till she fell dead asleep in the taxi, and Susy said to me at bedtime 'On *my* birthday, I'm going to the cinema. Me and some friends. No parents.'

> *. . . Alexandra started dancing on her own. We had such fun together, didn't we? So many of my memories are bound up with you –*

– I mean Mary, of course, but that mustn't be apparent.

> *So many of my memories are bound up with you two.*

Six o'clock, though the hugging fog makes it impossible to know what time it is. I've had the light on in here since noon. But my blood tells me it's six o'clock, my brain requires its alcohol, a little flame, a little devil, a little treat to spur the old man on. A glass of Chianti, a dish of olives, deliciously oily – the salt, the sour – the awakening tingle of the wine, the whispered lie that I'm still young . . .

Three score and ten. Time to go home.

> *Mary, you were always so kind to Susy.*

Mary was kind, full-stop. She would be kind to me, I know she would. She wouldn't notice how old I have grown. Once she told me I was attractive; I was touched, and surprised, for a moment I wondered if she wanted me to make a pass at her, but of course it was just Mary being truthful . . . or maybe just Mary being kind. I wonder if she would still find me attractive? How was I looking when we last met?

And God, I remember and drop my pen, it bounces away

across the marble floor and under the table, little and stupid as a dead match in all this expanse of solitude. I remember now when we last met and it makes me grind my teeth at my vanity (but before you judge me, try living alone. See if you don't grow vain and mad).

It was when I came back from Switzerland to see Susy, in 1998. It was ghastly, and we were in the dark. I had come alone; Alexandra refused; she acted as if I were committing a crime, but for once she couldn't change my mind.

I walked up the road with limbs of lead, feeling all the neighbours were looking at me, though I'm sure they had mostly moved away, and in any case they would have forgotten me. I didn't ring the doorbell, I'm not sure why, I let myself in and dragged upstairs, perhaps out of an obscure desire to claim that this was still my house, that I wasn't some stranger visiting, I was still her father, I was coming home (yet how passionately I wished not to be there!)

The house, as I corkscrewed up the staircase, smelled unnaturally clean, cleaner than it did when we were living there, but there were pale stains on the wood and curtains which surely hadn't been there before, and many things had vanished, plants, books, pictures ... an unfamiliar fresh smell of pine, less pleasing when I realised it was disinfectant.

The bedroom, they were in our bedroom. I pushed the door gently; it smelled of blood, stale air and menstrual blood. They were sitting together in the half-dark in the third-floor room which had once been our bedroom but was now clearly Susy's, holding hands, a moving tableau of mother and daughter, except that their sizes were transposed. Susy had swelled to a mountain of flesh; Mary the comforter, sitting on our bed, was dwarfed by the land-mass whose flanks she was stroking, her strong hand moving over Susy's fat pale one, for even her hands were fat, my God, and she must have been inside all summer, I'd never seen Susy look pale before. I took this in slowly; neither of them spoke; the curtains were only open a few feet so at first I saw only the outlines of their forms, almost allegorical in their silence.

Susy looked at me. She didn't seem surprised, as if she had been expecting me, though she couldn't have been waiting for eleven years. Mary didn't smile; she was never an actress. She half-rose from the bed, and touched my arm, I was grateful for the touch since her face was so grave, and she muttered 'Sorry, I just walked through the door, I haven't had a chance to clean up in here today, if you want to go away for a minute, Chris – '

But both of us interrupted her, my voice, phonily bluff, the father, saying 'Heavens, no, I want to see Susy,' and Susy, her voice surely not the same, or was I hearing it afresh after the long absence, flat and sibilant, a *fatter* voice, surely, hissing 'He can clean up. Let him stay.'

Then Mary slipped away, like a tactful shade, effacing herself so completely that somehow I'd forgotten she was there, I've suppressed that momentary monolithic tableau, the two female bodies in the menstrual dark, touching each other, excluding me, linked by mysteries I could never share.

– Except that when she'd gone, and my eyes had grown used to the dark, I saw that the mysteries were spread around the room, open to the eyes of whoever should come; the room reminded me of something half-forgotten; it was strewn with wads of drenched cotton-wool, sanitary towels soaked with dark blood, left wherever she had thrown them, bloody face uppermost, *see what I've done.*

– It reminded me of the hospital room where Penelope gave birth to Susy. The aftermath of a precipitous labour, before anyone had had time to clear up, and it lay all round us, bloody sheets and towels and tissues and the smell of iron, like a battlefield . . . but the baby was crying, we were laughing and crooning, we had a daughter, life was good, there was a sense of *rightness* in that room. I remember Penny saying, 'This is all I wanted.' Not that it was true, but she felt it then.

Whereas Susy, who had once been all we wanted, had just had her third abortion, and discharged herself against doctor's advice; her brother had summoned me against her wishes; everything was wrong, cross-grained.

How could I have forgotten seeing Mary there? I didn't try

154

to see the Browns before I flew back. I was too ashamed, of course. They'd done what I should have done. What crimes they must think I am guilty of. But Mary had a sweet nature, forgiving . . .

> *So many of my memories are bound up with you two. Mary, you were always so kind to Susy. How is she doing, do you know? If you see her, please give her my love . . .*

(too casual)

> *. . . please give her all my love, as ever.*
> *I am thinking of coming back to London. Venice is extraordinary, of course, but the perpetual damp can't be good for my health, and I miss . . .*

What shall I say? What do I miss so badly? I miss having anyone who minds about me, though that isn't a reason for going back to London, since I don't suppose anyone minds about me there (but perhaps they do. Perhaps Mary does. She always used to seem pleased to see me when I dropped in unexpectedly, with one or another child in tow, she nearly always agreed to look after them . . . My God, it's a quarter of a century ago).

I'd better not depend too much on Mary. Susy should mind about me. She's my daughter. I picked up her pads and threw them away, I cleared up the mess, that morning's mess, I did my best with it. I wasn't too proud. Nor angry, though that mess should have been my grandchild.

> *. . . I miss the Independent Times, which you hardly ever see here, and eggs for breakfast, and Earl Grey tea. If you're still at your old address, or wherever this letter finds you, drop me a line and tell me your news.*
> *Perhaps we shall meet before too long!*
> *Your affectionate friend*
>
> *Christopher*

– There's Lucia's bell ringing me to dinner. I'm pleased with myself, for here is my letter, a little achievement, signed and sealed, a little spurt of energy fed into the system, a tiny gesture against entropy. Something might change because of this . . . perhaps it will bring an answering wave. Perhaps it will clear the fog away.

Lucia has already opened a bottle, but I have brought my Chianti with me. Tonight I shall celebrate my letter by drinking two bottles of good red wine . . . I feel warmer now, less sorry for myself.

Good. *Fritti misti*, and a fine dressed salad gleaming red and green under the candelabra Lucia lights for me every evening. Life in Venice is not so bad. I think Lucia would miss me if I went home. That enormous table, just for the *padrone*. The salad glowing like a vegetable garden on its field of immaculate white linen. The breathing bottle of Amarone. Ah, my delectable Amarone. Forget the Chianti, push it aside . . .

And it lurches and tips across the white linen, pale bluish-purple as it soaks underneath, a terrible, garish red in great lagoons around my plate, going quickly darker, it's everywhere, I dab and squeeze with my linen napkin but the task is beyond me, I must ring for Lucia, spreading, staining, I have to help . . .

I tried to clear up but I wasn't very good at it. In the hospital, I held the baby – Penelope let me hold the baby – while the midwives sponged and washed and scoured.

Penelope cut her wrists nine years later, in the office one Friday evening, when everyone had gone home for the weekend. It had taken her a very long time to die. There was blood on every scrap of paper. She wrote a letter which was brief and competent; Penelope was always competent. She'd astonished me during our divorce by the coolness with which she refused custody of the children. 'I'm not going to be a single parent. I'm not going to wreck my life for you . . .' Her affairs were all left in perfect order, but the mess in the office was indescribable. Her secretary, who had been with her for a decade, took pleasure in telling me all the details.

'Lucia! Help!' For it was on my letter. The top pages looked

splotched with blood, I would have to rewrite it, all that work
... but women are never there when you need them, and when
she comes she will only scold.

Will Mary write?

Will Susy forgive me?

Part Three

17

Mary Brown: London, 2005

A letter came from Christopher Court. Beautiful writing, black italic. The first time he's ever written to us. I was struck by how like the man the writing was, the thick black strokes like his thick dark hair. It was – dashing. Elegant.

Though his hair can't be black any more. Last time I saw him was in the half-dark. He looked like death, pale and stricken, but even then he was handsome. I was furious with him, but he was still handsome. My heart still knocked in my chest to see him.

Stupid, all that should be in the past, I'm sixty-two years old, a grandmother, but nothing changes, my heart's still young. It beat faster just to see the name and address on the back of the envelope. Christopher in Venice; that seems right for him too. He wouldn't go to ground in Zurich or Brussels.

The letter itself was – what shall I say? I don't want to complain, but it was … elusive. I love getting letters, and they're so rare now, with everyone using wrist-phones, the bleepers going all day and all night … I have a wrist-phone, but I hardly ever use it. The most civilised people still write letters. I always answer the same day.

I sat down with the letter and a huge cup of tea, licking my lips at the thought of it. I didn't tell Matthew; it makes everything so slow, he's nearly blind and he won't wear his hearing aid, I meant to give him a precis of it later, but the more times I read it, the less there was in it.

It was affectionate. Warm. Very warm. But there was nothing to get hold of. No news, for heaven's sake, and I love news. Just the one passing mention of Alexandra. No mention of Isaac, or

Chris's time in prison. Perhaps he thinks we don't know about all that.

When I read it again, it seemed a bit empty. Urbane and charming, like Christopher. But sentimental, just remembering the good bits. Frankly, that river-trip on Jessica's birthday was a nightmare. Alexandra was over-excited – well, *drunk*; I seem to remember she took her clothes off, or flaunted herself in some outlandish way, and Matthew's eyes were out on stalks, and Christopher looked smug instead of stopping her, and the children and I wanted to sink through the floor.

– That's how she was. I suppose she couldn't help it. Matthew always said, 'But she's so alive . . .'

Now he's dying, slowly, he's been dying for ages, it's painful and messy and unglamorous, there isn't enough money, the basement is leaking, and London seems a very long way from Venice. Chris asked for our news, but would he want to hear it?

'So many of my memories are bound up with you.' I wonder how much he really remembers. He's clearly forgotten Dan's name, for example. Does he remember when we last saw each other? I doubt it; men aren't fond of mess. He flew straight back to Alex. That hurt my feelings. He didn't bother to contact us. I'd have thought he'd have wanted to hear my story –

– No, I knew he wouldn't want to hear my story. I only know about real things, and he's spent two decades escaping them. I cleared up the mess. It's what women do.

I should still be angry with him, but I'm not. I couldn't help feeling excited when I read that he was 'thinking of coming back to London'. 'Perhaps we shall meet before too long' – my cheeks were hot; I'm not too old to flush.

After all, Alexandra is out of the picture. After all, Matthew's only got a few months left . . .

– Oh God, I'm mad, I'm pathetic, forgive me. These terrible thoughts seem to think themselves, you get so exhausted when someone is dying that part of the brain has to plan an escape . . .

As if Christopher Court would ever look at me.

I'm 'good old Mary'. He thinks I'm 'kind'. He says so in the letter; I was 'kind to Susy'. I'm a woman, as well, but he never noticed. He doesn't know how often I pretended it was him when Matthew was making love to me. Sad little secrets. He'll never know . . .

Once I nerved myself to the sticking point and told him I thought he was very attractive. The Belsteads were having a party, and Alexandra was showing off, as usual, doing limbo dancing with a beautiful black boy, back to back, dipping down, two bows, their two arched bodies nearly touching at the head, her flaming hair hanging down to the carpet, and from a distance she looked as young as the boy, who was actually the boyfriend of the Belsteads' daughter.

Christopher sat on the sofa watching her. I'd come to sit beside him. 'Amazing, isn't she, Mary? I sometimes feel a lot more than fifteen years older than her . . . I sometimes feel an old man, watching Alex.'

I wanted to take his head in my hands. 'You don't look old. You're . . . very attractive . . . I think you're very attractive.'

'How kind.'

– He didn't notice how my voice shook, he didn't know how hard it was for me to say it, he didn't see I was sweating. He didn't see me, in fact; he was looking at Alex. Always at Alex, never at me.

Forget all that. Doesn't matter any more. I answer all my letters the same day. In any case I have some good news for Christopher (I do believe he cares about Susy deep down; I suppose I blame Alex for most of what's happened).

– It seems to me Susy's on the mend. I feel more hopeful about her than I have in years. I think she's going to be OK.

She asked me to lunch the other day. Jessica said she would sit with Matthew so I could have a rest from the sickroom.

It was a typical blazing late-October day. We ate in the kitchen, which was cool, as always – how often I had sat there with Alex and Chris, half-watching our children playing in the garden, sunlight, shrieks, happiness – and as I listened to Susy I realised how far she'd come from the pink-cheeked child who used to doze on the lawn; I'd always thought of her as an overgrown child, but at last that day she seemed adult. And after all she is nearly thirty-seven, as she was to remind me later that day. There were roses from the garden in a yellow jug, and a yellow table-cloth. 'How splendid . . . can't be just for me.'

'Don't be silly. I'm so happy to see you. And I like to show off my flowers – I'm getting the garden straight at last . . . but actually I am expecting someone else later. Someone you know. You'll have to guess.'

But I couldn't guess, and she wouldn't tell me.

'Let's have some food,' she said. And there was some food – real lunch-time food! Though she'd asked me to lunch, I expected no more than coffee and apples as I listened to her problems. But she laid out bread, cheese, salad, fruit on the sunny table-cloth, and actually ate some, a normal amount of it, wonder of wonders, and didn't witter on about her latest diet or gorge compulsively.

Because I'm a mother, and conventional in some ways – not all ways, I may surprise people yet – I couldn't help hoping that the 'someone' she expected would be a boyfriend, or manfriend, rather, some nice boy I had known in the past, a friend of Dan or Jessica, someone who would marry her and simplify her future – I knew too much about the messes of the past. But Susy didn't seem to want her future simplifying. She had finished her teacher training course at last, the one I never thought she would finish because she'd taken endless time off for illness; she was very enthusiastic about her first job, teaching two- and three-year-olds; I suppressed the wish that they were her children.

She was very interesting, actually. I think I know a lot about children from having brought up my two, but she had some ideas I had never considered. I began to look at her in a new light. We were eating Brie, and she was telling me why you couldn't 'teach' children how to draw, when I heard a key turn in the lock and feet came bounding down the hall.

The male 'someone' I was expecting to see turned into a frighteningly glamorous girl, with chestnut dreadlocks and a big red mouth and white cotton shorts on long, strong legs – in the old days we never wore shorts in October! – but with something familiar in the eyes and cheekbones, and she was smiling widely at me, big white teeth – 'Mrs Brown – Mary!' – and coming round the table to give me a kiss which I found uncomfortable; lots of perfume, hard bangles, soft skin.

'You remember Madonna,' Susy said. 'She's come to live in the basement. It's great. You can't imagine how empty the house felt before.'

I did remember her then, of course. My Dan's girlfriend. The heartbreaker. She had come on holiday with us twice, and the family were poor so we didn't let them pay (the father had abandoned them when she was only twelve or thirteen); she had always been a lively, lovely girl; then my Dan fell in love with her in their twenties and she broke his heart when she left for New York with a man old enough to be her father. I had to pick up the pieces. She was a journalist; she'd been mad for New York. I hadn't seen her since. Yet here she was back in London again, glowing with health and prosperity, looking quite different with her new long hair, and Dan was married, so I mustn't bear a grudge, yet for some reason the shadow which fell on me as she crossed the sunny window to embrace me made me shiver; it was darker in the kitchen for a moment.

Silly, because she was entirely charming. She asked after Matthew, who she'd always liked, and listened sympathetically to what I had to tell. She asked after Dan, and even his baby. In fact, she was delightful, as she always had been – Matthew always had a soft spot for her – and I was soon back under the spell of her charm.

When she went into the garden we talked about her. I could see her through the window, bending to pick up fallen apples with lithe athletic movements. 'She's lovely, isn't she,' Susy said. 'I'd forgotten how to have fun, before. And she's done so well. She's practically famous. She was on telsat last week, and they'll ask her again. She's deputy editor of *Karma Q* –'

'*What?*'

' – it's a really fashionable vidvox. And she works so hard.

She can dance half the night but she comes back and slaves away till morning to get her pieces in. Why are you frowning, Mary? She's been good to me. She encourages me with what I'm doing. Even though she's so busy. And she's really fond of children – '

The eulogy began to annoy me, and I asked meanly 'Has she got any, then?'

'You don't have to have one to love them. I love them and I haven't got any. She'd love to have one if she had time. But neither of us has got time at the moment.'

'Don't leave it too long. How old are you and Madonna?'

'I'm nearly thirty-seven.'

Perhaps she'd never have children. 'How old is Madonna?'

'Same age, of course.'

I didn't say *She looks so much younger*. Madonna looked not a day over thirty. But I had both my children before I was thirty. I changed the subject; it wasn't my business. The main thing was Susy was back on her feet.

It was the only slight damper on a marvellous lunch. 'Marvellous lunch,' I said as I left. 'Wonderful to see you looking so well.'

As I walked to the buzzerstop I realised who Madonna reminded me of. It was partly the new long hair and the confidence. She reminded me a little of Alexandra – but warmer, larger, and kinder, I hoped. Perhaps that was exactly what Susy still needed; a decent mother-figure to replace her stepmother, to make good the harm that Alex had done. I'd done my best for her over the years, but I had my own worries with Matthew and Dan – I wasn't around when the worst things happened.

I do believe women can help each other. My women friends have saved my life. We keep things ticking over, we oil the wheels, we worry about the environment, we collect the waste and do the gardening and write the letters and look after the dying.

Matthew's asleep, so I can write my letter. I wish Christopher had been there that day, he would have loved to see his daughter and Madonna talking, with the light from the table-cloth bright on their faces. That special loud cheerfulness of the young. The older we get, the more muted and careful . . . and the more we love youth, for a breath of fresh air . . .

Why don't I write on this lovely yellow paper that Jessica gave me for my birthday? *Christopher, Dear Christopher.* I want him to realise I'm not old.

18

Alexandra: São Benedicto, Brazil, 2005

I've been warned to be patient; it doesn't make me patient. Benjamin is much more patient than me, probably because he feels things less.

I'll hold you in my arms, little girl.

I'll never want to put her down. Whenever I sit down and think about her my arms move instinctively into a rocking, cradling shape, touching each other and holding each other because there is nothing else to hold, there is a space between my linked arms and my body, an emptiness aching to be filled. I sit and rock and think about her till I drive myself crazy and have to go out, walking for hours up and down the streets no matter how hot it is, no matter how humid, no matter how much weight I'm losing, no matter how much the locals stare at the gringo woman pursued by demons.

If I were younger with this burning hunger I could satisfy it quite naturally, I could make a baby from my own flesh to still the torment my body feels. But I wasn't hungry soon enough. I only wanted what I could no longer have. How could I have been so stupid? How could I have let my childbearing years slip by? How could Christopher have let it happen? He should have known that I needed a baby.

I forgive him, though. Perhaps it wasn't meant to be. The very first glimpse I had of Anna Maria I knew this was my baby. I was talking to her mother, yesterday; I saw her through the door, sitting on a stone, pulling at her hair which was glossy blue-black like a blackbird's wing, and I longed for babies and blackbirds and home, I longed to be young again and her

168

mother. I couldn't speak; tears filled my eyes; I thought *I have always misunderstood, I have always got everything hopelessly wrong, now at last I see my future.* In her hand was a flower like a marigold. Her skin was golden, her cheeks were round, she sat in a frame of brilliant sunlight and I stared at her from the stifling dark. When we actually met she seemed indifferent, but I'll never forget that transfiguring moment when I saw her and knew she would be mine. My baby. Mine. Come back to me.

For she will make up for what was lost, she will absolve my terrible folly – I admit I was foolish, but Christopher let me, he could have stopped me but he let me do it . . .

Never mind all that, I shall have my baby.

She isn't a baby, actually. She's three and a half, but she's very small, malnutrition and poverty keep them small. I'm glad; someone small is easier to love, easier to cradle in my arms.

I could sit with her for hours, just sitting looking at her little hands and feet, looking at her littleness. She seemed a still child, rather silent. I've spent all my time in rapid motion, rushing from one place to the next, fifty-five years of desperate hurry. Now I would like to stop and look.

I want to help her, hold her, feed her. I've never really done that for anyone, have I? If my father is to be believed, my mother never did it for me, either. He said she had no time for us girls as babies. And I was the youngest child, the least wanted. 'I always loved you, girl,' he said, 'I fed you with a bottle when she couldn't be bothered. I loved my two daughters, and you were my favourite, the brightest, the naughtiest, the prettiest. I wouldn't have been without you, Alex.' She would though. I think she never liked babies, though she loved the beliefs which meant she had to have them.

When I was fifteen or so I made her turn white with anger when I told her I didn't believe. I didn't; still don't; I shall die unshriven; Christopher and I were both unbelievers. Our religion was love, he said . . . hey ho.

And now I'm here posing as a virtuous Catholic! Thank heavens I remember enough of the cant.

169

How odd that I want to sit still with the baby. Because the thing I hated most about church was having to sit still, eyes to the front, not even allowed to scan the congregation without her finger digging into my back because we had to put on a good show. When she poked me I dug my nails into my hymn-book so hard they left little lines of scallops. It was easier when I had my own hymn-book, something of my own to hold on to at least, worst of all when I had to share with my sister and my nails had to dig into my own palms.

I never remember sitting on her lap. There were three of us, after all, competing, but I don't remember any of us sitting on her lap. I was never cradled, but I need to cradle. Perhaps it's a way of cradling myself. That's what I do now, as I wait for her, my two hands lightly stroking my wrists as they fold together across my body and tighten against me because she's not there. Hand upon hand, hand over hand. Her hand with the flower was so small in the sun, her fingers stubby when she came close and her mother tried to make her shake hands. Her eyes were brown and bright and impervious; she wanted to stay outside and play, of course she did, she is just a child. I took her small hand briefly in mine, hot, damp, stiff as a little starfish. Soon she'll relax and let me hold her.

Chris was a toucher, a holder. Chris cradled me when I wanted him to.

– Actually I do myself an injustice. I have held someone recently, I have cradled someone and helped them a little, though the year 2000 is no longer recent, it's slipping behind us with its weight of memories, that extraordinary, brilliant, savage year with its score of drama and blood and death . . .

It was Isaac I cradled, Isaac I held. Isaac, of all people. Yes.

19

Christopher: Venice, 2005

The nights are the worst, the foggy nights when the dark is solid, impenetrable. Everything dead and cold. No one in the world to care about me. No one to hold me in their arms.

I sent my letter into the void two weeks ago. Nothing's come back. Mary has forgotten me, or died.

They were all cold and hard, all the women I've known. Alexandra was worst, of course, the bitch. I get up at three in the morning and drink because there is warmth in a bottle of whisky . . .

I was good to Alexandra, damn her to hell. I loved her, protected her, comforted her. When I met her she wasn't much better than a tart, encrusted with mascara and sequins at the SFTA awards ceremony where she'd gone with some oily Greek millionaire . . . she didn't know a thing about broadcasting; she was expecting it all to be as glossy as the Oscars . . .

But she was so young. So heart-twistingly young. And sharp. And funny. And wild. And . . . wounded. She was like no one I had ever known, and she was in a mess; she needed me. Penelope had never needed me, or never admitted she needed me. I fell in love with Alex completely.

I held her, loved her, cradled her. I replaced her crazy Irish family.

Half-a-dozen years ago the fear began, or I began to notice it. I needed to be sure she loved me. I needed to be sure. I needed her.

Alexandra. And what did she do?

— She stared straight through me, betrayed me, left me.

20

Alexandria: São Benedicto, Brazil, 2005

It was Isaac I cradled. Isaac I held. Unlikely as it seemed, and still seems now, I held his hand for hours when he needed me. Or whoever it was that he really needed, it doesn't matter, I was there.

I did some good. I helped someone. I held a body like a very old man's, I fed him, sometimes, I cleaned him up . . . and that made me long for a baby even more. To care for a body that would not die.

I wonder now if he'd already tested positive when he came out to see us in Switzerland. I remember that unsettling sense I had that he was shrinking inside the overcoat of flesh. But no, I'm sure if he had had that knowledge he couldn't have resisted hitting us with it; he hated us so much that night.

Later on the telling was difficult. We had established an uneasy pattern of meetings, once every few months, when we were in the same continent. I think it was in 1998 that he came to see us in Sri Lanka, and booked a night at the same hotel (which his father paid for, despite his protests) so we could spend two days together on the lush green outskirts of Kandy.

The first evening was uneventful; he was on a health kick, and hardly drank, which kept our intercourse amicable, though he fussed a lot about the food, a perfectly delicious curry and sweet pancakes, and ended up by ordering a plate of raw vegetables, then panicking in case they weren't clean. He refused coffee and ordered boiled water, to which he added a vile-smelling herb tea-bag which he had brought along himself. In the soft evening light he looked a little puffy but pink and well; I suspect it was makeup.

Next day he appeared very late at breakfast and didn't look well at all. But then, perhaps none of us were looking our best in the bright Sri Lankan sunlight. He had never looked well; I thought nothing of it.

He waited till Chris had gone to swim in the pool – he did twenty lengths minimum every day, to excuse his inertia for the rest of it – and then bearded me in the downstairs lounge which had a beautiful view of the hotel gardens.

I love Sri Lanka, but in any case I had reason to feel very happy that day (I thought I had, thought I had). My period was five days late. My breasts were heavy in the hot sun; I told myself I felt very faintly nauseous, gloriously nauseous, glorious. I was avoiding coffee, although I love coffee, I proudly ordered fresh orange-juice – deluded, alas, as I know now, for it was one of the many times I 'knew' I was pregnant and took pride in my swollen breasts and belly, only to bleed just a few days late and bleed my happiness away.

I felt good until Isaac sat down heavily beside me, and asked if he could tell me something. I saw his face was grey in the sun; I saw his hand was shaking a little, though that may have been nerves, I'm sure it was nerves. At once I started to feel nervous too. The white fan hissed above my head.

'Do you mind if I tell you something? Something important? Have you got time?'

– Why did he tell me first? He told me first because he loved me least.

'Well yes, I'm honoured, but Chris is swimming – if it's important, don't you want to tell us both?'

'This isn't going to be fun to tell. It's something important. Bad.' His voice was not entirely steady.

My neck felt cold in the breeze from above; I gathered myself; I knew. I helped him by guessing what was wrong. It helped because it made him furious.

'Go on.'

'This isn't easy to say.'

173

'It's not about money?' I prayed it was.

'No.'

'I think I know what you're trying to tell me. Are you ill – ?'

'Yes – '

'Very ill.'

'Well . . .'

'You've got AIDS, haven't you. Oh God, Isaac . . .' My stomach twisted; I felt I was choking. I stared at the glossy tropical greenery outside the open window, so vigorously healthy, bursting with sap and shine and life, its veins and stems more insanely detailed the longer I looked, the harder I stared, the more I tried to avoid his eyes, till the sharpness suddenly dissolved and blurred and everything turned to a mess of tears. A bird sang a brilliant, liquid song. I hated it; I hated this. I wiped my eyes and looked at Isaac; he was staring venomously at me.

'How dare you assume that, just because I'm gay? As if it's *natural*. As if you *knew*. As if all gays die of AIDS. Well, I haven't the least intention of dying. I haven't got AIDS, in any case. I'm HIV-positive, that's all, but you're probably too ignorant to know the difference. I intend to live till I'm eighty at least . . . You might be HIV-positive too. How many men have you slept with, Alex?'

For once I didn't mind the injustice to myself. 'Thank God. You haven't actually got AIDS. Look, you don't have to get it, do you? Your father would pay for the very best treatment, anything at all to keep you well . . .'

Looming above us the fan sighed on, pale and heavy as an albatross.

'You and Dad always thought you could buy anything. You can't buy life, you know.'

I let the cheap philosophy pass. 'Can you explain a bit more to me? Do you have to stop doing things? Do you have to rest? Do you have to tell the people you're working for?'

' – I've told you before, Alex, I don't work for anyone, they work for me. I have three galleries, you understand. My galleries. The Isaac Court Galleries. I have twelve employees. I pay them money. I don't have to tell them I'm positive, I don't have sexual relationships with them. I'm telling you because you're married to Dad and I thought my family might take an interest.'

I hated the aggrieved, complaining tone that both of the children tended to adopt when they got a chance to remind us of our sins. It was in the past, all that; it was over. We were all grown-ups; they would just have to get on with it. And Isaac, as he kept on reminding me, had been very successful in life. He had galleries in London, San Francisco, Amsterdam. I knew the art circuit from long ago; I knew he must be making serious money. He was well-respected; he had several good artists . . . – so why play the whining child with us?

'Drop the irony. What do you want from me?'

There was a sudden harsh outburst of shrieks and screams from somewhere outside the window, bloodcurdling, hysterical. Both of us turned, to see a large peacock come barrelling across the hotel lawn as if there was a tiger behind him; he skidded to a halt a few yards from us and strutted up and down, squawking, indignant, slowly settling to a pompous pacing which seemed to say 'How dare they? How the hell dare they try it on with me?' I found myself smiling. Isaac didn't smile back.

'I want you to tell Dad. I can't face it.'

'I can't.' My response was immediate, unthinking, accompanied by a new gut-twist of fear.

'Why not? I don't mean anything to you, so why should you mind telling him?'

'Curiously enough, you do mean something. Why do you think I was in tears? I think of you and Susy as young. You were children, after all, when we lived together. I'm frightened, appalled, to think of you . . . *ill*. And your father . . . your father . . . you know how he'll feel.' I didn't say *I'm frightened to think of you dying*, but that was what I meant.

'So you won't even do one thing for me.'

'You're going to have to face him in the end. You can't run away – ' I saw his face, very white, suddenly, nostrils pinched, lips pulled back from his teeth in a frightful rictus, lost for words. His hand was a fist; he wanted to hit me. Then speech came spitting out, shaking with fury.

'You bitch. How dare you say that to me? It was you who ran away, remember? It was you who took my father away.'

I couldn't bear to look at his ugly face. I locked beyond the crowns of the coconut palms which waved regally above the rubber trees at the edge of the lawn, the edge of pain, beyond the pain there was clear blue sky, the innocent blue of holidays, baby blue, I wanted a baby, and as I looked back the peacock stopped, preened in the sunlight, spread its tail, performed the everyday miracle for me; the cone of turquoise became a fountain, the fountain spread out its jewelled eyes, the jewelled eyes stared into my future, I'd call my baby Emerald or Sapphire . . . This hideousness would quickly pass. Isaac wasn't my child; it didn't matter.

'You can't go on dragging that up for ever.' I sounded cool; I felt calm again. 'You'll have to tell him, I'm afraid. I can't do your dirty work for you.'

'I know you think that gays are dirty.'

'I don't have to sit here and listen to this shit. Having AIDS doesn't give you the right to abuse me.' I was talking too loudly; people stared, alarmed.

'I haven't *got* AIDS! You don't fucking listen!'

'OK! If I don't listen, don't waste your time talking to me.' I pushed back my chair, which squealed angrily, and walked out into the tactile heat of the garden, solid, fecund, animal heat, the heat of a womb, the heat of life. His pale face stared from the dark window. How glorious to get away from him. I mustn't get upset; it was bad for the baby, the minuscule life I was sure I was carrying, gradually unfurling in this bath of warm light. I nodded to the peacock, which stared back narrowly, lay down on a horizontal bamboo chair, closed my eyes and stroked my stomach.

The sun through my eyelids was terracotta red. Perhaps the tiny baby saw the selfsame colour as the sunlight poured through my thin cotton dress and the walls of my belly . . . perhaps, perhaps. If I wanted it enough . . .

176

I used to think everything came down to wanting; what I had wanted I'd always got — I just hadn't wanted a baby enough. Now I knew what I wanted, I could make it happen.

I wanted to give myself up to the heat. I had known for years that sunlight was dangerous but just for a minute I indulged myself, I pushed my sleeves right up to my shoulder and pulled my skirt right up to my thighs. I wanted the sun to sink into my bones, I wanted to be sure it warmed the baby, I wanted to say *I am with the living, I love my life, I love all this, I say yes to life and yes to a baby* . . .

Perhaps I fell asleep for a moment; I know I wasn't thinking about Isaac, I had consciously decided not to think, yet the next thing I remember is starting up as the peacock gently pecked my arm, someone was dying, the world was ending, the tears were running down my cheeks, I expected to see the blue crown of the peacock but in fact a muscular brown waiter stood beside me and his eyes were appraising, tender. And a little disappointed as I opened my eyes, or perhaps I imagined it . . . everyone looks younger, sleeping in the sunlight, but I wasn't even fifty then, how young must we be not to disappoint them?

His English was nearly perfect. 'Is Madam all right? May I bring you a drink?'

'I'm fine. I didn't . . . I fell asleep.'

'To sleep is dangerous, I think. I bring you an umbrella. Or I can show you a shadowy place . . .'

He was definitely slightly suggestive. Handsome, too, like many of the Hindu islanders, white teeth, clear eyes, young lips, *young*. He might be no more than eighteen. But a pregnant woman shouldn't flirt with teenagers.

'You can tell me something. Several things. Do you know about birds? Or trees?'

He was surprised. 'Yes. My uncle study them. Studies them. He works for big American scientists when they come here. I help him sometime.'

'I have two questions for you. Yesterday we walked a little way into the forest. There were some beautiful red birds, very high up, hovering like humming-birds, do you know humming-birds? Brilliant red. I couldn't see a nest. But as I watched, an egg fell to the ground. The shell was so pretty. Pale green. Mauve patches. I want to know what it was I saw.'

He was nodding, brown eyes bright.'Yes, it's a typical bird of Sri Lanka. Americans call it Scarlet Minivet. We call it – '

'Never mind. Scarlet Minivet. I have another question. That wonderful palm. Higher than everything, the coconuts, everything. With the queer drooping fringe of brown and the massive pale flower, it's practically all flower . . . do you know the real name, the American name?'

It was almost surreal; I gazed up at it, an explosion of cream above the dead brown leaves which hung down like a swagbag or a heavy brown scrotum, and the foaming cream poured out like sperm . . .

'This is also most interesting, our hotel's pride. You have come on the right week for this tree! Is the Talipot Palm, a curious tree. Flowers only once, and then it has died. We are very happy when Talipot Palm flowers.'

'Perhaps it will be lucky for me.'

'Yes, Madam.' He hovered, perhaps waiting for money, but I turned over on my stomach and he went away, silent feet on the well-mown grass. I remembered I had forgotten to say thank you, but it was too hot to call after him. Through my fingers I saw him aim a kick at the peacock which fluttered half-heartedly back towards the trees.

When he'd gone I got up and went to look for Chris. He would have to face Isaac later that day. Nothing had happened until he was told; we were all suspended in a quivering soap bubble, clinging for a moment to the still air. Until it burst, I wanted to be happy, I wanted to tell Chris the name of the bird, and the Talipot Palm, and our baby.

Looking back on the self of seven years ago I admit I feel a little – disconcerted. I was under tremendous stress, of course, but I didn't always behave as I meant to. I had good intentions, but things went wrong, they somehow twisted in my hands. I remember Stuart's valediction, a year before all this, I suppose, as he ran out into the sunlight after me, rapping on the window of the car and shouting 'You're a cow, aren't you! A selfish cow! The most selfish woman I've ever met!' – but then, he never met my mother.

At least I remember these things straight. I don't try to pretend I have been a saint. I pretend less than anyone I know. When I want something, I go for it; when I can't be bothered, I say so; I live the moment; I love the moment. I say what I think, even if it's not pleasant. I don't waste time, or other people's time, though Stuart thought I had wasted his time, but if he was happy, how can that be true? Being happy is never a waste of time.

Perhaps I wasn't always quite honest with Chris, but he never *asked* me if I was unfaithful. If he had asked me, I'd probably have told him, and yes, I admit that that's not true. I am honest to the last; I admit I lied.

But back to Isaac, poor unhappy Isaac. That was only the beginning of the story, remember. Don't judge me by the beginning. People can change, people can grow, Americans always insist they can grow, as if they all wanted to end up giants . . .

A mysterious change came over me as the longing for a child became more desperate, as desire was poisoned by the dread of failure, as I started to internalise (but never accept) the fact that this wasn't working – that I'd never carry out my perfect plan. I dreaded going to the loo each month; those cruel bright red splashes of blood that meant another egg was gone. It was worst when the period was latest and heaviest, when I'd hoped most, been happiest.

I found myself staring at entrails; I know it's pathetic, and disgusting, but I looked at the clots on the pale enamel, I looked at the clots on the cotton waste, trying to discern a tiny foetus, trying to give a form to loss, trying to think 'That would have been mine, I could have loved it if it hadn't died.' But there was never anything to be sure of. I imagined them, tiny, blood-soaked, curved.

Face the facts: there was never anything. Never anything, never any more.

Not long after I decided to get pregnant, I had visited a gynaecologist, a woman who I had been told was the most expensive gynaecologist in New York. She looked mildly surprised when I told her what I wanted, and more surprised when I told her my age, but she examined me without comment, questioned me minutely about my lifestyle, arranged for a battery of physical tests. I was favourably impressed by her thoroughness. She told me to come back in a week. As a matter of fact I was sure I was healthy; I'd always been healthy, hadn't I? What I wanted was an official rubber stamp; a blessing upon my enterprise. Since I could pay for it, I would have it.

Except that she wouldn't give it me. On that second visit I realised; she must have hated me on sight; I was prettier than her, younger than her, she was grim and plain and the envious type. She took pleasure in making me feel bad. Not that I felt bad, but I didn't feel good, I didn't feel the way I had paid to feel when I came down the stairs from her lofty office – in fact, let's be honest, I felt terrible. Humble, old and small.

She confirmed there was nothing physically wrong with me so far as the tests could show. 'But fertility's a subtle, complex thing. There's only one thing proves whether or not you're fertile, and that's getting pregnant. Which you're not. And age is heavily against you.' *She* was against me, I could hear that now. She spoke of the high risk of miscarriage, the high risk of certain genetic problems, problems in pregnancy, problems with delivery. I didn't discuss it, I just asked questions, pointed, specific, scientific questions based on hard reading of pregnancy books. To my disappointment she answered them all. I asked her finally if she could confirm that pregnancy was technically possible. There was an overlong pause; she steepled her fingers. 'Technically not impossible, no.' 'Thank you very much.' I had forced her to say it. That would have to serve as my blessing, then. But she fired a parting shot across my bows as I got up to leave in precarious triumph: 'Do you come from a long-lived family?' I told her no, not particularly (most Stoddys are fat, and die of heart attacks or strokes, but I am in no way a typical Stoddy). She said she 'hoped I had considered that aspect.'

The cheek of the woman. I was paying her, too. They like to interfere in other people's lives. It's a mistake to ask anyone for advice.

But her voice sounded horribly like the truth. It humbled me because I was afraid. Wanting something makes you humble.

It was all confused with what was happening to Isaac. My failure somehow made me . . . kinder. Not that I've ever been unkind, but it made me more able to identify with weakness . . . *Alexandra Court, a sterile woman . . .*

I wasn't omnipotent.

I wasn't immortal.

For nearly half a century I'd believed I was.

And so I came closer to Isaac. So I realised that something linked us. And found I could touch him, at last, without feeling he was alien to me.

His story began to move through its chapters. For what seemed like ages, but was only six months, we thought he was just HIV-positive; I'm an optimist, yes, I looked on the bright side, I kept telling Chris when he got depressed that Isaac would be one of the lucky ones, that not everyone went on to get AIDS, that Isaac would probably live till he was eighty, he'd told me so himself . . . but we stepped up our meetings, all the same, we tried to see Isaac every two months, and I never demurred, so perhaps I knew.

We were in Florence when he called us from a clinic in New York. 'Not good,' he repeated several times when we asked him how he was. He had a chest infection he couldn't throw off, he was losing weight, he was depressed. It hadn't been diagnosed as AIDS, not yet. 'But it's AIDS-related. They don't have to tell me. I must have been infected a long time ago. My prognosis is good, this time around. Don't bother to visit till I'm better.'

After putting the phone down, Christopher wept. 'There must be something we can do. Something. Has to be. He's *my son* . . . I can't help feeling it's all our fault.'

'Isaac would be delighted to hear you say so, but you know it's nonsense. He was always gay. We were too thick to notice. He didn't *turn* gay because we left him. Let's go out and buy him some wonderful presents and air-express them to the clinic. Florence is so marvellous for shopping . . .' Things twisted in my hands again. I meant to be kind, but something went wrong. '. . . And I need some new shoes. And a bag. And some novels. And then let's go to a gallery. Let's not go all mopey. Let's get going.'

Christopher never came to terms with Isaac's illness. I think it always puzzled him, as if he could never quite believe that each stage in the process was irrevocable, and this thinner, iller, older person was actually his clumsy, chubby son. I think he half-thought that one day the old Isaac would ring and say it was all a mistake, he wasn't ill, he wasn't gay. I gave up trying to educate him.

It irritated me; alienated me. We were going through a bad patch in any case. Not a patch, a tunnel, a long dark night, as month after month proved he was a failure – *we* were a failure; we couldn't conceive.

– *I* was a failure, deep-down I knew it, but I never admitted it to Christopher, it was too hideously dangerous to show my weakness. Marriage is a battle for survival, always; be strong and win, or go to the wall. In the end it was Christopher who went to the wall. Since one of us had to, I'm glad it was him. He sat in the dark watching endless movies, he sat and stared at ghosts on the wall.

But I didn't let Isaac go to the wall alone. It was an old debt; I hadn't long to pay it. Now I became the one who suggested meetings, who noticed the weeks were creeping by, while Chris was absent and forgetful, and silent when I talked about Isaac. We couldn't talk to each other about it; we talked to each other less and less. I knew we were coming to the end of the road, we were running out of life as the century did . . .

182

Yet Chris was my companion, my friend, my brother. If I lost him, I had no one else. That was the awful truth, there was no one else. We had left them all behind, you see. We had cast ourselves off into emptiness. In the middle of the night we clung dumbly together and fucked without passion, without hope; blind, wordless, regular, like moles grinding in their dark bunker (but I love the light; I'm a creature of day, and by day we couldn't meet each other's eyes and ate in silence like embittered pensioners).

We weren't talking about my pregnancy either, my absent pregnancy, my vanishing babies. I dreamed about them night after night. They vanished like dolls I had dropped in drawers, getting smaller and smaller as I searched for them with growing guilt and panic. I had one, cradled it, dropped it, picked it up and found it was no longer alive, its face was hard plastic or it had no face, as I stared it slipped yet again through my fingers, the carpet was covered with broken dolls, babies I'd been given but failed to look after, failed to love, failed, *failed*. I started to dream about Stuart again; he was ten years younger than Christopher; in life we had never fucked unprotected, but in dreams we fucked hungrily for a baby, in dream after dream Stuart made me pregnant and I woke orgasmic, on a crest of happiness, only to feel it trickle away, slipping away between my damp thighs . . .

But Christopher did make me pregnant. That's twice he did it, twenty years apart, two pregnancies ending in nothing, nothing. But no one can deny I got pregnant again; that at least they can't take away . . .

Surely I can bear to think about it now, now I know I'm going to have a daughter.

— I did get pregnant. I'm not deluded. I was forty-nine; that's quite an achievement. *So fuck that rat bitch gynaecologist.* I tested my urine twenty times, it made me so happy to be positive. I was positive! It was wonderful! No shadow of doubt infected my joy. I was furious with Chris when his response was muted.

'What's the matter with you? It's such wonderful news! It's a scientific test, we have to believe it. A little baby to travel with us. A little baby for us to play with. Baby, baby, baby . . . Oh *fuck*, I can't bear to look at your miserable face.'

'Look for God's sake, Alex, of course I'm happy, but you're forty-nine, and only five weeks' pregnant, I just hope everything goes right. You haven't got there yet, I dread disappointment . . .'

I admit I was unreasonable. 'Shut up! Shut up! You'll bring bad luck! You don't want me to be pregnant, you're hateful, hateful . . . we should tell the family. I want them to know.'

But the doubt had been sown, the little bad seed, and perhaps where it enters, disaster grows. I think I blamed Chris for what happened, though I'm wiser now, I am wiser now . . .

It got to ten and a half weeks. I said it was eleven, but it wasn't. Nearly three months, I told myself, and anyone else who would listen, strangers, waitresses, whoever I could find, the fact of my pregnancy had to be shared, perhaps because I could hardly believe it, perhaps because I feared it would end . . .

I had a deep need to tell 'the family' but alas, there was no family to tell. Doubtless my family had families by now; I had never been told; we had lost each other. My great mute solid pair of sibs, left in the past, stranded in the past. Or perhaps I was stranded, for they were still together, sharing their children, I suppose, playing aunts and uncles and nephews and nieces. But not with me. Never with me . . .

– I wished we had friends, I remember that. I wrote to Mary, and trembled as I posted it. She was always so solid, so gloriously maternal, one might have assumed she had six children. I think I feared she would disbelieve it; I think I felt she would see straight through me.

Dear Mary,
Surprise, surprise! Your old friend Alexandra is nearly

three months pregnant, and we are both so delighted about it . . .

Ten-and-a-half weeks isn't nearly three months. You grow less honest when you're mad with desire, and I longed for that baby with a monomanic love I have never felt before or since. Oh I wish the pregnancy had lasted longer, though everyone says late miscarriage is worse . . . if it had lasted longer it would have been more real. I would have *had* something, even if I lost it.

Ten-and-a-half weeks is nothing to the medics. 'It's a good job it didn't go any further,' said the doctor. 'It's nature's way, you know.'

– The profession is full of idiots, who should be muzzled, or preferably shot. But my anger was partly in abeyance, then. Most of what they said seemed to be beamed towards me from the other side of a huge sheet of glass; I was recording it all instead of talking back, only the very worst outrages made me talk back. Most of the time I just stared at them, numb, which is not like me, not like me at all. I was not like me. Part of me was dead.

I began to bleed one day in a car which was rattling through the hot Turkish hills. We'd had sex the night before; at first I just thought it was a leak of sperm, Christopher always had a lot of sperm even if it couldn't make live babies . . . Christopher felt too depressed to drive, since the latest reports from Isaac were bad, and I didn't want to bother, so we sat in the back of an old hire-car, suffering the driving of a crazy local. The roof of the car had been rolled back; the heat was intense, even through my straw hat, the road ahead shimmered and slurred in the heat; we threw up a cloud of dust and small stones; every now and then a fly whined by and was sucked into the past with dizzy speed; there was dust and resin in my mouth and lungs and ever since then I have never smelled pines without a cramping sense of dread.

All of a sudden I was afraid. 'Ask him to pull in to the side of the road,' I told Christopher. We screeched to a halt and I got out alone. In the trees it was stunningly dark and quiet after the rattling blaze of the open road. Once my eyes adjusted, it was beautiful; a few narrow sunbeams pierced the gloom; perfect yellow flowers underfoot, like buttercups but the leaves were wrong, the gold heads sang in a small pool of sunlight, telling me everything was still all right, but I looked all the same and there was blood, *at least it's dark, that can't be so dangerous*, but as I crouched there a bright splash fell.

— I remember I thought *funeral wreath*. They were mourning flowers, I knew they were. I walked back to the car like an old woman, trying to walk without moving too much, trying to protect the thing I carried. All at once it seemed infinitely fragile, infinitely open to our hurts. I asked the driver to go back to the hotel and screamed at him when he drove too fast; at every bump I winced and clutched Christopher, suffering the baby's imagined pain.

The doctor who examined me was reassuring. His English was good; he flattered me, unable to believe I was forty-nine; he said there was often a small amount of bleeding; I could rest if I chose to, but it wasn't essential. There was no point in tests. We had to wait and see.

I lay in bed for five whole days, I who could never bear to be still. Not far from my window a mournful bell rang out the hours; I lay and counted, lay very still in bed and prayed. When I lay still the bleeding stopped. My spirits rose; I hoped again. For twenty-four hours my towels were clean. Whiteness, cleanness was wonderful. I didn't read, didn't want to read, I became a still deep well of longing, a bowl of hope, perfectly blank. I talked to the baby, stroked my belly. 'I want you. I love you. Hang on, please. I'll do anything to keep you safe.' I couldn't talk to Chris; he was blank and closed; he dumbly brought me whatever I asked for, then went away and drank; I talked to the baby, talked to myself.

After five days I got up again and the sad, slow bleeding started at once, stopping and starting, brown not fresh. I lay down again; it was driving me mad.

'Let's fly back to London,' I said. 'The best gynaecologist. Stay at the Savoy. That's quite convenient for Harley Street.'

But things had ceased to follow my plan. I was destined to stay in hospital, flat on my back in the single bed, weeping into the stiff linen pillow, in a room full of florist's funeral flowers.

Christopher came with me for the ultrasound scan. First of all they listened for the heartbeat; there was a loud, long crackle like snow falling on all the telephone wires in the world, all of them listening for sounds of life; to me it sounded intensely alive, and hope surged hotly through me again. The heart must be tiny, immensely fast. No one said anything, though. Then the little machine slipped across my greased belly. We stared at the screen, heart in mouth. I knew it was no good when the picture steadied and the consultant stared at it, too long, going over and over it, saying nothing. A frozen swirl of meaningless silver. I couldn't see where the baby was. The pieces hung like a petrified snowstorm. A long silence; I was lying down; my voice had to come from some lost deep place; it broke as I asked, knowing it was hopeless, 'What can you see? Is it all right?'

They hate to tell bad news. 'I'm afraid — what should you have been, nine weeks — '

' — Ten and a half, ten and a half — '

'I'm afraid it doesn't look at all hopeful.'

I knew it, but the child in me couldn't bear it. 'What do you mean? There was a heartbeat, I heard it — '

'There was no heartbeat. That wasn't a heartbeat.'

'I heard it, I heard it, I heard it beating . . .' I was sobbing, now, turning over on my stomach, clutching Chris's hand because it was there, I hadn't looked at him but I needed to use him. He was saying something; I couldn't hear him. The consultant was answering him. They had taken over. I lay and wept; the tears were hot. They had taken it away, my beautiful heartbeat.

'I'm afraid we're ninety-nine per cent certain . . .'

'You mean there's some doubt? Could it still be all right?'

There was a silence. 'I'm afraid . . . this is a missed abortion.

Something we call a missed abortion. I think we should say one hundred per cent and act accordingly.'

I was admitted straightaway for a 'scrape'. They called it a 'scrape' and a 'missed abortion' ... The language was all horrible. All of it denied what had happened to me. As if I was pathetic, deluded, as if I had never really been pregnant, as if I was too old to be pregnant, and everyone else had known all along. The nurses and doctors never called it a baby. It hurt me that they never called it a baby. They called it 'your pregnancy', 'the products of conception', 'the foetus', 'the foetal sac'.

I asked to see my consultant, but he was overseeing a caesarian, some lucky woman who would have her baby, I would have been happy if they'd cut me in two so long as I could have had my baby ... I asked to speak to another doctor, anyone who could explain to me.

He was kind and sensible (cruel and stupid). He tried to be kind, but he was cruel. He tried to be sensible, which made him stupid.

'It's a good job it didn't go any further. It's nature's way, you know ...'

'Was the baby deformed? Could you see on the scan?'

'No, we couldn't see on the scan ... it may have died some time ago.'

Why did he have to tell me that? I wanted to think I had kept it alive for as long as possible.

'Why did this happen? I've been so careful ... I've rested, I ate healthy food ...'

'Nothing you'd have done could have made any difference. This pregnancy wasn't right from the start.'

He meant to comfort, but he tortured me. 'You can't know that. *You can't know that!* I felt absolutely fine, I felt very pregnant, I'd put on weight, my stomach swelled ... how can you know it wasn't right until you do the operation?'

'I'm ninety-nine per cent sure ...' – The stupidity of that. Why are they always ninety-nine per cent sure? Never ninety-three, never sixty-seven, the cliché-mongers, the morons – '... this was something called a blighted ovum. They're very

188

common. Much more than people realise. As many as one in four ... nearly every woman in her childbearing years ... no reason why there should be the slightest ill effects ... a very minor operation ...' His voice came at me in blaring surges, words I couldn't, didn't wish to, take in. He had a stupid red face, and thin mousey hair. Getting no response, he talked too much. His voice was common. I hated him.

'I have no further questions,' I said coldly, suddenly, as if he were a maid, in the middle of one of his bungling sentences. He reddened still further, nodded and left.

The room was painted a soothing peach which made me think of baby clothes. It was horribly quiet; Chris had gone to the shop. He returned with chocolates, perfume, orchids, a single perfect pearl-coloured orchid, coiled and curled like an elaborate shell, but in its tall glass on the bedside table it suddenly reminded me of a foetus, an aborted foetus hanging in a test-tube, I reached out my hand to touch it or stroke it and brought the whole thing crashing to the ground.

The worst thing was not knowing what to grieve for. I called it 'the baby' with a breaking heart, taking deep breaths before I said it, and all of them seemed to avoid my eyes.

The anaesthetist was tall and unreally handsome, pink-cheeked, blue-eyed, bursting with life, like an actor in a TV drama in his bright turquoise cap and gown. He chatted to me as we waited for theatre. I liked him; I like good-looking people; he didn't preach, or bore me to death; he asked me if my hair colour was natural, and complimented me on it. He said this was quite a routine operation, they did several of these every week. Since he hadn't examined me I didn't mind; somehow it didn't seem personal; I smiled and said I was glad I was routine, it was dangerous to be exotic in hospitals. When I told him I'd been out of the country he listened entranced, or apparently entranced, to my casually boastful itinerary, and we made each other laugh about foreign doctors, and I almost forgot, for the briefest moment, as he held my hand, why he was holding it, why I was here, why everything was ... – he was holding my hand to give me the injection.

'Now you'll feel a little prick on the back of your hand . . .'

And I knew with absolute urgency that I had one split second to correct a great wrong, to explain what everyone had misunderstood. 'Wait,' I said, and his eyes above the mask registered dismay, for this was not procedure; 'I just want to say one thing. I know I've been laughing and joking with you. But I really wanted this baby. I didn't want to lose this baby.' He nodded; his eyes were unreadable; the needle slipped into the back of my hand; I woke up in what they said was the recovery room, and the nurses were surprised by how clearheaded I was.

'Is it all gone?' I asked them.

The nurse held my hand and smiled vaguely. 'Yes, it's all over, no problems. In a minute you can have a nice cup of tea.'

'But what will they do with it? Will they examine it to find out what was wrong?' Why did they all evade my questions? I wanted to shake her, make her answer me.

'You'll have to ask your consultant.'

I asked my consultant next day.

He was a sensitive man, and I was paying him well to understand what I wanted of him. I could see he was sorry that he couldn't help me.

'I'm sorry, Mrs Court. I'm truly sorry. But we couldn't analyse . . . the products of conception. Whatever had been there . . . how can I explain . . . it is likely to have happened very early on . . . and then – the material – gets broken up . . . there really wasn't anything there to examine.'

I lay there silent, turned to stone, but the stone was a lump breaking out of my chest, breaking out of my throat, a stone, a sob, I turned to a single, terrible sob, a harsh inhuman croaking sound.

There was nothing there.

It never developed.

I was pregnant, but there was never a baby. There was nothing to lose; nothing to mourn. Only pure loss, pure emptiness.

Later I started to hate my body, I who had always loved my body. It went on leaking old brown blood, a miserable daily reminder of failure. I hated it for its stupid inability to do what women's bodies were made to do. It was weak and useless; I hated it. I hated Chris, I hated life, I hated death for dirtying me.

But I didn't hate Isaac. That was curious. I began to feel I needed to see him. I'd never been physical with those kids; their hands had always been messy and sticky; they didn't cuddle, they pawed at me, so naturally I pushed them away; but now I wanted to be close to Isaac. Now I had a positive urge to be close. I found myself wanting to hold his hand, I who was always horrified by illness, I wanted to hold him in my arms, I didn't do it but I wanted to.

Naturally Isaac was hostile and suspicious when I first began to visit alone. 'What's the matter with you, Alex? You're not after my money, so what is it, are you turning into a ghoul? You're a fucking ghoul! Fuck you, fuck you . . .'

He needed Christopher, not me. But Christopher couldn't bear it. Christopher would sit there, wrung with misery, making everyone feel worse, whereas I could go along and chat and smile if that was what Isaac wanted to do . . . More often, he needed to talk about dying. I could do that without flinching away, indeed the topic had some horrible attraction . . .

As if he were dying in my place, and I was more alive because he was dying; as if that ensured it wasn't my turn yet.

But it wasn't just that. I wanted to protect him. I wanted to hold him, and – *mother* him. I know it was too late, but it *wasn't* too late, as long as I let him rage at me. 'Don't try and pretend you understand, you bitch. You're a woman, you're smug, you're repulsively healthy. You think you're going to live forever. You won't, you know. That's what life means. It's not all bad, having a death sentence. I know more about life than an airhead like you . . .'

But he was too weak to be angry for long. He needed company, even me. And I needed him, I don't know why. I'm many things, but not a ghoul.

I know it was somehow connected to the baby; connected to the babies, all my lost babies, the adopted one, the aborted one, the one that they tell me hardly existed, the ones my body missed each month . . .

But don't ever think that Isaac was a substitute. Don't ever think that that thin, stiff body with its terrible purplish strawberry marks in any way replaced the small body I craved. There isn't a pattern, is there? That is the horror and the mercy of it all, that there isn't a pattern, things just happen, you make them happen or suffer them.

We kept on trying to make dates with Isaac, though he always sounded on the verge of sneering; an implicit 'What, you want to see *me*?' Yes, we wanted to see him. Soon. We would meet him anywhere, within reason. In retrospect those were the easier days; he was still able to travel then. Everything got harder, slowly, faster.

Seeing him was tough, but not seeing him was worse. Seeing him often lessened the shock, for nearly every time he was visibly weaker. Once when he'd been working very hard and then in the South Seas with Gus – (we had never met Gus; he kept saying we must meet him; we met others of his friends, painters, ex-boyfriends, but never the most important one; they had been together for nearly three years; we expressed enthusiasm, dutifully, but the promised meetings melted away) – we didn't see Isaac for over four months. We chased him from answerphone to answerphone and finally tracked him down in Sydney. Gus had gone home; Isaac had stayed; he was willing to see us, or not unwilling.

We met in a pub in The Rocks, just west of Sydney Cove, called The Hero of Waterloo; the hotel receptionist had recommended it. It was a Victorian simulacrum, with candleless candlesticks and pointless imitation fires. By the time we got there we were almost past caring, for the most notable thing about The Hero, which Chris's informant had neglected to mention, was its situation right at the top of a very steep hill. Chris and I were quite fit – I was very fit – but we had to rest halfway up. Isaac wasn't there. We ordered beers. Our silence was more nervous than usual.

When Isaac burst in, he looked terrible. He was puffing like a steam-train, wheezing, gasping, as he steadied himself against a table and looked round wildly, blind after the sunlight. He was papery-white, his skin shone with sweat, beads of moisture and strange dark patches he never had before.

'Isaac, over here,' Chris called, but I got up and ran over to him. It was unpremeditated; I tried to kiss him. He looked at me as if I had attacked him with a knife, but perhaps he was in pain.

Now it was clear he was ill, things were simpler in my mind, if not in his. It removed some walls of sulky dignity; his illness seemed to invite me to touch him. Maybe Isaac himself just felt less defended. He certainly felt the cold. It was very hot, but he wore a jumper, and as soon as he stopped sweating he was shivering. There was a look on his face I did not remember, a brief strained look when he seemed not to focus or to stare into the unfocused distance, and I think he saw death, and was afraid; yet for the first time since the reunion in Switzerland I wasn't afraid of him.

— Everyone else was afraid of him, or afraid of what they could see he had. We soon had a vacant table. Half-a-dozen heads had stopped blocking the light. He wasn't puffing any more, but there was still a faint sound of wheezing. He seemed unwilling to look at us, perhaps because he didn't want to read our expressions, and as he stared down at his orange-juice I got a proper look at him in the harsh daylight that poured through the window.

— He had aged ten years in the last four months. His skin was drawn tightly across his bones (I half-remembered something I'd once told him: *You're like your father, you've got good bones. The girls will be wild for you in your late thirties*). Now the bones were getting ready to come out and dance. Around his eyes the skin seemed to have retracted, and had a brownish tinge. His mouth was slightly open, allowing him to breathe, and it twitched into strange accidental half-smiles completely devoid of humour or pleasure.

Only four months had passed. I wondered how long was left. Suddenly he looked up, his sharp blue eyes entirely intelligent, and caught me staring.

'I know I look fucking awful,' he wheezed. 'But I'm going to live to see the year 2000.'

'Of course you are – ' 'We never doubted it – ' After an awkward pause, we carolled reassurance, shocked by the littleness of his hopes. It was the first time he had admitted, even tacitly, that he was going to die.

Chris moved on hurriedly to small talk, comparing notes with Isaac about Micronesia. They were prosing on about whether it mattered that something called 'outriggers' were disappearing, that the young no longer wanted to fish or grow *taro*, that Guam was a nightmare of soldiers and tourists – it was boring, and I cut across them. There were things about Isaac's trip which interested me much more.

'I really had hoped we'd get together with Gus. Did you say he went back to New York early?'

'Yes . . .' his voice trailed downwards.

'Is he OK?' I was fumbling this. 'I mean, he hasn't got . . .?'

'He hasn't, no. His latest test was still negative. But he can't stand the pressure of my being ill. We've been rowing a lot. I told him to go.'

'You mean he left you when you needed him?'

He didn't answer; he smiled at me, a smile of purest irony, looking almost like himself again, letting my own words ring in my ears.

'Oh Alexandra. You're priceless. Yes, Gus took a leaf out of you and Dad's book . . . actually I didn't really need him. In the end I might need people to look after me, but I've got a lot of friends. We're good to each other. Gus was never that sort of guy. It's OK, really . . .' I'd begun to apologise. 'Don't justify yourself. I've started to feel more forgiving towards you. Nothing seems to make much difference, now.'

– And perhaps his smile did become more forgiving.

He liked to be asked about his illness; he liked to describe the fluctuating symptoms, the little details which made up his new life, the new short life he had been given to live. He wanted us to know he was learning things; he also wanted us to feel his pain. I would say he was a hypochondriac, except that people with AIDS aren't hypochondriacs, but he had that same loving, compendious interest in every facet of his body's decline. I understood that, and was happy to listen; I've always been interested in bodies. And sometimes the disease seemed almost playful. He got better, he got worse, but there was always something different, some new cause for hope or despair, a new drug, a new symptom, a new horror to tease us with. But Chris couldn't bear those conversations; he never joined in, just sat there, frozen, staring at the carpet, or out of the window, while Isaac and I rattled on about Kaposi's sarcoma, or he tried to tell us the meaning of life, and God knows we needed someone to do that, for sometimes our lives seemed meaningless – yet how could *death* give a meaning to life? He insisted it did, and I listened, politely.

After each meeting, I felt better, but Chris withdrew into his private suffering.

We were in touch with Susy, too. Susy's attitude to Isaac was not always appealing. I suppose that whenever she contacted us we must have talked about Isaac too much, but then, she was his sister.

'You really love all this, don't you, Alex,' she hissed at me one day, long distance to Australia, soon after we met Isaac in the pub at West Rocks. The long distance silences made her seem brain-damaged. 'You're really excited by what's happening to Isaac.'

'That's – *sick* – '

'Maybe it is. I have been sick. I had a lot of abortions, remember. Nobody seems to care about me. All I ever hear about is Isaac's latest symptoms . . .'

Actually her attitude was thoroughly normal. Sibling rivalry is thoroughly normal. For the last two years of the twentieth century we were once again more like an ordinary family, richer than most, perhaps, less happy than some, keeping in touch with our grown-up children, seeing them occasionally, bickering, bargaining . . .

I was becoming more ordinary, too. I could never be ordinary, of course, but age is ordinary, and I was growing older, I was forty-eight, I was forty-nine, I wanted something I couldn't have, I who had always had everything I wanted; I hardly talked to my husband, which is normal, and I hadn't a lover, and I wasn't happy.

It didn't suit me. It couldn't last. It was the lull before the millennial explosion; guns and love and death and dancing and fireworks spattering the skies with rubies . . .

They fell in the bay around the Statue of Liberty in sprays of bright new blood. Isaac kept his word, and saw in the new century. And he made me a present: Benjamin.

Benjamin was his friend – young enough to be my son, you see. Benjamin was Isaac's protégé. He had his first two private shows at Isaac's London gallery. Then he started selling, and being noticed. Isaac encouraged him to move to New York, and found him a studio with nominal rent. Perhaps Isaac was in love with him, for he left his diaries to Benjamin.

I read them, of course, without Benjamin's consent, though I told him afterwards what I'd done, I'm not dishonest, I thought I should tell him. It turned out he hadn't read them himself; Benjamin's incurious in certain ways. I told him not to bother, they were rather depressing.

Isaac wasn't as forgiving in private as he sometimes seemed when we were together, but of course the diary petered out in the end, and the end was the time when we came closest.

There are passages I can't forget. There are passages his father couldn't bear to read, but luckily his father will never read them. (*Is it possible that I shall never see Chris again?*)

– The mistakes we made, we made together.

I should like to live to see the twenty-first century. I know it's arbitrary, even cute, but I've started to focus on that wish.

196

Once I took it for granted, of course. I'll only be thirty-three, after all.

Eighteen months ago I was more ambitious. I wanted to outlive my bastard father. I wanted to see that motherfucker dead. Then I got hep, and pneumonia, and had to give up my acupuncture, my positive imaging, my homeopathy, lie flat on my back and accept heavy drugs. They said I would die without PFA. And it worked, I rallied. But I know I'm weaker. I know from looking in the mirror that I haven't got so long to go.

The year 2000 is like a beacon. Blazing figures on the grey horizon. I know there will be amazing parties, vast carnivals where the healthy and lucky ones will take possession of the future. Too bad, because the dying will go too. Millions of the dying will attend. They try to forget the dying, but we'll go on dying across their future, men and women dying together . . . now the women know they haven't escaped.

My father and Alex will probably already have booked themselves into some fabulous event. On a plane or a yacht or the top of a mountain; Dad always had a thing about mountains. Something romantic for the two of them. There were only two people in their world. There wasn't any space for anyone else. They didn't care whether I lived or died; sometimes I think that's why I grew ill. They didn't leave any room for me. They didn't see that I was different. They didn't see any need for difference.

Love meant love between a man and a woman. There were only crumbs for their kids and their friends. Sometimes I feel so angry with them I wish Alex had HIV as well.

My analyst thinks I must go beyond this if I am ever to get well. He doesn't mean that I won't die. No one will tell me I won't die. Perhaps he means die well. Not such a bad idea, to die well. With a life as short as mine will be, a lot of emphasis falls at the end.

Analysts won't tell you what they mean. I feel that he wants me to go beyond anger, but he only asks me if that's *what I want. I think I need my anger. I think my anger keeps me alive.*

And yet, if I could be bigger than my anger, perhaps I should not feel so small, perhaps I should not shrink so much, for the frightening fact is, I'm shrinking.

And I feel the cold now I've got so thin, I get tired in the street and puffed on stairs. So I'm spending too much time up here, in the penthouse flat I was so proud of affording (I've done fucking well: no thanks to anyone, no use to anyone now). I look out over New York through the veil of fumes and pick out crawling files of cars two hundred feet below the sunlight. They don't know I'm up here watching them. They haven't a clue that I'm still here, up in the sky with the skyscrapers, staring across a solid mosaic of dirty streets to the distant horizon, with the oily glitter of the sea to the right and those bloody great waste barges floating and stinking . . . it makes me see I'm not alone, though I've always felt terribly alone, and I blame my parents for my loneliness, I blame them for not loving me – but at last I don't have to feel so lonely, since it's clear the world is dying with me.

Melodramatic, isn't it. The first time I read it I was furious, naturally enough, about the reference to me, then I realised he didn't mean it. I read it again and felt depressed. Today I'm just impatient for my child, impatient for Anna Maria to come, and it makes me impatient with Isaac's moaning. He was just the same as a teenager, attracted to James Dean and Jim Morrison and all those beautiful self-destroyers . . . It's dated so quickly, hasn't it, all that doom-ridden apocalyptic stuff. They churned it out by the cubic tonne in the run-up to the millennium. Before we pulled our socks up . . . (we have to be hopeful. There must be a future.)

I stick to what my own eyes can see, and the world hasn't changed much since I was twenty. Somewhat hotter, I admit, but two degrees doesn't sound very much. Africa has suffered terribly, but Africa has always suffered . . . and I suppose there have been more famines and fires and hurricanes and droughts in some parts of the world, but of course you can avoid them if you're halfway intelligent. And there was no occasion for breast-beating on our part, which Chris would have engaged in if I had gone along with it. I could never see that it was our fault; *we* didn't cut down any rain-forests or kill any whales or pollute any rivers, we didn't even have a car of our own for the twenty years we were away, so Christopher was wasting his time feeling guilty. All we did was to go on holiday. Was it so wicked to go on holiday? We saw a few sights, we ate a few meals, but we paid our bills.

Of course. We were rich.

I was never susceptible to all that preaching. Christopher, poor darling, read too many books which thundered on about the state of the world (I read books as well, but mainly novels, which don't waste pages on tosh like that).

— I'm sorry for Isaac. Oh, I'm sorry for him. I'm wracked with grief when I remember that diary. And I'm frightened, sometimes, about the earth. All the things I love. All the beautiful things. What if it just gets hotter and hotter?

If only Benjamin had hidden that diary. He should have guessed it would be painful for me. But there you are, the young haven't suffered, they can't understand what they haven't lived.

Even my joy over Anna Maria seems excessive to Benjamin. He's busy being cautious and nervous, in some ways he's just like Christopher was, always warning me against getting too excited in case I'm disappointed again, and as they start carping my joy leaks away, I imagine disappointment, I'm disappointed.

Not this time. This time nothing can stop me. This time my certainty is too great. This time I'm ready; I have suffered; I have paid. And the child is real, not a hope in the dark. This one won't die or slip away. As I looked at the child yesterday the sun came out and displayed the blue-black silks of her hair and I knew she was meant to be my daughter, the sun reached out and linked us together, my past and my future, a life in the sun, and the little girl with the marigold. She's a child of the sun; she's meant for me.

The sun is our friend. It wouldn't burn us up.

I don't think I can bear to wait much longer. After all, I've been waiting half my life. I've been trying for a child since the twentieth century.

Perhaps it's a mercy I didn't conceive, so the child didn't suffer the millennium and all its terrifying *grand guignol*.

But if I'd conceived . . . if we could have managed it, by one of the ordinary little miracles that happen to other women all the time . . . None of the rest would have happened, of course. Benjamin and I would have remained just friends, or perhaps I'd have fucked him once or twice and nobody would have known anything about it. Christopher would never have wrecked his life. Christopher and I would still have been together. He wasn't a bad man. He was the best.

It would be five minutes' work to find out where he is; a simple phone call; the bank always knows. Maybe, perhaps, just to tell him my news . . .

But of course it would hurt him. He'd be jealous. He would wish she was ours, little Anna Maria. I can never face him. Over, finished.

This aching desire to tell someone. The stupid wish that there was someone to tell, for at last I am going to be happy again. Life should be happy; I was meant to be happy.

21

Susy: London, 2005

That fucking woman wrote to me! Just as if nothing had happened. She *dropped me a line* after a five-year silence. Not mentioning Dad, as if he was dead. The letter was a sort of honeyed hiss.

> *Dear Susy,*
> *Bet you're surprised to see my writing, if you still remember it, if you're still living at 9 Devereux Avenue. I hope so; it was a lovely house.*
> *I've been thinking about the old days a lot. You were a sweet girl; I didn't deserve you. I'm going in for motherhood again, and hope to do better this time around. A glorious Brazilian three-year-old from a desperately poor family. Black hair, black eyes, beautiful. You will have to meet her when I next come through London. I'm so excited about it all.*
> *How are you? I'm sorry I'm so out of touch. You're probably married by now with twins, or else headmistress of some marvellous school. In any case I wanted to drop you a line. Do write and tell me all your news. We'll be staying for a month at the New York Plaza when we finally get out of here.*
> *Your loving stepmother*
> *Alexandra*

Your loving stepmother! I couldn't believe it. I was so angry I burst out crying. After the way she treated Dad. That was her thing, though, leaving people. After the way she wrecked our lives.

We didn't deserve you, Alex. Nobody's bad enough for that. Dad was crazy to do what he did but you must have pushed him till he snapped. He was a gentle man. He wasn't violent. He never smacked me; he rarely shouted.

He loved her so much, she should have felt lucky, but it wasn't enough for her, she wanted someone else, or however many other lovers she had. When I remember how she went on at me about sex! . . . that's what I can't stand; she's such a liar. Alex never thought I was a *sweet girl*. I'm sure she never *thinks about the old days*.

Everything was lying and acting. All that mattered was appearances. The way I dressed used to drive her insane. She looked at Isaac's spots as if they were plague sores — later, of course, they were. And then she acted the angel of mercy! Who was she trying to impress? There must have been something in it for her . . .

She ran off with that young boy. I heard he was really great-looking. Perfect for Alex, she was such a looks snob. But by now she must be getting on . . .

I last saw her at the funeral, looking wrecked, frightful, at least forty.

— Come to think of it, she must have been older than that. She was thirty-six when they went away. My God, so she was fifty then. I admit she didn't look fifty. And she was as brilliantly done-up as ever. She was still as skinny, and her hair as red. But she was a dead white, a real snow-white, as if they had drained away her blood, as if she were the corpse, not Isaac. It must have been powder, laid on with a trowel. She sat at the back, but a lot of people gawped. She stared straight ahead, and didn't look at anyone. I hated her so much for that. It was a pose, of course, like all her poses, trying to look like a Japanese mask, all stiff and grieved beneath the spotted net veil. She looked barmy and loathsome, but as smart as ever, like a drawing in very sharp black and white pencil. It was one of the horrible things about Alex. The world would end, and she'd still look smart.

I hated her for daring to show up when all that had happened to us was her fault.

She was late; I thought she wouldn't show, I thought the bitch had lost her nerve. Dad was there with a trio of hard-eyed men with bull-like necks and suits like safes. Surely they realised he wasn't a crook? Surely they realised it was a mistake? He was sitting in the front row, like me, and if the suits had been absent he'd have been beside me, we could have held hands and had a cry together, but no one could fit in the pew with them so I sat alone on the other side, turning to look at him, all the time hoping he would catch my eye. But he was staring up at the stained-glass window, a horribly gory saint stuck with arrows, thin chicken body, fat drops of blood. Some of that religious art is *gruesome*. Dad's profile was old. He looked small between his minders. I longed to touch him, but the church was too cold, I didn't know how close you were allowed to go to prisoners, I didn't want the suits to push me away, I didn't want a scene for the paparazzi . . .

But all the reasons were bad. I should have touched him, and I failed.

We were all too stuck in our stupid roles. My family has always been broken, frozen. Only Isaac and I really loved each other in an uncomplicated way. We made each other laugh. We were fond of each other. And later, of course, he was all I had left. We argued a lot and he was jealous of me – maybe I was sometimes jealous of him – but he was my friend and I miss him still.

It hurts, it hurts. And the guilt makes it worse, because I hadn't seen him as much as I should have done since he was ill. I can't forgive myself for being so stupid. I knew he would die, but I couldn't believe it, *wouldn't* believe it, I suppose. I was busy, *busy*, when my brother was dying.

The thing is, it was true. I *was* too busy. I was starting to come out of a long dark tunnel, deciding to finish my training or bust, get a job, get on with my life . . . I didn't want to be dragged down again. Besides, it cost money to fly to New York, and Dad didn't send me any extra money –

– I'm like Alexandra, always making excuses, never admitting anything's my fault. All right, it was my fucking fault. I didn't make the effort when I should have done, I kept putting it off into the future, and when the future arrived, he'd gone. I felt such an idiot; why didn't I realise? Once people are dead, nothing can be mended.

The funeral was the very last family occasion. The last time we would ever all be together. Not with our real mother, of course, but with the bitch who had replaced her – and oh, why must life be such a muddle, because she wasn't always a bitch, she could be kind, she could be generous, sometimes she even made me laugh, but once they ran away I forgot all that. Why do I have to remember all that? At the funeral I was praying she wouldn't be there, but maybe one per cent of me hoped she would. And I couldn't help looking round for Isaac. Logically I knew he was in the coffin, but I couldn't help thinking he might turn up, panting in at the last moment, as usual, clumsy, apologising, *my brother*, peering shortsightedly round the dark church. My brother aged twenty. My brother aged eight. He was kind to me, he cared. My brother.

But he didn't come. Of course he didn't. It was her who came, moving in a weird stiff way, acting her idea of a mourner, wasn't she. A little ripple, or sigh, or whisper ran round the church as she came in, and for a moment I thought it would turn to a hiss, and they would all stand and hiss her down, I wanted that, I was dying for it, so at last she'd be made to see she couldn't get away with everything . . . but the noise died away. The church settled down.

And Alexandra didn't look for us. She sat at the back in her dead white makeup (it must have been makeup, I can't be wrong. Alex never cared about any of us, she never even cared about Dad. I don't want to be wrong, it makes life harder).

My father turned round, as I knew he would, he looked like a tortoise, sort of hopelessly craning. He saw her, and his face crumpled. The mouth was working. I didn't want to lip-read. They held his arms. He was trying to rise. They held his arms, they held him down! My father held like a murderer.

At the end of the short, false service – all read in a nasal Californian voice which made death seem like a cold in the head, something to whine about — I saw his head shoot round again, I heard him groan as he half-rose to his feet. He must have seen her go. I saw her go. Just a glimpse of her back, a jet-black matchstick slipping through the door. A final flash of that carroty hair.

— And now that woman writes to me!

What does she want? Is she fucking crazy? How can she bear to write my name?

Come to think of it, it's still her name as well since she hasn't actually divorced him. I remember how ecstatic Isaac and I were when we found out her maiden name was Stoddy. It was written in a copy of some crappy novel — *Gone with the Wind* I think — she had before she married Dad. That bloody woman was a Stoddy! Our stepmother a Stoddy! We pissed ourselves with laughter. Alexandra was furious.

But the thought of the Stoddys cheered me up whenever I had to put up with her carping about my clothes or my laziness.

I suppose she wants to keep on being a Court. Part of the family she split up. My *loving stepmother*, Alexandra. Just looking at the envelope made me feel sick.

If only I still had my real mother. If only I could remember her better. I don't even have a clear memory of Penelope, as if all the tears had washed it away. I remember losing her, of course. Days of howling. Dad silent and grim. Alexandra rushing round like a headless chicken, snapping at Dad, and ignoring us. Another death that Alex caused. Mum would never have died if Dad hadn't left her.

— And perhaps if Mum was still alive I wouldn't have done the things I did. Things which will always be on my conscience. However many children I help at school, however many children I might have myself — and I don't suppose I will; there's almost no time left — those deaths are on my conscience. I hated the idea of abortion always, but I went and had three. It was all like a dream. Then afterwards you wake up, and they're gone, and the misery stays, and the longing for them. Feminists tell me I'm mad, or feeble, but I sometimes feel like a murderess.

Alexandra should watch her back. I'm like my father, murderous.

And there it goes sprawling into the bin, letter and envelope and all, her clawed black hand, her false bloody kisses, *thinking about the old days . . . sweet girl . . .*

I'm not very sweet any more, Alexandra.

I lost my sweetness years ago.

— Ah, there's Madonna coming up for breakfast. She must have smelled coffee, great . . .

I'm terribly fond of Madonna of course but I sometimes wonder about her judgement. She's fascinated by Dad and Alex. She thinks it's an incredibly romantic story, which I suppose it is, in a way, if you don't happen to have lived in the shadow of it. When I told her Alexandra had written she snatched the letter out of the bin. She managed to put me back in a good temper — it's one of her talents, cheering me up. She can make me feel my background is picturesque rather than a series of appalling fuck-ups. It doesn't last but it helps for a bit.

'At least your stepmother isn't dull! All those men fighting over her . . . death and mayhem wherever she goes . . . and always smart as paint, you say. She's stunning in those photos upstairs. *Definitely* a role model for me. I'm so bored with working non-stop for stardom . . . When I do have time for a personal life, I'm going to go for it, wow . . . something fabulously melodramatic like hers.'

I could never get mad with Madonna. She's so full of life, she makes me crack up with laughter . . . she sometimes comes on like a real bitch but I know it's just a game.

'Why not write back. Go on. To the Plaza. It's so great that she's going to be at the Plaza, as a final gesture when I left Armand I took him to dinner at the Plaza — saved my wages for a week to do it and told him I was leaving him over the *petits pots au chocolat*, and he threw it, my darling, on the tablecloth, a man of sixty acting like a child . . . Everyone stared. I didn't care a bit. I mean, I cared about him, I suppose, but not the

206

stares, and I thought the farewell meal was a brilliant idea. I think things *should* have theatrical endings.'

Armand was the man who she followed to New York, breaking Dan Brown's heart in the process. 'Was he really sixty? You're so over the top. Your older men are older than anyone else's . . .'

'He *said* he was sixty. I suspect he was more. I don't give a shit. I adore older men. They spoil one so. As long as they can still do it . . .'

'Can they?'

'*Mine* can. I make sure of that.'

'What do you like about them?'

'They've lived. I want to find out what they know, I want to suck it out of them . . .'

We both shrieked with laughter at the same time. 'No wonder they like you if you suck it out of them.'

'You can go on making love till you die.' She was serious now. 'I do like old men. I find them terribly sexy. Everyone thinks it's because of Dad walking out but it isn't, I never much cared for my Dad, I just find those rugged, silver-haired types incredibly appealing . . . besides, to be frank, they're unlikely to be poor. Men my own age are mostly poorer than me, and I work bloody hard for my money, I don't fancy spending it on other p — . . . I don't fancy spending it on my boyfriends.'

Money is a bit of an awkward topic. Household expenses have got out of hand. Madonna earns good money, and often buys treats – champagne, strawberries, scrummy organic meat from the wildly expensive butcher near her offices – but never remembers we have to have washing-up liquid, and bread, and potatoes, and have to pay the gas and the phone. I've been overspending on the garden, even though Dad sent money for the garden last year, which paid for a shed and some new shrubs and trees to replace the ones we lost in the gales. But there've been more gales since then, and in any case I'm mad on growing things, I really love to make new things live and grow, baby tomatoes, miniature roses . . . It's my passion, the one thing I spend money on. I don't spend a lot of money on myself. But teachers don't earn much, either. And life seems more expensive, now Madonna lives here, though I'm sure she is contributing . . .

In any case she had a brilliant idea. If she came up and shared the top four floors with me, we could convert the basement, and rent it. That would rake in a lot of geld. Except the conversion would cost a fortune.

A fortune to us, but not to Dad.

And so I'm going to make myself write to him.

In any case, Madonna's right, it's sad not to be in touch. He's in Venice, just a half-hour flight away. I've been mad at him – I suppose I've been sulking – ever since he wouldn't let me visit him in prison. He never answered my letters properly. And at the funeral he stared straight through me; so he never explained the whole dreadful mess. Mary Brown says he must have been in shock, but at the time it just seemed he didn't give a fuck. So I decided not to care about him. I've only written once since he came out of prison, and that was to ask him for money. I did it on a postcard to hurt him, a four-line postcard with a stupid picture.

We go on and on, tit for tat, all the time. He hurts me, I hurt him, it's so bloody childish, and I'm in my late thirties, as Madonna reminded me. Coming up forty. Oh God, getting old . . .

This time I'll write a proper letter. Nice. Be nice. And full of news. Asking him for money for the basement, OK, but also asking him – why not? – asking him if we could maybe get together. He is my father. I – . . . yes, it's true. I'd like to see him. I long to see him, when I think about it. It's just that I don't expect it any more. I don't expect to see my family. I learned the hard way what not to expect. I expect them to die, or abandon me.

The letter is Madonna's idea, but I'm keen. He's never said No when I ask for money.

– And he might be lonely. P'raps he wants to see me. P'raps it's the shame that's stopping him.

He's still never told me what really happened. The newspaper stories were such junk.

'How can you *bear* not knowing?' That's Madonna, shrieking, clutching her forehead. She's in a lather of anticipation. She wants me to get him here at once so she can give her hero the fourth degree.

Dad a hero!

Dad was never a hero.

He and Alexandra and their hammy old love story. (*But how could she write and never mention Dad?*)

She knows what happened on the day of the killing. She was there, and I'm positive she drove him to it – and now she's living another novel with another man in South America, and Dad's still mourning her in Venice . . . I bet he's faithful to her memory.

I wish he would tell me what really happened.

22

Alexandra: São Benedicto, Brazil, 2005

Middle of the night. I've never liked night. Night-life, yes, parties, dancing, black satin and candlelight . . .

But in the wilds of Brazil. After they put out the lights. After the clothes come off. And my companion goes to sleep . . . (why do other people sleep more than me, better than me, dream-lessly?) . . . I feel so terribly alone. And the past comes back. The past claws back. By day I am alight with the glorious future, but at night there is only . . . *what I have done.*

I no longer know what these thoughts mean, these phrases that come like tiny stones tossed across the floor of my aching brain. *What I have done, what I have done.* It means nothing to me, for I've done nothing – nothing, that is, to agonise over, but the words mutter on of their own accord, and at night there is nothing to drive them away.

At night the child seems unreal. I can't believe she will ever be there, with us, near us, a breathing presence, a little body entrusted to us. Do they wake at night, at three years old? Will she call for me? Shall we hear her calling? What a mercy it will be to hear the voice of a child instead of these crazy, meaningless echoes.

What have you done . . . what have you done? . . .

What I have done . . . what I have done . . .

– God in heaven! It's the end of the world! Benjamin, wake up, save me, they're shooting, it's a revolution, we'll be killed in our beds . . .

The pig. He turns over, scratches himself, grunts like an animal, snores again. I'd better go and look. I'm not a coward.

– Firecrackers. How stupid of me. Of course they are always playing with fireworks, there's always a *santo* to celebrate or some primitive ritual like christening a lorry . . . lots of black shapes, stamping, dancing, a fire, firecrackers – nothing special. I must be nervous. It's the strain of waiting.

For a second I went back five years. I was sure it was gunfire, I was sure I'd be killed, I could almost smell that peculiar singed metallic smell that hung on the air. In that shabby little room in New York City where I'd tried to be happy, where we were happy . . .

Christopher. Christopher, my love. Why did you do it? Why didn't you wait? I would have got bored with him if you had waited. I'm bored with him now, bored to death. What you did only forced us together . . .

I don't really know what's true any more.

What did I do . . . what have I done?

Isaac rallied and relapsed innumerable times. He'd had every bit of medical help that could be bought with his money, or with ours, he had taken up cycling when he could hardly walk, he'd gone on working, slumped in his office, then moved all the computers up into his flat, where there were always paintings coming and going, and Isaac dragging round, always tired, but still eager, turning up one, dismissing another.

I was amazed to see how many friends he had. Perhaps it was just us who made him truculent and vengeful; perhaps he had never been like that with his friends. They embraced freely; they laughed a lot, often at jokes I didn't understand. Some of them wore peculiar clothes and some of them did not look well, but they really seemed to care for Isaac. Sometimes I almost felt envious. Perhaps it was friendship that kept him alive.

When he was finally bedridden, when he was too thin and weak to get up, he went on talking, talking, to them, a torrent of life from the propped-up death's-head.

I liked to buy presents for the children. It made it easy when they asked for things. But when someone's dying, there's nothing, nothing. Or nothing you can know about. Perhaps there was something, but I never found it.

One day I realised he had changed so much he no longer looked like Isaac at all. No link to the solid boy we once knew in the face pared down to the form of a skull, the lids and lips pulled tightly back, grinning and staring as his voice ground on, the painfully naked, sinewed neck which poked like a wrist from his dressing-gown. Life had its bit between his teeth; will and adrenalin were driving him on down the final strait towards the year 2000.

As Isaac neared death, in some geometrical but entirely unjustifiable way, so did my hopes of his father.

We didn't talk about conceiving any more, but then, there were so many things we didn't talk about. Chief among them, love and death had slipped off the agenda. I thought about it all the time, but so differently from how I did at first, when everything seemed so miraculously hopeful . . . I remember with astonishment now how at first when we started to fuck for a baby I used to imagine I could feel Chris's sperm swimming up inside me, tiny explosive presences, small stars electric with future life, sweeping up through my welcoming body . . . except that the welcome didn't come off. Now I no longer expected it.

Yet I couldn't stop hoping entirely; those were unusual times, crazy times, in the frenetic run-up to the millennium everything seemed fluid, fantastic, there were prophecies of apocalypse, promises of the Second Coming, technological miracles as the first group of rocket-borne sightseers shuttled round the earth and looked down on us, returning amazed and voluble . . . in the best private laboratory they tried with our dreams for over two years, they took my eggs, they took his sperm, they tried to perform the most mundane of tricks that street children manage at the age of thirteen and they failed, they failed, and we failed too. Each month the bleeding still made me sad, I walked round too fast, clumsy and furious, knocking things over, growling at servants; roses spilled, doors banged, I wept. At those times Chris was always kind.

But one month he snapped when I shouted at him, perhaps because Isaac had just given up work. 'You're not the only one in the world with problems. You shut me out of everything. Have you forgotten I wanted us to have a child over twenty years ago, when you really could have got pregnant . . .? Not just this bloody . . . *nonsense* . . . and *misery*.'

So he thought the whole enterprise nonsensical. That hurt, hurt. That was dangerous. Christopher was fifteen years older than me. I had started to think about that a lot. His energy was flagging, clearly. Was it fair for a baby to have a father in his sixties, even if Chris could manage it?

I clung on to my hope of a child with Chris, but there were two of me, and the other one was making alternative plans. *I admit I'm nearly fifty, but that's not old, especially if the father were younger than me . . . I would be giving myself the best chance, that's all. A lovely young man, it wouldn't be impossible* . . . The second self started to look about her.

– Meanwhile, Chris was planning, and I was applauding, a spectacular millennial celebration. We would greet the year 2000 together. By then we'd have managed a quarter of a century! It would be a monument to our love! So he told me, a little uncertainly, and I agreed, the first self agreed.

The rich went mad over the millennium. The rich love parties; count me in. The mega-rich and mega-great competed to hold their parties in places that symbolised richness and greatness, the Eiffel Tower, the Taj Mahal, the Pyramids, Ceausescu's Palace – all of them had their parties planned. The Millennium Society hired ultrasonic aircraft to chase the dawn of the year 2000 around the world on a cloud of champagne. Millions of bottles of the stuff were selling, far too many for them all to be real. I suppose the poor who knew no better must have bought inferior imitations.

Isaac was on a drip by now. He hadn't eaten solids for several weeks. He lay there, inhuman, frighteningly human, the merest contraption of skin and bone, but in his eyes was burning will. It was no longer possible to read his emotions. All you could see was fire. His remains – they were already his remains, the emaciated husk of him – were held from the edge of death by that single blaze of will and fear.

Christopher had finalised our plans. Perhaps they were corny, but all the millennial ideas were corny, the idea of celebrating is corny – we have to do it, though, or else we die . . . Chris had booked for the party in the Statue of Liberty as soon as it was clear we couldn't leave New York, for Isaac would never leave New York, Isaac would be buried in New York. Every place had been taken for over two years, but Chris paid five hundred times the going price.

We asked Isaac if he would like us to stay with him. He said there was no need. We offered to take him anywhere he wanted; all of us knew what that offer meant in terms of the medics, the drips, the machines which would have to come with us on any expedition; all of us knew it was impossible. Isaac declined impatiently. 'My friend Benjamin's coming back. He's been away painting for months; I've missed him. I'm going to give a little party. I'll just drink some champagne,' he gasped, in the peculiar, rasping voice which had started to take over from his proper one. 'A thimbleful. So what if it kills me. Not through a drip. The regular way. With my friends. My friends are all coming round. They're my family. They won't desert me.'

I was terribly relieved that we didn't have to take him. My feelings about Isaac were changing. At first it had been easy to love him ill, because I knew the demand wouldn't go on for ever. But his dying was terribly long. How could he look so ill and still not be dead? There was nothing left of him, yet he was still here. Angry, triumphant, elated by turns, insisting that we listen.

Feelings I'm not proud of surfaced. There was a terrible monotony about his voice, rasping, coughing, yet still roaring on, trying to talk himself into the future. The room had a familiar, sickening smell, sickening because I spent so much time there, rubber, disinfectant, more disinfectant, ecological air-fresh, orange-juice, and if the nurse hadn't taken the bedpan away, urine and shit; all life was here. I felt claustrophobic in that room; he felt the cold, so all windows were shut; his was the most powerful face in the room, and I was fascinated and appalled by the glaring gargoyle which stared at me. *My name is death* it said. *Hallo. Once you didn't believe in me.*

Most shamefully, I became afraid of infection, though I hadn't been afraid all through his illness. Though I knew intellectually there was no risk, though I know what the doctors worried about was us infecting him. As his body collapsed further into itself it was as if all the barriers that kept us separate had melted away, leaving me utterly exposed. When he spat out words, I watched the drops of spittle spraying out in the bedside light. When he wiped his nose on his hand I blenched, because now he liked to hold my hand, after resisting my touch all through his illness he suddenly needed to hold my hand, he lay there gripping it, roaring at the darkness, long rambling monologues about the past.

I gave my hand like a long-ago present. I never complained. I sat there and listened. I was glad that at last I had something to give. I paid the old debts, day after day.

But another part of me didn't hear a word. Another part of me longed to get away. I was thinking about babies, and the twenty-first century, and what it would mean to be fifty years old, and whether I would ever take another lover, and what I would wear to the Statue of Liberty. This other part of me wanted him to die . . .

No, all of me wanted Isaac to die; he should be released, he had suffered enough; I should be released, I had done my best.

– I longed for December 31st. I wanted to forget every depressing thing. I wanted to drown myself in Guerlain. I wanted to drape my still-girlish body in flame-red taffeta, ready to dance. I wanted the music to pick me up and fly me over the towers of Manhattan, diamanté strips against the roof of the night, whirl me up and around the globe, over all the places where we had been happy, and perhaps I should start to love Chris again . . . I wanted to be in love again.

I was bubbling, high, as I dressed for the ball. Christopher and I were high together, the occasion was bigger than our misery, the pain dissolved, we could laugh again. We stepped into a taxi and fought our way through the honking crowds with their millennial streamers, banners, hats to the queue for the boat. The Statue of Liberty had been lit up with rainbow lasers for the occasion; it looked vulgar, actually, a little unreal, a cartoon version of its statuesque self. It's the whiteness we love, the startling whiteness. But everything had to be dressed for the party; money had to be seen to be spent, given the money they were charging us.

The whole waterfront was alive with people who couldn't have afforded to join our party; every stone was trampled by dozens of feet, every lamp-post and litterbin and seat was leant-on, the bottles and cans were open already and the dry surfaces were damp with life, breathing, kissing, drinking, spilling. There were shouts and bursts of singing in the foreground, cabs honking, vendors yelling, people with hotdogs and popcorn and balloons and masks and drugs and sex to sell, faces and accents from all over the world, all the countries that we had visited, people I would normally never have noticed, because there's not time to look at them all, they pass down the margins of one's life without ever attracting one's attention – but tonight everyone felt special; everyone was shouting 'Look at me': I looked, since the chartered boat still hadn't come, and was amazed at first by how many they were, the faceless masses I usually ignored, how many faces they actually had, how boldly they seemed to look back at me, how many of them looked carefree and happy, how they surged back and forwards like the sea, as if they were all part of each other . . . the queue for the boat remained a little outside, trying to keep a space of our own since there wouldn't be room for everyone to join us . . . the larger crowd had shining faces, shining with sweat, black pores, red

216

lips, smoke, onions, sudden leaping bursts of jazz from a wireless but no, it was a jazz band playing their souls out in the middle distance, oblivious to everything, faces contorted with effort and joy (and sometimes I wish I had worked at something, worked my heart out like those trumpeters, I wished it, briefly but painfully, then . . .)

The foreground noise was deafening but all the same I made out something else in the background. Something like music, but without a tune, a kind of communal sighing, or whispering, something like prayer but without any words, a sigh like the corks coming out of champagne, millions of corks, millions of bottles. Then I realised what it was. It was all the earth's people holding their breath, laughing softly, sighing with excitement, standing together, chattering, dreaming; Chris said there were armistices in so many wars, they would end tomorrow but tonight there was peace, and this distant whisper was infinitely peaceful . . .

I wonder why it made me sad; I wonder why tears sprang to my eyes; I wonder why I felt left out, as if I had missed out on life's great secret, as if it was me who had been out in the cold and not these millions of faceless people . . .

But the sadness was the merest moment. We were all together. It was beautiful. As the boat took us across the light-tipped water the night was all round, a black satin night, a night that couldn't frighten me; it felt cool, for once, and clear for stars, a night which would magnify and not dampen, a night which could hide the rubbish barges and the piles of junk, the addicts, the derelicts, a night which would be our theatre.

'Did you see the children?' Christopher asked.

'No. Isn't it rather late for children?'

'There were some schools with banners. Hundreds of children. Waiting for the fireworks – you didn't hear them singing?'

'There was so much noise – I'm sorry I missed that. You should have pointed them out, darling.'

Looking back across the strait I did glimpse a banner, a brave red splash dipping and swooping above the crowd, but the faces were too small, we were too far away, the pity was that I couldn't see the children, but I smiled in their direction as the boat bumped the jetty, and a few minutes later as we stroked our hair and patted our clothes before entering the Statue we both turned for a second and looked back at the waving, shimmering mass of humanity stretched out along the water-front, waiting for fireworks and comets and marvels and blessings upon the rest of their life, waiting for the street party of a lifetime, and I think we both felt reluctant to leave them; but we had already made our decision, Christopher had paid an exorbitant price, we'd bought our tickets, now we had to use them. We kissed and went in out of the night.

But we left the best of it all outside. Inside all was planned, and therefore banal. Remember that Christopher and I had had two decades of eating in the best restaurants all over the world. We were very hard to please, or surprise. Now we were faced with festive food, spectacular but tasting of dust.

The centrepiece was an enormous cake in the shape of the earth, carefully iced with seas and continents, prettily coloured, suspended on a plinth with considerable art; it hadn't crumbled yet, though the first guests inside the Statue must have flung themselves upon it with great fervour for a lot of the cake had already been eaten, much of the polar regions gone, Europe nibbled, the green patched with brown where the icing had been stolen; around it were similar but smaller set-pieces, a mountain of caviare shaped like a whale, terrines and pâtés in the form of a rhino, a kangaroo, an elephant . . . star-shaped dishes, moon-shaped dishes, dishes based on every national flag with stripes of radish and tomato and salsify that rapidly became indecipher-able as spoons plunged in and broke them up; there were rather appealing marzipan mock-ups of famous buildings from all over the world, from the Leaning Tower of Pisa to the Sydney Opera House, all looking less clichéd in sepia miniature, there were meat-loaves like primitive space rockets, a shortcrust steam-train pulling carriages of cheese, jellies and mousses like passion-flowers or peonies, wonderfully life-like but smelling of soap, an icecream model of the Palace of Versailles which began to melt as the mob pressed round, and many other fantasies I must have forgotten, for even at the time my head was spinning . . .

Everything was there that anyone might want but all of it was in fancy dress — and so were we, so who were we to complain?

On a long side-table there was a display of glazed bread baked into the form of Twentieth Century Immortals; I know that's what they were because the legend told me so, but they were an ill-assorted and misshapen crew, who ranged from Charlie Chaplin and Albert Einstein to Michelle Pfeiffer and Samuel Beckett (that posturing Frenchman a Human Immortal! At college he had made my first year modern languages course a misery, he *was* a misery, endlessly banging on about poverty and despair), Michael Jackson, Lucille Dupont, Mikhail Gorbachev, Margaret Thatcher — Margaret Thatcher! — I have never had the slightest interest in politics, but everything about her offended me — her joylessness, her sexlessness. She was the Britain we had left behind. Her long mean nose had been overglazed and bore a tiny accidental dewdrop of dough. I cut myself a slice of Margaret Thatcher and a larger piece of Samuel Beckett, but they sat like cardboard on the tongue, they were probably immortal because they were inedible!

Chris said, 'We're pathetic creatures, aren't we?' and for once I could agree with him. This peculiar feast was someone's idea of what mattered about life on earth, what was worth admiring and celebrating, but the symbols seemed random and disproportionate, a star and a rocket, the moon and a steam-train, everything now being broken up and swallowed in a giant orgy of consumption.

We were still in a good mood with each other; it was only an armistice, but it felt like peace. We laughed at the food and drank a lot of champagne. All over the world we knew that bottles of champagne were being turned into alcohol in the bloodstream, into gaiety and hope and excitable behaviour and not until much later, but inevitably, quarrels, headaches, hangovers, and who wouldn't take the former and never mind the latter? . . . we always had; we did, we did, we took our pleasures and the consequences —

(Except that I wonder. Now. Alone. In the heart of the sweaty Brazilian night. I wonder where all the pleasures have gone. All I can feel are consequences ... what have I done, what have I done?)

We wandered about, arm in arm, smiling with delight at the few young faces there, few because few of the young could afford it, and smiling in a different way at the overdecked, overlifted old, not wishing them ill, just glad we were different. We still weren't old. *I wasn't old.* My hair and my dress were flaming red, when I danced my body felt like a young girl's, and I danced that night for hours and hours, enjoying the way men looked at me, for I still had power, I could still make them want me ...

(Only five years ago. How slowly time begins to speed up.)

Chris grew tired of dancing. Chris grew tired. He was fifteen years older than me, remember. 'Let's find a good seat to see the fireworks.'

A stupendous firework display was promised for midnight; everyone in New York would be watching. The champagne — too much, for they were pouring it like water — made me more wilful than usual. 'I'm not ready to sit down yet. You go, darling.'

'But we have to see in the New Year together – '

'Of course I'll come, but not yet, don't fuss ...'

In fact, I didn't know the precise time, because the watch that matched the flame-red dress had been snatched from my wrist on the wide sunlit sidewalk of Kalakaua Avenue, Hawaii, and I'd never found another precisely right, but I intended to dance into the twenty-first century, I was too young to sit down yet.

— And so it happened that I missed the moment and we didn't celebrate it side by side; I was spinning round the suddenly surprisingly vacant dance-floor, admiring myself in the enormous mirrors brought into the Statue for the occasion, a scarlet woman, spinning like a leaf, when I suddenly heard shooting; a tremendous fusillade of guns; the figure in the mirror stopped dead in her tracks; the orchestra, which I later realised had gone on playing just for me, lurched to a ragged halt; after a millisecond's pause they struck up Auld Lang Syne, and I knew that the firing had been for midnight as the sky outside the high strips of window burst into a tracery of brilliant colours, everyone was cheering, I was alone.

I walked forward on my own across the gleaming floor into the twenty-first century, looking for Christopher, Christopher, the love of my life, Christopher who was looking for me.

After the fireworks ended my energy ebbed. The champagne had undermined vast tracts of my brain; at a certain moment, the whole subsided, gaiety crumbled, I wanted to escape. I had a nagging sense of sadness; it was childish to bother about a mere ritual, but how had I managed to miss the moment? How had we failed to live it together? It seemed like an omen, or a proof of something. The twenty-first century had started badly. I wanted to go home, though the hotel wasn't home, I wanted to sleep and wake up different, I wanted to abandon the attempt to be happy and try again in another life.

But Christopher wanted to look in on Isaac, Christopher who never suggested visits to his son and avoided them whenever he could. I said I'd take a cab back to the flat alone, but it soon became clear, when we got back to the mainland, that no one was going anywhere except on foot.

'Come with me, Alex. He'd like to see you. He's done what he said he would; he's made it.'

We were only four blocks from Isaac's penthouse apartment, but just this one time I wasn't ready to face it.

'It's you he loves. You're his father. Go.'

'Things change, Alexandra. He loves you now.'

And for some reason, probably the champagne, I remember my eyes filling with tears, though I'd known for a long time that Isaac had grown to love me; the fact of Chris saying it, his father saying it, seemed to me inexpressibly moving, as if he was saying I was . . . *motherly*, but by that stage why did it matter to me, when I'd more or less abandoned hope of Chris and of mothering? Whatever the reason, the tears welled up, and the extraordinary scene on the waterfront all round us of thousands of people jostling and swaying, screaming and singing, kissing and dancing, black and yellow and pink and brown, all the wonderful colours of flesh, very young and very old, people with Giancarlo Ongaro dresses and people in rags and carrier-bags, yes even the derelicts, cheering and fighting – blurred into a swelling river of colours, I hugged my husband, I entered the river. I no longer knew where the edges were, my sadness spilled into a larger feeling which felt like love; for Chris, for Isaac? For life, as well, and for myself.

'Of course I'll come. I felt tired for a moment.'

So we went together to call on Isaac. There was an English voice on the entryphone. A tall young man answered the door. Strikingly tall, strikingly handsome. Perhaps it was the friend, the English painter. Isaac had warned me he was beautiful. The voices of the others floated down the stairs, happy voices, slightly tipsy.

'Hi,' he said, 'I'm Benjamin. Happy Millennium. Good to meet you.'

He took my hand, and held on to it. *Why are all the best-looking men homosexual?* I remember thinking as he smiled at me in the merciless light of the lobby. I wished that my skin were as perfect as his. Marvellous eyes, very large, deep brown. The pupils seemed to widen as he looked at me. Luminous, black. He pulled me inside.

Isaac lasted until April, to the doctors' astonishment. There was one last rally in the first week of February when Benjamin began to draw him; Isaac insisted he be propped up on pillows, and his heavy skull strained up like an eagle. Talking was too much of an effort by then, but Benjamin talked to him about painting and I sat and listened by the side of the bed. At the end of one visit Isaac wrote me a note: *Munch. The Dance of Life. Book?*

At last, at last I could get him something. I felt as if *he* had given *me* a present. I wanted to hug him tight as I left, but remembered his fragility. Instead I put my arms round him – it was so easy to put my arms right round him, lifting him from the pillows like an egg-shell – and kissed him gently on the lips, though it was teeth that my lips encountered. Maybe I shouldn't have done it – a virus would have killed him – but I felt too full of life to do harm. As I straightened and turned I found Benjamin looking at me with peculiar intensity. I'd realised by then that he wasn't homosexual. I saw he was falling in love with me. I went out to a bookstore and came straight back with a mammoth biography of Edvard Munch that contained a double-spread print of 'The Dance of Life', terribly excited and pleased with myself, but Benjamin had left and Isaac was asleep.

Next day Chris decided to come with me; I couldn't dissuade him. The book lay there still wrapped in its pale tissue paper. Isaac had relapsed. He stared at me as if I were the Reaper come to fetch him, but then I realised he was staring straight through me. It was a relief when his eyelids closed. We sat by his bed for almost an hour in the stony silence he inspired in us. Then Benjamin arrived to join the congregation; our eyes slid uneasily over each other, Chris's eyes, my eyes, Benjamin's eyes, a nervous ballet of fear and desire. Isaac showed no sign of waking. The room was becoming intolerably stuffy.

Benjamin suggested that Chris and I might like to go out and get a coffee. Chris declined; he would sit with his son. 'Maybe you and I could go then,' I said to Benjamin, breathing hard, that familiar, that wonderful, forgotten little tremor beginning in my stomach as I said the words not looking at the boy, then looking at him, his golden skin, his magnificent eyes, all of him saying *yes* – whereas Chris and I only said *no* to each other, no baby, no hope, no fun.

In the coffee-bar Benjamin told me he loved me, as I had known he would. He said two things which went straight to my heart.

'You're so *beautiful*, Alexandra. Your hair, your eyes, your skin, the way you move in that room, where there isn't any room to move gracefully with all the shit Isaac has to have, but you manage it, you're lithe as a cat, I'm mad to paint you, will you let me, please – ' So that was one thing; I could still be beautiful. Fifty years old, but still fit to be painted.

There was something more important, though. Benjamin thought me *sweet* and *kind*. 'I can't believe that someone so good-looking is so gentle and maternal, too. You're a wonderful woman, Alexandra.'

It was balm to my wounds. Oil on the waters. Oil on the waters of old regrets. Marvellous to be thought good by someone, marvellous, enlivening to be praised. I needed praise; I have never had enough.

Even Chris was too depressed to praise me any more (why should he praise me? I made him unhappy). Our love-making was dogged by the shadow of failure. Recently he had had difficulty coming; he found it depressing, but what about me? It's insulting to a woman when a man doesn't come . . . worse, Chris knew that I felt that way, so now when he did come I suspected he was faking. I had never thought sex could abandon us; but if it did, if it had . . . I might look elsewhere, if he forced me to. I looked, and Benjamin looked back.

March was already baking hot, the hottest spring for the last five years. In Isaac's room the air-conditioning rushed and so did the rise and fall of his breathing; he'd refused to go into hospital – he wanted to stay with his plants and his pictures. He no longer talked, but his eyes opened. I wondered if he noticed what was happening, how often my visits coincided with Benjamin's, how our eyes swerved together across the room above the top of the surgical masks we sporadically wore to protect him from colds . . . it was rather a joke, wearing that mask, after Benjamin told me it made me seem like a woman in a harem.

Maybe death makes life seem more acute. That must be part of the point of it, to frighten and excite the living. The first time we fucked was extraordinary.

– And I never thought about AIDS, not once, not as something which could apply to me. I was lucky, wasn't I? I couldn't die. Sex had always meant pleasing myself, and later, much too much later, babies. It didn't mean death. It couldn't mean death. I never realised the two were related.

*

We couldn't go back to our apartment, of course, but nor could we go to Benjamin's place which he shared with a crotchety Bulgarian sculptor who exhibited his work to all Benjy's visitors. So we ended up in a dark little room that Benjamin found, in a hotel straight out of the nineteenth century, with *stairs*, and no telephones in the rooms, and no security in reception, no lounge, but we didn't need a lounge, no room service, but we serviced ourselves, no air-conditioning, but we didn't notice. A view of pigeons and fire-escapes. (Benjamin was not very rich just then; he hadn't found a dealer to replace Isaac; so perhaps it was the money as much as the romance that took us to the Arlington.) In any case it was ours, it was perfect, and the first time we fucked was unforgettable.

We fucked, and laughed, and smoked, and talked, and fucked again, for hours. His impatience was glorious, glorious. As soon as we had turned the key in the lock – a mortice key! a rusty little lock – and shut the door again behind us, his hands were pushing up under my blouse, he was kissing my breasts, he was holding my arms, his voice was shaking as he said my name, he had pulled my pants down over my feet and was down on his knees on the threadbare carpet, moaning as he breathed in the smell of my sex, as his mouth pushed up between my thighs and his tongue found the hard little tongue at my centre; I begged him to stop, I was falling, dying, we had to lie down, we tore our clothes off, saying nothing, clumsy, furious, clasped each other on the bed at last, naked at last, nothing could stop us – I groaned as I felt his heavy penis nudging against me like a dog, I pulled him inside me, I had to be filled. He came in seconds, roaring, helpless, and lay for a few minutes stunned in my arms. Then we both started laughing. 'Your turn next. I want to have you four times today.' Actually I think it was only three, but it was like being young, I was young again.

It was boiling hot. We had stripped the bed. We lay together, smoking, naked. I always smoked for births and deaths; this felt like the birth of the rest of my life. The sunset light on our flanks was red. His cock was big; he was a big young man; his balls were beautiful, heavy, hard; his hands were big, but extremely gentle, as if they had known and touched me for ever. The window was open, and life flowed in. It was so different from where we usually met, with everything covered, carpeted, masked, disinfected, hushed, restricted, dead. No one opens windows in New York, but we flung them wide, though the air is lethal, it was air from the sky, not a filtering system, and in the quiet moments when we lay and smoked a lifetime of fragments of remembered sound floated up above the traffic's dull roar, laughter, screams, doors banging, a dog, church bells escaped from long-ago Europe, the horns of taxis blaring for someone – and rich smells of frying onions and liver, everything cheap and anarchic and young, his hot young skin against my hot skin, and what did it matter if his were younger?

Behind the hotel was a long strip of wasteland, a makeshift garden, raggedly green. Very faintly, we heard those noises too, green noises from another world, the thwacks and screams of a game of baseball, children shouting, an icecream van, then louder, clearer, a baby crying. Benjamin and I made love again.

– I thought, *I could leave Christopher. When Isaac has died. When Chris is over it.*

I stopped pursuing Chris for sex. If I wasn't so happy, I'd have been more cunning. I had all the sex I wanted, now. I was nice to him, though. I was kind to him. I knew he had found no way through to Isaac, and he would only accept that once Isaac was dead. The suspended possibility was horribly painful, even though Isaac could communicate with no one, only drips and drugs got through to him. He could signal only by blinking his eyes: there would be no more rallies, no more presents. But he wasn't dead. Chris suffered it. I was sorry for him, doubly sorry.

And yet, he bored me, he irritated me, he slept in my bed, a weight of gloom, wordlessly asking me for something. I longed for everything to be over. We were in the twenty-first century now; I was ready for it, I was glowing with life, but the past hung dying round my neck.

I failed to conceal my happiness.

One day I came in from an afternoon of visiting Isaac and fucking Benjamin and found Chris sobbing on the bed. A horrible sound, strangled, despairing, head down on the pillow, deaf to the world. The video screen was a forgotten snowstorm reminding me of something bad, something heartbreaking from the past. Either he hadn't heard me come in or he didn't care. His shoulders heaved. Perhaps he wanted me to find him, wanted me to love and comfort him. My stomach contracted with dread.

I couldn't do it. I felt like a stranger. I was no longer the woman he was waiting for. He was waiting for me, but I had moved on. In some terrible way I didn't care, though another part of me was shocked, frightened. But my capacity for pity was dulled by joy; all afternoon I had been so happy.

The same old truth about long marriages; it all reduces to a struggle for power. I had lived with Chris for twenty-six years, I'd been happy with him, I'd suffered with him, and now it seemed we had come to an end I was glad that he, and not I, was weeping. After twenty-six years there was bound to be weeping.

– I pretended, of course, because he frightened me. I pretended that he was crying for Isaac. 'Poor darling,' I said, the solicitous nurse, I sat on the bed, I stroked his hair, I looked away but I stroked his hair. 'It'll soon be over. This week, maybe. The doctor reckons the end of the week. You could come with me if it would make you feel better.' (I was safe saying that; it made him feel worse; he never visited without feeling worse.)

But the sobbing went on. He didn't play. 'Alex,' he sobbed. 'Alex, Alex.' Not sobbing for Isaac, sobbing for me. The devastating smell of another body that he had somehow sensed on me.

It was twenty minutes before he stopped. I walked about doing unnecessary things with exaggerated concentration, speaking calmly and gently, as if to a child, always of Isaac, never of us. When he managed to stop, he said nothing. Because we said nothing, both of us knew. It was as clear as accusation and confession.

But still I knew I could not walk out. Not possible, with Isaac dying.

And so things moved towards their end. So we moved towards our end.

And five years later I don't understand: why was the choice so clear to me? Why was I so sure I could be happy with Benjy? Why did I think that leaving would be easy, that everything would go according to plan?

I think I could no longer imagine Christopher. We lived side by side, but I never saw him, I stopped myself feeling what he felt because that was difficult, painful. Now the same thing has happened with Benjamin.

In my mind Chris became an old man, an invalid, someone who suffered, and would suffer from me, but who would have to accept what I did to him.

I didn't realise how much he loved me. I didn't see that he was half-crazy. I didn't know he would kill for me.

What have I done, what have I done?

23

Christopher: Venice, 2005

Lucia doesn't realise who she's working for. She thinks her master is old and frail. Her soups get thinner, her coffee weaker. She talks a lot about my heart and frets if the windows are left open at night because of 'unhealthy airs' from the canal; she tells me I'll *prendere un raffredore*, as if I would expire at a breath of wind. If I walk in the sun it's just as bad – 'Wear your hat,' she shouts from the door, 'the sun is cruel to grandfathers.'

Grandfathers! Christopher a grandfather! I lack grand-children to soften the sting of that . . . I'd show her who was a grandfather if she would come upstairs with me.

And yet she is right. I'm a cold old man.

Why does loneliness increase desire? My wishes are hot, but my heart is cold. It's true, I have grown colder, cruder. I was once a nice man, so Alex told me. She even said I was a feminist. But now I hate all women, now I detest the whole gang of them! Why shouldn't I hate them, since none of them loves me?

Inside my good clothes, which are as elegant as ever, perhaps more showy than when I was younger (but then, I have to display myself, for no one knows me for what I am) – beneath my silk shirts and perfect jackets I sometimes feel that I am nothing. Unlovely and unloved. Night after night I lie on my own, and my nakedness is no longer what it was when Alex lay beside me. Then there was . . . – a simplicity, a perfect comfort, a sense of rightness; here I was, undisguised, unprotected, and there she was, she saw me and loved me. We seemed to expand as we took off our clothes, taking possession of our shared space. Infinitely precious, those nights together, the sleeping together as much as the sex, the way our skins breathed into each other, the way our dreams must have crossed and touched even when we were no longer speaking to each other (and we didn't once sleep in separate beds, I was her pillow, she was my sheets), a quarter of a century of shared oblivion.

Now I feel small and exposed. I curl in bed like an elderly foetus, feeling my knees, touching my shins, checking that I'm still there. My heart is too loud in my eardrum where the ear is pressed against the pillow. There are strange little pains in my limbs, creeping reminders of trouble to come, little promises that things will get worse. If I've drunk too much coffee (or too much wine too early in the day to be soporific), the tide of wakefulness roars in my veins. That and the voices. Regrets, worries. Shots, screams, sirens blaring. The same shots, screams, sirens, from the same day in the unforgiving past, sounds I shall hear for the rest of my life. And memories of prison. The shit, the urine, the endless locking and unlocking of doors, the men who howled like animals. And the older, slyer, whispering memories of the other corridors I've never quite escaped, the fluorescent corridors I lived my life in in the days when I was like other men, when I had a job, when I had ambition. When I was still part of the race for prizes, when adrenalin still flooded my veins, when I fought and drank and talked with men . . . in the small hours I hear them laughing at the bar, Terry Fraser, my old mate Ian, Graham Healey who did so well after I left, the old male crowd I was once a part of before I gave everything up for that woman. I lie here and listen to them laughing at me.

– And the real noises of the Venetian night. Sounds of strange falls, of the tide sucking, of distant thrashing commotions of water which could be waterbirds taking off or could be the bodies of small children drowning . . . or perhaps the very first faint flurries of the final cataclysmic collapse which will draw us all down into the hungry mud. The great flood barriers have been a disaster; it's as sure as death, we know it will come, Venetians have been hoping for a hundred years that nothing will happen till tomorrow, and tomorrow . . .

I think it will come one night, when human beings are easier to drown, all those white bodies laid out sleeping, ready. Sometimes at night I feel a trembling which I think is the world, and not me. A very faint series of shudders, as if the millions of wooden piles on which Venice is built were settling lower, finding their level, a level a little nearer the end.

It's suicide to stay, of course. I stay because I deserve no better. I'm too much of a coward for suicide, but I shouldn't protest if death came for me.

I would like to stand with my eyes open and face the wall of water. I'd like not to run away. I would like to be brave like the amazing Chinese students in Tiananmen Square sixteen years ago, who stood unarmed and faced the wall of bullets, others replacing them as they fell, and looked it in the eyes, the end of their future.

— You see, I still weep when I think of them. Perhaps part of it is that it makes me feel lonely; there's no one to stand with me, no one to replace me, no one to notice if I die well. In my life there have been no causes, not since the early days in television news when I felt there was truth to be fought for. Later the truth grew more complicated, tatty, piecemeal, a compromise, accepting other people's notions of 'priorities', accepting other people's view of 'balance', accepting that we shouldn't be 'negative'. In short, accepting a lie. And then the only truthful thing left seemed to be my feeling for Alex. She was my own, specific, immediate. The air between us wasn't fogged with consensus. I never had to lie when I told her I loved her, because I always loved her, you see.

I didn't have a cause, but I had an idea. Living for Alex was my idea. Loving another finite, time-bound individual. To go on loving her through time, to go on loving her till death. So love was dignified by death, since death is what makes us unique and precious, the fact we shall not come again. It makes us more interesting than worms or amoebae, endlessly splitting or redu-plicating, all those life-forms which never die.

And I think about love. Romantic love. Maybe love is romantic because we die; to love *this* person, this once-and-only person, on her single journey from birth to death . . . to stay faithful as you start to die yourself. Two unique individuals, facing life and death together. What painful rubbish, what a mockery when I think what a mess our lives became, and how stupidly death entered it . . .

I meant to love Alex until she died. That would have been a truthful life. OK, we never had children together, OK, we didn't give much to the world, we were individuals, that's all we were, bourgeois individuals, prigs might say – what do they know? What does anyone know? I *knew* my wife, I *loved* my wife, my lovely wife who will never come again.

And none of those students will come again, though now what they did is greatly honoured, though they have their place in the history books. They were all at the beginning of their lives. Most of them unmarried, they didn't leave children. I was fifty-four when those students died. I went on living, and I'm worth nothing.

Especially now Alex has gone. So the idea on which I based my life is valueless, since I've outlived it. I'm just an old man with too much money and too much time to dislike myself, waiting for death in a dying city.

Out, out, I must get out, a flash of sun on a seagull's wings. I must avoid Lucia on the stairs or she'll nag me to wear my Panama, which is not quite right for what I have in mind, it makes me look like a distinguished old gentleman, but it doesn't make me look much fun. I have to get out and find some fun, how dreadfully unfunny it is to need fun. Out into the daylight or go mad with gloom . . .

Buon giorno, Lucia. Good day, my dear. You're looking well, wonderfully well. Yes, *risotto alle vongole* would be delicious (God knows what filth those clams have grown in, but they still taste delicious, tossed in butter . . . everything swims in human shit). No, I shan't be needing my Panama. Thank you, Lucia. Until this evening . . .

And she lets me go, she gives me up, shaking her head in disapproval, her handsome head of blue-black hair so well restrained with invisible hairpins. They would fall on the ground like a barrage of hail if she would only let me have her. Sometimes I'm sure she's fond of me. Sometimes I think it's a little more . . . a hint of aggression, a hint of challenge in the way her brown eyes stare at me.

Besides, Lucia's here. Right on the premises, every day. If she would love me, I could stay at home. I shouldn't have to roam the dangerous streets, searching for some tart to milk my juice.

– There she is waving from my dark doorway, shouting something I can't hear, so I nod and smile and pretend I do, I don't want her to think I'm deaf and ancient, and I know from experience what she is saying as her large pale arms wave about like wings, she is probably pointing to last night's flood-mark, the fresh green stains on her ground-floor empire, or else she is warning me not to get robbed, there is a new young population of footpads squatting in the flooded, abandoned houses . . . What energy in those large pale waves. I screw up my eyes to see her better.

Aha, there's something in her hand! Letters, two of them, that's what she's shouting! Hope swells up within my heart. I won't go back now and open them in case they are only a disappointment, in case they are only bills or bank statements. No, she is stupid but not that stupid, she wouldn't wave a bill at me. They must be personal! Must be. At last!

I know that Mary has written to me. I'm sure, but not quite sure enough to test it . . . good God, it's taken her long enough. I posted mine four weeks ago – why did I think she would write at once? I'll take the pleasure of anticipation with me.

Goodbye, Lucia, you splendid woman. Perhaps we shall celebrate when I come home.

Abandoned!

Now I am entirely abandoned! Floods, come up and suck me down. A day of extraordinary reverses, great events, triumphs, catastrophes, more has happened to me today than in three years of existing in Venice . . .

I was a hero.

I was a clown.

I went, as usual pretending to myself that I had nothing

particular in mind, towards the waterfront behind the casino, facing the sulphurous lagoon, a region which is deserted now except for prostitutes. They seem to hold their life so cheap that they don't mind living by a lake of effluent, ammonia, naphtha, chlorine, cyanide, human sewage, detergents, oil . . . after all, we men put our rubbish inside them. What's outside must be nothing to them.

The flash of sun proved illusory. A dank rain started as I strolled through the streets. I stopped and bought an umbrella, then continued my apparently casual walk, drawn, as I knew but the cats and old women who silently watched me pass did not, towards the dark passes of the waterfront. They'd be fluttering there even if it were raining, bright little birds with welcoming eyes, girls in red stockings and daggerish heels which remind me of youth and the 1960s . . .

Funny that cats like Venice, when they don't like water or rain. It must be the promise of cadavers that does it. As I got away from the more populated streets and approached the edge of the red light district, the rain was so dense that it began to seem dark, and I started to notice the crying of a cat, locked out, I suppose, by a forgetful mistress, or abandoned by a family who had saved themselves.

The rain hammered down on the stone and the water. The cat kept crying against the rain. It was getting louder, not quieter.

— Till I realised it was a child, or a woman. Someone in a long reach of terror, or pain, for the cries had been coming for nearly five minutes. I ran towards them, or felt I was running, I forgot my age and slipped as I ran, landing hard on my rheumatic hips, jolting pain, green slime on my trousers, I wanted to sit there and suffer a little, but the cries were more desperate. I got up and ran on.

There was a half-open door in the blackened walls of a tenement house which looked deserted. Blistered paint. I hesitated, but the screams were definitely coming from there, and just as I pushed inside they quietened, a tiny, stinking porch full of bodies, the back of a man, a hulking brute, the face of a thin

234

terrified woman, red as a chicken's, he was wringing her neck, bulging eyes, bloated tongue, was she staring at me or staring through me? There was no room to see, no room to fight, I shouted the vilest curses I could think of and got his head in an elbow-lock, I was half on his back, being shaken against the slimy walls of the hall like a rat, one foot off the ground, the other slithering; but he couldn't have seen how old I was, we hadn't seen each other's faces, and all he wanted was to get away, just as all I wanted was to let him go, but I couldn't let go of his hold on my throat or I would have been flung headlong to the ground, he was battering my head and shoulders on the wall in a desperate attempt to fling me off . . .

The ridiculous struggle seemed to last for ever. He was cursing, too, in a steady stream. I kept my eyes fixed on the face of the woman who lay slumped on the ground where he had released her, a face which slowly became almost human as the gross distortions he had made relaxed, a face which registered nothing at first except a hunger to breathe again. Then something gathered. Concentrated hatred. She pulled herself up by the stairs behind her and drove her nails at her attacker's eyes. He staggered back, we staggered back, we were suddenly out in the rain again, then all the breath was knocked out of my body and I found myself flat on my back in the street with the girl yelling curses on her knees beside me. We were alone. The man had gone.

She started to weep, in the grey rain. She had a pretty face, badly bruised and swollen where he had battered her. But she smiled as she wept, a marvellous smile (though rather crooked and the teeth discoloured) because it was full of authentic feeling, every kind of feeling, relief, surprise, love, she looked at me as if she loved me, and perhaps she did love me, for saving her.

She took me – or rather I took her, for she was trembling so much she could hardly walk, whereas I felt full of adrenalin, I didn't feel my bruises until much later – back to her tiny room at the top of another damp and deserted tenement which smelled of urine and cheap scent, and she tried to sponge my suit, which was smeared black and green, ignoring her own cuts and bruises and the snail-path of blood on her cheap white jacket.

She made some coffee. Her name was Elisa. I sat on the chair. There was only one chair, but she insisted I have it, she perched on the bed, laughing and crying and stretching each limb to check that she was really still alive, telling the story of the attack and breaking off every other sentence to say how brave I was and mop at my trousers; was I really all right? How could she ever thank me . . .? Did I know that I had saved her life?

And it seems that I really did save her life, for the last few months had seen a succession of murders among the girls of the waterfront. 'Seven deaths,' she said, pursing her lips, her pretty mouth which had begun to swell up. 'And you're not young,' she kept saying, as she filled my coffee-cup and wondered at my bruises.

We sat together for over an hour. Violence linked us, and the glow of relief. The rain grew quieter. We grew quieter. I stood up to go, a hero.

She offered to thank me in the only way she knew, with the only thing she had to offer. I was almost shocked. It was impossible. I had been a gentleman to her. I had done battle for her, protected her. She was not a prostitute, she was my daughter. 'You don't need to thank me. Please don't thank me. I'm thankful I could be of service. How fortunate that I took a detour on my way to visit my family.'

Her eyes were amazed. They shone with tears. I gave her money. She didn't believe it.

But she couldn't know how grateful I was. It was I who was grateful, I who was lucky. I walked back home a different man. I had done some good. There was some point to me. I had saved a life. I had saved myself.

Lucia was putting some final touch to circles of pastry as I came in. I came into the kitchen so that she could see me, hear my story, admire me, care for me. She spoke to me without raising her eyes.

'Did you understand me, signor? I shouted. There was a telephone call from England. A woman called Susy. She doesn't speak Italian, but she keeps saying Susy. It wasn't a wrong number, she knows your name. Oh, and two letters this morning . . .' She turned to find the letters and was shocked to see me. A torrent of Italian unleashed itself, my clothes, my bruises, my age, my morals . . . out in the rain with no hat, no umbrella . . .

I didn't know where to begin to explain, how to turn blame into the praise I craved. 'I bought an umbrella, but I left it behind. I got into a fight on the waterfront . . .' (I admit I couldn't resist that phrase. It was so very ungrandfatherly, 'got into a fight'.)

'You have been running after those bad women again!. . .' And so it poured on, a deluge of words, a torrent of maternal disapproval. She came upstairs and found me clean clothes. I had to restrain her from calling the doctor and bringing me supper on a tray in bed. I kept trying to tell her what had really happened but she wasn't willing to believe a word, she thought I was spinning a tale to cover up being robbed and beaten by some pimp . . . I didn't care. I sank into it blissfully, the great warm bosom of Mamma Lucia.

I needed a drink, of course. I awarded myself two Martinis for heroism, very large Martinis very short on ice, I didn't want to cool down too much. Lucia had gone back to her risotto, life was almost normal again, but better in every way than normal, brighter, lighter, younger, hotter. The Martini was wonderful, sweet, dark, herby. It raced into my excited blood. My cheeks stung pleasantly where Lucia had anointed them with surgical spirit, lamenting. My clean collar pulled at my sore neck. My knees were stiffening; my shoulder ached. Every one of these wounds was a glorious memento. I drank to myself. I drank to the girl. I drank to goodness, and probably beauty. I meant to ring Susy after one Martini, but the need for Martini somehow seemed more pressing, and after two Martinis I thought it wiser to wait till I'd settled my stomach with dinner. Susy had always been something of a puritan where drink was concerned; I didn't want to spoil things.

I thought of my daughter. I drank to her. It was her I had saved; I had saved my daughter, I treated that prostitute like my daughter, I was there when I was needed, I was a good father. She had telephoned. We should be reconciled. I would call her back when I was utterly sober.

Time for my letters! Time for Mary! I could face it, now, if it wasn't from Mary; today had proved there was always hope; if there was nothing today, it would come tomorrow.

But one of the letters was from Mary; the other was some dull word-processed thing. I saw the envelope and didn't bother . . . I filled up my glass and opened Mary's.

Yellow paper. Not Mary, surely. Or not the Mary I used to know. If I ever knew her, which I doubt. A bit bright for my eyes, but beautiful, in my present mood it's beautiful, a thoroughly cheerful daffodil yellow. Makes the writing jig about a bit, swimming into focus then darting away . . . Hard to make sense of, but I'll try. The main thing is she has written, of course. *My dear Christopher*. . . That's affectionate; I don't think she wrote like that before . . . missing us both . . . that's standard, she always used to miss us both . . . very sorry to hear about the tragic events . . . yes, we were all pretty sorry about those, get to the point, how's Matthew? You say he's *unfortunately very gravely ill*, but is he dying, that's the question? Doesn't commit herself on that.

Susy. She writes about Susy. Heart in my mouth; may it be all right. Good news – excellent – turn for the better – garden flourishing, who cares about the garden, I want to know if my daughter still hates me, I want to know if she's all right – living with someone her own age, oh God, another frightful boyfriend – a girl! Really, she's living with a girl! Madonna – God, I remember Madonna, ravishingly pretty teenager, of course she's not a teenager any more . . . Wonderful news, what could be better? Two girls sharing, I thoroughly approve . . .

She asks – She asks. I hardly dare to believe it. *She asks if I ever think of coming home.* She says she thinks Susy would like to see me. But perhaps she means *she* would like to see me. All of my women are waiting for me! Christopher, Christopher, you are beloved! *Affectionately, as ever, Mary.*

Delightful woman. Charming woman!

238

I sat there reading and re-reading, entranced, unable entirely to follow the thread but lingering over every phrase that seemed friendly or affectionate, and all of them did, to me, last night.

I was in that heightened, nervous state where you don't know entirely what you're doing but you have to do something, you can't sit still, hungry for action, for anything . . . I ripped open the other envelope, the word-processed rubbish, hungry for food but dinner was late, it would be Lucia's fault if I ended up tipsy . . .

I ripped, and stared, and couldn't believe it.

My God, it was Susy. Susy!

Since when has she been using a word processor? Susy. And postmarked four weeks ago, even for Italian mail that's rather excessive . . .

Susy. My Susy. Voluble. Fond! Susy telling me news, and gossip. Madonna – yes, just as Mary says. She's very happy. This is marvellous. Ah – asking for money. Ah well, predictable. One's children always ask for money. At least she's asking politely this time. Wants to convert the basement . . . Wants to let the basement. Our house let to an outsider, I'm not so sure I like that idea, our house where we were a family, and happy . . .

Some of the time we weren't unhappy . . .

I'll think about it. I suppose I'll agree.

What's this? She *wants to see me*? She says *it would be lovely to see me*?

I think I have been forgiven at last. I must be the luckiest man in the world. It must be a reward for what I did today, though this was written weeks ago. But God arranged for it to arrive today; he forgave me for not believing in him.

Lots of love, Susy. Darling girl. And then an illegible hand-written postscript, scrubbed out, cross-hatched with black ink till there's a dent in the paper. Never mind. I prefer it to end *lots of love*.

And she rang, as well. Perhaps just about the money . . .

But if they really want to see me. If she and Mary really want to see me. What scalding happiness I should feel then.

If I could be loved again.

I sat there gloating, drinking, smiling. I read both letters over again. I squinnied at Susy's crossed-out postscript, right-way up, upside-down, through the thin paper with the candle behind it. I was drunk, of course, I was sentimental, but one of the letters was taller than the others, taller and pointed, an *A*, surely. *A* for *Alexandra*, perhaps. I was playing, giggling, life was fun, from now on everything was possible.

It was a wonderful evening till it all went wrong.

There was a bottle of Amarone with the clams. Lucia didn't know I had already been drinking; Amarone is a very heady wine. She commended it to me for its iron content, excellent for someone who had lost a little blood, and I acceded, meekly, dutifully, poured a large glass, and then another, and somehow I was on my fourth. The clams were delicious, and I gobbled them down.

I couldn't find the bell; I yelled for second helpings, and she came in, looking rather flustered, bearing a yellow tureen of rice. I asked her, with what I thought were perfect manners, a little flowery but wonderfully polite, to sit down and join me. I was a king, I motioned the beggar-maid to sit beside me. She was too shy to accept; that must be the reason, or so I thought, so I honestly thought. I became insistent, masterful.

I took her hand. *I took her hand!* After three years of looking at those hands day after day – the firm white arms, the solid hands, very smooth for her age and occupation, one particular blue vein on each inner arm, a delicate blue river dividing, diving, I'd watched them so often as she cared for me – placed steaming plates of food before me – ironed my clothes or poured my wine, and all she offered me was good and wholesome, I knew them so well I could have mapped those veins – after three years of watching Lucia, I took her hand, I touched her flesh.

I decided to try and say all this, I spoke to her eloquently of her goodness, her wholesomeness, her hands, her veins, but something wasn't right, she hadn't understood, there was a problem with my Italian, perhaps, I held her tighter and spilled more words.

Perhaps I mentioned I was a hero. Perhaps I had drunk rather too much wine. Alas, I am sure I spoke of love, and even as I said it the flood tide was draining, my certainties were on the wane, the rice was cold, I had spilled some wine, there were splashes of it all over her apron, I tried to take her apron off; I asked her, I think (and the timing was wrong, as I pulled at her apron-strings, absurdly knotted), if she would marry me – and because her expression was not encouraging, because she was getting very red in the face and her bulging eyes reminded me unpleasantly of the poor woman I had saved that day, I rushed on to explain that although I was married, I was willing to get divorced tomorrow, my wife was a bitch who had abandoned me, and now at last Lucia was becoming compliant, her fingers clasped mine on the apron-strings – she shouted that she was a married woman. She pushed me away. I pulled her back. I tried to kiss her. She boxed my ears. She battered my ears which were already painful. I don't want to remember the things she said.

(– I remember perfectly. She called me a dog. She called me a stupid drunken old man. She said she wasn't surprised my wife had left me. She said she was leaving now, at once, I would have to get my own breakfast tomorrow.)

Now I am in bed. It's four in the morning. I fell into bed like a stick or stone and unconsciousness swallowed me up at once. Now it has sicked me up again. I must have been too tired to brush my teeth, my mouth is a sticky, salty cave, fluffed with dust when I try to breathe. The drink has faded but its dying echoes send memories crashing round my head, jolting from nothingness to frightful clarity. I shall not sleep again tonight.

Perhaps my motives weren't wholly romantic. Returning sobriety casts all into doubt. It makes me wince. It makes me smile.

– I remember that after she boxed my ears and said she was going to leave at once my attention fell on the dirty table, the greasy plate, the cooling rice, the bottle of wine, which for some puzzling reason was lying empty on its side, with a thin lagoon of blood beside it – *I believe I begged her to stay and clear up.*

One last clear shot of her outraged back.

Goodbye, Lucia. Try to forgive. Think of me again as a foolish old grandfather.

(But I can't help wishing she'd believed my story. I was brave today. I know it's true.)

Whatever I have failed to do in the world; whatever I have stinted, or omitted; whoever I've insulted, or let down, this afternoon I wasn't a failure. I stood my ground, I saved someone. I was a man . . . I was serious. Whatever it means, to be a man.

Once, I remember, it did have a meaning. Something my father said to me. I had been involved in some bullying at school. I was a passive spectator on the fringes, not really an aggressor but still implicated, still one of the names the desperate victim finally gave to the headmaster. My father was summoned to see him – my mother was summoned but my father went, because my mother thought the headmaster a bore and his yellow buck teeth made her want to giggle – in some ways my mother was a limited woman.

My father and I had a long talk when I came home, intensely painful to both of us. I was both ashamed and eager to insist I didn't have that much to be ashamed of. 'I want you to be a man,' he said, his dark eyes turned on the ground as they always were when he talked of anything important. 'A better man than I am. I want my son to be a man. I want you to stand up for what's right. Even if it's only one single person. If you had stood up for that one person.'

And then he went on, as if talking to himself, looking out of the window now, over the garden he'd never cared for. 'It doesn't have to be a great, grand cause. I never trust causes, or abstract things. You can be very wrong about abstract things. Wars and cruelty come from causes. But if you see people suffering. Suffering things. People, animals. You know it's right to stand up for them. And then I would have been proud of you. You could have been proud of yourself.'

I was a man today. I am proud of myself. If my father saw, he is proud of me.

I find myself thinking of my son. I find myself wishing that he had seen, too. I don't think I helped him to be a man. I don't think I gave him a very good example. And it seems he shied away from being like me, my kind of man, a normal man . . . if that murderer down by the water was normal. I'm sorry, Isaac, for my stupid thoughts, I know homosexuals are normal too, Alex lost her temper with me so often when I let remarks like that slip out . . . but you shied away from being heterosexual, and I can't help feeling that was my fault. Is that what the father of every gay man feels?

I felt my son had rejected me. But of course it was us who rejected him, running off just as he was growing to manhood . . . by then I suppose it was already too late.

Was he a kind person? – I think he was. To various young painters, the obituaries said. To Susy. He always protected her. He came back covered in blood one day when a bigger boy had snatched her Sony Walkman and squeezed her breasts when she tried to get it back. So perhaps he was a better man than me, no matter if he was homosexual.

If he'd seen me today, he would not have been ashamed.

Half-past four. Too late for sleep. But I have done great deeds today. For once I feel almost cheerful.

Off to the bathroom. Clean my teeth. Inspect myself in the bathroom mirror. The cuts look clean, Lucia did well. I see a *man* in the bathroom mirror.

Carry the dirty pots downstairs. Scalding water. Salving water. Scrub all surfaces till they are clean. I stand, light-headed, in the middle of the night, in my brilliant kitchen above the black water, a bubble of brightness above the dark, though dawn smears pink along the line of the roof-tops.

And now I know I can go home.

Nothing to stay for, no one to stay for. In London, Mary is thinking of me. In London, I still have a daughter. They know about me, they care about me. They know about the past.

That *A* for *Alexandra*.
I'll phone Susy at nine o'clock.

But the phone rang at 8.15, jolting me out of a light doze, and it was Susy, sounding tired and strained, ringing before she left for work. Instantly everything became mundane, as if we had never been out of touch. I wasn't a hero, or a prodigal father.

She wanted me to know that Matthew was dying. 'The children both happen to be abroad, Mary is exhausted – '

I was upstaged. 'She wrote to me. Only yesterday. Sounding very cheery. I mean, he's been dying for some time – '

'His other kidney packed up three days ago. I just thought you might like to say goodbye. I want to relieve Mary, but it's the last week of term, I'm working flat out, she said you wrote to her – '

'Yes. Look, I've been thinking about moving back to London . . . but I'll have to tie up a lot of loose ends here – '

'How long?'

'A month or two, maybe – '

'If you want to see Matthew, you've got less than a week. Two weeks if we're lucky. Are you going to come back?'

'I . . . I don't know.'

And I didn't know. I was afraid of them. Am I a hero, or a coward?

24

Alexandra: Paris, 2005

Grey, grey. Grey and cool. Outside the window, the silver-grey world I know so well and had nearly forgotten. I shall stay inside today again. One more day then perhaps I'll be ready. Pale cool sheets where I could float forever. I have been floating, I have slept for days, helped by the drugs the doctor gave me. Today I'll try and do without.

The man who brought breakfast said it was Friday. How many weeks – it must be months – can it be less than two weeks since we took her away? How long did I have her? Less than two weeks. Just over a week. Shrinking, shrinking. Less than two weeks for the greatest adventure in my life to begin, and run its course?

I had waited for years. I yearned and waited. With Christopher, with Benjamin, with a galaxy of different pipettes and test-tubes, waiting and hoping for my boat to come in. I grew old as I waited. We all grew old. I travelled the world to find what I craved. I festered in hideously awful places. I hung on to Benjamin, when all was lost, because the child would need a father.

Then all of a sudden she was there, she was ours, with hardly any warning the miracle happened. We had fallen asleep, and the boat came in, all light and colour and music playing . . . *she smelled of mangoes and salt and honey. She played a clay bird whistle the first day we had her, when she was still happy, she sang like a bird . . . before she realised she was ours forever . . .* Then before we'd really taken it in, the thing we had waited and prayed for was over.

Nothing seems real except this grey. Maybe I came here because it's grey.

*

She was a beautiful child, Anna Maria. I have covered the top of the vast dressing-table in this vast pale room with pictures of her. We took so many photographs, trying to capture her, as if we knew she would not stay. Towards the end we only took her sleeping, because then you couldn't see her eyes, when she was sleeping she still looked child-like, contented.

But at first she was so beautiful, and her eyes most beautiful of all. Her coal-black eyes with the lovely clear whites, white as clouds, white as stars, her plumpling lips so red they looked painted, her short straight nose, so pure in its form, straight, disdainful, Indian. Some of the photographs catch her beauty but they lack the quality which made me adore her, the simple thing I shall never have again. Her presence. She was there.

Anna Maria was *there*. Suddenly one morning she was brought to us, plump, foursquare, staring at us, then away, smelling of mangoes and salt and honey, her dimpled hands, golden hands, her head of blue-black shiny hair. The child I'd first seen on the step of the hut in a beam of sunlight, playing with a marigold, and the sunlight had linked us, had made me a promise . . .

There isn't any sun in Paris.

I've lived my life according to whim, superstition, wishful thinking, rubbish. Sunlight doesn't promise things. Children don't make good presents. Can't be given, can't be bought.

She was decked in her best, a shiny red nylon dress, a little too big for her. Her upper lip gleamed with sweat. She wore orange and blue necklaces which clashed with the dress. She had only brought two toys with her – but perhaps she only had two toys. I am sure she only had two toys. There was a bird whistle and a painted wooden bird on a stick with wings that flapped as you pushed it along, but one wheel was broken, so the bird limped. I thought of all the things I could buy her; it isn't so wicked to want to give presents, to want to give when you have so much (*but now she is gone I have nothing, nothing*).

We stood outside their little hut, lined up like two families meeting for a wedding except that Benjy and I were two and they were seven, they had five children, too many to feed; we inspected each other, smiling too much, except the child who didn't smile at all. They had too many children so they sold us one. Now I see it clearly, they sold us one.

Little Anna Maria. They pushed her forward. She put her head down and clung to them. My heart was wrung. I protested, and yet I knew they were doing this for me, doing it for my money. I took a photograph of them all together to delay the moment when she screamed. We delayed the moment, but then she screamed.

She cheered up a bit when she saw our car and realised she was going to ride in it. 'It's your car now,' I said, taking her hand and placing the palm against the side that was in shade. 'It's Anna Maria's. Well, it's rented. You can have the next car too . . .' My Portuguese is good, it's always been good, but she looked at me as though she didn't understand me; when she finally did start speaking that night her intonations and vocabulary were so far from *Portuguese* Portuguese that I didn't understand her either. Oddly enough, Benjamin did better at talking to her, with only Spanish he did better than me, so perhaps it was the timbre of a woman's voice, perhaps Anna Maria was afraid of women, the terrible thing was we knew nothing about her, and even now I don't know much more. Except her body. At least I know that. How to look after her little body. *It's a lie, though, isn't it, I couldn't look after her, now I shall grieve for the rest of my life.*

All the same, she smiled as she looked at the car. She consented to climb inside. I told Benjamin to put the car radio on. He turned it up. She was fascinated. It was playing some sentimental song, some dance-band tune from the 1930s, 'These Foolish Things', I think it was, something that made my heart light up and the inside of the car, which smelled of hot plastic, suddenly filled with the scent of wallflowers. I knew how happy we were going to be.

It was very hot, near the end of the siesta, but the dust on the road was so appalling that I told Benjamin to put the windows up as we swung round in a half-circle in front of the sprawling row of huts. He turned the radio down, and tried to close the window, but the remote control for the window was broken. He wound the window up by hand.

Two things happened in quick succession. As the volume of the radio sank towards inaudibility, the keening of the family rose to our ears, a cry like the noise of massed distant sea-birds, but as he shut the window it faded away. Anna Maria sat upright staring at us.

She hadn't understood what was happening. Her first day with us was her best, because she still thought it was an outing of some kind she'd never had before, and that we would take her home later.

We wanted to get to an airport, fast. We were intending to make for Manaus, but we couldn't get to know her driving through the heat so we'd decided to go back to our hotel for the day. I'd had doubts about that, which Benjamin dismissed.

'We can't bring her here. It's so squalid. The *flies* . . .'

'There are an awful lot of flies where she comes from.'

We'd prepared at the hotel, after a fashion. We had gone to the nearby market to buy toys. It was a very poor town; there weren't many toys, and none of the sort I had in mind, large comforting toys, enormous teddy-bears or dolls to cuddle. There were drums made from gourds and pipes made from clay that I thought might blow bubbles, but they were for tobacco, there were wildly expressive devil masks that I thought might frighten her . . . I realised we didn't know much about toys and we didn't know a thing about what this child wanted. Sweets were safe. So we went for sweets. Benjy bought lots of baked marzipan sweetmeats in acid pinks and yellows to make up for the toys. We piled them ready on the bedroom table. We had rented an extra room for her, but we thought she would have her presents in ours.

She inspected everything without a word. For me? she gestured. We nodded, and stood there watching like nervous scientists. She started to eat the sweets. She ate them, solemnly, one after another.

'Shouldn't we stop her?' asked Benjamin, but we were so

248

happy she was eating our sweets, at least she wasn't rejecting us.

I showed her the ramshackle baño. She looked frightened. She stayed on the threshold, staring at the bath.

Benjamin said, 'She's never seen one before.'

'Of course she has. This is the twenty-first century.' – It wasn't, though, in Brazil. How could I have been so stupid? I wonder sometimes if I've always been stupid, always failed to understand what mattered. Now I'm fifty-five and it's all too late.

'I hope she knows how to use the loo.' He was thinking aloud, sparing me nothing. Enormous doubts began to gather.

It was hard to know what to do that day. If we'd been in a city, with bookshops, I could have read her stories in Portuguese. (Had she seen books before? Would she like them? Would she like me? Would she ever love me?) We were perilously near her home, only three or four miles away, and I was jumpy, fearing her family would change their mind, we had paid them the money now, after all, they might come to the hotel with the chief of police, or come to the hotel and weep and plead . . . I took her for a walk, and everything felt dangerous. She wouldn't hold my hand; she stumped along, hanging a few feet behind me, so I had to keep turning round in terror that I'd lose her, and I soon found the walk too tiring; so different from striding along on my own. Besides, it was too hot for a pale English woman . . . she was evidently used to being too hot. She would have walked for ever, but I took her back, still hanging behind me, pale gold, impassive.

When we'd nearly got to the hotel, she ran away behind some flame-coloured eucalyptus trees which lined the abandoned railway track; there her scarlet nylon was almost invisible, and my heart thumped in wild alarm, thinking she had run back to Mummy and Daddy, but when I spotted her she was crouching down and peeing. A lot of things were going to have to be explained.

'What time does a three-year-old go to bed?' Benjamin wondered. We didn't know. We decided on eight o'clock. We looked in her bag for pyjamas. There were no pyjamas, of course. It would have seemed uncaring, or faintly indecent, to let her sleep without pyjamas, though neither of us ever wore pyjamas; I found her a small silk vest of mine.

I took her for a bath. She screamed. She wouldn't let me take her clothes off. I think she thought I was going to murder her, penned in this blank foreign place. Her fear of me was terrifying. If I inspired such fear, what kind of person must I really be? I felt I was forced up against some naked truth, in the horrible bathroom which smelled of drains. Anna Maria was not polite; Anna Maria couldn't lie to me, or understand what I wanted her to think ... It was as if she pierced to what I really was, instinctively, and it was monstrous, but I told myself to stop thinking these things.

I gave up on the bath. I sponged her face. I remember enjoying that intensely, sponging her small arms and face. I knelt on the floor. I sponged her feet. Surely she must see I only meant to love her. Small broad feet engrained with black. Her smallness, innocence, helplessness. I found myself weeping though the smell was sour, the immemorial cheesey smell that I'd turned away from all over the world wherever the poor confronted us. I sponged her feet till they were clean. Then I smiled up at her, triumphant, but her eyes were closed, she was pretending to be dead, perhaps she was less frightened if she pretended that the worst had already happened to her, or perhaps she was just exhausted, just sleeping.

I took her by the hand, led her to her bedroom, showed her her bed, shut the shutters. I blew her a kiss, I didn't want to rush her though I longed to hold her in my arms. I made to leave. She ran after me, screaming. A torrent of Brazilian Portuguese, she wanted her mother, her father, her sisters. She was small, but her grief and her will were huge. I pointed to myself, and said 'New mother. Mother. I'm your mother.' She hit me, with furious small hands, tried to push past me and run away.

It was one in the morning before we slept, in our bed which creaked whenever she moved, curled between me and Benjamin.

250

She had not stopped protesting, not for one moment. She had merely collapsed, in the end, exhausted, in the middle of saying, for the hundredth time, 'You're not my mother! You're not, you're not!'

I lay there listening to her fast shallow breath. I could feel its heat on my shoulder, faintly. The bed was too narrow for the three of us. At four in the morning she woke up again, shivering, and started to cry, this time very quietly, and it happened as I had hoped and dreamed, she let me hold her against my body – I cradled her to me, her head in my arm, and listened to her breathing change, she fell asleep, I lay and marvelled, and in a little we slept together.

In the morning we were woken by an unaccustomed noise and saw her bare bottom underneath my pink silk perched on the window-ledge above the sheer drop; she had wrestled the shutters open, she was struggling with the window catch, we were fifteen feet up but she was going to jump out – we pulled her in again and tried to console her. Her screams were so shrill, they tore at my guts ... what if people thought we were murdering her? 'Please, please,' I found myself begging her. 'Please don't cry. *Please*. You're safe with us. You'll be happy with us.'

Then she was sick; perhaps yesterday's sweets, perhaps terror at what she had seen of her future. She was sick on the table, on her only dress, on our case, on Benjamin's shoes, on the carpet. We had no cloth to wipe it up. I had to do it with Benjamin's shirt, wrung out in tepid tap water, while he held the child on his knee and rocked her, and she quietened a little, from screams to sobs, hiccupy sobs with long silences between them. After I'd finished I threw the shirt in the bin.

The sight of them together, curled together, provoked an odd emotion I still haven't understood, his bigness curled around her littleness, he looked happy, remember I had loved him once – 'I'll take her now,' I said, I insisted. But she wouldn't come to me.

My life as a mother lasted less than two weeks. It was no time at all, yet it seemed like for ever once I knew that things were going wrong.

We set off on the drive to the airport, a five-day drive if we went flat out. Perhaps everything would have been all right if Benjy and I could have got her out of South America. Even after eighteen months we were strangers there, we didn't know how to find toys or doctors or children's clothes or food she would eat. We didn't know anyone else with children who would have helped us with all these things, shown us how to be mother and father, let their children play with her. I never saw her playing with other children. So many things I never saw her do, I have the rest of my life to realise how many.

She stopped eating. We offered her fruit. Half-eaten fruit lay around the hotel room, pocked with small white tooth-marks soon going brown; it littered the floor of the car, and stank. We were short of sleep, and too tired to clean up, too tired even to keep ourselves clean. One morning as we were packing to go I noticed Benjamin smelled of sweat; I've always liked clean men, I was indignant, amazed; 'Benjamin! Your armpits smell!'

His eyes were red. 'OK, Alexandra.'

'Well go and have a shower. It's disgusting.'

'I'm trying to clean this child's teeth . . .'

'I bet she doesn't like the smell either.'

He suddenly lost his temper. 'Fuck *off*, you bitch. Try sniffing yourself. You might learn something about yourself.'

The terrible thing was, he was right. I found that I smelled too. The truth was that neither of us washed any more. How could a single three-year-old child make two adults both too tired to wash?

She was about to become less tiring.

She became docile. She became ill. After only two days it was doctors we needed. She had diarrhoea, and fouled our bed, since she still refused to sleep in her own. (What a fool I was, what I fool I am. She had always shared a bed with three others, as she explained to Benjamin.)

The sorrow of it; she preferred him to me, she liked to sit

near him, she talked to him, though it was I who had longed and planned for her, I who had crossed the world to find her.

Her docility was unnerving. She no longer wept and screamed for her mother. She too seemed tired; now we were all tired. (Only the childless aren't tired. Why have I never understood, why didn't someone bother to tell me?) I delayed calling a doctor because I was afraid. An ordinary doctor might say she must stay in a Brazilian hospital until she was better; they might try and make us take her home . . . If only we could get her on to the plane, only another day's drive if we drove non-stop, if only we could get her back to civilised places with private doctors and properly trained nannies, I thought I would employ one for a month or so, just to show me the ropes, then I'd be able to sack her . . .

Then the silly dreams and fantasies ended. On the third day we stopped at a hotel and found she could not walk from the car. She wasn't sleepy; she was too weak.

I wanted to carry her. *I wanted to*. But I wasn't used to carrying things. I was good at running, dancing, walking, or I had been only recently, I have only recently grown older . . . I have never had to carry things. Servants or men have always carried things. Dead weights are incredibly heavy. She was so quiet, so mute, so good. She wasn't unconscious, but she seemed not to see me. Her eyes were losing the brightness of water, they were drying up, becoming opaque . . . suddenly I was very afraid, more afraid than I'd ever been . . . only once before had I been as afraid, and that was in New York when I knew what had happened, when I saw what Christopher had done, when I realised it was irrevocable . . .

I sat and clutched her on the hot plastic seat. I wanted to carry her but oh, I couldn't. With her on top of me I could not move. I would have sat there holding her for ever, and no one could have separated us . . . But Benjamin saw, and saw I was crying. Benjamin took over.

We paid the hotel for a room. We paid the hotel to find us a doctor. We paid them more to get him there fast. The doctor came, and tutted and swore. He was a small fat man with a sweat-blackened shirt and his breath was a horrible fug of old drink. He gave us medicine. We paid him well. He threatened us. We paid him better. He told us we should take her home. With surprising tenderness (for he was a crook) he held her hand, and talked to her, and she almost smiled, she was briefly alive before the apathy came back. He held her hand, and insulted us. He said we were selfish, and stupid. He said we knew nothing about children, and nothing about Brazil, and nothing about the world. We were stupid, spoiled gringos. He folded the money we had given him and said we could keep her, if we wanted, if we wanted to be murderers.

What he said was true, and made him feel less dishonest. He staggered off for another drink.

The drive back was a worse nightmare. Benjamin told her she was going home, but I don't think she believed she could ever go home. Still she rallied a little with the medicine. She drank water like a dog, slurping, desperate, and the diarrhoea grew less thin and persistent. She was easier to love when she didn't smell, but I never stopped loving her, adoring her, as the car sped nearer to São Benedicto I loved her more and more.

I wept a lot. Benjamin drove. I held Anna Maria, and she let me hold her. I stroked her hair, I kissed her head, the burning, living crown of her head with its prickling of hot silky hair, she was still alive, she mustn't die. Wherever our skins touched, we ran with sweat, but it didn't matter, we touched each other. I knew I had to hold her enough in those four days to last me for ever. She was my child. I had lost the others; she was my last chance to be a mother.

(*And yet, we almost murdered her*. I haven't yet managed to understand. I shall suffer it through again and again, I shall make myself think till I understand. *What have I done; what have I done?*)

When we found the family, they were glum and scared after the first unthinking joy at seeing her. They could see she was ill; did we think she was no good? Had Anna Maria disappointed us? Would the rich foreigners be angry with them? Would we be asking for our money back?

254

Instead we gave them more money. They would need a lot of money for the rest of her life. We couldn't give enough to ensure that she got it, but we gave as much as our grief was worth, and that was a fortune to them. They couldn't take in what was happening. I told them we were giving them money for Anna Maria's education, that in our country it would have cost twice as much. But they stayed subdued. It was too much money.

I had to say goodbye to her. I had done it once in the car, before we saw them and they looked at me, and looked at her, and saw what we – what all of us had done to Anna Maria; before she was back with the family that proved I was not her mother and had never been her mother.

– I was her mother, all the same. I may be deluded but I still think it's true. For those seven or eight days I was her mother, I was all the mother that she had. She slept beside me, she let me hold her, she let me sponge her and comb her hair. I washed the red dress out every night, I brushed the dust from her plastic sandals, I washed her feet, I kissed her feet.

I said goodbye to her out in the car. She had still not realised where she was. She sat forlornly on my lap, looking out of the window without seeing anything. I hugged her, awkwardly, shoulders, elbows, hard to hug someone who doesn't hug back. I kissed her head, the thousandth, hundred-thousandth time I had kissed her head as we bumped across Brazil and she stared into the distance. I wanted to kiss her face, her lips, but she didn't turn towards me.

'We ought to go in,' said Benjamin, tense with unhappiness.

'Shut up. I have to say goodbye.' – I forgot he hadn't said goodbye.

I was going to give up, but at the last moment she realised where we had stopped, and a look of unbelieving joy startled her face, lit up her eyes – she turned towards me for confirmation and I kissed her cheek, I kissed her lips, my cheek was blessed by her small smooth cheek, she allowed me to kiss her face to face as she was transfigured by the hope of leaving me.

Although I had kissed her goodbye in the car I thought I would die if I left the hut without a gesture. It was my last chance of touching her. And yet I was ashamed, in the face of all those witnesses. But Anna Maria had slipped out of the back, into the yard where I first fell in love with her. Benjamin was talking to the parents; I went to look for her. Through the doorway I saw her sitting on the step. Her baby brother crawled beside her, patting and poking at her thigh. I watched her lift him as if he wasn't heavy, I watched her jig him on her knee. It was a different girl from the girl in the car, more like the child with the marigold who lived here until she met me.

I was going outside to say some nonsense when something froze me in the doorway, before my shadow had fallen on her. I thought, *she might be frightened. She might think I've come to take her again.* It was clear to me I must leave her alone. I left her sitting in the sun with her brother.

I sent Benjamin away. Only two days ago. It was quite easy, after all that had happened. We were ashamed to look at each other: unable to comfort each other. He protested very little, but he hated me, silently, I felt his hatred as I said we should part. I knew he had begun to blame me for what we had done to the child. Perhaps he still loved me – he had passionate feelings, I could feel the force of them contorting his brows and clenching his fists as he packed to go, as he slammed the doors and banged the cases, though I was too numb to wince or quail – perhaps he still loved me, if love means hatred. I hadn't loved him for years and years, so I should have managed to feel a little pity, but he seemed irrelevant, that's all. I tried to be kind; I think I thanked him; he brushed me away, furious.

Now I'm alone I can see him better. There were good things about him that weren't imaginary – his tenderness, his sense of humour, a practicality Chris lacked – but I didn't want him for those reasons. I wanted him to be a son and a father, a son for me, a father for my baby. I asked him to promise eternal youth. Instead we aged and failed together.

He hardly painted in the years with me. You see, I don't make people happy, I'm not good for them, I don't encourage them.

There are women who are good for people. Mary Brown was good for people. She had a good marriage and good children. I suppose she has them still; they turned out well, thanks to Mary. Matthew and Dan and Jessica. I could have had Matthew if I'd beckoned, but something stopped me, I don't know quite what. She wrote so kindly after I miscarried, even though I believe she knew about the abortion I had all those years ago; I think Chris told her at a drunken party; I know he was desperate to talk to someone; when he didn't deny telling her I slapped his face, the only time I ever slapped a man, my sense of betrayal was so great.

Or perhaps it was guilt, guilt, guilt, I've always denied that I feel guilt, yes I am guilty, god, I'm guilty, *what have I done, what have I done?* – I am sure she listened, and comforted him.

Perhaps she would listen to me now. I'm nearer home than I've been for three years. I came to Paris because it isn't foreign, it's safe and cool and civilised, I suppose I knew it was time to go home . . . but not *home*, of course. I could never do that. I haven't a home. But sometimes I wish . . . other women are home-makers. Mary was. I bet they still live there, I bet that nothing has happened to the Browns, I bet they stayed there quiet as mice while Christopher and I lived our great adventure . . .

How can I still fool myself? – *while Christopher and I were wrecking our lives.*

If I could only talk to Mary. If I had the courage to pick up the phone I don't think she'd refuse me. She was a good friend . . .

The terrible crying begins again. A lifetime ago, a lifetime has gone, my life has slipped away through the gap since I saw her, all the loved things have slipped away, youth, Christopher, Anna Maria, Isaac and the baby who was never born. I was thirty-five; now I'm approaching sixty. It can't have happened, it can't be true. Other people grow old, not Alexandra . . .

There are sirens blaring in the street below. Quick, have a look . . . but I can see nothing. I hear them, though. I always hear them. Whenever things go wrong, the sirens come, the sirens from the millennium, and the terrible sequence begins again, *what have I done, what have I done. . .*

At least Anna Maria didn't die.

Once it is done it can never be changed. Once they are gone they can never come back. But they live in your brain. They infect your brain . . .

— The truth is, Christopher killed someone. In the year 2000 we killed someone.

25

Susy: London, 2005

Poor Mary. I saw her yesterday. I didn't know whether to go round or not and then I thought sod it, she's so often been there when terrible things have happened to me, I'll go just so's she knows I care – I went round after school and rang the bell, Jessica answered, we kissed each other, we hadn't kissed since we were little girls, then I followed her into their front room and Mary sat there, unrecognisable, puffy and red from hours of weeping, as if she'd been beaten up or run down by a car, and she tried to stand up to say hallo and couldn't.

I hate funerals. The hymns make me bawl whether I cared about the person or not, crying for myself I suppose and the fact that we're all going to die in the end. I always feel icy cold at funerals, no matter how many clothes I wear. And I feel lonely. Which is silly, except in Isaac's case of course, because he was my friend and my brother, and losing him made a difference to my life. But I always feel lonely, even when it's just an uncle or aunt that I haven't seen for years . . .

I started to explain that to Phil at school. He comes in twice a week to do gym with the children; it's a mixture of dancing and wrestling, which they love. He's very easy with them, and easy to talk to. Odd that he's so relaxed, I used to think, when he's really a marathon runner, which takes so much concentration and will to win. But he says no; you have to go with the pain, relax into the pain of it.

Phil said, 'When is the funeral?'

'Monday morning. I get nervous in advance, I know there's still the weekend to go . . .'

'I'll come with you. My training partner's sprained his ankle, I'll give myself a morning off.'

I was so surprised I nearly spilled one of the beakers of dilute orange juice we were drinking with the children. *Did* people go with one to funerals? People who didn't know the dead?

'. . . Well . . .'

'Then you won't feel lonely, at any rate. I'd love to come with you. Don't say no.'

I looked into his frank grey eyes, with the nest of laughter lines all round, his weather-beaten, lightly-tanned face, his smiling lips, slightly cracked from the sun, and thought how comforting he was; the children loved him; I said, 'Yes. Thanks, Phil. You're a friend.'

Now I'm a bit embarrassed that he's coming. I'm bound to cry, whether he's there or not, and he'll see me crying and hopeless, with eye makeup all down my cheeks, whereas at school he sees me cool, calm and collected, in charge of things, a rock for the children. It's lovely when someone thinks you're calm.

And Jessica and Dan will wonder who he is. And Madonna will tease me afterwards. (I suppose she's coming to the funeral – Matthew was very fond of her, but when I asked her last night she said she was working, though she never gets to work before lunchtime on Mondays. Perhaps she doesn't want to upset Dan, or make his wife jealous – Anne's rather plain and enormously pregnant.)

Phil's been round to the house a couple of times, once with some newspapers for a *papier maché* model I was doing for the kids, once because he was training nearby, and he took me for a pint at my local. I don't know why I didn't ask him in. Maybe because Madonna was there.

Is it that I'm ashamed of him? He's completely unaware of what he looks like. He usually has old tracksuit bottoms, non-matching top, and that weird hair – his hair is the texture of a scrubbing brush, so no wonder he just lets it stick out of his head, he must have despaired of doing anything about it. But he's got a lovely humorous face. Looks older than he is because of all the weather. In any case given that he's not my boyfriend, why should I bother to feel ashamed?

260

I'm glad there'll be someone to turn up with. You're never quite sure that Madonna will show, or if she'll be late, or get the day wrong. Whereas if Phil says he'll be there, he will.

My father let us down, of course. He didn't come back in time to see Matthew. According to Mary they were very good mates. And I remember the four of them when I was tiny, sitting in the kitchen together and laughing, usually at our house because it was bigger, the four of them together on so many outings.

Matthew and Mary were Dad's friends. So why didn't he come and say goodbye? Doesn't he care about anybody? Wouldn't he come if I was dying?

I did my best, I rang him in Venice even though he hadn't bothered to answer my letter. I was horribly nervous, but I telephoned him, and I shook like a leaf when I heard his voice, my Dad's voice after nearly five years . . . but he sounded just the same, plummy and leisurely, and I felt pissed off, he wasn't pleased enough to hear me, I was brisk and cold and told him the news. I told him Matthew would die within days and he gave me some bullshit about how Matthew had been dying for years, nothing to worry about, he didn't know if he could make it.

All the same, I couldn't help hoping he would. I thought he'd think it over, and come. I even tidied the house in case he stayed. Madonna had encouraged me to ring him, but she didn't help me to tidy the house. Recently I've slightly gone off Madonna; maybe I'm jealous because she's got a man, Madonna always has a string of men though she's always talking about settling down . . .

I don't really want her to settle here. She *is* good company, but not for ever.

We have a lot in common, though. We talk about babies. Wanting them. Madonna's got it bad, she loves them to death. That's why she's got to settle down. She wouldn't stop working, of course, but she'd like three children, a year apart. She's planned it all; she'd stop working for a month, then get a really good nanny to take over. She knows lots of people who've done it like that. Of course she'd still spend lots of time with the children, at weekends and after she gets home in the evening, though she often doesn't get home till ten. But she says it would be *fun* time, quality time.

Her ideas are much more worked out than mine. With me it's more of a steady hunger, knowing I want a baby to live with, and being sad I don't have a father yet. Wanting to love it and look after it. And I'm less energetic than Madonna. I know I'd need at least six months off. We go on and on about all this. It's almost as good as having the babies. But sometimes I get really freaked out about our age; both of us are thirty-seven, getting on, though Madonna says that's irrelevant with all the break-throughs in techbirths now.

— Thing is, I don't want a techbirth . . . I want a baby the old-fashioned way, I sort of want to complete the cycle I kept cutting off when I had the abortions. I'm sure it will happen, some time soon. I don't know why; I just feel it will, and even now with the funeral on my mind I've got this secret, growing happiness deep down inside me at the thought of it, tingling my breasts, tickling my belly. To have a family of my own.

I suppose I'm still trying to replace my family.

On the phone Dad wasn't sure, and I half-thought he'd soften, but Matthew died on Wednesday and no word had come. Dad didn't even telephone me or Mary.

The funeral is his last chance to make it up to the Browns, but I remember he and Alex didn't like funerals, it reminded them of stuff they preferred not to think about. They went together on sufferance when they couldn't possibly get out of it, overdressed, ridiculously smart, and when they came home they went hysterical with laughter and made horrible remarks about the other guests.

Silly to kid myself. There's no chance he'll turn up at the funeral. I wasn't even going to tell him about it but Madonna said I might as well. So I rang him in a fury and got a strange man — a contract cleaner who was cleaning the flat — I just left a brief note of the time and place. He was Italian, I don't s'pose he passed on the message.

Poor Mary. She looked like someone else. She looked like an animal, actually. Mary, who'd always looked so clean and careful. As if she'd been beaten half to death. As if she would have just fallen down at our feet if she'd had to suffer another bit of pain.

'I've known for years,' she said. 'I've known he was ill since the late 1980s. Since just after . . . your parents . . . went away.' (I've told her I don't think of Alex as a parent, but she can never think what else to call her.) 'He was deaf and half-blind. It wasn't fun for him. So why am I being so silly? Why do I feel — why am I so — ' She couldn't get it out, she was sobbing again, the snot was all running down, and tears.

I don't know why I was surprised she was like this; Matthew and Mary were happily married . . . but I knew she was fagged out with all the nursing, and she didn't want Matthew to suffer any more. She had talked so calmly about him dying. But now it had happened she was mad with pain. Jessica sat with her arm round her shoulders. She seemed OK, but her eyes were wet. Dan's son George was trailing a battered teddy bear round behind the sofa, making ambulance noises, and every now and then saying 'Poor Grandpa. Grandpa go to heaven. Amb'ance take Grandpa to heaven now.' Anne was in the kitchen, making tea, Dan was upstairs going through his father's clothes; when we were quiet downstairs I heard another noise, like a motor throbbing or an engine chugging a long way away, but it was Dan, upstairs, the whole house was at it, they couldn't stop bawling.

I was desperately sorry for them, I swear. Mary had always been so nice to me, and Matthew, in his more distant way. And yet I felt jealous. Sick with envy. They were a family, even in this. They were still together. They could cry together. It made me feel lonely, and hate my father.

Tonight I can't sleep. It's the funeral tomorrow. I know it's stupid, but I'l never learn, I've been watching the clock getting later and later, some part of me still hoping Dad will ring and say *Don't worry, I'll be there. Don't worry, we'll go together.* But now it's midnight. Hope's run out.

God! The phone! I nearly died, I can't find the bloody receiver in the dark, but it's him, it must be, now I've dropped it on the floor . . .

'Susy? It's Phil. Sorry to ring so late . . . I just wanted to ask you, what should I wear? I don't want to let you down.'

It isn't a big funeral. Thirty or so expected. We got there early to show solidarity. I told him not to worry, but Phil's wearing a suit, a fairly dreadful suit I suppose, though I've never been very up on these things, it has a vaguely '90s air, but I think he looks terrific, actually, I'm proud he got out his suit for me.

The family are gathered in little knots, quiet-ish but livening up every now and then as they see someone they haven't seen for years and forget for a moment that we're here to be gloomy. Most of these people I've never seen; I knew Matthew and Mary and Dan and Jessica, but otherwise only the occasional aunt who came to London on a shopping trip – ah, hallo, you must be Aunty Katharine, we met a year or two ago, sorry I don't know your proper name . . .

She was a Smith. That's Mary's side. There are Smiths and Browns, basically, whatever name they go under now. Alexandra thought it was unspeakably comic that Mary was a Smith who ended up a Brown. But then Alexandra was a Stoddy, so nothing she says has to be taken too seriously . . .

I explain some of this to Phil, under my breath. It means I have to tell him a little bit more and then a little bit more about my family . . . At first he doesn't seem to be taking it in.

'Mad how women used to change their names,' he says. 'My mother was a Windsor, of all things. Not that kind of Windsor, of course. But she changed her name to Sparrow. I ask you. Would *you* change your name to Sparrow?' Then he runs on in the same breath, 'I think what you told me is appalling. To be abandoned at seventeen. And I want to say – I think you're remarkable. You're absolutely remarkable. To have survived something like that, and be like you.' That *like you* is said in such a lovely way that I think confusedly *he's sorry for me. He is ever so sorry for me. How comforting.* And I really am in a muddle, because another part of me's still thinking about what he said before, and enjoying it: *Would I change my name to Sparrow? . . . Yes, because I hate being a Court.* And *Yes, Susy Sparrow . . . I could marry Phil.*

Dan has his arm round Mary. She's a bit like me; doesn't care about clothes, and she usually dresses in scrappy layers that seem to have sort of blown on by accident, and make her look fatter than she is. Today she's in a plain black dress and coat and I see she's actually not fat at all; she's very upright despite Dan's arm, it's as if Dan's hanging round her neck, not holding her up at all. She looks – solid, and calm again, and graceful. She isn't red and raw, any more. She's pale and almost radiant, her skin with a sort of milky shine.

'Who's that woman? The beautiful one,' Phil asks me, and I see he means Mary. Mary Brown beautiful! Alexandra always used to laugh at Mary; if Dad tried to get Alex to go out with him in a hurry and she wanted time to make herself glamorous (though even at home, she was always glamorous), she would say, 'For heaven's sake! I can't go out looking like Mary Brown!' And it was Mary's name Alex flung at me when she thought I looked particularly horrendous: 'Susy! Do you want to grow up looking like Mary Brown?' – and then she would add, but it can't have been true, ' – of course I'm very fond of her.'

'That's Mary Brown. The widow,' I say. What a horrible word, sort of pompous and queenly, whereas Mary had always been – *ordinary*, extraordinarily ordinary, really, safe and comfortable and warm. And linked to people; never on her own. All the same, I'm amazed to see that what Phil says is true; Mary looks beautiful today.

It seems to have been a good week for dying. Outside the window we see the lot before us shuffling away, awkward, embarrassed, an old man cracking up with laughter, two old women with their arms round each other, the wind and the sun making a halo of their white hair . . . Not so many people as there are at Matthew's. I'm glad people have bothered to show

265

up. It might make Mary feel a bit better, that people loved Matthew and turned out for him.

Off we march towards the chapel. But of course my family *hasn't* bothered to turn out. Nor Madonna either, not that Mary would care ... I'm really glad that Phil has come. I shall introduce him to everyone afterwards. Now Dan and Anna and Jessica are all pressing close around their mother, the door creaks open, and organ music – ooh, I love it, it's 'The Lord's my Shepherd' – flows sweetly out to draw us in, and at once I feel my eyes going prickly, my heart starts thudding, I want to cry, not just for Matthew but for everyone lost, even Dad I suppose, even my father, he'll die in the end and who will care?

– Not Alexandra, that's for sure, not my 'loving stepmother'. With her toyboy and her new Brazilian baby.

I'll let the family go to the front, I don't want to seem pushy. These must be sister and brothers I suppose, they're really old, same age as Matthew. He was something like a dozen years older than Mary. How ancient they look. All stiff and slow. It's like a queue lining up for the grave.

– Would my Dad look as old as that? I last saw him properly six years ago, and he was already old of course, in his sixties at any rate, but he wasn't all twisted and crabby and bloodless, he didn't look like these people. He looked quite good, in an actorish way. He always was a bit of an actor. That thick silver hair, and his queer hooded eyes. And still tall and solid, not dried out.

But prison dries you out, I expect. And being alone. And missing your wife. Dad lived for Alexandra.

Massive shufflings of bags and shoes and hymn-books. The priest looks like a bloodhound but with black beetling brows. He stares at us as if we don't come up to scratch. I squeeze Phil's arm and want to giggle, but I also want to cry as I look at Mary's straight strong back in her black coat, the column of her neck and her grey-streaked hair in the unflattering bun she always wears, but somehow with the black it looks – posh, aristocratic; Mary, the least grand and nicest of people; Mary who so often dragged me out of messes I was in; all the same her bare neck looks sort of defenceless, it's almost like watching someone asleep, now she can't look after herself, so we have to. I really love Mary.

We stand up to sing Hymn No 134. The organ crashes. So does the door. *Dad*, it could be, my heart lurches and I half turn round, I can't see the door between the shoulders of pensioners searching their hymn-books, please may it be Dad, it's his very last chance . . .

Then I see her, and feel very cold. Encased in immaculate black velvet, skin-tight; she is matchstick thin; a black hat with a black spotted veil that completely covers her long hair, and her face underneath it is a blur of white, coal-black eyes, blood-red lips. I have to sit down, my knees won't hold me up, and Phil looks anxiously at me; it's the ghost who came to my brother's funeral, it's her, the bitch, it's Alexandra.

Then the door bangs again. This time I know exactly who it will be, I see that everything was fixed from the start, I know they will get back together, my heart is drowning in sadness and terror and the surging, soaring chords make it worse, and in he comes, looking thin and hunted, eyes darting round the dark interior, handsome as ever, but oh, so much thinner, my white-haired father, Christopher. I want to kiss him and stroke his white hair.

Christopher and Alexandra. Not together yet, but I know it's going to happen. Alexandra and Christopher. And everyone else will be fucking irrelevant, no one else will get a fucking look-in.

The hymn is over. Everyone sits down. Three things happen in quick succession. The black-veiled woman turns to stare at Dad, who's sitting by himself three pews from the door; Dad is peering at Mary's back; Mary turns, as if she feels his eyes, sees him, and gives a small half-smile, a shiver of shock then a small Mary smile, and Mary's smiles are lovely, the best; the black-veiled woman raises her veil to get a better look at him, and I see it's not Alexandra at all, it was just the clothes that confused me for a moment, it's *Madonna*, my friend Madonna, for Christ's sake, dressed to kill, and staring at my father.

26

Alexandra: Paris, 2005

We killed someone. I have to live with it. I ran off with Benjamin
to escape.

 — In the year 2000, we killed someone, Christopher and
Benjamin and I. Christopher and I. Christopher.

Christopher killed, but I drove him to it.

I don't want the pills. I have to remember.

What have I done. What have I done.

We had just unlocked our little room. They had got to know us
at the hotel, the thin receptionist smiled at us —

The thin receptionist. I know her name, I should know her
name, it was Consuela Harbert, her name is stamped upon my
brain. She was narrow, Latin, fiftyish — even now I don't think
of myself as fiftyish, even now that I'm fifty-five, but Consuela
Harbert looked prematurely elderly, boot-blacked hair and fans
of wrinkles. After an initial sharpness she grew kind to us; she
liked Benjamin; she would try to give us the room we had first
because we said we liked the window, the steel-framed window
we could open wide. 'You again,' she always said, in a grainy,
humorous voice that we grew to like because we associated it
with love-making. I suppose that's why I noticed her. She was
the sort of woman I didn't notice; the sort of person I never
notice, not particularly beautiful or interesting, a marginal figure
in my life.

That day we talked. I arrived alone because Benjamin had
stopped for cigarettes; she said, 'He's a handsome boy,' as if we
would understand each other, and I realised she thought she
and I were the same age, which was blatantly ridiculous (until

the court case proved it was true) but I didn't protest, I was proud of possessing him.

'Yes. I'm lucky.' I thought I was.

'Got any kids?' She was curious.

'No. Yes. I don't know.'

'Got problems with 'em? They teenagers?'

'One of them died,' I said. My aborted son, my lost one. I don't know why it came out like that, I had never said that to anyone before. Perhaps I assumed she was Catholic. Her eyes, which were very dark, very Spanish, looked vast and sad in her wizened face.

'I'm sorry,' she said.

'Yes. One of them I had adopted.' Her face changed, shocked, less friendly. 'I was only twenty-two. Too young. Now I miss them.' I think I wanted her to like me, though why I should have bothered I still don't know.

'I got six,' she said. 'Four boys.' She was proud to tell me that she had a life, she had something I would never have. I had Benjamin, but she had sons. 'One still at home. One going through college. Six bright kids.'

'Uh-huh.'

— I wasn't going to admire her. I should have done out of sheer politeness, but it hurt too much, that casual boast; she had six kids and she was ordinary, and I was special, and I had none. It was my fault for getting into conversation, nothing could be gained from such conversations, as we went round the world I had made a rule of not wasting time gossiping to servants; sometimes one needed to talk to them, to find out certain things about the country one was in, but even then they would often tell one too much or not enough of what one wanted to hear; better to keep one's distance. Better for them, better for us. Yet lately I had grown lonely.

— I thought she was triumphing over me, and I wished her harm, I admit I did, but then Benjamin came springing through the door, her smile widened into a beam and I realised I was imagining things.

'Mr Ash.' She reached behind her and picked out the key. 'Your regular room.'

'Thanks, Consuela. You're looking great.' (She looked tired, and old, and ordinary.) 'How's everything?'

'Good, sir. Good. Well, except for my daughter . . .'

I wanted to fuck. I wanted it now. I didn't want to hear about her daughter. 'I haven't got much time,' I said to Benjamin, cutting across the receptionist, only registering her words as I stopped speaking – 'She's going blind. Some germs from dogshit. Dogshit! I ask you, *Jesus* . . . you can't get away from it in this town. She's fourteen years old. She's a great kid. It's kinda hard to take, but we manage.'

I thought about the daughter I had had adopted. In my head she was still a teenager, though actually she would have been nearly thirty. I imagined her going blind. I said, 'I'm sorry. I'm really sorry.' I meant, I'm sorry I had horrible thoughts, I'm sorry life can be so horrible, I'm glad nothing bad ever happens to me. 'That's terrible.'

'We're doing OK.'

We smiled at each other, a real smile, not the formal grimace I usually gave her. She started to explain to Benjamin. Benjamin was a wonderful listener. I stared out of the door, no longer impatient, the glittering windows across the street, the flash of a yellow taxi passing, the blue sky, extravagantly blue in the chasms between towering clouds, bluer from inside this dark narrow building where Consuela sat all day. The light before a storm had the stagey quality of sunset light, melancholy, golden, making the ordinary brownstone walls of a warehouse facing the hotel as rich and red and remarkable as any of the wonders I'd seen on my travels. I could *see* all this. I was very lucky.

We went upstairs. I tried to forget her. Going upstairs with Benjamin, the excitement of his big young body, walking behind him, watching him, his thick soft hair which smelled new-washed, the tang of fresh sweat, his hard buttocks . . . he ran without thinking, eager to get there, and I ran too, but not quite so easily . . . not quite so easily as before.

270

It would have been better if she hadn't liked us, better for her, better for me. Better for him, for Christopher.

But *we* don't matter. We don't deserve to. That tired woman was all that mattered. And I thought they didn't matter at all, people like her on the edges of life. We were the centre; I was so sure . . .

We had just unlocked our little room, the one we had used on our very first tryst, with the daring window over the street, the window that seemed to let in the world, the opening that said we could go anywhere at all as long as we could be together, places where Christopher had never taken me, *younger* places, *freer* places . . .

(See what a betrayer I am. Christopher and I were once young and free . . .)

We hadn't long unlocked our little room when theatrical clouds piled over the sun, leaving the heat, taking the light, except for the occasional long golden lance which pierced the blackness, flickered, died. I think our mood changed with the weather.

There were sirens in the streets. Something had happened. The noises were different from before; no bells, no children, just the sirens wailing and angry cars using their horns. There was a smell of something burning; rubber? flesh? I was going to close the window, but there wasn't time.

'Take off your clothes,' said Benjamin. 'I'm desperate for you . . . I'm dying for you.'

That day Isaac's breathing had changed in some horrible way, long labouring in-breaths which took for ever and then violent, explosive out-breaths. The nursing staff were grave; they warned us we were near the end. Benjamin and I and Herbie and Ken, who ran what had once been Isaac's favourite restaurant, sat there together on the edge of hysteria, for Isaac had turned into some clockwork toy, his parts agitated by something outside him, and I knew that the force which was driving him was no longer a life-force, it was death.

Herbie and Ken had to go back to work. We sat there for hours; nothing changed. The nurse had said this could last for days. Our eyes kept meeting over his body. We had to make ourselves forget. We had pawed each other in the taxi, frantic.

Benjy pulled off my t-shirt and pants. I saw myself in the narrow mirror of the antediluvian dark wood wardrobe. My red hair hung below my shoulders, my breasts hung down but they were full and pale, I still had a girl's indented waist. Benjy stood behind me; he made me look small. Taller than Christopher; I like to look small. My face looked haunted, full fifty years old. His young brown hands slipped over my breasts.

I could feel his erection nudging at my buttocks. My nipples contracted, hardened, darkened, stuck out at our reflection like tiny guns; my cheeks had flushed into excited life. I was ready for him, I wanted him, I wanted his beautiful cock inside me, I needed his hand between my legs, I groaned with pleasure as he played with me, oh I wanted to die doing this with him, oh come inside me, Benjamin, come . . .

Then someone was hammering at the door. We stood immobile, a photo in a frame, watching our faces exposed in fear. Unfocused fear; we were in New York; it was full of maniacs with knives and guns; we were in a sleazy, shabby hotel . . .

All the same, my fear was nine-tenths guilt. I should not be here. They had found me here. Fate had come hammering at the door.

'Who is it?' called Benjamin. I tried to hush him. No one must know he was here with me. His voice wasn't his own; he was frightened. I knew he would be brave, but he was frightened now. He tried to put his pants on; they stuck out, absurdly. No answer, but the hammering intensified, it was definitely someone insane, the whole door shook with the force of the blows . . .

– The door splintered. The door crashed in. My heart stopped beating. Someone was screaming, hideous screams going on and on, it was I who was screaming and holding my breasts, Christopher, it was Christopher, he had kicked the door in, he stood there panting, old, triumphant, terrible. He looked at me in my nakedness, his eyes were on mine, we saw each other, I saw he knew me for what I was, a cheat and a liar, our life was over, he was trying to speak, he went red then pale, I thought perhaps he was having a stroke, the sirens wailed for another murder down in the street where I longed to be, and then I saw what he had in his hands and my bowels turned to water.

(Someone was calling up from downstairs, a woman was calling, but I hardly heard her.)

Christopher was shouting, hoarse with rage. 'I'll fucking kill you! Both of you! You bloody – awful – lying – *bitch* –'

I looked at him; it might be enough; he must see the truth written in my eyes; *it's me, Alexandra. I know you love me. Christopher, please. I never stopped loving you –* We'd moved, both of us, Benjamin and I, across to the window, as if we could escape, as if we could have flown like Superman four floors down to where the world was normal – Benjamin put his hand on my arm, perhaps to protect me, perhaps to restrain me –

Somebody else came through the door. I didn't see who. There was a shattering explosion, the sound of everything coming to an end. Another and another. I was crouched on the floor, an animal was moaning, Christopher had me by the hair, Benjamin lay half on top of me, dead, blood pouring out of a hole by his ear.

Christopher was making strange horrible noises, my arm was crimson with someone's blood, *my* blood, *God oh God I'm bleeding*, blood was welling from a wound in my side, but Christopher was still hurting me, dragging my head from side to side, and I realised what he was trying to do, he was trying to pull me out from under Benjy's body, I made to help him, Benjy's head fell back, his eyes rolled upwards, he was dead, dead, oh I didn't want to die myself, Chris pulled again and then let go, I lurched forward, staggered on to my feet, lost my balance and fell sideways so my forehead butted the bloody mess where Benjy's ear and cheek had been. There was silence, briefly, except for Chris's panting and my small sobbing breaths of incredulous terror, this couldn't have happened, he couldn't be serious, Christopher could never have hurt me . . .

It must have been a minute at least before I saw there was another body. Prostrate on the floorboards by the door. Thin, sexless, in shapeless grey. She must have been poor, I realise

273

that now, Consuela Harbert must have been poor – with her kind smile and her six kids and her part-time job in a two-bit doss-house.

Benjamin and Christopher and I were alive, sprayed with blood but superficially wounded. Consuela Harbert was stone dead, hit through the head by a ricochet off the steel window we had been so fond of, Consuela Harbert who had liked us both and had taken the foolishly courageous course of following Christopher upstairs . . .

(In court he had to explain it all. He had bluffed her into giving him our room number, pretending he was Benjamin's brother bringing an urgent message from home. She must have suddenly sensed his rage. She was ordinary, but extraordinarily brave.)

Consuela Harbert. We killed someone. I didn't dare go over to her. I no longer knew what was happening.

Outside the window, the sirens grew louder. Perhaps for us. Perhaps they would save us, Christopher and me, from all this horror. The police would come and whisk us away . . .

I remembered. No, they were coming for him. Christopher was a murderer.

We heard them running upstairs. The last hotel in New York with stairs. Chris faced the door, gun still in his hands. I wanted to put my arms around him, I wanted to touch him, hold him – Christopher, not Benjamin; but when I tried to raise my hands only one of them moved, I felt suddenly weak, I sat on the ground, it pulled me down, the splintery floor with its thin stained carpets, I bled on the wood, I bled on the carpet, I sat in a faint as the drama ended, as the policemen shouted from outside on the landing, as Christopher threw his weapon out with a noise that made me clutch my heart, and suddenly an army of men rushed in and bundled Chris out, arms twisted up behind him.

Everything happened in another world. He was an old man, silver-haired, in tears, and small compared to the giants who held him, tooled to the gills with guns and truncheons. He looked back at me. I stared at him. Consuela Harbert lay where she had fallen; a police officer was massaging her heart, hissing 'Jesus, *Jesus*, come on, lady . . .'

I knew already it was no good. *What had I done, what had I done?*

I was mad as a hatter for two or three months. I blamed myself entirely; I sat in a darkened room and wept. Benjamin was far from dead; he had a deep but not dangerous wound by his ear where the bullet had sliced past his head. My upper arm had been pierced by mistake – at least Chris claimed it was by mistake in his confession, and I believe him.

Isaac slipped into a coma the very next day. Whatever had happened, he still had to be visited. Benjamin couldn't leave hospital, Chris was in prison. I went alone.

They had managed to do something about his breathing, but his eyes had the same unfocused look. I wasn't sure he knew me, but he did. 'Blink if you know me,' I said. He did; he wanted to hold my hand; how could it be the same hand after all that had happened since yesterday? His eyes signalled at my wounded arm, which happened to be nearest to his own freckled claw, but I gave him the other, un-painful one and began to babble nervously, stupidly, I started to tell him a torrent of lies lest he spotted the bulge underneath my blouse where the bandage pressed into my flesh; I had been in a road accident, Benjamin too, we had been mowed down by a drunken driver as we walked away from visiting Isaac, so Benjamin couldn't visit today, I was sure he would try and be back tomorrow, I thought drunken drivers should go to prison, I thought they should treat them like murderers . . . as if he knew or cared about all this shit.

And as I skidded on down a long slope of rubbish I watched Isaac leave; it was as simple as that; consciousness was there, and then it was gone, and I had an absolute intuition that it would not come back again.

Sometimes I know I am a worthless person. On the day I die I shall still remember how my lies were the last thing Isaac ever heard. He was trying to get clear, to be free of us all, and I poured out garbage on top of him. And when soon after that I became confused, and they had to take me and sedate me, I think I was still talking about that last morning, though of course nobody could understand. 'If only I'd shut up, and just said I loved him . . .' They thought I was talking about Chris, or Benjamin.

If only I'd shut up, and just said I loved him.

I went to the funeral, doped to the eyeballs. I felt I was mourning the whole of my life. The ghosts were there, through a cold sea-mist, staring out from the other end of the church where Isaac was buried. Christopher's back, I saw Christopher's back, sandwiched between the policemen's vast ones; it made me shiver with a fierce emotion, love, hatred, pity, guilt? Then the spasm died and the world returned to its general state of frozen grey.

Out of that greyness, Susy stared. She was up at the front, level with Christopher. His escort of gigantic policemen entirely occupied the right-hand pew, so Susy sat alone in the left-hand one. Her eyes tracked me down as I entered; she stared at me; she wanted me to see her; she wanted me to see the message she gave; she didn't realise that I was frozen.

The message was that she hated me. The message was that it was all my fault. I had killed her brother and imprisoned her father. Her pale green eyes burned out of the grey.

The terrible millennium. For most of the summer I was not at home. I stopped seeing Benjamin for a bit. I gave evidence to the police; they looked at me appraisingly, hostilely, staring at the bags underneath my eyes, their faces saying *What do you do? What tricks do you turn to make them fight over you?* And the other message I read everywhere: *You dirty bitch, it was all your fault.*

I visited my doctors for medication. I took my pills and then visited Christopher, knowing the pills stopped you feeling things; I sat and stared at him, curious; he sat and stared at me,

276

in turn, his face a screen of fleeting emotions, but his words were prosaic, careful, and mine were dull and careful too. Did he want chocolate? Newspapers? Pens? After three of these visits he forbade me to come. The wonderful pills stopped me suffering and helped me sleep and eat.

Benjamin was young, he recovered quickly. Then he wanted me back again. He came and found me, full of hope. And he wanted me back from the frozen north. At his urging I came off the pills. The effect was to make me talk and talk, hours and hours of breastbeating.

Benjamin denied my guilt. He prevented me from feeling what I felt.

Yet what I felt – what I felt – . . . I know now I was right to feel, I had to feel it – I should have suffered. I was guilty, guilty. Christopher was guilty, but so was I, we were both guilty. But Benjamin wanted so much to love me. He wanted me to deserve his love. And if I was guilty, so was he. Benjamin insisted I wasn't guilty. He reminded me that he'd fallen in love with me because of my kindness, my gentleness. I was a good person; I'd been good to Isaac. Whereas Christopher had hardly visited his son. He was obviously an uncaring father; more to the point, he was a maniac . . .

In the end I listened to what Benjamin told me. He told me what I wanted to hear. I didn't want to die of guilt, and shame. I didn't want to think of myself as a killer.

I told myself all sorts of nonsense as life began to return to my body. I had a right to happiness, I had a right to find myself (yet I'd travelled the world for nearly two decades; I should have found myself by then . . .)

We would go away together, just the two of us. Anywhere in the world to escape. We'd find another life where everything was light. Freedom, freedom. We were going to be free . . .

It reminded me of something a long time ago, and the memory was certainly a happy one, so why did I feel such terrible sadness?

*

We waited for the trial, in any case. The newspapers had fun with us. Isaac's was the famous name, not ours; the shorthand for him was *AIDS ART KING*. We were of interest as his adulterous parents. How quickly we slip into the past! Why hadn't we realised how well-known he was? Perhaps he had hinted, and we hadn't listened.

Christopher Court, of Islington, London, England, but actually of no fixed address, was charged with malicious wounding and murder. (Did anyone really think he meant to kill her? Why would he have bothered to murder her?) Deals were made; dollars were paid, immense amounts of money to improbable lawyers who looked and talked like film actors.

Christopher appeared looking pale and distinguished, thinner, older than before, surely too delicate to wound or murder — *surely too old to be a husband for me?*

The charge was changed to manslaughter. His previous good character was adduced, though it's hard to find witnesses to the good character of someone who's spent the last two decades travelling. (It made me think, even then. Had anyone cause to stand up for us? Had we done any good to anyone? Mary and Matthew would have obliged, but we'd lost touch with them; we'd lost them.)

I think *I* gave evidence to his good character, or else to my bad character, which meant the same thing — as I've said, after twenty-six years of marriage, everything comes down to the struggle between you.

Benjamin wanted to escort me to court; I pointed out that this was madness. As it was the cameras never stopped clicking on days when I had to be in the dock. I had to resort to the pills again. There were photos of me looking rich and disdainful; I was still a *beautiful redhead* to the papers.

It's thanks to the papers that I know that Consuela Harbert's family were in court every day. She had six children; she had told me so; I remember with pain how I envied her. I remember the blind fourteen-year-old daughter.

It may have been one of Consuela's kids but it wasn't the blind fourteen-year-old who spat at me one day as I clicked up the steps to the courtroom, numb but dressed in my best, and hit me full in the face at close range with what felt like a jugful of warm saliva . . . pills don't protect you from everything.

'The day the trial ends, we're leaving,' I vowed.

I thought, I will do nothing scandalous, ever again, nothing that might make me famous, or hated, nothing that might make another human being spit. With Benjamin I could be ordinary. Benjamin wanted a wife and a mother; I wanted a child and a new young husband, though I didn't actually mean to marry him.

I wanted to forget the imprisoned and the dead, I wanted to forget that I had been spat at, I wanted to forget Susy's terrible face, turning me to stone as she stared her hatred through the frozen seas that concealed Isaac's coffin . . .

Five years later, her face is still with me. And the thing that was beginning with Benjamin, the life that was so full of sap and hope, is dead and shrivelled like the rest. And all the years I was with him I was trying to shut out the memory. The one memory that matters absolutely. The moment when we killed someone . . .

Why am I able to face it now, even though the pillow is soaked with tears, even though my whole body aches for some drugs that will take away the pain and terror? They're on the bedside table, but I think I can resist them.

Something to do with Anna Maria. Some mysterious gift she left behind. Though I'm torn with longing when I think of her, though I'd give up everything to have her back, here in the bed as she slept before, whimpering softly as she dreamed of home — though half of me feels nothing but sorrow and hunger, the other half is glad that we took her back. Proud that we took her back before we killed her. Proud, I suppose, that we didn't kill her.

Not much to be proud of, is it?

I wish I could talk to Christopher.

Part Four

27

Susy: London, 2007

Becky is placid, pink and round, with a little cap of soft brown hair, getting thicker now, ragged at the edges, sticking out like feathers.

When she was born she was practically bald. There was a sort of swirling pattern of dark hair on her red wrinkly scalp, and Phil looked at it and said it was like magnetised iron filings, but they weren't filings, they were little threads of duck-down. When she was born she was incredibly tiny. Six pounds four ounces, the size of a bird, a chicken, perhaps, or a large pigeon, warm as the breast of a nesting bird. She was bird-boned, our darling little Becky, she lay light as a bird along Phil's arm, her head in his hand, like an egg in an egg-cup, her tiny toy feet in the crook of his elbow.

The first time she heard her father's voice she just stared at him, she looked amazed. She opened her tiny toothless mouth, opened her blue eyes very wide and stared. We'd talked to her all through pregnancy, so she knew his voice already, you see. The only other person she stared at was me. We were her parents. She was our daughter. We all belonged. We belonged to each other. I'd never felt – what do I mean? I'd never ever felt *complete* before. Completely at home. And at home in the world.

Becky is six months old. I've kept her alive for six whole months! She seems so big and solid, now. She isn't, actually, she's normal weight, but I feel so proud of having helped her grow from that beaky little scrap to a dimpled baby with nice round cheeks and chubby wrists and ankles.

Those six months seemed full of incredible dramas, the

biggest dramas of my whole life. Everything else in the past and future pales beside what I've just lived.

— There was the jaundice. We helped her get over that. Our tiny daughter developed a tan, she looked brown and healthy but really it was jaundice, they said it was 'common in the first days of life' but I couldn't let my baby have jaundice. She needed liquids. The nurses in the hospital wanted me to give her water in a bottle, but I didn't want her to get used to a bottle, I let her live on my breast instead, I let her sleep there, wake there, hang there, I made sure my breasts were hardly ever covered and she was hardly ever in the clear plastic cot in which all the other babies lay in a row. One midwife disapproved, the stupid cow. 'You'll make yourself sore,' she said. 'Ten minutes each side is all she needs. And remember to write it on your chart.'

Once upon a time I would have done what she said. Once upon a time I did whatever people told me, but I've grown up, in the last five years, I've learned that what I think is worth something. And my body's worth something, and the love I have to give. So maybe Phil's lucky to have me – maybe Becky's lucky to have me as her Mum – I try and tell myself that sometimes, since I nearly always feel I'm the lucky one.

The jaundice got better. We took her home, and lay her basket in the basement window where the February sun poured in from the garden. Becky was made better by sunlight and milk. When the jaundice was quite gone I felt enormous pride. And she put on half a pound, then a pound, then another, after the scarey two-pound dip straight after she was born. The midwife came each day and weighed her and each time it went up a little bit more, and it was milk from my tits that was making her grow.

Then there was the drama of the little stub of cord where her belly was once joined to mine. It didn't heal. I thought it must hurt her. When we bathed her it looked red and raw. The wound was so sort of – *primal*. It had to heal for her to be a person, not just a torn-off part of me. I'd been sent home from the hospital with some sterile wipes in those little individual sachets, but I felt they were hopeless, they were so dry and hard . . .

I rang up Mary. Mary Brown. My light in the dark, my comfort. Mother of two healthy grown-up babies, Mary who came and visited Becky only three hours after she was born. Mary recommended surgical spirit, swabbed on the wound with cotton-wool. Within twenty-four hours it looked less angry. Within three days it was drying up fast, and the little tag of cord fell off when I bathed her, and suddenly my Becky had a belly-button, the neat little navel she'll have all her life, and she'd taken her first step towards growing up. Not that I want her to grow up, not yet, I want these baby days to last for ever, I want to use up all the kisses and strokes and hugs I've been saving for a baby . . . but I want her to be herself, a *person*. Becky Court-Sparrow, not chained to me.

I've just gone back to work part-time. The old nursery-school couldn't take me back, so I'm supposed to be teaching eight-year-olds English, in a mediocre school ten minutes away. I dreaded it. I thought I'd be hopeless; I was never that brilliant at English myself, and I don't read much, after all who does?

But as soon as I got there things started to go well. I manage to make them laugh a lot. And books are great once you get into them. I always did like fairy-stories; so do they. We read them together, we read poems aloud, I've got them to write some stuff for themselves and read it out, they seem to trust me. I arrive out of breath at the last minute, because leaving home's harder than it ever used to be, with a heap of things to remember to do, and thousands of things to tell the babysitter – but in such a good mood, because of having Becky, the wonderful secret I have to go back to, that I want to hug them all. I smile at them instead like the Cheshire Cat in *Alice in Wonderland* which we're just reading, and it seems to make them smile too. I know it's sentimental, I know it's my hormones – at any rate that's what Madonna says – but all the same I feel I have a right to love them. Because I'm a mother. *(Extraordinary. Susy Court is a mother!)* Because I love my own daughter. I'm drunk with motherhood, drunk with my baby.

In a funny way, it's as if she's been my mother too – and God knows I needed one. I've had a new life since Becky was born. I feel as though I've been given a new body, despite the little scars from having a baby, the floppy muscles, the stitches, the numbness. Because now at last I like my body. I'm proud of it. See what it can do! Thirty-nine years old, and it made a baby! I'm still breast-feeding. I never want to stop. But until I had Becky, I didn't know I could, I didn't know these huge bloody tits were useful. They were just there, they went around with me, they drove men mad, they would never lie down. It was nice when a man I wanted liked them, but the trouble was that all men liked them, they turned men into demented morons who never looked me in the eye. Now I'm not embarrassed by them any more. I was swimming with milk right from the start, I had no more problems once the milk came in, and I couldn't help feeling a little bit smug when I heard the other mothers worrying, had they got enough, was the baby hungry, should they be giving him supplementary feeds, should they be stepping up his solids . . . I'm so proud of myself for keeping Becky happy.

Becky really is a contented baby. She loves the breast. She loves me. When she's just been fed, and lies in my arms, or on my lap on her tummy while I stroke and pat her little back and marvel at her heavy head, you can see the shape so clearly under the soft hair as she lifts it up and looks out at the world – she *sings*; there's no other word to describe it. She sings, in a clear sweet milky arpeggio, a high-pitched gentle croon of content-ment that Phil and I call her 'milk song'.

You see, I make my baby sing. I must be a good mother; songs flow from me.

And the world seems to be changing as well. I remember thinking, when I was pregnant, and Becky was already very much there, I knew her name and sex, I loved her – *What if she can never spend time in the sun? What if that ozone hole gets worse? What if she can never play in a field, or sit by the sea in her swimsuit?* She was still inside my belly, and I wondered if it would ever be safe to come out.

But the news seems to be a little better. The ozone whatsit

seems to have slowed. The hole isn't mended, but it isn't spreading. Perhaps the old fridges and perfume sprays have done their worst and released all their poison . . . But it's sooner than anyone thought that would happen. Perhaps it's the earth, finding some new pattern of healing itself.

– Or perhaps the results are being faked by someone who wants to sell fridges and perfumes . . .

No, I want to believe the worst is over. For the last two years the temperature's stayed nearly the same, though they say they can only be sure of that after ten or twenty years; but hope is free. You can't live without hope, can you? Not with a baby. I have to be hopeful.

As long as the world isn't completely ruined. We'll never be able to stay outside all day in August again without a sun-hat and suncream and shade to cool down in, but we aren't yet doomed to live in burrows, looking at films of grass and flowers. Becky will have real grass and real flowers. I'm ever so grateful. Life is good.

Of course, I get tired and furious sometimes when she won't go to sleep and I don't know what's wrong, or when she wakes an hour earlier than I can bear, at half-past five when I'm deep asleep and have to drag myself up from a blissful warm daze into a cold early morning that's all scratchy with crying. I hated her when she bit my breast, with her first sharp tooth, two painful bites. How could she bite the thing she loved? How could she hurt her Mum who loved her? I get irritable when we want to take her out and have to stop and change everything again because she's dirtied a brand new nappy. But Phil does more nappies than me, when he's here. He can't breast-feed, so he does the nappies.

(He worships Becky. He actually worships her. He babbles at her in a voice I've never heard him use before, his own kind of singing, I suppose, but he never sings in everyday life. It's soft, playful, higher than usual. 'Little little little,' he sings. 'Who's my little little little?')

The first time I ever took her out in her pram, which I didn't dare do till she was six weeks old, lying on her sheepskin, wrapped against spring winds in a soft white coat with a tiny hood which held her little head like a hand, I watched her staring up amazed at the blue and white splotches above her. They say they can't focus, but I watched her take in the wonderful blue stretch of light, and I'm sure she knew there was a world opening up, a world without any walls or curtains . . . her small blue eyes had the sky inside. And as I watched her I held it too. It was as if I found the world again through Becky.

Nothing can change the past, people say, but Phil doesn't agree, and I'm undecided. You can change what it does to you, he says. The past can be shifted as you understand it better. Some of the pain and heaviness go out of it. You can be kinder to who you were. You can be kinder to other people. If you hate yourself less, you can hate them less too.

— Becky should have had three brothers or sisters. I should have been a mother of four. Phil has listened to me for hours about this; in the end he thinks enough is enough, enough grieving, enough suffering. Nothing will bring them back again. He's wrong on that one, I know he is. I'll always have to talk about them.

I think I do believe in penance. I've suffered enough over those babies, I've wept enough about their unlived lives. I suppose I've purged my guilt, though on two occasions when Becky's been ill, once crying for days with persistent diarrhoea, once with a sudden astronomical temperature, and just for a moment I feared she would die, the shadow crept back. The horrible shadow. I no longer torture myself with blame but for the rest of my life I'll miss those children.

Looking back, the shadow that came with the abortions seems to stretch down into the distant past. As if I was always unhappy, and the abortions just happened to confirm it. As if I'd always lived in the dark. Perhaps it was when Mum died. Perhaps the shadow was my terrible anger. Because if parents run away, or kill themselves, what hope is there for the children? Even after that there were sunny patches, times with Isaac or times with Dad, or even occasionally with Alex, or days when I had fun with my friends, but then they went away and I had to grow up and the shadow came over me for good.

Except now I know it wasn't for good. It's like crawling out from under a stone. I'm just like Becky, amazed by the view.

And it's not all down to Phil and Becky, either. He didn't save me, I was saving myself. He just happened to come along at the right moment. I'd finished my training. I'd got my first job, I was enjoying living in the house with Madonna, the garden was getting over years of neglect, I'd done a lot of pruning and planting . . . Phil came to Matthew's funeral. That was the start. Quite slowly, really, we fell in love. I was ready for it, you see.

And now my life is glorious. She grew inside me. I kept her warm. My size was absolutely right for her. Madonna had gone on at me to try and lose weight, and she was just the last in an endless line. All through my teenage years people said I was plump, Alexandra could hardly bear to look at me, Dad got embarrassed and suggested more salads, even Phil once teased me about my belly . . . but my belly was a good home for Becky. I put on weight in a steady curve which the doctors approved. *Nobody* criticised! My belly stuck out and my breasts were big like all the other pregnant women waiting at the clinic.

And all of us were bursting with female hormones, but nobody raped us with their eyes. Our great big bellies protected us. I became a person, not a thing that provoked.

– That was when I really knew there was goodness in me. That discovery has changed so much . . . – whatever it means, to be good; I can't define it, I was never intellectual, but I know what it feels like. I feel what it means. Being good for people, or good to people. Good for the baby, *good*.

I missed my darling when she first left my body. I cried on the day when they told me I'd cry, but I wasn't depressed, as they'd warned me, how could I be depressed when Becky lay there asleep, on my pillow in the hospital bed? In twenty-four hours the tears had gone. And it stayed, the sense of completeness, and the knowledge that my body is a good body.

Now I start to miss her in a different way because it's possible for me to leave her. I'm glad I can be alone for a bit because it proves my happiness isn't an illusion, it doesn't disappear when Becky does. Actually I enjoy a few hours of being freer. Then I start to miss her. I long for her, the nice kind of hunger when you know you will be fed.

It's four o'clock. Nearly time for her feed. My breasts are full. They're aching, prickly. I think of her mouth, so tiny and fierce, and a trickle of milk leaks out of one nipple. Becky, my darling. They'll be home soon.

Then I hear them coming up the garden path, three floors below but the sound carries up on the hot midsummer wind with the grass and the pollen; I sneeze, as she calls me, there's a heavy scent of roses, he's singing to her and she's singing back.

Yes, there they are. I can see them now. His snow-white head bent over the pram adjusting the flowered canopy. Her grand-father, my Dad. Dad dotes on her. He adores her. Mary stands slightly to one side, head cocked, laughing a bit at the fuss he makes. They look like parents who've suddenly grown old, but he is the mother, and she is the father.

People are amazed to hear he's back after all these years, and living in the basement. We did convert it after all, but into a flat for Christopher. He's been living here since I was three months pregnant. He bought a house in Chelsea, but he was lonely. I let him be lonely, just for a bit. I thought it would be good for him to be lonely. But because I was happy, I began to forgive him. When I didn't hate myself, I couldn't hate him. Besides, I was on my own. Madonna had gone; she'd found a new man, the married man who'd bought up her firm, a rich Japanese, Yukio Oshima, and I still hadn't decided to live with Phil, I didn't dare risk it till the very last moment. I thought my Dad would be company.

Besides, he was seeing Mary. I didn't quite know what 'seeing' meant. I still don't quite know what 'seeing' means. Surely they don't – but surely they must. It isn't proper – but of course it is. I live near Mary. I wanted to encourage them. If they got married, I'd have a real mother. How funny; just when I don't need one so much . . .

Dad's deeply conventional, in his way. Odd when you think what sort of life he's led. He said of course I should live with Phil. Phil loved me, and he'd love the baby. Dad said we should get married before she was born (but we didn't – still haven't. I haven't quite dared . . .).

Dad's a different man from what he was. Older, humbler. Slower, not so strong. Phil's very fond of him, and can't quite believe me when I tell him how much I used to despise him. To Phil the whole story is fantastic, unbelievable, the world travels, the shooting in New York . . . it's a novel, or a film, to him. I think he half-thinks Dad is a hero.

I don't press the point. The anger is going. The man in the garden is a different man. I hear him laughing. An old man's laugh. Of course, my Dad is seventy-two – The great lover is seventy-two.

And now he's come home to be a grandfather. I run downstairs on a tide of love. For Becky, but there's some left for him.

Before I get to the door, the telephone rings.

28

Alexandra: Mexico City, 2007

I've been living alone for nearly two years. In a city of thirty million people, the biggest city in the world.

I don't know why I came to Mexico City. I knew I must come to Mexico, though, once I had realised I couldn't go home. I'll never go home. I know that now.

I wanted to be alone. I wanted to be with crowds of people. So many millions of us live here, in a curious milky bowl of bad air kept in by the ring of mountains; snow-covered mountains, but we never see them, because the air we breathe is opaque. You get used to it. I've got used to it. I haven't lost hope; one day I'll see them. One amazing morning they will be there.

Everything else is here. Everything human is in this city. People of bronze, they call themselves, but actually every human colour, permutations of Spanish, Indian, African, Mayan, Aztec . . . I sometimes feel like a ghost among them, so pale that no one notices me.

I know this city is right for me. It's old, like me. It was built on a lake, it was once another Venice, the glittering Tenochtitlán, but the canals and waterways have long dried up and the tower buildings have sunk and settled. Some of them lean a little, now, as if they're trying to get back to the water which must still run deep underground. Decades ago I dreamed of living in Venice . . . but that was with Christopher, and I am alone.

I bought a flat – a modest flat – in a tower block within walking distance of the Alameda Gardens. The vendor himself tried to dissuade me; surely I wanted something larger, smarter . . .? But it suited me fine. It was curiously . . . homely.

No more hotels. No more moving on. Now I know my way

in the half-dark. When I wake in the night and can't get back to sleep, I can feel my way from room to room without having to put the light on. The flat is quite new but the furniture is old, heavy dark shapes that I seem to have known forever, and glide around by instinct.

I've begun to belong to these dim spaces.

Two years ago in Paris I so nearly went home, I so nearly went back to what was once home . . . I didn't, so I suppose I never shall.

This flat will have to be my home.

I was in Paris grieving for Anna Maria. Fresh from the disaster in Brazil. I dumbly, unreasonably felt it was time. Time to go home, to crawl back home, now I'd lost my child and parted with Benjamin. Time to go back to London. I was half-crazy of course, I deluded myself. I thought I might talk to Mary Brown, I thought I could tell her everything . . . I was within an ace of picking up the phone.

But I suddenly knew it was no good. Paris is so near London, but it was no good. I thought of Mary and only saw blackness. I had a feeling of terrible foreboding; Mary or her family was dying, I knew; no one would have any time for me. I'm borderline psychic, always have been. I couldn't have borne to ring up and be rejected. I thought, I can manage on my own, I have to.

Then something happened to steel my nerve. Something trivial, a casual pick-up, an unlikeable man whose name I've forgotten . . . but it got me on the next plane for Mexico City. Not for a holiday. To stay. I still don't understand what happened . . .

I'd begun to feel a little better, I remember. I'd skulked in the hotel for nearly three days, paralysed with misery, but I slowly started to feel life creeping back, and with it came the old hunger for Paris. The silver avenues, the dreamy attics.

I dragged myself up and went for a walk, dressed up in my most beautiful clothes to disguise that I still felt ill and old . . .

I went, as so often, over the decades, with Christopher, to the Jardin du Luxembourg. The chestnut trees were still there. And replicas of the green iron chairs, and the boating lake, my old favourite, though the children were playing with amazing remote-controlled submarines . . . But the children were playing. Their clear high voices. I sat on a chair to watch for a bit. I wasn't in Paris, I was in Brazil, hearing the voice of Anna Maria . . . When the uniformed man came to sell me a ticket I didn't notice he was there . . . then a boy came to sit beside me. He was watching me, sidelong. I arranged my face, I crossed my long legs above the knee. I was not averse to being looked at.

What was his name? . . . Jean-Claude, Jean-Pierre? I remember his hanks of blue-black hair which reminded me of Anna Maria's, his brooding eyes, his full red lips. He was skinny, wiry, dressed in bright blue cotton from head to toe, as had just become the fashion then. He was anything from eighteen to twenty-five, not just young, *young* young.

I'm afraid my first thoughts were straightforwardly sexual. Benjamin and I hadn't had sex for weeks, with the tension as we waited for the child, then Anna Maria sleeping in our bed. I had so much on my mind that my body had gone hungry. The body is important. It must be looked after, or else it will start to turn against you. Long ago I used to look after my body. For the past two years I haven't bothered, but that day in Paris I considered the boy, I stroked my thighs, I uncrossed my legs, I felt a tingle in the centre of me, I thought *my body might enjoy you.*

We talked inconsequentially. He was a student, he said, a graduate. His parents were rich; I knew that from his clothes, from the confidence that fought with his shyness. He asked about me. I said I was a mystery. I said at my age too much had happened; to tell him everything would take all day. 'And all night,' I added, looking hard at him. I saw something there; pride, resistance. Perhaps he wanted to make the moves. He was very attractive; that wiry grace, the shining teeth behind his full lips. Fifty-year-old teeth don't shine so much. His eyes were thick-lashed, almost black.

We walked a little in the summer heat which didn't feel at all hot to me; I enjoyed the spaces, the measured greenness, the way that everything was planned, I looked forward to a game I hadn't played in ages. There was a breeze, a real breeze that day, not a gale, which we are all afraid of, nor the sticky stillness of the tropical forest; a green summer breeze, which lifted my hair, blew my red hair out into the sunlight, whipped a few strands across his face, and he laughed, enjoyed it, brushed it away, and my skirt lifted too, we were floating, flying . . .

I suggested we lunch together, I would pay. He seemed to stiffen, then agree. I don't know how long it takes those heavy tranquillisers to leave the system completely; I wasn't supposed to drink with them, but I hadn't taken pills for nearly two days.

– Maybe I shouldn't blame the tranquillisers. Maybe I just wanted to be drunk. I should blame my desperate wish to forget, at the very moment in my life when I'd just understood *in theory* that no good would come from forgetting, no hope of forgiveness, no happiness.

We settled at a table in dappled sunlight. The place was expensive, and used to be good. The linen was amazing, after Brazil, thick as snow and blinding white, sticking out stiffly over our knees. I thought of Christopher; I thought of the mountains; I forced myself not to think these things.

'Beautiful linen,' I said to Jean-Claude.

'Too much bleach,' he frowned.

'I didn't know you were so strict . . .'

He smiled again, entirely charming.

'You're so delightful I can't be strict. But you know these bleaches are so bad for the water . . . let's order some wine and forget about the water.'

Everything shone with anticipation, the silver, the glasses, the linen. The bread – French bread, not coarse Brazilian! – was blonde and crusty with a tender warm centre, the butter white and sweet as a kiss. I wanted my little friend to be happy; I was actually feeling happy myself. I passed him the wine list with a deferential smile, and without looking at it he ordered champagne. *It was going to be fun. I could still have fun.*

And I started to tell him about my wonderful life. My extraordinary travels all over the world. I drank deep of the champagne, and showed off for him. I wanted him to know what a prize he was getting, if I should decide to give myself. I reeled off names and recommendations.

At first he went through the motions of listening, handsome head angled attentively, inserting the required amounts of curiosity to keep my gazeteer unfolding. Indeed I thought he was very impressed. I thought he was virtually stunned into silence; I reined myself in, a little; I wanted to dazzle, but not frighten, the boy. I paused, and sucked in another three snails drenched in heavenly garlic butter. A little of it ran down my chin; I wiped it, flirtatiously, on the napkin.

'And you,' I said. 'Do you travel at all?'

'I'm not a tourist,' he said. That was it. He stared down at his plate, refusing me. His charcoal-thick lashes hid his eyes. I asked him if I'd said something wrong.

'I think you've lived your whole life wrong, but that's only my opinion, Madame, and I really don't want to upset you . . . Let's change the subject. Have some dessert. Have you seen any theatre in Paris?'

Naturally I couldn't leave it at that. I was completely rattled. What could he mean? I begged him to explain, I pleaded with him. I saw him enjoying his power, then.

We went back to my hotel to talk further. I was tipsy enough not to want to talk, by the time we got to the high-ceilinged room with the vast pale bed and the view over Paris; I wanted to shut out the rest of the world, I wanted to crawl into bed with him, I wanted to be given the treat I craved and then to wake up and find him gone.

But he wasn't so easily disposed of. Jean-Claude was an anthropologist; Jean-Claude was a philosopher. He was a Marxist too, and in the twenty-first century how often does one meet one of those? He was a pedagogue, once he got started; he had the absolutism of youth; and – as I found out at the end of the day, when I started to get a swingeing headache and to long for sleep, solitary sleep, without his voice boring on in my ear –

his attitude to women was an awkward mixture of shyness, lust and cruelty.

Yet for all that, what he told me was true. I knew as he spoke that it was all true. I must have known it before, in some part of me, and that arrogant boy just put it into words as he tossed his black cow-lick away from his black eyes. How handsome he was, this prince of darkness, how sure he was of his own virtue. How he enjoyed despising me! How he wanted to fuck me, though.

He said I had never travelled at all. He said Christopher and I had been nowhere, done nothing. We had fed an industry, that was all. We had failed to see the simplest facts. Did I know that tourism was the biggest industry in the world at the beginning of the twenty-first century? He said Christopher and I were archetypal tourists. We had tried to buy the world, and missed it.

He asked me if I'd met the local people; eaten their food; stayed in their houses; been in their houses, even. (I had, when we were trying to buy the child, but I didn't tell him about that.) He asked me if I realised that all the hotels we'd stayed in were the same. I denied that, furiously, and started to describe them in detail, the most spectacularly eccentric ones, built in old castles or old monasteries, built on piles over picturesque lakes . . . I could feel myself getting red in the face, but Jean-Claude, or Jean-Pierre, just laughed at me. 'Window-dressing. It's not the real world. You floated about in a fantasy space invented to please you foreigners . . . You spent most of your time with other English people, or rich Americans, or Japanese . . .' He was getting actively angry now, warming to his theme as he drank the brandy a blank-faced waiter had brought to the room. '. . . You probably spent most of your time with your husband. Your nice fat bourgeois English husband. Drinking and fucking and stuffing yourselves, and then going out to buy souvenirs which were fabricated with you in mind. Tourism is a gigantic con-trick –'

' – We weren't *tourists*, we travelled on our own, we never went on package tours, we never asked for fish and chips – *we looked at things*. That's not a crime.'

297

'But everything's getting worn away by all you people *looking at things*. Not understanding, just looking, touching, because you want to feel you possess them, you've been there, done that, stolen their soul . . . Except you know nothing about their soul. You only know what you read in your guide-book, some glib bit of nonsense written for tourists. Then you stroll back to your luxury hotel and start pressing your wrist-phone for another destination, another airport, another hotel . . . And the people who it all belongs to – the real people, the ordinary people – the people who live and work in these places – probably poor people living simple lives – you only meet them as servants. People you never notice or look at, like the waiter who brought up these drinks. Don't deny it, I saw how you hardly said thank you – '

' – But *he* ignored *me*, for goodness' sake, you Parisians are always so snooty – '

'We don't like English people much. Stupid, materialistic, soulless – ' (this was getting out of hand, I should have to get rid of him, but I saw he was getting excited, now, staring at my breasts as he insulted me) ' – in any case, that's not the point. The point is, your travel was just a hobby. The world was reduced to an accessory. You looked at whatever flattered you. You were blind to everything that mattered. Poverty, disease would have upset you. You would have been bored by people's real lives – '

'That's not true! That really isn't true! It was one of the things I missed. Something real – whatever that might be. Not all the time, but occasionally. I did sometimes feel our lives were unreal, there's a lot of truth in what you say – I just didn't know where to begin. My husband was always watching films, or swimming. At least I walked. I seemed to walk endlessly. I never knew quite where to go. I did want to see things, I was interested, I wanted the names of birds and trees – but there weren't any books about them in English, there weren't any books about them in Spanish, there weren't any books, period – I suppose I could have tried to get the locals to explain, but I didn't know how to get through to them – they were often hostile, or suspicious – ' I was flapping about like a nervous hen, justifying things that required no justifying, telling him things he didn't need to know. Why was I letting him do this to me? He was the merest stripling, spoiled and aggressive – and he, unlike me, had been rich from birth. Why should I let him rattle me?

Now he was taking out his penis. It was engorged, a shiny, rosy toadstool; he held it towards me with his fingers, indicating that I should masturbate him. His dark eyes were hard, excited. Make the bitch feel small, then fuck her. But I wasn't going to play that game. I have never been a masochist. I realised that I no longer felt drunk, whereas he was lit up with Armagnac. I had a headache, but I was sober.

'OK, you've made your point. Which must be why I'm bothering to justify myself. There's no point in quarrelling, is there? If a life has been wasted, it's mine, not yours . . . look, I'm older than you. I know things you don't. Recently I've suffered a great deal. And I shan't make love while you're being aggressive. I'm too old for that. It's a mug's game, little one.'

Then because he looked so crestfallen – because he had shrivelled to the size of a wren, a fledgeling abandoned on his blue cotton trousers, because his red mouth was on the verge of tears – I took pity on him, and ordered coffee and omelettes to be sent to the room. I took his hand, and sat him down in the window where we could look over the rooftops, the eccentric and magical rooftops of Paris, their silver-grey slowly darkening, the sky becoming an indigo blue, the first stars coming, so old and so young – and I said 'Have you travelled? Do you know about travelling? Tell me how I should have travelled.'

And for the next two hours he did just that. He didn't understand about talking and listening, men and women, give and take, even in the twenty-first century there are cave men still; yet his principles were wonderful; sharing, learning, avoiding exploitation, respecting others, respecting the earth.

The theory was not of much interest to me. I always go to sleep when men talk theory. But one thing was absolutely wonderful. He talked about a trip he made to the Himalayas.

my friend and occasional boyfriend who has a silver shop in the Zona Rosa, gets very angry with the squatters, although almost nothing makes him angry. I love the trees, but I'm quite sorry for the people, and sorry I have to think about them; that's one of the problems of settling down; if you keep moving you never have to think.

I've grown very attached to that garden. Just one small window of air and light, then a jumble of buildings eats up the world all the way to its curving edge, which wavers in a grey-blue haze. Not unattractive to the eye, but poisonous.

I've boxed myself in, I suppose. No easy exits from this city. Here I am, alone with myself at last, in the biggest city in the world.

— I've read. I've thought. I am capable of thought. I've written letters that I've never posted, to Mary, to Susy, to Christopher, even to the garrulous Parisian boy who started me thinking about our travels, but I tore that one up; it would make him vain, and he was quite vain enough already.

I've made some friends, just by staying put. Juanita, the retired teacher in the flat next door, who I thought at first was terribly dull because of her grey hair and matronly clothes, turned out to be kind-hearted and funny. She's got a beaky face like a humorous parrot, flashing gold teeth when she laughs, which is often, and rather remarkable topaz eyes which it took me months to notice. She long ago despaired of Mexico City. 'It's dying, darling, you must see that; the more it grows, the sicker it gets; all cities are bad, but this one is madness.'

Yet the Alameda park survives. We admire it together as the seasons change, Juanita and I, my friend and I, from our adjoining fourth-floor balconies. Tiny people come and garden, watering and weeding, raking and planting, though the water supply is so often cut off, and official regulations ban hose-pipes; but the gardeners keep on watering. No one has dared to build on it yet. It's always there to welcome me when I open my curtains at six in the morning.

Juanita loves the garden too, though she wouldn't put it in the same words. At first she used to laugh in a kind of uproarious terror if I said anything that might be called strange. I was the first Englishwoman she had really known. Occasionally we met down at ground level, in the ugly foyer by the creaking lift. I always made her stop and talk to me. She was a widow; I'd lost my husband. Single people need each other. I know she was sometimes lonely, too. We sat on a seat and watched the finches. She'd had three husbands, and five kids, but she'd never married her favourite lover. We laughed about sex, and men, and ageing. I confided in her when Manuel began to court me, poor formal Manuel with his passion for ties and his sweet temper and his love of sweet rolls.

One day I discovered we were both fifty-six, though at first I'd thought Juanita two decades older. I was mildly piqued that she wasn't surprised. But later when I went and had a good look in the mirror, I saw how much I'd let myself change. There was no way back. One day I'd be sixty. Too old to look like a young girl. I couldn't be bothered with makeup here; I'd let the grey grow into my hair; I didn't know anywhere to buy the henna that Benjamin never knew I used.

Besides, the grey is mine. Red and grey mixed is my colour now. I shall never grow younger, or be more beautiful. But I can survive. I've decided to survive. I can make friends. I can relax. I can sit and play cards with Juanita, I can linger over *la comida* with Manuel, I can teach English to Juanita's grandchild, I can shop with Emilia, the caretaker's wife, who stops them cheating me at the market – not that I buy much more than bread and beans.

I've learned there are many ways of being with people, that people can like me and like to be with me, that I don't have to try and make all men want me and all women envy me – not that I could, even if I tried. I'm tired, you see. All that is over.

But I'm not over. I'm not finished. There's a lot of unfinished business yet.

At night I don't close the shutters. No one can see me, four floors up, and I like to look over the glittering city, diminishing into the far night sky with its ominously beautiful orange-lit clouds; down there every light means three or four people, in

303

cafes and clubs maybe thirty, a hundred, and the lights themselves are innumerable, it would take the rest of my life to count
them — I started so late, you see.

Every morning I see the people clearly. Down in the streets,
in cars, on bikes, trudging along under dirty bundles, carrying
flowers, briefcases, babies — so many of them carrying babies —
running, walking, staggering, skipping, lying in the gutter with
a bottle of *mezcal*, sitting on the pavements with giggling friends
or pyramids of fruit or shoe-shine stands, miniature people with
dust-blackened faces — fathers of families going to the office,
mothers of families going to the factory, sleepy schoolchildren
trotting to school, grandfathers going to buy tobacco, grand-
mothers going for milk and bread, whistling street-sweepers,
swaggering policemen — and the poor, of course. The poor,
going nowhere. *So many of them. So unimaginably many.*

They were always there, but I never saw them. Going down
among them I am almost overwhelmed; now I am old I'm
invisible; the people swarm along the shining streets, alive with
the sum of all their separate energies, pouring forward, pouring
outwards, gathering speed as I run down. They are so many, we
are so many. So many people I had never seen, so many people
I had never felt part of.

I thought we were different, special, golden. Alexandra and
Christopher. I thought we were the golden ones. I wanted
everyone to look at me; I never bothered to look at them, not
unless they were beautiful or interesting. But we weren't special,
were we? We were just rich.

Inside the flat, when my friends aren't there, the voices come for
me.

— I can't alter what I've been and done. Too late to change its
littleness; I was clever, creative; I could have done more . . . I
tried to do more, but nothing came. Instead I did damage. Quite
a lot of damage. I missed opportunities, let things escape me,
wrecked them because I didn't know what they were . . .

It's not so much that I had my daughter adopted — I was so

very young, unrecognisably young, I can hardly remember what I was like, only that life was desperate, and she didn't look like me, not a bit, she had a squashed head and never seemed to stop crying, her poor little head was squashed by the forceps, even her birth I couldn't get right . . . It's not the abortion, even, though I still sometimes cry when I think of it, inextricably entangled in my mind with the miscarriage two decades later, Christopher's two miscarried children – it's not so much those stupid messes as the two children I failed to see. The two who were there, who needed me.

– Isaac and Susy. They were still so young when they first began to live with me. I couldn't see that they were children. I saw them as problems that went with Christopher, things that always got in the way and stopped the two of us enjoying ourselves. They were five and eight, but I fought them like adults. Susy at five was lovable, I can see that now, remembering her, but at twenty-four I had no love to give, and I wanted all Chris's love for myself. She wanted to cuddle, she wanted to talk, she wanted her dolls when she missed her mother, she missed her dolls when I threw them away – she screamed at me without the power to hurt me. I was cool and adult; I was mad as a hatter, but no one dared to tell me so.

How could I have taken her dolls away?

Now I can see that they were all babies, I just couldn't bear to think about babies, I'd lost two babies in the last four years, but Susy was too young to understand, *I* was too young to understand . . . only now do I begin to understand, but it's a lifetime too late for Susy.

I suppose that nothing will go right for her. I suppose she'll go on as she began, disliking herself, hurting herself, all because I disliked her and hurt her. I suppose she's the one I've damaged the most, if I leave out Christopher. Susy and I haven't spoken since the shooting. I've never dared to pick up the phone. I sent her a postcard about Anna Maria, when everything seemed so hopeful. Odd I should write to her about that. Or maybe not so odd, alas. In some shameful way I felt competitive with Susy; she looked so . . . fecund, so bursting with babies . . . so I wrote to tell her I was going to be a mother. She didn't answer, naturally. And I never wrote to tell her that I failed. Like her, I failed to be a mother. If it was a competition, nobody won.

In the moments when I'm not reading or sleeping or spending time with Mexican friends, I think about them, my family, all the people who have touched my life, whether they're related to me or not – the nearest thing I have to a family, God help me, since I lost my first family, I cut them off, they cut me off, I was amputated. Susy, Penelope, Benjamin. Mary and Matthew; they mattered once. Stuart, but I don't like to think about Kirsty. Anna Maria. Oh Anna Maria. Isaac, yes. And Christopher.

All of them gone. *What have I done?*

The trial is endless, the verdicts shift.

– I forgive myself for what I did to Isaac, because *he* forgave me, in the end. I forgive myself for what happened to Penelope; I tell myself that one is Christopher's fault, and anyway she was a sick woman. And Benjamin was young, he needed to suffer, he wanted to suffer, he was madly in love, and a painter needs a grand passion, he said so. One day I'll probably appear in his paintings, a De Kooning harpy with scarlet hair . . .

But then I remember Susy, at the funeral, Susy's eyes bear down on me, and the verdict is always *Guilty, guilty* . . .

It whispers on, accusations, denials, when the flat is empty, when my mind is empty, when I stare across the city at dusk, before the colours drain away, pinks and greys and the dove-blue haze, as isolated lights start to pierce the evening, as the sirens start to wail, then die – as I stare across miles of crowded streets which know nothing at all about my ghosts. They are my ghosts, mind; I have to care for them. I hear the voices as I do my housework, all the small tasks that go with living, polishing, cleaning, cooking, washing, for I can look after myself, you see, I'm doing it to prove I can – I review the evidence, I sentence myself, I sentence myself to yet another trial.

Possibly the voices are getting quieter. I've been here two years; are they running down? – I always leave out Christopher, because his case is so fundamental. By Christopher I stand or fall . . . how can I extricate myself from him? How much was

306

my fault, how much his? I suppose we're in the dock together, except that we're so far apart. We lived together. We should be together.

We lived together, we should die together.

But I'll never make a move, of course. I'm afraid of rejection. I did betray him. I wanted to escape the sense of failure, I wanted fun and sex and passion and cigarettes with Benjy in the sunset light; I forgot I loved Chris, I managed to forget him, how could I forget all those years together? I saw something I wanted, and traded Chris in . . .

But Chris was the one who went to prison, and Consuela Harbert was the one who died. I got off scot free, except for the voices, *what have I done, what have I done* . . .

Maybe Anna Maria was my punishment. Loving her so much was my punishment.

Chris is out there somewhere. He's still alive. Someone would have told me if he had died. Mary would have told me, good old Mary, Mary Brown would have found me, somehow, Mary would never let me down, though we haven't written for nearly five years . . .

When I think of it like that . . . that he's living somewhere, the same man, Christopher, my lover; my friend, my brother, who I slept beside, who slept so close to me for twenty-six years, we heard each other snore and sleep-talk and snuffle, we knew each other's bodies as if they were our own – the little hairs on my arms bristle, I stare at the horizon with such stupid longing, because somewhere behind it he's still there, and until people die, everything is possible – he's never divorced me, has he? He's never tried to find me, but he's never divorced me –

And yet it's not possible. I know it's not. I shall never be calm until I accept it.

But sometimes things seem so simple. I just want to hold him in my arms. I want to stroke his hair, and tell him I'm sorry. After the shooting I never said sorry.

I think I just have to shelve it all, put off the reckoning into the future. There's plenty of time. I'm only fifty-seven.

— But Christopher is seventy-two. People can die at seventy-two.

It's been a day of rare, headachey heat, one of those days when the sky screws down like a lid on a jarful of captured insects and the whole city longs for rain. I've had all the windows open, despite the fumes, but not a breath of air has come to me — it's the weather, you see. That's why I brood so much. Manuel is on holiday in Acapulco. I could have gone with him but I'm tired of holidays. Twenty years of holidays is quite enough. And Juanita's gone away to see her daughter. I'll watch night come; that always calms me.

Tomorrow there's a fair in the Alameda. There are so many feast days I lose count, but tomorrow I'll go and enjoy myself. Be with people. That's the answer. I'm all right really. I'm fine in myself. I watch my garden, morning and evening, holding the sun at the end of the day, and I think *I'm surviving, I'm doing well.*

And another little voice thinks, *something will happen. There's unfinished business. Something will happen.*

— And something has happened. It can't be undone. Now the rest of my life will be measured from that.

The day of the fiesta was two weeks ago. I've lived that two weeks hour by hour. I'm so afraid. So alone.

Hard to re-create how I felt that morning. I'd slept soundly; my headache was gone; I woke up excited about the fair. It had rained in the night and the air felt fresher. My depression had lifted; I felt optimistic.

But everything's not in the mind. I thought I was resting, but my body had been busy. The housework wasn't enough for it. That day I stretched in the bedroom mirror as I often did, like a figurehead, stretching the stiffness from my bones, pulling my thin arms back like wings, when I thought one breast moved a little differently.

Imagine my indignation and surprise when I found a tiny

lump, no bigger than a seed, a buried seed-pearl or a birth-control pill, on the edge of my breast. It was very small. Perhaps I was imagining it. All morning I kept testing, my fingers compelled to creep back to my breast again and again, sure that this time it would have gone away, or transformed itself into a wart, or a pimple. One time I couldn't find it, and broke into a sweat, a wonderful sweat of joy and relief, but I'd simply looked in the wrong place. The little stone was hiding half-an-inch away.

So then I wasn't quite so sure there was time. The horizon seemed to have moved a little closer, the sirens sounded sharper, nearer. I was only fifty-seven, too young for this. All my life I had been unimpeachably healthy. I had never breast-fed; surely that made me safer? Breast-feeding must put your breasts at risk. I'd read something about it, but I couldn't remember, and when I did remember, I'd got it all wrong, because breast-feeding protected you, and I had never managed to feed a baby . . . Surely this was happening to somebody else.

But there was no one else. I was on my own. I knew what was happening, and to whom.

Out of the window, the gardens had vanished. The green had gone under a riot of stalls, and brightly-coloured bodies surged and retreated, looking from up here like a single life-form with complicated rhythms of its own. I didn't want to be alone. Juanita wouldn't be back for a week, Miguel should be back but wasn't answering the phone, perhaps he was down there with all the others.

I had spent the morning sitting numbly in my night-dress, but I dragged on some clothes, and went down to the street.

I've always loved dancing. It's a little like fucking, but people can admire you doing it . . . for the past two years, though, I'd hardly danced. Today everyone was dancing. As I neared the garden the music came to meet me, pulsing, vibrating salsa music, and just for a moment it lifted my heart, just for a moment my feet were twitching . . . but then I understood it was for the others, the painted crowd with their vivid life, the magic circle of the living, and I wouldn't dance, because I'd stepped outside. Besides, I no longer had anyone to dance with.

The noise and movement were so violent that my solitary terror was blown away. There were orange and green dragons with gaping nostrils, red and purple cocks with flaming crests, all of them soaring up and down on poles with hysterical women on their backs, clinging on helpless, entirely happy. Two skeletons wandered arm in arm, almost genial when there were two of them and their ghastly grins were aimed at each other; perhaps they were going off duty for a bit. Children screamed on a big dipper which never seemed to stop, whirling for ever against the sky, faster than normal, was something wrong? They must be getting tired, I was getting tired . . . no one else but me was watching, no one else but me was tired, everyone was in perpetual motion, buying or selling, laughing, shouting, changing partners, disguising themselves, hiding from someone who was looking for them, hiding from something which was tracking them down . . . I stood for a while and watched the dancers, in bright satin skirts split to the crotch or trousers so tight that their genitals wagged, drunk with their bodies, with sex, with life . . . one couple, less flamboyantly dressed than the others, middle-aged, I saw, when I glimpsed their faces, danced in a style less extrovert than most but so meltingly sexual I could hardly watch; every inch of their bodies was turned to the other; they rubbed, they clung, they kissed, they pressed, only the barrier of skin stopped them flowing together, and their heads, as they kissed again, gently, seriously, expressed such hypnotised tenderness that they seemed to be miming a long-lost love-story, they showed me what Christopher and I once had; I longed to be touched; I turned away.

Somebody touched me on the arm. I saw the hand first, a white-gloved hand. I turned to face whoever it was.

The skeleton had come back on duty. He was alone, and no longer looked genial, and I was alone, and I had to face him. 'Give me something,' he said, softly. 'You have to give me something, now.' I gave him money. 'Not enough.' I gave him more money, and ran away, but I knew I still hadn't given enough, I hoped to lose him among all the dancers.

As I panted into the foyer of the flats I still had a feeling he was behind me. The lift rose noisily, familiar noises, *stop this, you're just imagining things . . .*

But as the blare of the fiesta faded away, I was left alone with the new normality, I walked into the horror of the empty flat and slipped my fingers under my blouse, feeling for the thing I had not imagined.

I thought I had only been out half-an-hour, but somehow two hours had rushed past. I had the sensation of time speeding up. Certain things became clearer, more certain.

I would die if I didn't talk to him.

(And yet the lump was so little, so dainty, tucked so demurely under my armpit. And I knew most lumps weren't cancerous; why should I be among the unlucky few? – But I had never been one of the many. I had *always* been one of the few.)

I hardly ever wore my wrist-phone – almost no one did in Mexico City, and indeed most people still used old-fashioned handsets; they didn't want their mothers to follow them around – the problem was I could never find it when I really needed to make a call. I wasted another hour searching and cursing; I had used the bloody thing only that morning . . . By the time I found it I was on the edge of tears, and the certainty I'd felt was leaking away.

It was nine o'clock in Mexico City. I pressed for the time in faraway London. Four o'clock. What an English time. It would be tea-time in England now.

– After all these years, the house would be sold. That was why Susy hadn't answered my cards, it wasn't because she was angry with me. As I dialled I already knew what would happen; the little lapse in time for a trip round the world, the twenty-first century hadn't changed that, my hunger to hear him wouldn't change that; then the long despairing howl of Number Obsolete. Or the bell would ring in the familiar house or on the wrist of someone eating muffins in the garden, I would gasp out my name, I would ask for Chris, and an unfamiliar voice would say 'Sorry, wrong number.'

The little lapse in time seemed longer than usual. I imagined my hope running under grey oceans where everyone I'd ever known was drowned, and the wire just missed him, floating face downwards, while a nightmare version of Susy screamed 'He's *rotten*, you fool. He died *years* ago.' Someone picked up the phone. My heart thudded.

The 'Hallo' that followed was curious, hopeful, but still recognisably Susy. But I wasn't sure. I asked her, terrified, deferring the moment when I had to say my name and explain what my business could possibly be; in any case I no longer knew, in my guilt and fear I knew nothing clearly except that I badly wanted to ring off before she started to abuse me.

'Is that Susy Court?'

'Speaking.' A long silence. 'Hallo?'

'Yes. It's . . . Alexandra. Alexandra, your stepmother.'

Then it was her turn to be silent. 'Oh . . . I got your postcard. Congratulations.' She sounded as apprehensive as me.

'What do you mean, congratulations?'

'You were just about to adopt a child – '

'Never mind that, it's not important. I mean – never mind what I mean. Do you know – I suppose you don't know – do you have a phone number for your father?' I said 'your father' to propitiate her, to say I acknowledged her prior claim.

Another long pause. I could hear her breathing, I could hear our breathing, my chest had tightened, I prepared myself for her refusal.

'Well – as a matter of fact he's here . . . with Mary Brown. Do you remember her?' – and I swear her voice had an edge of anger; I swear she knew she was punishing me – 'She's a widow now. She's going out with Dad. He's very well and very happy. We're all *all right*, you know. I've got a baby. Things are going well – '

– She didn't say it, but I heard the conclusion; *so don't upset us. We're doing fine without you.* She didn't need to say anything, actually; I was poleaxed with grief and jealousy.

Mary Brown. *Mary Brown!* She was always sly; she had always wanted him, pretending to be so demure and kind. And all the time she was after Chris. I was fighting to breathe and to speak without crying.

'Oh. That's – lovely.' *I said it was lovely!* 'I'm – glad to hear you're all OK. I'm glad to hear you've had a baby.' The tears were coming, but not yet in my voice, pouring down my cheeks, the world was dissolving. 'Actually I won't bother Chris. If he's busy with Mary. But send my regards. Say – say – *I thought about him.* I've got to go now. Goodbye, Susy – ' My nose pricked; my sinuses gushed, but the words came out with hardly a tremor, thank God to be fifty, and not fifteen –

She broke in, alarmed. 'You should speak to him. I really think you should speak to him – '

What did she want? She wanted me to suffer, they wanted me to suffer, I was dying, dying, they wanted to rub my nose in my loss – 'No, it's OK, another time, there's someone at the door, I'm just going out – ' There was no one at the door, everyone had left me, I would never be asked to go out again.

'Alexandra, don't be ridiculous. You know he'll blame me if you just ring off – '

'This is too expensive, I'm in Mexico City – ' But she knew I never worried about expense. 'There's no point, I'm leaving for Europe soon . . .'

'Give me your number! Stop playing with us!' She was suddenly furious, the same old Susy who had glared at me at the funeral; perhaps she did think I was playing with them; I no longer cared what Susy thought, I only cared about finding some tissues and getting off the phone before I sobbed.

Yet Christopher might be only inches away. With Mary Brown. With that ugly old cow.

'Goodbye, Susy.' I flicked the off-switch, and fell on my knees in a passion of sobs. I clutched myself, I rocked myself. There was no one else to comfort me. But the hands that hugged me with such hopeless strength could not keep still, had not forgotten; as I knelt on the floor and howled at the darkness my fingers were feeling for the lump.

They say the best doctors are still in Europe.

29

Christopher: London, 2007

Happy man; lucky man. Christopher, beloved of the gods. After the years of hell in a New York prison and the years living like a rat in Venice, waiting to go down when the city did, I've been forgiven; I've been reclaimed. I wake up unable to believe it's true. I wake in my sun-drenched basement bedroom, so clean and light with its pale new wood, look up through the windows at the dancing blackthorn and behind it the shimmering columns of the poplars, silver green in the morning light, and the gross black fingers of the monkey-puzzle tree, and the nodding roses, such pinks, such creams – the sights of home. I've been allowed to come home. I'm clean again. I've been forgiven.

But more than that, I am loved, loved. Loved by my daughter, loved by my granddaughter. *(I have a granddaughter! A grandfather at last!)*

– I'm a real grandfather. I'm useful. A working grandfather, not honorary. I babysit for Susy whenever she needs me. I can change nappies. I can give bottles. (Penelope took charge of the nappies and bottles, and when she was working, the nanny did it; I'd never changed a single nappy.) The child gurgles when she sees me coming, my darling girl, my little Becky, perhaps she has seen the resemblance between us, for she is pure Court, she's exactly like me. Susy has given me a granddaughter.

And then there's Mary. Sweet Mary Brown. Just as I had wished. Just as I had dreamed! – Not quite as I had dreamed, but marvellous.

I came back to Matthew's funeral, desperately nervous, expecting nothing, but homesick, so homesick I had to risk it, I knew everyone who mattered would be there, Mary and her family, Susy –

Perhaps not *everyone* who mattered.

For one mad moment I thought she was here, I saw a ghost in an elegant veil with Alex's mouth and stick-thin figure – but it was Madonna, Susy's friend. Why is the brain so predictable? – I have sighted Alexandra a million times since the last day I saw her in that echoing prison, when a fly landed on her crimson shoulder, and she swatted it, and it slowly died there. I've seen her escaping down Venetian alleyways, waving at me from distant gondolas, flitting down the side of a foggy canal – it was never her. It's never her. Now I've found a way of controlling the ache – but enough of that. It's too early in the day. Don't think of that, don't spoil things. Reality is enough for me; I'm happy, so happy; be grateful for that. It wasn't her, it was a trick of memory.

– Mary turned round and smiled at me. There was no shadow; she smiled at me. She's accepted me back, right from the start. There's a clear radiance about her thinking, a total inability to lie or waste time. She knows what she wants. But she wants *me!* And she could hardly believe I wanted her.

She was looking beautiful that day, classically dressed in her funeral blacks, with her hair pulled back from that milky forehead. (I wish she dressed like that more often; most of the time she looks a mess; occasionally it irritates me.) After the service I went to Susy; she took my hand, she held my hand, then she put her arms round me and leaned against me. Phil stood beside us, smiling all the time, smiling the smile of an idiot, actually, but now I know him I know he's quite normal; athletes are probably never superbright . . . (that's unfair. He's just different from me. Not educated at Oxford in the last century.) Most of me was wrapped up in my daughter; I was truly moved by our embrace, but my eyes still strayed over to the corner of the room where the elegant widow stood among her children, Jessica weeping, the magic circle, I longed but feared to speak to her . . .

Then she caught my eye, hugged Jessica, said something to them and they all came over; as simply as that; I went to shake her hand, her pale hand with all the rings, square and lined but

315

smooth to the touch, and instead she reached up her face and kissed me, her cool soft mouth, right on the lips, the gentle kiss I did not deserve, for I hadn't got back in time to see him . . .

'Mary, I'm so sorry . . .'

'Christopher, you've had a terrible time . . .'

And that set the tone of things, right from the start; she worried about me; she cared about me. Perhaps it distracted her from her grief, for Susy says she was half-mad with grief, but perhaps Susy exaggerates, for Mary seems very fond indeed of me.

I'm afraid I talk and she listens. She's led a very quiet life, you see. Nothing's happened to her; she says so herself. Whereas I have decades of drama to talk out. The horrors of the prison. I've told no one. One particular warder who hated limeys, who spat whenever he heard my voice, who went in before me when I had to clean the latrines and peed on the floor, spraying all over, as steady as a mechanical sprinkler, and then he showed me his big slack penis and said 'Don't complain or you'll have to lick it up, and you'll have to lick this, you stuck-up asshole . . .' There are too many things like that to tell. She's lived a sheltered life, but she seems unshockable; she listens, and her mild blue eyes fill with sorrow.

Of course I don't want her to pity me. Well, only a little, when I need pity. I talk about all the other things too, the marvellous years of travelling, the things we saw, the things we did . . . I try not to talk about Alex too much; I don't entirely like it when she talks about Matthew, and I don't want to make her jealous, though she shows no signs of jealousy . . .

She doesn't talk about her feelings. Admittedly I don't pry. But she's happy with me. I think so; I know so. She sits half-smiling in the window and listens, perhaps sewing something, perhaps knitting something, perhaps shelling peas for a light summer lunch, any one of her quaint twentieth-century habits which I admit can sometimes get under my skin; but most of the time they're soothing . . .

One day I had somehow strayed on to the topic of Alex and how she had deceived me. It does no good to go on about it, it isn't tactful, I know I shouldn't, but nevertheless it's a painful subject and the rhythm of her fingers, inexorably shuttling, pausing not at all as I stripped my soul, suddenly became unbearable to me, and I broke off my story and said a little sharply, 'Why do you always have to do that?'

She looked up steadily, but didn't stop knitting. 'Because I don't like to waste my time.' For a moment I saw a glint of something steely, but then she was smiling; I'd imagined it. After a life like mine, one imagines things.

In any case, I know she loves me.

— The question of love-making. At our age, the issue is not a simple one, for all I knew she had given it up, Matthew had been ill for a very long time, for all I knew she would slap my face, she had never struck me as a libidinous woman . . . I, alas, am a libidinous man, but I wouldn't have risked upsetting her. I have adequate ways of relieving my lust, more than adequate, of which more later, but fantasy cannot supply a friend, and she was my friend, and precious to me. I wrestled with the problem; best not to ask her. I left politely at the end of each evening.

Until four or five months after Matthew's death. I had just moved into the house in Chelsea, a long way away from Islington. I kissed her as I made for the door, as usual, warmly but respectfully on both cheeks . . . when she took my head between her two hands, looked me in the eye, smiled at me, and said, 'You don't want to trek back all that way. Stay the night. Sleep with me.'

I was flabbergasted. I swallowed hard. But I was already pulling my coat off. 'Do you mean it, Mary?'

'Why else would I say it?'

In the bedroom she delighted me with the grace of her heavy body. I had always been attracted to thin women, but now I saw the beauty of solid flesh, her big pale breasts, her curving hips. Indeed I felt too thin myself. I was uneasily aware of my bony knees. Maybe less fashionable women aged better.

And she was passionate! Why had I feared she was not sexual? She was tender and direct, and very active. I took her in my arms; she took me in her arms. Her arms were big and

317

strong and smooth. I pulled her to the bed; she pulled me to the bed. I kissed her passionately, masterfully, and felt her tongue push between my lips. Then Mary climbed on top of me.

It wasn't just duty; she wanted to come; I wasn't used to her, remember, and after all I am seventy-two, and I didn't move quite fast enough for her, leaving her panting with desire, and she made me finish her off with my fingers when I was lying stunned by my own orgasm, so contented that it made me forgetful.

(Which never happens with the Simulator. Sometimes it spoils you for real life.)

I felt triumphant, all the same, that night. Now I had a mistress. Perhaps we would marry. Admittedly I was still married to Alex . . . why the hell was I still married to Alex? She was infinitely small and far away, and Mary was here, and she smelled of lavender, not chemical lavender but garden lavender, for that night she'd been making lavender bags as we sat in the lamplight and talked of the past, her gentle fingers sorting and bunching . . .

'Are you happy, Mary?' I asked her later. She wasn't asleep; the light was still on; we were in the double bed she must have shared with Matthew. I was smoking, and she was staring at the ceiling; her large blue eyes looked far away. I was happy, so she must be happy.

'Uhn.' Her grunt evaded the issue.

I had to know that she was happy; could I still make a woman happy?

'But are you? – I feel completely happy.' Perhaps it wasn't true, but I believed it.

She sat up abruptly and stared at me. Her steady eyes could be unnerving. 'How could I be completely happy? Matt only died a few months ago.'

– I had the sudden sense of being nothing, nobody, the merest bit-part in a mighty opera. Silly, of course. I know she adores me – it was just a case of post-coital blues.

No one has mentioned marriage yet, though we've been going out together now for nearly two years. No one has mentioned living together. Perhaps it's because we're both so busy. I wasn't happy in the Chelsea house; I was lonely in the Chelsea house. I stuck it for less than eighteen months; a year or so ago I gave it up.

I mentioned my unhappiness to Mary, and waited to see if she'd suggest some change – perhaps we should buy a house together; perhaps I could move in with her, but I wanted it to come from Mary. I didn't want to be turned down.

'I don't think you should live on your own,' she said. I waited eagerly. 'I think you should go and live with Susy. Talk to her. She's on her own. That woman – Madonna – has just let her down, ran off to live with a married man . . .'

– Mary is marvellous, but a trifle cold. And always thinking about other people, trying to help till it makes you feel tired.

But in fact, it's all worked out wonderfully well. Susy did want me to live with her, she was pregnant, she wanted company. Seeing my granddaughter is utterly marvellous. She's a lovely baby, a remarkable baby, particularly advanced for her age, and that's not just a proud grandfather talking . . . I'm teaching her to crawl. I make myself useful.

All the same, in the basement I'm completely independent. I have my bedroom, my kitchenette, my bathroom, my study with video and IRD . . . And it might be awkward, if I lived with Mary. She might not tolerate my IRD habit. It's more than a habit, I know, it's a need.

I love my Interactive ReCreative Device, my Simulator, my 4-D Goggles, my dancing Dreamsoles, my Globesweep Gloves. Everything here is state of the art. Madonna, the darling, who got some of the stuff for me, because it's her world, she knows where it's at, thinks it's really smart to be a user at my age when most people can't stand the stuff (and Mary's one of them; won't even discuss it; she says IRD is 'a waste of time'. In some ways Mary is a narrow woman).

'You're a real Yardie, Christopher,' Madonna said, the last time she dropped in, bringing me a new Sensory Feedback Module, for which she only charged me half-price. I felt boyishly pleased by the compliment; a real IRD freak at seventy-two! Perhaps I was the oldest Yardie in London!

– Then I stopped feeling pleased, and just felt old.

But when I'm using, I never feel old. With the IRD I can be anything I wish. And with anyone I wish, wherever I wish, and doing anything I wish to them . . . If I think of it too much I'll have to go and use it, and that's not possible at present, I'm sitting in the garden with a sleeping Becky, waiting for Mary to take us for a walk, and if I start to use I wouldn't hear the child crying or the doorbell ringing or the house burning down . . . I almost wish Mary weren't coming.

And that's the trouble with yarding. It's more absorbing than anything real. That's the real reason people like Mary dislike it, I think; its power to drain the colour from the real world. She told me Dan is using too much while Anne and their three-year-old are in Sweden. I said, 'Don't blame IRD. It's because the real world is cold and lonely that he's using so much, not vice versa.'

'I still don't like it,' Mary said. 'Enthuse to Madonna, not to me. You're wasting your time converting me. To me it's a con, inhuman, hateful.'

But then, Mary is a very strong person. The better I know her, the more I realise. Mary can look life full in the face, probably because she's got nothing on her conscience.

Whereas I, I . . .

But never mind that. If she weren't going to call, if Becky weren't beside me, under her fringed canopy, turning her round head slightly as she dreams, I would go and escape, like Dan. I would go and sit down in my computer-room, not big enough to be a real cyberary, where all my cyberware sits and waits, dull on the outside, technical, restrained, but if I slip on my IRD helmet, my goggles, gauntlets and dreamsoles, if I switch on the computer and set to *ReCreate*, and then to *Multiple-Image-Copy*; if I reach into the secret drawer in the table and take out my envelope of photographs, poor still photographs, worn by now, handled too much, milked of their life, as my poor throbbing penis will be milked of its life – if I show those thin

320

facsimiles of life to the screen, and sit back and wait, unzipping myself – in five seconds or so she'll be there before me, almost perfect, moving, breathing, and if I speak to her she'll answer, though the voice isn't hers, it's just the one I've created by using the voxkit again and again, modifying, tuning, softening, but it's still a doll's voice, not a woman's.

Not Alexandra's. Not her beautiful voice, husky, thrilling, almost hoarse. But the rest is Alexandra, Alexandra to the life, Alexandra to the death, I love her still. And in a minute, as I flick the switch, Christopher will appear beside her. A younger, stronger Christopher, for the photos I use are always young. And whatever he does on the screen I feel through my gauntlets, my helmet, my dreamsoles, and as I shift my body, he moves, we move. And she is more mine than she ever was, for I created her, I can unmake her, I summon her at will, and he uses her, Christopher uses her, I watch, we use her, we use her until her doll's voice squeals, we use her until I can bear no more and reality this side of the screen takes over, I freeze the image and tear off my gauntlets . . .

When I've come, of course, it all looks different. Then the frozen image on the screen looks cold; the cyberary is lonely; she is just a cartoon, she feels nothing, nothing, she was never here, neither of those people are satisfied, they are just condemned to eternal repetition, and the cooling sperm on my leg feels sad because it is the only thing that was warm. And each time I vow not to do it again.

Today there's no danger, at any rate. Ah, here she is, my darling Mary, late, as usual, scruffy, laughing, admiring Becky only slightly less than I do . . . And we wander down a road not completely changed since the days when there were four of us, when it was Matthew and Mary and Christopher and Alexandra, when we were all young, before we went away, thirty years ago precisely. When there were four children; now there are three. Nothing is sadder than outliving your children.

But when I'm with Mary I'm rarely mournful. Trundling the pram, talking, laughing. Not too far, just a gentle stroll, because

Becky has a feed at four, and Susy will have finished preparing her lesson and be panting to see her daughter.

(Such mothers, the women of today! Neither Penelope nor Alex was ever like Susy! I love my daughter. I'm proud of her.)

Mary is going to stay for tea. She doesn't often do that, I must make a fuss of her. The temperature, as usual, is in the nineties but she adores crumpets even in summer and I keep them in the freezer just for her ... The baby is burping, bubbling, grinning. That wonderful smile is just for me.

'It's no good, monkey, you're too young for crumpets, you won't get round your grandpa like that ...'

I hear the telephone ringing in the house. Mary tenses; there's some problem with Jessica which she was explaining, but I missed the details. A little delay, then Susy comes from the house. She is rosier than usual. She stoops to the baby, scoops her up, cuddles her, whispers to her, then remembers Mary and I are here.

'Dad. Mary. Thanks so much.' Closely inspected, she looks a little strange, distracted; maybe her breasts are hurting her.

'That wasn't for me? The phone?' asks Mary. There's a long pause. Susy stares at the baby.

'It was a wrong number,' she says, finally.

30

Susy: London, 2007

Why am I such an idiot? Why do I kid myself everything's fine? Today I feel as if the roof's fallen in and I suddenly see it's all black out there . . . Yet I was so smug, only three days ago when the phone call came from Alexandra. I thought I'd handled it brilliantly with my lightning decision to keep it quiet, not to disturb our happy family, not to upset my happy father. When I saw him with Mary and the baby in the garden, they looked so sunny and peaceful together . . .

Now I suppose I'll have to tell him after all. Things are sadder than I thought. I'm wrong about things. I always was. And I'm still not safe – none of us are. Things can be snatched away in a moment.

This afternoon for about sixty seconds I hated Madonna more than anyone on earth. I still can't think of her without a stab of anger. I don't think she realises what she did. She never admits she's wrong, Madonna. She did say 'Sorry, sorry' – but sulkily, as if placating someone mad, in the first few minutes when I was screaming at her and everyone in the Terminus was watching, shopping trolleys stalled, frightened faces . . . I didn't give a monkey's what other people thought, I only stopped screaming because of Becky; I actually wanted to slap Madonna.

I'm not sure I'll ever forgive her. Every time I drive to the megaterminus to collect my computer-order of shopping I'll hear Becky crying again.

Although Madonna moved out years ago to live with her dreadful Japanese billionaire, she still acts as if this house were her own, dropping in on me and Dad without warning and sort of claiming territory; she'll go into the garden, or take a bath, without so much as a by-your-leave, and return with an armful of roses for herself or a dripping towel for me to deal with. She raids the fridge. She cooks herself meals. Dad is tickled by her, but I don't care, after today that's it, she's had it.

I suppose things have been going wrong between us ever since Becky was born, after the first crazy exhilaration and Madonna's dramatic exhibition of joy, arriving at the hospital with armfuls of lilies and staying till nightfall drinking champagne. Later her visits were less welcome. She never managed to grasp Becky's bath-times or feeding-times; she got irritated when I was so busy with Becky that I missed the thread of her narrative. On the phone she was worse, never understanding that a screaming baby in the background meant I couldn't talk to her, or that silence meant Becky was probably asleep, in which case my time was unspeakably precious.

This afternoon she did at least warn me she was coming, ten minutes before she came. I had to pick up a load of shopping, and said she could come with me, which she did, grudgingly, as if I shouldn't have arranged to go shopping just in case she happened to visit me.

The traffic was appalling, as usual. We sat in a jam on the motorway with the fumes all round our heads. 'I can think of better ways to spend an afternoon,' said Madonna, as if I couldn't. Becky was asleep in the back, and I wanted her to stay that way, but Madonna talked loudly and laughed a lot.

We started to talk about Dad, or she did. She's always been so nosey about Dad. I suspect her of having a tremendous crush on him, which is an odd thing for me to suspect, given that he's seventy-two and in major need of a techfix, and she's only thirty-nine like me; but she's so weird, Madonna; she loves old men. Luckily she's already got a sixty-three-year-old, the Japanese IRD billionaire who left his wife and kids for her, so her interest in Dad is just recreational.

I think it is. It had better be.

I wasn't entirely listening to her. Sometimes I don't mind traffic-jams; they give you a chance to doze off, if Becky does. Suddenly I heard her saying, 'You probably think I shouldn't encourage him.'

324

'Who?'

'Christopher.'

I shot up in my seat. 'What do you mean?'

'I mean, with his IRD habit. Don't bark at me. What's the matter with you? You don't use yourself, so I thought maybe you hated all that . . . And you're so down on Alexandra . . . We've never really talked about IRD.'

'It's your job, it's OK, I'm not going to give you a hard time for doing it. I suppose you need some money of your own.'

'Oh thanks very much. Thanks very much. Well we can't all afford to work two days a week. We haven't all got a rich father . . . sorry, sorry, didn't mean to say that.'

We crawled in silence for another ten minutes. Then I remembered something she had said.

'What's Alexandra got to do with IRD? You said I was very down on Alexandra as if she had something to do with it. Did she start Dad using, then? Doesn't seem like her, somehow. She could never sit still, he was the screen junky.'

There was a pause. Then she said 'Oh nothing' in a deliberately infuriating way, letting me know as clearly as she could that there was something, but she wasn't telling.

'Madonna! Don't play games!'

'I'd tell you, but I think you might be upset.' Licking her lips, a tiny smile. 'Besides, your father might not want you to know.'

'Madonna, I shall drive your side of the car into a lorry if you don't tell me whatever it is . . .' The car jerked into life for a brief minute. 'On second thoughts, don't bother. I don't want to know Dad's little secrets. I'm happy he's happy, and that's it.'

What a fool I was; that's never it. Nothing is really as simple as that.

'I'd better tell you. You'd better know. Your father is still obsessed with Alexandra –'

'Balls! He's told me he loves Mary –'

'Maybe he does. People are complicated. Your world's so black and white. Even more so since you settled with Phil and had the baby. Your world's more unreal than IRD.'

'He hardly ever talks about Alexandra. The pictures have all come down from the wall. I just don't believe you, Madonna . . .'

'I can tell you where the pictures are. Don't keep saying you don't believe me. They're all in a drawer in your father's cyberary. He uses her all the time. He ReCreates her, and they do things together – '

'What do you mean? What sort of things?'

I took my eyes off the road and looked at her, and she looked at me pityingly, as if I were an idiot.

'Well. They travel together of course. He uses the Globesweep programme. He's got the discs for almost half the world . . .'

'And?'

'Well. I don't want to upset you. But there are other things users do to the people they ReCreate. Little boys shoot their teachers and their fathers. Big boys – darling, boys will be boys.'

I drove on grimly, my stomach turning. I'm not a puritan, I'm not, but I don't like to think of my father . . . I've never even liked to think of him and Mary, but I certainly don't like to think of Dad down in the basement endlessly *doing that* . . . Besides, how does Madonna know about it? If he tells her that, then she's flirting with him, talking dirty with him, I know she is . . .

'I haven't upset you, have I?'

'Nope.'

'In any case, your Dad is so *moral*. He's only used Alexandra for years. I've been telling him off about that. It seems to me a bit claustrophobic, know what I mean?'

'Don't tell me any more.' I wanted to cry, but I wouldn't give her the satisfaction. 'I've got to pick up one or two things from the Personal Shoppers, OK? I left a few things off the list . . .'

'Can I take Becky out of the car?' Madonna asked, and I wanted to say No, *don't touch my baby, don't touch my father,* but I said Yes, because after all, I didn't want to be unkind, I knew she was lonely. I'd been lonely myself. Yukio would not divorce his wife, Madonna was no nearer to having her baby.

When she holds Becky she gets a really weird, possessive look, as if she was going into a trance, not particularly endearing to Becky who likes people to smile and talk, but I know what it means – Madonna wants her. On the other hand, she knows nothing about her. She's never shown herself remotely competent with nappies or with feeding bottles.

We went into the Terminus with Becky in her pushchair. Madonna wanted to carry her, but I said it wasn't practical for shopping. Madonna pushed the pushchair, and gazed under the hood.

'You should leave Yukio,' I said. 'You do want a baby. I can see.'

'Don't pity me,' she said. 'Don't patronise me.'

'Look, I didn't mean to . . . Madonna. You're my friend. Let's not quarrel. I was just really shocked by what you said about Dad. I didn't realise he still felt that way about Alex. Maybe he always will. I suppose it ought to be touching in a way. I detest her, but I admire my Dad for being faithful, after a fashion . . .'

And I was doing it again, I can see that now, building the walls painfully back up again, trying to make everything good as new, trying to make everybody happy happy happy . . . Becky was beginning to wake up. The atrium was enormously high, darkness sort of loomed above the blinding lights, the echoes were like musicians tuning up. Becky's nose began to wrinkle, her eyes opened a crack. The place always reminds me of a Paris station, except that nothing's beautiful.

'If I give you my card, could you go and pick up the order? I'll stay with Becky.'

'I'll stay with Becky, you go and get the stuff.' Madonna was not one for heavy duties, though she was taller and stronger than me.

'She's not used to you. She'll cry. I'll take her in with me to pick up the Personals. It's never as bad as the computer queues.'

But today Personal Shopping was full to the brim with people like me who had left things off their list. I took one look in and decided I couldn't fight my way in there with Becky in tow. She seemed in a good mood, though she was chewing on nothing; I gave her her teething ring. I only wanted two or three things, I knew I could be in and out in a second. I left her by the door, near a kindly-looking lady who waved at her and smiled. I dashed inside. I was down the other end when I heard a cry that I was sure was Becky's. I fled back towards the door but the crush was appalling, there was no way out without going through the checkout, the crying had stopped but my heart still thumped and I ran through the door and found her gone.

So had the kindly-looking lady.

My body caved in, I couldn't get my breath, but I started to screech, 'My baby, my baby, someone's taken my baby,' and I started to run in stupid small half-circles, looking round the horrible atrium as if there were possibly some corner where she could have rolled by mistake, but there were only people, thousands of people, cruel, indifferent-looking people, every one of them murderers or child molesters, and I ran back into Personal, grabbed the first checkout worker by the arm and sobbed my story in his ear.

The whole apparatus came down around my head. Assistant managers and welfare workers and security officers and nosey parkers all pushed around me in the atrium. I had become an event, a disaster. I'd lost my baby, myself, my body. My stomach felt like a drum of cold metal, my chest was bursting with heavy terror. I had no idea how much time had gone by.

Then someone was pushing through the crowd towards me. 'Susy,' said Madonna, 'for goodness' sake, what happened to you? I got worried – '

In her arms she carried Becky. Red-faced, tear-stained, but quiet and asleep. She'd clearly cried herself to sleep. I began to scream again. I don't know what I said. The crowd stayed around for a bit to listen and then drifted away, satisfied.

Madonna had collected my shopping, come over to Personal, seen Becky on her own, and picked her up. When Madonna picked her up Becky started crying, there were too many people, and Madonna decided to take her to the car. This seemed to her perfectly reasonable. In later versions she had picked Becky up *because* she was crying, and comforted her. In all of these versions Madonna was blameless.

328

'Do you never think about anybody else?'

'She was *crying*. You shouldn't have left her on her own.'

'I know that, I know that, for God's sake! That doesn't excuse what you did! I was *terrified*, I was *dying* of fear . . .'

'I'm not going to get in the car with you if you're going to go on screaming at me.'

'I don't want you to get in the car with us!' I made myself breathe deeply, and the anger steadied. I wanted her to know that I meant what I said. 'I don't want you to come to the house any more! You've exploited me in any case – just stay away for a bit, Madonna.'

She stared at me, white now, unlike herself, almost frightening with her snake-like hair. She gave me a curious contorted smile, just possibly, no certainly, controlling tears. 'It's not your house. It's Christopher's house. He likes to see me. I shall come to see him. I'm in your house already, anyway. He's not all that faithful to Alexandra, actually. Last week I offered him some photos of me for his IRD, and he accepted. I expect he ReCreates me all the time.'

I don't believe a word of that. She sounded fifteen years old, and about to cry, and she ran off through the car park like a teenager, her dark curls flying out behind her, head down, one hand covering her face.

I don't care what she says. I don't care about her.

I care about Becky, and my father. When I told Phil, he said, 'Good riddance.' He's never liked Madonna. I didn't tell him what she had said. I've told no one, as yet, about Alexandra's phone call.

But now I know I must. Now I know I'll have to tell Dad.

Partly to say thank you for getting Becky back. She's back where I can see her, sitting on the carpet, playing with a squeaky velvet mouse, dribbling and bubbling, perfectly happy . . . and now she wants Mum, and she's in my arms, her solid weight, her warmth, her smell. Being without her was like falling forever. I can't bear to think of Dad having that pain.

To think of him longing for Alexandra, and missing her, and knowing she's lost, thinking he'll never see her again, thinking she'll die without him seeing her, thinking all of the dreadful unthinkable things that I thought about Becky this afternoon, but I only suffered that for half an hour, whereas he must have lived with it for years.

At least I can tell him Alexandra's alive. She sounded well. She was in Mexico City, but 'coming to Europe soon'. There was something she said, some message for him, but it was vague as hell, and I can't remember . . .

He'll be crazy to know. I'll have to remember.

Oh yes. It was just that she *thought about him*.

Alexandra *thought about him*.

31

Christopher: London, 2007

How can I sleep? How can I eat? How can I ever get back to normal? I enjoyed normal, normal was good, I had made a life that was comfortable, I slept like the dead and woke feeling calm ... there were sometimes bad dreams, but everyone dreams, everyone wakes up crying sometimes. I was happy, wasn't I?

Never again.

Now I toss all night and wake in a fury. I've quarrelled with my daughter; I've annoyed Mary. My only friend is Madonna, who won't come to the house because of Susy. Things were so peaceful – now it's chaos, no one is speaking, even Becky is ill.

My granddaughter. I could show her to Alex ... she would see at once that she's just like me ...

There I go again, madness, folly, I can think of nothing but Alexandra. She's escaped from the screen, she's tormenting me. I torment myself. I torment other people.

When Susy told me she had phoned, I tormented her with questions about it. Susy couldn't recall their exact words; she couldn't explain why Alexandra rang off; I'm sure that Susy was nasty to her, but she denies it, she would deny it, those children never appreciated her ...

I must get a grip on myself. They were only children. She wasn't the perfect mother to them.

The trouble is, the appalling thing is, after all these years, after all that she did, the cheating, the lying, using my son – for I'm sure she hardly ever visited him; she was fucking herself silly with that overgrown gigolo, I'm sure they never bothered to look in on Isaac – despite all that, I love her, dammit. I still love her. I still want her back.

If I could have spoken to her, person to person, voice to voice, her real voice, not the dreadful mockery I get from my machines – oh her sensuous, smoky, husky, voice, which grew more wonderful as she got older, though who knows what the last seven years have done – if I could speak to her; if I could see her; I'm sure – I'm not sure, but I half-believe – I don't dare to believe, but I sense in my heart, my stupid heart, that she'd come back to me. And then I'd give up everything. I'd have to give up everything. My daughter, my home, my peace of mind, dear Mary Brown, my little games with Madonna – I'd give up all of them without a second thought if I could be back with Alexandra.

She is my wife. We should be together. How dare Susy try to keep us apart? Why didn't she call me straight away? How could she have failed to take her number?

How dare Susy even dream of not telling me! – Protecting me like some aged neurotic who can't face up to reality. It doesn't make sense, in any case. Two years ago my daughter was happy enough to tell me Alexandra had written from Brazil, saying she was adopting a baby. With the gigolo, of course. She didn't protect me from knowing all that (if only I'd killed him, if only it had worked . . .). And it hurt, it hurt, a brick in the gullet, a sack of lead hanging down from my heart, for I'd wanted so much to give Alex a child.

The gigolo couldn't do it either, there's some satisfaction in knowing that. And I'm sure that's why Alex wanted him. And now he's failed, she must be bored. She can't be happy with a teenager. Why would she ring unless she's unhappy?

Susy must have said *something* to frighten her away.

She was living in Mexico City. Why would she be there? Too crowded, too dirty, too uncouth for her, it means that no one's looking after her. *I* looked after her, it was an honour, I did everything I could to make her happy . . .

I would go out to look for her, like a shot. Mexico City goes on for ever, but somehow I'd find her, I know I would, my love for her would lead me to her. And the child (I would love her.

She would be our child). And the gigolo (I would get rid of him, if Alex hasn't done that already).

But I can't do that. I can't do anything, because she told Susy she was 'coming to Europe', and Europe could mean anywhere, couldn't it? I can't comb Europe looking for her.

– Toledo. Would she come back to Toledo? She always wanted to return to Toledo, year after year when we were travelling together I would wait for the moment when she'd pronounce its name with a particular emphasis, caressive, loving, slightly softening the 'T' and the 'd', she'd say 'It's spring in Europe – I'd love to be in Toledo in May.'

Such a beautiful city, the city on the hill. Rose-pink, sand-yellow. Beautiful and treacherous, the flesh-coloured city where things first went wrong – *and yet, there was such love between us then*. We were in Toledo in the warm spring, when there were still springs, not just baking summers, we were in Toledo in the springtime of our lives, and perhaps she would go back to find us again . . .

Or to Paris, where one day in the Louvre she told me she'd noticed we were getting older, the first time she'd ever considered it; she said it with amazed tenderness, as if that meant we must love each other more, as if that meant we must prepare our bed, the bed where we would lie together, the bed where we could die together . . .

Could it still happen? Could the lost be found?

Could my broken life be made whole again?

Nothing can happen until I find her, she finds me, we find each other, but I can do nothing to make it happen, the agony is I can do nothing to help.

She could come to me though. She knows where I am. Come, Alexandra. I'm an old man now but I'm waiting for you . . .

I've questioned Susy again and again and she's almost positive Alex said 'I', 'I'm leaving for Europe' not 'We're leaving for Europe', she's coming alone, and that surely means . . .

*

Means nothing but torture and despair, means nothing for me but a hell of hope. It matters so much to me, that phone call, but what if it meant nothing at all to her, if she was just bored, or did it on a whim, while riffling through the phone numbers in her phone file . . .?

And at other times since I've known about the phone call I've felt nothing but indifferent anger. She wrecked things, she was a wrecker. Now I've got a new life and she wants to wreck that . . .

Besides, she'd be old now, not herself, not the immaculate Alex I ReCreate. She'd be selfish as before, and blind as before, but no longer beautiful to sweeten the pill . . . she'd probably have lost her craziness, her wonderful laugh, her pleasure in everything . . . She wouldn't be calm, and calming, like Mary, she wouldn't . . . *care for me.*

Mary cares for me, and takes care of me a little, and I of her, and we're happy, I think. Or we were, before I annoyed her. I would lose all that, if Alexandra came back. She's a good woman, Mary. She's good for me. It would hurt her so much if I left her now, though she had to pretend – she's strong, and proud – that Alex's phone call didn't upset her, she wasn't jealous, I was being absurd – for the first time ever she got cross with me. I know it was really because she loves me. We love each other; a steady fondness; though she's more passionate than me.

And if something is missing – some spice, some wickedness – there's always Madonna. Lovely Madonna. Lovely, wicked, feline Madonna, who likes to come round and tease me a little. Madonna and I understand each other. She's got her Yukio, I've got my Mary, but we like to pretend that one day, maybe . . . I *think* she's pretending, at any rate.

You see, I am happy.
I don't need Alex.

334

32

Mary Brown: Paris, 2007

These days are rather a strain for me. I usually like Paris, but now it leaves me cold. I must admit I can't wait for it all to be over. I think about it all the time, especially now there's nothing practical to do. So I kick my heels and wait for things to happen.

And if it's hard for me at the moment, what must it be like for Jessica? My daughter is five days overdue; she's huge; she can't sleep a wink with her amazing belly, though at least the baby's grown too big to kick, he lies in her belly like a giant pea about to burst out of its skin-tight pod. I can't do that much for her, except for being here, and making sure that everything's ready. Even my being here sometimes gets on her nerves. She's so used to being alone. Only Jessica would do this thing alone.

It seems a lifetime ago, though it's in my lifetime, that single parenthood was all the thing, and there were endless articles in long-ago forgotten newspapers about the single woman's right to bear a child . . . but in the last decade people have grown positively shrill about the child's right to two consenting parents, as if people didn't ever die, or divorce.

I see both sides, as usual. And I see my daughter, my darling Jessica, who's done so brilliantly in her career, suddenly start to feel lonely. Suddenly she felt incomplete. She hasn't told me who the father is. Doesn't want him to be involved. And she says she's part of a trend; she says lots of her friends are going to do it, friends with money enough for nannies, friends who don't want to be dominated by men. She says they call themselves the New Feminists, and I wonder how feminism managed to grow old . . .

I wonder how all of us managed to grow old.

Christopher. He was my *beau idéal*. My ideal beau, in another world (my French is poor, we were badly taught. I belong to the generation of dinosaurs who didn't learn to speak even one language well . . . it must be part of why I've never really travelled, though I don't think I really missed travelling much until Alexandra and Christopher went away).

I burned with passion for him then. I sensed he was a sexual man, a man who liked to make love a lot, you could feel the heat of it coming off them, Alex and him, that electric heat, something that held them tightly together and left the rest of us out in the cold.

He was so handsome. He was . . . devastating. I have photos of him with thick dark hair, smiling eyes, wide sensual lips, a face just this side of fleshiness, the face of a big man – Christopher was big – whereas Matt, poor darling, was thin, and bald . . .

Once or twice recently I've looked at those photos, although I've been seeing him every other day. Because the memory of the Christopher I fell half in love with is slowly fading, shrinking away, in the face of the Christopher who came back from the dead. Who came to the funeral, and came for me.

– We've had lots of fun together. It's been good for my ego to have a man want me, and good for my body to have regular sex. At first it all seemed overwhelmingly romantic, before it had sunk in that he wanted me, before he became a fact of my life . . . before we actually made love.

But when we did, he was old. I know that's a heartless thing to say, I know I'm in my sixties myself, only eight years or so younger than him. I know age shouldn't matter; Matt was old. Old like Chris. Just a year younger, in fact. He was seventy-one, and blind, and I adored him. I never thought of him as old. But then, Matt and I had grown old together.

Whereas Chris had come back a different man. Thinner, frailer, a little shrunken, still not a small man, but no longer large, no longer large and splendid and comforting. His hair isn't all that much thinner, but it's white as snow, and dry to the touch. And so is his skin, thin and dry, and I can sometimes feel the bones underneath. And he worries a lot; he's frail and

336

nervous. And a little forgetful, sometimes, in bed. Not quite as passionate as I had hoped, but then, I'm not Alexandra – and he is no longer middle-aged.

I am grateful to have him, of course. I didn't want to be alone for ever. We're company for each other. And in his clothes he's still very imposing, a handsome man, a fine figure of a man.

But I can't help feeling it's come too late. I wanted him before, when he was with her, and she took the best of him, sucked him dry, and spat out the husk upon my table . . .

I took him in. I looked after him. He's a happier man because of me. I've grown used to him, and looking after him. It's Christopher and Mary, and Mary and Christopher. Not the Mary and Christopher I dreamed of, but still a partnership. A loving friendship.

And now we've quarrelled over Alexandra. Swanning in by phone from Mexico City. I hope she had phoned for a purpose. I hope she had phoned because she cared. In that case she had a right to phone. She has a right to phone if she cares for him.

But I saw the damage that phone call did. Christopher was completely thrown; didn't know what to do with himself, couldn't think of anything else but her, couldn't stop thinking and dreaming about it, drawing wildly over-optimistic conclusions, oblivious to the real world, oblivious to everyone else – oblivious to me.

– But not entirely oblivious. He made it worse by remembering me. 'Oh Mary, you must think me such a pig. I know how lucky I am to have you. I know how much you love me. I don't want to break your heart over Alex – '

'Why do you think you're breaking my heart?'

'You don't have to be proud with me – '

'Nevertheless, I'm sixty-four, I'm too old to break my heart over you. It's true I'm faintly annoyed that you've talked about nothing else but Alex for the last three days. It's true my vanity is piqued. But I'm sorry for you, as well. Because I think you're building castles in Spain over this. It might have been a perfectly casual call. She has a penchant for casual behaviour. You're a fool to assume she wants to come back.'

337

Poor Christopher. He looked so crestfallen. He muttered something and went away.

All the same, I don't think he really took it in, or else he didn't choose to believe me. Because the next time we spoke he was still apologising for the frightful wrong he was preparing to do me, had already done me in his fevered brain. I got cross again, but silently this time, and rang off as soon as I decently could without explaining why I was going to Paris, just saying I would be going away.

Maybe it's good for him to suffer a bit. Maybe he's a little too pleased with himself.

– Coming to Paris has been good for me. This is the first time I've thought of him since I left. Almost the first time. Not the first time. But Jessica's baby is the main thing on my mind. Soon there'll be another life to look after, how exciting, I adore new babies – I love to look after people, daughters, granddaughters, it doesn't have to be a silly old man!

But today Jessica has sent me out. I'm annoying her by constantly cleaning, cooking for the freezer, putting clothes ready, and although I tell her that after it's born there won't be any time for anything at all, she tells me I'm driving her crazy.

So she's sent me out to see an exhibition. She put me in a cab, and told him where to go, and ordered me to go shopping afterwards and buy some clothes for myself, not the baby, and not to come back until tea-time.

(Lovely to have children to take charge of one. Nice to be looked after as well as looking after . . .)

I've always wanted to see the Louvre. Sixty-four years old and not seen the Louvre. But it's a whole city, a whole vast world. You could live your whole life in a building like this. It makes me feel tiny, and marginal. And the big exhibition of Edvard Munch that Jessica's so sure I'll enjoy was flagged with gigantic posters outside, but inside there is no mention of it, in this huge cathedral with its oversized stone heads and endless ranks of fractured bodies, broken arms, ruined legs . . . why do the heads survive the best?

I suppose people's minds survive the best, what they do with

338

their minds, their ideas, their inventions – I sometimes wish I had used my mind more. Instead I've loved bodies. Matthew's, my children's. I've loved and cared for human bodies. That's what most women do, I suppose. I've enjoyed my own flesh, I enjoy it still. Odd to look around at so much wreckage, such cracked and battered human bodies, and see how tenderly they are preserved, mounted on plinths, gazed at, exclaimed over . . .

Why don't people love their own bodies more? The marvel of unbroken bodies? I've always felt if people loved their bodies they wouldn't be unhappy and full of hatred . . .

But Alexandra and Christopher became unhappy, although their bodies seemed to crackle with pleasure. I suppose I'm no philosopher, or else they didn't love each other as much as I thought. They weren't faithful, were they? I think I believe in faithful love.

The guard pretends not to understand my French, but nods disdainfully when I write 'Edvard Munch svp' on a piece of paper. The exhibition is miles from the entrance.

As I tip-tap across the echoing salons, treading my own path through the crowds, I realise how strange it is to go out alone. Even now Matthew's dead, I am rarely alone, unless I am at home with all the friendly ghosts, and even then almost certainly there will be one or other of my children, or Susy, or one of my widowed women friends. I have a lot of friends now. I'm lucky. More than I had when I was married. More than I had in the decade when Christopher and Alexandra were our friends, and because they were so exciting, so special, we somehow let all the others drop, and missed them terribly when they ran off . . .

I won't make that mistake again. I try and value all my friends. My family and my many friends. I am grateful for them. Thanks to them, I don't feel like someone who's been left behind.

And now because for once I am on my own I start to glimpse them everywhere, a head turns and I think it's Dan, his gaunt boy's face, his dear thin neck; over there is surely Henrietta Pickering, laughing at a satyr and shaking her hair; that woman bent over two young children is Susy, not long in the future;

339

there's Christopher, an old man, haunted-looking, arm round a woman who might be his daughter.

I think I could have a perfectly nice time just wandering about and looking at people, but I see EDVARD MUNCH announced over there, so I leave them behind, my crowd of friends. If I don't see the Munchs my daughter will be furious.

The first dozen pictures are an unpleasant shock.

All the women on the walls are Alexandra.

Munch has painted her again and again, a sinuous siren with flaming hair. Great heavy heads of crimson hair you would think would make their shoulders ache.

Why are so many men obsessed with redheads?

Why are painters obsessed with redheads?

He loves the body, this Munch, like me. He paints beautiful, joyous, sexual bodies. But the soul always seems to weigh them down, staring out of the skull behind their eyes. Most of the men are lustful or jealous; the women are seductive or haunted or sad ... actually everything in life seems sad. I really don't think I like this painter.

I don't believe all life is sad ... but then, I'm a body person, not a head person.

'The Frieze of Life', the caption reads; the blurb underneath is full of superlatives. Apparently these are his master-works ...

Alexandra. Always Alexandra. I didn't come here to see bloody Alexandra. All the muses are Alexandra. She's always the figure at the centre of the story, right in the thick of the drama, radiant. Aware that everyone's eyes are on her but not looking at anyone. Not bothering. She doesn't have to, she's there to be seen. And she makes all the other people shadowy, they all fade away into her penumbra.

I hated her when Matthew wanted her. In my heart I hated her. I disapproved of myself, but I wanted to kill her. She had Christopher, she held him as tightly as if they had married the day before, he was a great dog panting after her, and I wanted him, his big heavy body, his hotness, the roughness of the kiss I once saw him give her when she had been limbo dancing at a party, oblivious to him and all of us, with another man, a handsome black boy, and he stopped her laughing with a passionate kiss, crushing her thin body against his body – I wanted him then, not now! I wanted him then, and she had it all! I say I believe in faithful love, but how I burned to make Christopher unfaithful.

Only he wouldn't have wanted me then. Whereas Matthew wanted Alex. She could have had Matthew if she'd lifted her finger; perhaps she thought him not worth having, how dare Alexandra despise my husband? But in the end she tired of everyone; she tired of Christopher. Even him. And then he came running back home to me, a thin old dog, beaten, exhausted.

'The Dance of Life' from 'The Frieze of Life'. What a strange picture . . . and yet, when I look back over my life, it *is* like a dance, with us all changing partners.

A dozen people at twilight dancing by the sea, with the moon carving a path over the waves. There are couples and a few single people. In the foreground, there are two women watching, one on the left, young and pretty, obviously just waiting to join in, but not quite ready to make her move. The other on the right is a lot older. Munch has made her a straight black column, her face not unbeautiful, quite beautiful really, but desolate because she has already left the dance. She must have been replaced by someone else, or else her partner has died and left her . . . She's staring in a steady, melancholy way at the couple at the centre of the picture.

And there centre-stage is that accursed Alexandra, with her red-gold hair, her scarlet dress. And the tense dark figure of the man who holds her. He's unsmiling, in a trance, a dream of love, and their linked bare hands at thigh level somehow suggest they are already fucking, his arm and hand invade the shape of her dress, but her eyes seem to gaze away over his shoulder . . .

That must be me, the tall woman in black. The widow watching them. Knowing it's too late. It's too late for me, Alexandra will come back, in triumph, still red-headed and beautiful, and Christopher will have no time for me . . .

Rubbish, nonsense, what self-pitying rubbish. The picture makes me impatient too.

The air of tragedy hanging over them all. They are dancing, for God's sake! They are in love! They are all dancing by the moonlit summer sea! Why must they look so sad about it? Is life really such a tragic business? I'm a happy woman. I've led a happy life. If Matt were still alive I'd be completely happy.

I walk hurriedly on into the next room and at once I see the peculiar thing, the thing that is wrong and out of place, but the room is so big, and my eyes so imperfect, that I can't quite make out what it is, and I think it's of no importance.

The room holds the largest pieces on display, murals Munch did for Oslo University, photographs on canvas, since the originals can't travel.

At the far end is a magnificent sun, rising in glory over the sea, brilliant, dazzling, holding my eyes, the rays painted in as broken lines of gold, red, orange, pale lemon, blue, the centre of the sun a burning white. That must be what they mean by 'incandescent'. The moment after the sun has risen, but as if the painter had half-closed his eyes to protect his brain against the light. The light is so stunning; can it really be painted?

I love that painting. I don't know if it's good, I don't know if art critics think it's good, but I, Mary Brown, think it's wonderful. The best painting in the whole exhibition, the most important, surely. The sun gives life to everything, after all. It giveth, and it taketh away. The meaning of life isn't those self-indulgent dancers.

There are no human figures in the mural; nothing could stand up to the heat of that sun, anything else would look trivial, pathetic.

Like the thing on the floor in front of it. The thing I half saw when I first came into the room. The bundle of dark clothes at its feet, which I can now see is a person, not a thing.

It's a kneeling person, head down on the floor. The head was invisible from the door and even now I can only see the back of it, a grizzled old head lying flat on the marble, the hair partly hidden by the dark cape which covers the rest of the body. He

342

has fallen, or he's praying — is he in some kind of religious trance? Is he in pain? Is he doubled up with pain?

Why is everyone staying down the other end of the room? Oh God, I'll have to help, as usual, because no one else can be bothered to help. — Is he having a breakdown? Is he crazy?

I've really had enough of other people's problems. Today I am supposed to be having a rest. Having a rest and 'recharging my batteries'. That marvellous sun might be doing it for me if I didn't have to worry about that poor man . . .

If I try and speak to him, he won't understand me. I'll leave it to a native to sort it out.

Still I stand a moment, undecided, my eyes drawn down from the Sun to the body, from the glory above to the wretched thing below. As I stand there hovering three apparent natives pass by without a single glance, their eyes fixed firmly on higher things, and in the end I have no choice. I am human, whatever that means — what if it were Jessica kneeling there, giving birth with no one to care for her . . .?

I touch the person gently on the shoulder. No response. I see the hair which the cowled neck hides is long. It's a woman; I feel a small rush of relief. Women are less frightening. I bend over and touch the grey hair. 'Pardon . . .'

As I say it I remember that's not what you say. But she stirs from the ground, her spine unbends, with reluctance and a slight creaking of wrists the thin arms lift the heavy torso; an old woman; long wavy grey hair, the lightless yellowish-grey of the poor who can never afford to get their hair done; a tired face, very thin; perhaps a faint remnant of crazy beauty; of course I have never seen her before, but as I look into the startled pale eyes I see a horror beginning there, a look of terrified recognition, as if I am a monster come to torment her, a terrible monster who's been pursuing her, and she staggers away from me on her knees, which refuse to unbend after kneeling so long, she is half-crawling, half-scuttling away with a peculiar crab-like motion, saying 'No . . . no' as she does so, and she goes ten yards in this terrifying manner before she manages to get to her feet, she looks round once briefly, then

343

runs away, and by the time she has got to the end of the room her gait is quite normal, she's not crippled at all.

I stand there feeling horribly disturbed. As if I had prised someone from under a shell. Why should she have felt such fear? Perhaps she just couldn't bear to be touched, but it was as if she recognised me, her eyes — which were a rather striking colour, a pale hazel-ish brown in the chalk-white face — had a look of riveted, shocked attention which only then turned to absolute terror.

I'm sure I didn't know her. Unless it was someone from the distant past, but there's no one in the world who's afraid of me.

Now I feel afraid as well. What can be in me that I don't know about to inspire another human being with such fear? I think of myself as good, and kind ... But you would have thought I was a murderess.

Going back through the galleries I feel less sure that Munch's version of human life is so morbid. Perhaps he sees the mysteries. Perhaps he understands the terror. Perhaps something unspeakable is waiting in the end for the glamorous redhead at the centre of his pictures.

I suddenly start to worry about Jessica, and in seconds the worry turns to blind fear, I know that something has gone wrong, I know she has gone into labour on her own, I know she needs me, she's calling for me ...

I pant through the halls of uncaring strangers to the exit, and fling myself into a taxi.

— Jessica is perfectly all right, of course, and upbraids me for 'fussing' and 'coming back early'. She's decided to clean the floor, and wanted to finish it before I came back and started interfering and telling her to stop.

I try to tell her my story, but she can't see anything remarkable about it. She is terribly intelligent, Jessica, but a little bit short on imagination. She points out that Paris is full of tramps, and many of them are women, and unfortunately the museum administration haven't thought of a way of excluding them, on the days of *admission gratuite*, at least.

'Why shouldn't tramps look at pictures? In any case, she wasn't a tramp. She was praying, or something, or feeling ill, I'm still not sure . . . but her clothes weren't poor, they looked quite expensive . . .'

'So why are you bothering about her? Honestly Mum, I've thought of you as a tower of strength all my life, but since you got a boyfriend you've grown positively flighty, I don't know what Dad would think of you . . .'

This was a favourite theme of both my children; they had not adjusted to Christopher yet. I didn't want to be diverted. 'But she seemed to recognise me. That was what was so spooky.'

'The world is full of people who think they recognise people. Quite often they're wrong, so what?'

Something occurs to me. 'Cleaning the floor is a very good sign. It probably means you're about to go into labour.'

'You've gone mad,' says Jessica, rubbing her back.

'Getting down on all fours. Always has been. Good, I'll go and make sure your bag is ready . . . *God!*'

'What's the matter now?' asks Jessica, sounding just as resigned as I once had when she tried to tell me things twenty years ago.

'I've just realised what she said! She said "No, no", not "Non, non", she was English, she probably did recognise me . . .'

'She was an English maniac, not a French one. Get out of my way or I'll scrub your feet.'

Jessica has given birth. We have lived through an extraordinary ten days. It was a two-day labour with a sudden end in emergency Caesarian. I've been by her bedside day and night; time's had no meaning, or the world outside, only the red-faced, mewling baby, my infinitely absorbing grandson.

And yet only half of me is here and now. The rest has been dragging back through the years, living so many things over again, searching my heart, trawling my conscience, thinking

345

about Christopher far too much, asking myself if I want him; asking myself how much I want him. Asking myself what I should do . . .

For everything has to be thought out again.

— It happened in the middle of the night, you see. It happened only hours before labour began. I was lying there replaying the scene in the Louvre for the hundredth time when I understood.

I realised, on a wave of incredulous emotion, that the old woman was Alexandra. She had grey hair, that was why I couldn't see her. I never expected her to have grey hair.

I never expected her to grow old.

I shot out of bed and stood by the window, staring down at the empty moonlit street, every hair on my body rigid with shock, putting them together, trying it out, the face I remembered from a lifetime ago and the face which had turned its suffering towards me, the face with the terrified hazel eyes, the face with its glove of crepe-white skin.

That woman was Alexandra.

33

Alexandra: Paris, 2007

I was happy, as always, to arrive in Paris. The nearest to homecoming I dared. Paris is the city I love best, partly because it's always different.

I had last been there two years ago in a time of grey summer rain and sunshine. With the cocky boy who lectured me. This time it was fresh and dry and white, dazzling bright in windows and mirrors, shocking me a little with what I've become, although I accept what I have become.

The Government had instituted a massive programme of sandblasting to try and bring the tourists back after the nuclear disaster at Cap Le Hague in 2002, which had blown a great plume of radiation over Paris. The white was uplifting, it sang with life. The statues had wings again.

The fashion was for white as well, unbleached white, the white of the stone. In the rich streets of the 5th Arondissement people walked about looking brisk and faintly medical, ready for an operation, perhaps, for Camille Lemonnet, the designer who counted, had decreed that they be covered in white from head to toe, hats, gloves, high collars, goggles, it was both comic and ghoulish to me; perhaps these people had something to hide – they might all be robots, or have terrible burns – and although I rather admired Lemonnet, who was the sort of designer that years ago I would have waxed ecstatic about, I began to feel hunger, in the end, for the body that had been hidden from view. To see a little nakedness. A calf, a bare arm, the top of a neck, a heart beating, a hand held out . . .

On my way to my appointment at the hospital I felt entirely hopeful. In Mexico a brief mini-scan had established the lump was cancerous. But it was so tiny, after all, and my health was good, or had once been good, I exercised – had once exercised – of course I tired more easily now – I ate the best food, but that wasn't true, for the last two years I'd lived on beans because *tortilla y frijoles* was so easy to cook ... all the same I felt hopeful, in these white streets, because I was lucky, and had always been lucky – usually, usually I had been lucky, only recently had my luck worn thin – and nothing truly bad would happen to me. Not today, with the whole city shining at me.

He would probably say it was no longer active.

He would certainly say there were no secondaries. It would be treatable by drugs, or by gentle radiation, there would certainly be no need to – no need to. I couldn't finish the sentence, I've never been able to think about surgery. When I was young surgeons cut in through the skin, now the instruments inch along under the surface like tiny insects with razor jaws, but that doesn't make it less frightening ... I was too old for that, and my problem too slight. In two months the little lump hadn't grown. Indeed I was almost sure it was smaller.

My consultant introduced himself with the kind of smile that still makes me feel beautiful, although I have learned it's only charm. But he smiled at me as if I were healthy, as if our meeting was good news. I went through that day's battery of tests without too much discomfort; I felt jaunty, and joked with the nurses, though I was a bit sharp with a glamorous young woman who I assumed was a bossy nurse, until she turned out to be a senior doctor. Even a feminist can make these slips.

It was tea-time before I was brought back to the consultant's room. I knocked and came in; he was standing at the window, staring out at something fascinating I couldn't see. I was eager to get this over with, to have my good news and go away, back into the fresh white day again. I wanted him to turn and smile at me.

He turned, and spoke. 'My colleagues tell me ...'

I didn't understand. It wasn't good news, it wasn't the news I knew he would give me. I listened with a growing sense of disbelief. There were secondaries in my spine. He was asking whether I had had any pain. I looked at him, stunned, and did not answer, but I thought about the question, and yes, of course, my back had sometimes been painful, but all backs were painful, weren't they, all middle-aged backs ached once in a while . . .

I thought, *it's because I annoyed that doctor;* and then, *they've confused me with someone else,* and then, *how silly, I'm going to die, just when I'd decided to get better again.*

He was eager that I start treatment at once. I said I had to think about things. He said there was really no time for delay; every day I wasted, the cancer was spreading. A terrible phrase; *the cancer was spreading . . .*

He had such power. They have such power. They can tell you the thing you most want to know, they are fortune-tellers with scans and scalpels, staring into breasts and hearts and bones, and to someone else he would say 'You will live,' he would give them the world with a charming smile, and to me he had said 'You will probably die. You will die unless you give in to me.'

I resisted him. It took all my courage; I was alone, he was stronger than me, the weight of the building massed behind him, the rows of figures, irrefutable; I told him I needed a week. Not much could go wrong in a week, surely. Perhaps I would decide tomorrow, who knows, but I said seven days; a breathing space; in seven days God created the world, seven days was enough to remake myself.

I left buoyed up by resisting him. I floated the three blocks back to the hotel; through the cotton-wool I was aware it was cold, with the sudden fierce winds that are common now, I don't remember them when I was younger, they weren't so cruel when I was young.

Up in the lift. It seemed cold and dark. The door of my room closed behind me like death. My brief buoyancy drained away. I was alone. I would always be alone. No one to tell. No one to care. The maid had been in and made the bed. It was a double bed, but no one would join me. She had turned back the covers in a ruler-straight line, lifting the lid of loneliness.

Once I had thought I would lie with him for the rest of my life, die with him . . .

Now he slept with . . . *madness*. Madness to think of him now.

I missed my darling. I missed my love.

I lived for love. Love left me.

Inside the room I was trapped with loss, a tightening noose of lonely terror, for nothing would change for me now; I had burned my boats, there was no one to turn to . . . Outside, the winds were freezing cold. I chose outside without a flicker of doubt. I wrapped myself in the black cowled cape I had bought for cool evenings in Mexico City, phoned for a taxi and ran downstairs, down the sweeping Cinderella staircase because I didn't want to be boxed in the lift, falling through the series of gold-framed mirrors that lined the pale pink walls of the staircase, and I was in the wrong fairy-story, I wasn't young, I hadn't been dancing, I was a small black shrivelled thing running from what was hunting me.

I flung myself into the taxi, and realised I didn't know where I was going.

'The Louvre' I said to the bored driver. And indeed there had been something I wanted to see, something I'd made a note of already . . . I couldn't remember. My brain had frozen. When I got there, though, the posters were everywhere. 'Edvard Munch,' they said. *'You're going to die,'* the thin faces whispered. They reminded me sharply of Isaac's drawn flesh and the biography of Munch I bought with such joy when for once he'd managed to ask me for something. But he was dying too quickly to look at it. I hurried past the posters into the building.

I'd always liked painters who painted redheads. When I was younger – when I was young – I used to enjoy taking Isaac to galleries and passing in front of the painted sirens, shaking my own prolific red hair – *but I'm not a redhead any more*. I wasn't the figure at the heart of the paintings.

There was Isaac's painting. 'The Dance of Life'. Once I might have found the title faintly laughable, but now I found my eyes filling with tears. Life was a dance, I agreed with that, I wanted to stay part of it, I wanted so much to go on dancing, I still loved life, although I'd lost everything . . . – I was no longer the woman with the flaming red hair, locked in an embrace with the thickset man. I stood to one side, in widow's weeds. I had become an onlooker. Even so, life was too interesting to die, and the gnawing fear pressed under my ribs and made me walk on clumsily.

I did love life. Looking at life. Very recently I had been looking more. Once my vision was so selective; I looked at what I thought was beautiful, I looked at what I thought was distinguished. I was so sure, you see, that I myself was distinguished, different from the others, better than the others – but age makes everyone ordinary. And so I grew more interested in ordinary things – and found that none of it was ordinary, all of it was life, and life was miraculous, especially now I knew I might have to leave it, I didn't want to, I didn't, *oh* –

I half-ran into an enormous room, and at first I didn't see what was there because I was too locked in my own terror, I was hurrying straight through to the other side, trying to escape, for it was pursuing me, they were pursuing me, where could I hide? – Then I saw the sun; so beautiful; an enormous sun rising from the sea, the rays coming out to pierce and embrace me, a white-gold sun which was waiting for me, a sun which had been painted for me; it was the sun itself, life itself, I hurried towards it, my hands held out, it held my eyes, it held the secret, we held each other, I was still alive, I knelt at its feet, eyes blurred with tears, and wished as I had never wished before, prayed as I'd never prayed before; *help me, help me, I want to live. Perhaps I'm too late, but I want to live. I'm sorry, forgive me for what I have done* . . .

And then she tapped me on the shoulder. I started, expecting a museum guard, I turned, and knew her instantly. She had hardly aged, but she was different. No longer plain. More frightening. She looked strong and tall. Stronger than me. Her face was a torment; pity, puzzlement . . .

I hated her. Oh, I hated her!

She was once my friend. I hated her. Mary Brown. I hated her. She had everything, and she came to crow. They had come to crow. He must be here somewhere, Christopher and she were here together, and would always be together, and I was alone.

I ran from her. I ran away. Once I would have faced her, but now I ran, because I had nothing to face her with. Only the proof of all I had lost.

— Now all of them are hunting me. Death, the doctors, Christopher and Mary, come to throw their happiness in my face, come to stare and pity me. Things are speeding up, time's running out . . . my precious seven days are leaking away.

I've wasted hours over the last two days getting myself back into battle-gear, getting myself ready to face the camera. My hair is red again, not a bad colour, a fraction too dark, but I look years younger. I've bought some lipstick and some new clothes.

To face Christopher. To let him see me. To hide from him what I've become. That woman's seen me, but he won't believe her, he'll think she's jealous, how ironic.

For no one would be jealous of me any more. Once I thought everyone envied me . . .

She looked so different. Stronger, prouder. Her face had lost its puddingy look. Her hair was grey, like mine, but drawn back in a rather imposing knot. She looked younger than I am. How could that be? She always looked at least a decade older . . .

It's a quiet life, I suppose. The quiet life of the virtuous matron. I expect she bakes for him. Bloody sponges. I expect she still makes lavender bags, I remember one day how amazed I was, I dropped round to see her to borrow some apples one Sunday after the shops were shut and she was sitting on the lawn, sorting lavender heads, little grey moth-bodies, hundreds of them, and she said she was making lavender-bags. To go in her drawers! Did she mean her knickers? Are her bloody knickers full of stinking moths? I hope they're unhappy, I hope they don't do it, I hope he can never do it again, since I can never have him again . . .

I don't want to see him, I daren't let him see me.

352

I have to see him or I shall die.

I'll have to leave Paris; I can't leave Paris. I can't leave Paris till I've made up my mind.

To fight or float.

Death or the doctors?

34

Mary: Paris, 2007

I let two weeks pass before I telephoned him. It was easy not to phone; I was so terribly busy, and besides, he had my number. Christopher could have telephoned me.

And I said to myself, *You imagined it. You hadn't seen her for twenty years. Why unsettle him for nothing?*

Or I said to myself, *She knew it was you. She didn't want anything to do with you. It would be a kindness to leave her alone. Leave Christopher with his illusions.*

But I didn't want him with his illusions. With his illusions he would never love me – not properly, not completely.

Besides, I wanted to talk to him. I began to miss him and want him back. It was marvellous to be with Jessica and Sam but I was beginning to get exhausted; at first I had spent the nights with Jessica, since there was no one else to do the nights, sleeping in the same room as them and bringing the child to her when he woke, then changing the nappy and putting him down, but the tiredness was cumulative. I was sixty-four, not a young mother, and as Jessica began to get her strength back I started to feel mine draining away. I wanted to have my quiet life back. I wanted my life with Christopher, the things we did, which were right for our age, the quiet evenings, the little treats, the gentle pace of two elderly people. I missed our love-making, too.

I rang him. He was pleased to hear me, perhaps not quite as pleased as he should have been but the warmth and love in his voice were soothing . . .

– He hadn't been *desperate*, though. He hadn't been *dying* to hear me. He asked about Jessica; I told him. I gave him five minutes of Jessica and Sam, more than I usually talked about myself but I had been living it very intensively; babies are absorbing – to parents, or grandparents. Christopher was mad about his granddaughter, of course, but he didn't show all that much interest in Sam, after checking the address to send Jessica flowers . . .

I knew I had something of more interest to tell him but I put it off; Chris was mine, for the moment, even if he wasn't entirely listening. Once I mentioned Alexandra I'd be pushed aside . . .

And all of a sudden I thought, *No. I'm much too old to worry about that. He's very lucky to have me. If he doesn't know that, he's a fool. And she was a wreck. As she probably deserves to be. Wreckers get wrecked, in the end. If he wants her, fine. I don't care. I'm not lonely. I'll do fine on my own.*

'Alexandra is in Paris,' I said.

35

Alexandra: Paris, 2007

Together we travelled all over the world, a glittering, shifting mosaic of places. Odd how few end up meaning anything. And so I come back again and again to the same ones, because they have meaning. Not because they are exotic, or strange. Because I loved them. Because life was here. I loved the place in Mexico City, because it was mine, and ordinary. Paris, so banally beautiful. The little place we stayed in in Western Samoa where no one realised we were rich, we were staying in a family home where we shared one small room with a view of palms and the creamy surf through the glass-less window, our tiny, sunlit shanty . . . But when we went back the fourth year running it had been knocked down to make room for a hotel.

– Looking back now from twenty years later I realise I loved the house in Islington, even though I went round the world to escape it. I did love it. I knew it, I lived there, I could rest there and not notice it. It folded around me like a body. Every corner had memories. The monkey-puzzle tree, the red hibiscus, which always seemed to promise escape and adventure . . .

And now, in my mind, I come back to them all, the well-known places, and there aren't so many, for now I can't escape any more, now I have to find somewhere to die.

Christopher didn't come looking for me. It was only vanity to think he might. If he'd come looking, he would have found me, for I went to all our favourite places, and at first I looked immaculate, I brushed my henna-ed hair till it shone, I put on my painful high-heeled shoes which went oddly with the fashionable cotton but Christopher always loved high heels, Christopher loved my legs in high heels, and even now my legs are good, long and sinewy and almost too thin . . . I staggered gamely in my dated high heels to the Ile de la Cité, the Quai aux Fleurs, the Jeu de Paume where the Van Goghs still flamed, and my lips were painted as brightly as them, and I stopped every hour to look in the mirror, for I did not want him to find me defenceless.

In the end I got tired, for he never came. They never came. They had both lost interest. Of course he did not. He would have run a mile. She would have told him she saw me, mad, pathetic, a crawling wreck on the floor of the Louvre.

Perhaps he stayed away because he loved me. Perhaps he wanted to remember me the way I was when we were together. Chrisopher was always a romantic . . .

But what about me; what about me? I am real, and dying, and need him now. I am all that is left of the woman he loved; surely he owes it me to come and find me? Wouldn't that be the romantic thing to do?

The ultimatum I'd agreed with the doctors slipped past unnoticed. I had done nothing. After another two weeks of wandering Paris, my clothes less smart, my hair less glossy, the high heels abandoned for walking shoes, my ports of call more frequently a bottle of good red in a friendly cafe than a sentimental *point de repère*, I decided I had to go home. My real home, not my imaginary home. Hope was exhausting; I had run out. Time to limp back to Mexico City.

In any case, *they* would have gone home by now. Christopher and Mary would be home together, loving, domestic, forgetting me.

There were one or two places to say goodbye to, since I would not be coming back. I had saved for the very last morning the Jardin du Luxembourg. The last time I'd visited was two years ago, I was fifty-five, only two years younger, but how different things were; I was mourning the child, bereft of my darling Anna Maria, but I still had my health, and some of my looks, and the blue-clad student had wanted me, and as far as I knew

357

I would live for ever. This time I knew that no one would want me.

The world would be there even when I was gone. It would be, wouldn't it? We hadn't quite destroyed it. There were my chestnut trees, in full green leaf, though in close-up some of them looked a little sickly. They were still cared for, still geometrically polled, never mind that there were only a fraction of the numbers of strolling people who once thronged through these avenues. Walking was less popular now; the sprinklers whirled in solitary splendour. Paris seemed to live its life inside.

The green iron chairs gleamed in the sun, standing in fragile lines along the water's edge like thin old people, nearly all of them empty. The edge of the metal dug into my thighs, I could feel the dull pain in my spine which would wake up and sharpen later. Those empty chairs. Once we came here together, we ate a huge sausage and he made me laugh, and everywhere there were children playing, the lake was covered with scudding toy boats and the thin-legged kids in their formal French clothes stood along the railings anxiously watching as their favourite boat set off across the waves. Christopher loved it, he loved young children, I didn't see that because I didn't want to, I didn't take it in till it was too late, and even when I did I only thought about *my* hunger, *my* loss ... He wanted children. I left it too late.

The chair was too painful, without conscious decision I found myself crouching on the grass, if only Chrisopher could come again, if only I could be young again, but not such a fool, such a stupid fool, I crouched by the lake in the blinding sunlight, an old woman crouching, face streaming with tears, and a gendarme came and questioned me in a tone more indignant than solicitous.

I said I had tripped; he didn't seem surprised; old women fell down all the time, but (his expression seemed to say) they shouldn't do it in a public place. He helped me up, rather forcefully. A pigeon came and crapped on my handbag as I stood by the railings, collecting myself.

My plane was at six o'clock that evening. My luggage was

packed; I had checked out of my hotel. Once I had walked everywhere in Paris. I loved this city because it was small, a human size, small enough to walk through. In my mind I strode athletically through Paris, to the Marais or the Botanical Gardens, the Petit Palais or the Musée Rodin, but my body couldn't follow; I hailed a cab.

'To the Trocadéro,' I said.

When we got there the bounty of water and whiteness and diamond-bright light made me young again. The Trocadéro fountains had just been mended; they soared in the sun in an endless arc; I was running like a young girl towards them. The wind whipped the water across my face, ice-cold, knife-sharp as I ran up the steps, I did not remember there had been so many, a mountain of steps, so white, so wet, and I was going well, I began like a sprinter, for the first twenty steps I was a dancer, and young, but the truth pulled me back even as I ran on, the pain pulled me back even as I walked on, I panted on, limped on, sank down, deafened by my heart and the roar of the water.

— People were shouting. I heard them, dimly. There *were* people in Paris, after all. But they were shouting at me. I was alone. There was danger, perhaps they were stragglers from the rumoured armies of beggars who haunted the peripheries of Paris. I thought, dimly, *Not so bad to die here. Christopher and I were once happy here. On the steps of these fountains he told me he loved me, and I didn't hear him because of the noise* . . . By the waters of Paris I sat down and wept. I was too tired to run away.

— Hands on my shoulders. I closed my eyes. He pulled me round. It was Christopher. I was dead, or dreaming. It was Christopher.

He had been here looking for me for two weeks.

'I knew I would find you. I went to all the old places. But you weren't in any of the big hotels . . .' He gabbled it out, staring at me, and I didn't see horror or contempt.

He was an old man, in the surgical sun. He was old, but he

was a white-haired eagle. Still elegant, where I was not, I was wearing comfortable travelling clothes; my legs were hidden; I wore old gym-shoes; he'd never seen me travel like this. He was immensely, frighteningly elegant, when he had straightened his jacket and tie, all awry from running after me (but later I found he had dressed for me; he'd set out each day dressed like a king; in Islington it would have been tracksuit and slippers).

Underneath all this, we were flesh and bone, the bodies which had loved each other. I forgot my pain. I walked with him.

We didn't know where we were going. We walked along the Seine for almost a mile, the loud traffic preventing speech, before we realised we didn't know; we had been walking like the blind, him clutching me, me clutching him; I followed Chris; Chris followed Alex.

'Come back to my hotel,' he said.

He hailed a taxi. He was still a gentleman, Christopher had always been a gentleman. He ushered me in through hotel reception as if I were a returning queen. He ordered champagne to be sent up. As I watched him talking to the barman I saw that his gestures had grown slightly stiff, as if the film was jerking into slow motion, but he came back smiling and everything was normal, to see him smiling at me was so *normal*. I knew that this story had only one ending. I knew we would go upstairs and make love.

We were back in yet another of the endless series of hotel rooms which had been our life. We were slipping off our shoes and coats, so simply, as we had done thousands of times before, we lay side by side on the enormous bed, so quiet and natural, it was all so familiar, an amazed happiness flowed through me (though I kept thinking there was something I should say, something I'd forgotten, but I mustn't upset him).

The champagne was delivered. We sat up on the bed. He opened the champagne, that hiss of relief. He opened the champagne, but he didn't pour it. He was staring at my face as if he was drowning.

'I want to kiss your breasts,' he said. With that intent stare he was still terribly handsome. I remembered what I had to tell,

360

but I didn't tell him; I was afraid; I wasn't whole; it made me vulnerable. He might not want me, if I told. His body, as he stripped, was still the same body, thinner, frailer, but a beautiful body. Christopher could hurt me so absolutely . . .

I took off all my clothes. I didn't look at him, or the mirrors that enclosed us like walls of ice, trying to freeze us into old age; these rooms were meant for the young and vain; I took off my clothes and bowed my head.

I knelt down. I found him. I took him in my mouth, Christopher's prick, so small and soft. So warm. So human. I had longed for him. I had longed for this for so many years.

I kissed, I sucked, I teased, I rolled. (I was tired; my shoulder was hurting me. My shoulder, and perhaps my arm.) My knees began to ache; the carpet was thick, but I was too thin. His prick stayed small. I looked up at him. I couldn't read the expression on his face.

'Never mind,' I said, he said, we said. I smiled, not seeing him, I started to cry, I went to the bathroom so he should not see; he poured champagne, I put my clothes on.

I felt humiliation. Never before. It had never happened. In all our years together, never before. It was because I was old. He didn't want me. How could I expect anyone to want me? This was my punishment, not to be wanted, for all the times I had had what I wanted.

We didn't speak of it. We had grown formal. We remembered the things we should have asked each other.

I asked him if he was living with Mary. He said he was very fond of Mary. I asked him again if he was living with her; I remarked how much I had always liked her, 'although she was so very sensible'. He said he loved and respected her. I kept the scalding tears at bay. *So what was he doing here with me? Why had he bothered to look for me, just to tell me he loved Mary Brown . . .?* My back began to hurt again. I asked after Susy, not listening to the answer.

He asked me about Benjamin. He asked me if it was true I had a daughter, and if so, where had I left her? His voice was cold, as if I might have forgotten her, left her on her own in some distant hotel. I answered as briefly as I could; I dared not reveal my suffering, if I'd told him the truth I should have sobbed; I told him the adoption had gone wrong.

I drank the champagne, looking at my glass. It tasted sour, and I was cold, the air-conditioning was turned up too high. I buttoned my blouse up to the neck. I slipped on my shoes, and thought about dying. Suddenly I recognised his look. He was smiling and staring at the ground, a wooden smile that meant enormous misery. I'd known that smile since I was twenty-three.

Of course, it was *he* who was humiliated. He thought he was too old for me. I got up; went over; stroked his cheek; laid my hand along his cheek-bone.

'I'm sorry, Alex. I do want you. Terribly.'

I knelt at his feet. I had done him wrong. In our life together I had done him great wrong. I knelt at his feet to show I was sorry. And then I told him. There was nothing to hide. I didn't weep; it was a present for him. I always like to give people presents. I gave him my need, my frailty. I gave him the fact that I would die.

It was he who wept. It was he who knelt. It was he who took my glass away. Christopher took me in his arms, he lay on me gently, he loosened our clothes, we pulled our clothes from our ageing limbs, he kissed my arms, he kissed my breasts, weeping and gasping he entered me, entered our home, this dying body.

36

Christopher: London, 2007

I left her in Paris, very reluctantly. I came back to London to make arrangements. She longed to 'go home'. And didn't know what it meant, but perhaps the house in Islington. No, she wouldn't come with me now. She was afraid of Susy, afraid of the past. 'I'm terrified of how she'll look at me. You go on ahead and prepare the ground. Tell her I've changed. Tell her . . . everything.' She was adamant; I flew home alone, trying to decide where we should go.

The basement wouldn't do for the two of us and all the equipment she might need later if – whenever – if – . . . I still couldn't quite believe what must happen. All the equipment she might need. Susy and Phil lived on four floors with Becky. They would have to draw in their horns severely.

In Paris this seemed completely reasonable, but on the London flight I began to have doubts. Susy disliked her step-mother. Phil disliked any kind of change. One of the floors upstairs had been converted into a gym for him. They liked their space; they'd grown used to it, and it was my fault they'd grown used to it. I had offered it them without conditions.

But surely they would see this was life and death. Surely Susy would forgive her now. But the past had claws. Susy was in its grip.

'She got round you, didn't she?'

'What do you mean, "got round me"?'

'You were always a sucker for that woman. Never mind your responsibilities here – '

'What do you mean, *responsibilities?* At thirty-nine years old

363

you are not a responsibility, and I'm sure that Alex will love the baby . . .'

'Goo goo goo over babies, is it? That's the line she's shooting you . . . She's a liar, she always was. Every word she speaks is a lie. If you bring her back she'll hurt you again – '

'She's *dying*, Susy. You're out of date. You're imagining someone completely different. She's old now. She looks ill. She's beautiful to me, but she looks very ill. I have to look after her.'

'And how about Mary? You just dump her, do you? Mary was a mother to me. And she's been so good to you, Daddy. Now you toss her aside like a – used dishcloth – '

'Susy! That's enough rubbish! Mary knew I was going to look for Alex. It was Mary who told me she was there. She's a strong person. She's not a doormat. She's strong enough to take care of herself – '

'So why haven't you telephoned her? Why haven't you seen her since you came back? You phoned Madonna, but not her. I found Madonna's message on the answerphone, purring like a disgusting little kitten – '

'For God's sake, Susy. Madonna's not important. She cheers me up, that's why I rang her. It's difficult with Mary, of course it is. I'll ring her now. You're right about that.'

Mary was grave, but friendly. Could I come to see her? There was a pause. 'If you like,' she said, equably enough. 'Do you want to?'

'Yes.'

'Then come' – much warmer.

She looked serene, healthy, lovely. She looked so well compared to Alex. She looked younger than her. Once she'd looked older. She was wearing an old blue cotton dress with a plain round neck that showed off her skin. She took me into the drawing-room, perhaps the grandest of her rooms, perhaps we were to say something momentous, but I just felt tired, and sorry, and sad, and I wished we could go upstairs and make love, without having to talk, or explain, or grieve.

'Tell me,' she said, 'tell me everything,' and I felt a rush of tenderness, for Alex never asked me to tell her everything, Alex was usually talking herself.

I began to explain. Nothing came out right. My collar hurt me. I loosened it. 'I couldn't have a drink, could I, Mary. A large whisky. That's so kind – ' Yet her face, as she handed the drink to me, was a little severe, not entirely kind, and she was right, I never usually drank before lunch. I wished she would get drunk with me. Suddenly nothing seemed serious, my whole story seemed a fabrication, Alex's illness, her reappearance, even, the grand choices I had to make – I wished it were last year again, and we were walking in Regent's Park.

But Mary was serious enough. 'So you're going to bring her back here. You've decided.'

'Isn't it the right thing to do?'

'It's your decision, not mine. Remember you're making the decision.' There was a long pause; she looked out of the window, calm blue eyes on the distant blue. 'But yes, I suppose you're right. It is the right thing to do. That's probably not why you're doing it, though.'

'What do you mean?'

'You love her, don't you? You've always been in love with her.'

'Well – but I love you too, Mary – '

'In a different way. I know. Just as long as you know that this is your choice. I won't be waiting on her death. I'm proud enough not to do that.'

'There you are, you're strong. You're such a strong person. I know you'll be able to look after yourself. Whereas Alex can't, she needs me – '

She held my eyes, her mouth a little narrow, her firm jaw set more decidedly than usual. 'It's a pity, isn't it, that I'm so strong. It's a pity that I've taken care of you. Because in the end that's not what you want. You want someone demanding and a little crazy. I'm too good for you, aren't I . . .? Men don't like that. But I'll survive.' She stood up, gracefully. Could it be over? Was she telling me to go? I felt confusedly I ought to say more, I hadn't even finished my whisky –

But she was walking towards the door. I swigged the rest of my whisky, indignant. But also ashamed, and very small. She was better than me. She had told me so. Perhaps she was relieved I had chosen Alexandra (but as I padded through the hall I saw it on the table, a bottle of champagne still in its paper, and I knew she had bought it just in case, part of her had gambled, part of her had lost).

I kissed her cheek, I missed her firm mouth because she turned her head away. As I went down the path she called to me. 'I wish I had got you when you were younger.'

Back home still smarting from that encounter, and yet it had gone off better than it might have done, she hadn't wept, and nor had I, we hadn't accused or insulted each other – but Mary knew she was better than me. She wouldn't be there after Alex died. Not that I wanted her there, but still . . . I wished fiercely that Alex had come home with me, to keep her living image with me and banish these stupid small discomforts; she was starting to fade a little already. I tried to phone her; she was not at the hotel; but phoning brought a rush of love, a passionate wish to talk to her.

– All the same, the discomforts were real enough. My life was in chaos because of Alex. She had always caused chaos, always; I had lost my family because of her, only luck had brought Susy back to me, and now we were quarrelling again –

There was a tap at the window like a cat, but it would be Susy, she'd forgotten her key, and Becky would be with her, I glowed with pleasure – and perhaps a little with the rather large whisky, because I was delighted to find it was Madonna.

'Come into the garden, Maud,' I said. She looked blank; we had a culture gap, despite the shared front of IRD. 'Come into the garden and hear my troubles.'

'Gossip, amazing, I love it,' she said. She smelled very strongly of something musky and yet growing, earthy, like tobacco-plants, perhaps. Her nipples poked out at me through her blouse. She was radiant, carefree, bursting with life.

366

'You've been drinking,' she said, as she gave me a hug. 'Give me some at once. No, more than that. I'm not your daughter, you know, Chris . . .'

'You know I know.' She was extremely attractive. She squeezed my arm as she went into the garden. I followed her bum, her long bronzed legs. I felt something I had not felt in months; *cheerful*, yes; I hadn't felt cheerful; happy, ecstatic, tormented, wracked, but not actually cheerful, and – yes. It was shameful, given the drama I was living, but Madonna made me feel randy. The bliss of uncomplicated randiness. The garden was hot, we sat side by side, the grass prickled and swarmed beneath our legs, the earth felt alive, and so were we.

I told her my story. She adored it. To her it was a book, a love story. To her the whole thing was intensely romantic.

'But does she really look old?'

' – Well, yes.'

'In the photographs she looked so young.'

'She's ill, remember – '

'But you still love her?'

She seemed to find this incredible. How could I love someone who looked old? Madonna thought only men should grow old. She didn't believe in death, or illness. And when I was with her, nor did I.

'I've got some news as well, you know. I've given Yukio the boot. I was bored with him. It's great.'

The sun poured down from an immense height. She was pressing her thigh against my thigh. I closed my eyes and let the heat pour through me, the red living heat poured through my eyelids, through my veins, through my old bones. The sun was life. I wanted to live.

'We should run away,' purred Madonna. 'We could run away. Wherever you wanted. I'm sick of England. We could be free.'

Her hand was creeping across my trousers. The heat was in my cock, it began to stand up, I was not an old man, I was proud of it.

'We could have babies,' she said. 'I want to have children

now, at once. I've wasted enough time waiting for Yukio. I want to have three boys who look like you. You'd be a wonderful father, I've seen you with Becky – '

'But I'm seventy-two. I'm much too old – '

Her hand was pressing, kneading, caressing. Her eyes were bright, her cheeks were red, the line of her arm was beautifully round, her hair was a mop of varnished curls. We hardly moved; just her hand and my penis; the heat of the sun held us fast, mesmerised, dreaming of brilliant, distant futures. She offered me everything; freedom, and babies, and a hold on youth, and sex, and fun. Madonna offered me my dreams. But she was not impractical.

'When you were trying for a baby with Alex. You must have tried IVF, I suppose.'

'Yes. Why?'

'That's great. That means they must have freeze-dried some sperm – '

'What are you talking about?'

'It's standard practice. They have to. It's the law. Since 1996. I know about it. I was trying then, with another man – '

'But why couldn't we try the regular way?'

'Oh, I hope there'd be lots and lots of *trying*. I hope I'd be able to tire you out – ' Her fingers tightened on my cock, almost painfully. 'But for children, we should use the freeze-dried sperm. Younger, you see. Less chance of defects.' She caught my expression of frank dismay, and laughed, and got up, showing me her crotch. 'Just leave all that to me, I'm an expert at this. Come inside with me. Let's have some fun.'

The telephone rang from the house.

'Let's not answer it,' she said, as she preceded me into the darkness.

'I have to. It might be Alex – '

'Even more reason not to answer it.'

She was warm and damp with sweat from the sun. The smell of her was overpowering. She pulled off her t-shirt with a fluid movement and they bobbed before me, round as apples but with toffee-brown nipples that stuck out like sweets. They

368

brushed my arm. I heard myself groaning. But the phone was still ringing. Alexandra needed me – I pushed her away with more force than I meant, more force than I knew I still had in my body, and went for the phone; but the phone stopped ringing just as I snatched it up to my mouth. It stopped ringing! I started to curse, I snapped on the 'TRACE CALL' button and got the number; a Paris number, not her hotel; I dialled it, my fingers banana-huge and clumsy from sun and lust and whisky, and it rang and rang in an emptiness, a horrible dead metallic sound. I checked; the number was a call-box. Of course it was Alex, but what was she doing? Why not ring from her hotel? Don't say she was wandering, half-insane, the way she looked when Mary saw her –

I turned back into the room, and there was Madonna, stripped to her pants, the briefest thong. There was something unpleasant about her mouth. She was angry; I had pushed her away. Nobody pushed Madonna away. Her nostrils were slightly flared, sulky.

'You see? I told you not to answer it.' She came towards me, golden-brown, nimble as a spider with her two bobbing breasts.

'This is not a good idea,' I said, feebly. 'You're a beautiful girl, but I – Alexandra – '

'Wasn't she always unfaithful to you?'

'No. Not always. Oh. Oh. Oh that's so nice. Please don't, I mustn't . . .

For the next five hours I didn't think of Alexandra. I'm ashamed to admit it, but it's true. I shot the bolt on the door to upstairs, I shot the bolt on the door to memory. I sealed the decision with a lot more whisky. We took some zoots that Madonna had in her wristpack; she said they would make sex even better, and perhaps they did, for it was wonderful. I hadn't been with a woman with a body like that since too long ago for me to remember (I couldn't bear to, for the woman was Alex, Alex before we both grew old). She knew exactly how to make an old man happy; she knew exactly how to make any man happy.

I was laughably happy, with the whisky as well, and as we floated together on the golden river I realised how I missed excess; I couldn't remember when I'd last got drunk, I'd been leading a life of awful moderation, seeing things grimly as they were; drink gave me the wisdom to know all this; I explained it to Madonna, who laughed a lot, she laughed a lot, we laughed a lot, we drank some more, we were suddenly silent.

'Let's use,' she said. 'Do you want to use? If we live together, we can use a lot. Let's take some more zoots and use.'

We took some more zoots. We switched on the machines. She had brought her own goggles, earphones, dreamsoles. We were naked but covered with machinery. 'Let's go to Chile,' she said. 'I've never been to Chile. I've got it in my bag. They say it's fantastic.'

We materialised in virtual space. She made herself slightly smaller than me, slightly smaller than she was in fact. I made myself younger, but she complained, so I gave myself grey hair again. We decided to start in Santiago.

The telephone rang; I ignored it. It rang and rang. I didn't care. I was going to Santiago with Madonna, it was summer in the middle of the last century, there was snow on the Andes above the city, fruit on Santa Lucia's vines, warm wine shining in cafe windows. Our figures walked down the street hand-in-hand, I had escaped into a different world where no one was in pain or lonely. The phone stopped. It started again.

'Shall I go and switch it off?' Madonna mouthed, for we were listening to Andean music that was being played in a little bar, poignant flutes and shimmering strings; in a moment we would go inside.

It was my decision, but I said nothing, and she went and switched the telephone off.

I had made my decision by saying nothing. Now time began to have no meaning; it happens when you use a lot, especially when you're using with someone else; we wandered around Santiago for hours, it was magical, perfect in every detail, the posters on the walls, exquisitely shabby, peeling in delicate sun-faded colours, the shadows of the houses, which actually moved

370

as the programmed sun moved in the sky – everything was there which had ever been there, except, of course, that the doors didn't open to most of the private houses, so we could only go into cafes or churches, and the churches seemed lifeless, I don't know why.

'But we don't need other people, do we?' said Madonna, and on screen a small Madonna kissed me. 'That's what I like, not knowing anyone. So we can escape. We can really be free.'

(Had I thought the same thing, a lifetime ago? I didn't know; it didn't matter; the zoots and the whisky said *here* and *now*, the IRD said *there* and *then* . . .)

I had fallen asleep. I dimly remember Madonna pushing me into bed, a glimpse of her face looking hard in the lamplight, but she curled beside me, and we slept like the dead, the punishing sleep of the used-up Yardie, a dark tunnel in which phones rang and rang forever in the echoing distance.

I was woken up by a woman screaming. Before I could remember anything a shrieking harridan was upon me, dragging open curtains, dragging off bedclothes. Becky was there. Becky was crying.

'What are you doing?' my daughter screamed. 'You disgusting, disgraceful, immoral old man. I've had Alexandra on the phone. She's been trying to reach you since yesterday. She sounded dreadful. I was sorry for her. And here you are with this – ' Words failed her. 'This tramp. This dirty creature.'

Only one thing in the room was real: Becky, hanging on to the edge of my bed, Becky, her round face blotchy with crying, reaching out her hand to touch her grandpa. Becky, frightened by us grown-up people.

I tried to sit up. I was a hundred years old. 'I'm ill,' I said, and lay down again. Madonna was dressing, swiftly, silently. Susy was throwing open windows as if the place had had the plague. Suddenly she turned on Madonna and grabbed her by the shoulders. Madonna was taller and stronger than her. Susy shook her like a rat. Becky stopped snuffling and screamed, an acute high sound of extreme terror. Susy let go and picked up her daughter.

Madonna was gathering her things. She ignored Susy and spoke to me. Susy carried Becky out into the garden.

'You'll feel bad today. It's the zoots. I've left some Re-Treads in the bathroom. Take three. By teatime you'll feel fine. I'm flying to New York at six this evening. Meet me at five at Heathrow airport. Come away with me. We'll never come back.'

Unmadeup, Madonna looked girlish and lovely. It was real, last night had really happened. Her kiss was sweeter for not being scented. She looked at me as though she loved me and left, a slim figure but curved like a dancer, the wonder of that youthful body – and she was prepared to grow heavy for me. She would let her belly grow big for me.

Yet something was wrong. I saw Alex's face. White and tired, and those scruffy gym-shoes.

I lay in bed not listening to Susy, who had run back inside when she heard the door close, furious to miss the chance of battle. As a girl she had been sweet and slow –

I turned my head and the whole world rolled, and a terrible anxiety gripped my stomach. I spoke quickly to stifle it.

'I might be going away for a bit. To think things out, you know . . .'

'With Madonna, or with Alexandra?'

I didn't answer. I couldn't answer.

'What shall I say to Alexandra? I'll say you've gone away for a while, but you'll almost certainly be back, you're planning to be back before she dies, you're only going for a holiday . . . that was the line you spun to us.'

I lay there wincing at the light. 'Go away please, I have to get dressed.'

I didn't want Susy to see me naked. But perhaps she already had.

The Re-Treads worked in a curious way. They wiped out the headache with a suffocating ice-pack that turned your whole brain to hard-trodden snow. It didn't hurt, but it was dead. Like that, I functioned, got dressed, cleaned up. Like that I began to pack my bags. Like that I picked up the phone to ring Paris. The phone lines sang with frozen wind. She spoke to me from the bottom of an iceberg, vastly diminished, a tiny doll.

'Christopher. Thank God to get you.'

'Alexandra, my dear. How are you?' I sounded odd even to myself, mannered and distant, an arch grandee. The Re-Treads were moving on to their second stage; I began to feel larger, more powerful.

'I rang you yesterday. I went for a walk. I was suddenly so tired. So dreadfully tired. I crawled into a phonebox, but you were out . . . I want you to come back, right away, I feel things are going faster than I thought, maybe I've left it too late to come back, I just want you to come here and be with me – '

So far away, she was ridiculous. As if I could go to her just like that! A little old lady under so much ice!

'But I have a little trip to make. I'm sorting things out so we can all be happy – '

'What do you mean *we can all be happy*? Are you talking about Mary Brown? Are you going away with her, Christopher? I can't bear it, I really can't – '

'Don't be ridiculous.' And I sniggered; I actually sniggered, God forgive me, the Re-Treads told me how smart I was, for I told her no lie, I wasn't going with Mary. I heard Alex's fingernails scratching at the ice. I wanted it to stop before I put the phone down.

'Everything's all right. I'll be back very soon. Take care of yourself, not too much walking – '

'Do you miss me?'

'Yes.'

Did it sound convincing? At any rate, she let me go.

By tea-time an adrenalin high had come. There was the faintest hint, just under the surface, that there were things half-dead, half-mangled, bruised and damaged by the night's excess, that were trying to crawl back into the light, but the Re-Treads kept them safely down. As I drove to the airport I was a king.

Madonna was waiting for me in the Presidents' Lounge. She looked astonishing in silver sello but I saw from her face that she had been nervous, and she'd chosen a chair with a view of the door. How wonderful to be waited for by a woman who all the other men wanted! I expanded under their envious glances. I got her a gin. I got me a gin. We clinked our glasses, silvery, icy, the pleasant sound of fun and money. We were entering our fantasy.

But something in the gin didn't suit the Re-Treads, or else the Re-Treads didn't suit the gin. The air began to drain from the bubble. A very slow quiet headache began, far away at first, in someone else's brain, but then it began to knock, very gently, the head it was knocking to enter was mine.

Alexandra's face. Alexandra.

'How many Re-Treads can you take?' I asked Madonna.

'No more,' she said. 'You might hallucinate. It's not always nice. And this isn't the place. Are you feeling dreadful?' She kissed my cheek, but absently, automatically. Perhaps her own head was hurting too. 'I've got something you can have on the plane. An hour after drinking, minimum.'

My feet began to move on their own. My hands were itchy too. I looked at my watch, and the indicators. 'Why are they late?' I asked Madonna, accusingly, as if it was her fault.

'Don't ask. They're always late.' She had put on headphones; she had gone away. She left one hand on my arm, in casual possession. I couldn't stand it, I shook it off, as unobtrusively as possible. I started to pace around the room, trying to quiet the dreadful panic. Why didn't the plane come? Now, at once? If it didn't come soon it would be too late. I would be too late, I would be stuck for ever, I wanted to vanish into the sky but they would not let me, they kept me here, if I stayed I would die, and be still for ever, lie and be still . . . still for ever –

I suddenly realised I wanted that, we didn't have to keep travelling, but the drug in my blood stream twitched, insisted.

I walked round the lounge some twenty times. The call came

at last; we all lurched to our feet. Madonna had put on dark glasses. She was definitely wan, and she smiled at me, the smile of a fellow-sufferer. I wondered what I was doing here.

We were walking rather fast towards the plane. I was part of a caravan of travellers, all of them looking tired and jaded, carried along by their travel habits. I wondered how many of them wanted to go home.

We passed the last line of little perspex phone-booths at the end of the tunnel leading down to the tarmac. Suddenly one of them began to ring. The phone rang furiously, a dentist's drill, straight to the nerve, it could not stop, and all of us jumped, in our docile queue, all of us somehow knew we should answer, for whatever guilt we were leaving behind was taking its very last chance to reach us. But we all filed past the ringing phone, and as more and more of us abandoned it it no longer sounded peremptory, it sounded frantic, lost, pathetic. I was twenty yards out across the tarmac when it stopped. The plane gleamed snowy-white in the twilight.

But I turned to Madonna, touched her arm. 'I'm sorry,' I said, but I wasn't sorry, I was transfused with absolute certainty. One single person, one suffering person . . . I heard what my father had once said to me. And I saw her face. Alexandra's face. Her beautiful, withered, sorrowful face. 'I'm sorry, I can't. I can't leave her.'

Madonna's face was contorted with violent emotion, and then it smoothed out, as smooth as water. 'You're a fool,' she said, and made herself smile, put down her case, put on her headphones, plugged into a world where she needed nobody, where she could no longer hear my words.

I said, but I knew she couldn't hear me, 'I know I'm a fool. But not for this reason.'

– She was already gone, padding on across the tarmac like a beast of burden in perpetual motion, a little bowed under her electronic yoke.

I walked back inside and booked a ticket to Alex.

36

Alexandra: Home, 2007

I asked him to take me to the snows at last. He promised me that when we were first together, that he'd take me back to the Himalayas where he made his film a lifetime ago. There's still snow there. It might be peaceful there.

I won't be alive when he takes me, of course. It's all a matter of time, and perception. Christopher never leaves me now. We left the children and we left each other; we abandoned the world, and the snows melted. We used the world until it grew tired. Now I want to be given back to it.

We travelled to escape ourselves, I think. We travelled to escape our littleness. If we kept moving we would never die. We left the world to die instead. Susy's generation will be more careful.

I've seen Becky, and she's lovely, alas. I pitied Susy, now she pities me. I'm glad for her. She's done better than me. Her generation will have to do better.

They offered me a thirty per cent chance. Massive chemotherapy, thirty per cent. I think that must mean twenty per cent. And I don't want to fight; it's time to die. I'm so tired now, it's time to sleep. No more techfixes. My own tired body.

I want to die into this dream. It's dreamed me two nights running; both times I woke up, but tonight I don't think so.

Christopher is taking me into the mountains. We come to a hut. It's small from the outside, but we go inside and I feel lost, it's rough and medieval and very cold, an enormous hall of many chambers. None of the shadowy figures see me; I stumble through to the opposite side, and I find a room with a low window, a long low slit along the wall; I look through into another world, a world in miniature, but it's our world, not an icy world but a green garden, green and blue and multiform; everything is here, but hidden; all possibilities are folded here; all we have to do is look after it, and I want to stay, it's so beautiful, I'm happy at last to understand, but it's too late, I am swept on past it, and outside the walls I see them coming, pouring up the mountainside like a river, their vivid life carrying them up against gravity a certain distance before they sink down, and then the others carry them on or they fall and melt into the fluid chain, a great skein of people, dancing, touching, Christopher and I and all the others, and all the strangers are no longer strangers, here are all the faces I failed to see, all the lives I failed to notice, stretching back as far as my vision reaches – the snow is blinding; we hang in the light; we stream uphill towards the light, and I clutch Chris's hand, I say I'm not ready, I want to slip back and see the green garden, if only we weren't old, if we had another chance – but he tells me *Alexandra, go towards the light*, and we move over the snows towards the light.